Pulitzer-prize winning journalist John Sandford is the author of eighteen *Prey* novels, four *Kidd* novels and the stand-alone thriller *Dead Watch*. He lives in Minnesota. Visit www.johnsandford.org

Praise for John Sandford and the *Prey* series

'Tough, engrossing and engaging, Sandford writes superb thrillers' *Literary Review*

'Delivers twists to the very last sentence' *Daily Mail*

'That rare beast – a series writer who reads like a breath of fresh air' *Daily Mirror*

'Few do it better than Sandford' *Daily Telegraph*

'An exciting and superbly elegant demonstration of the intelligent crime writing that has helped John Sandford to sell an estimated 33 million books' *Guardian*

'A winner in every possible way' *Independent on Sunday*

'His effortlessly fluid writing and plotting really impress and his pithy characterisation is often sensational . . . Do yourself a favour and invest in all 17 Prey novels, take a week off work and enjoy' *London Lite*

'Sandford is a cunning writer. He constantly avoids the routine or expected with intelligent and surprising new wrinkles' *Washington Post*

D1393143

Also by John Sandford

Winter Prey
Mind Prey
Sudden Prey
The Night Crew
Secret Prey
Certain Prey
Easy Prey
Chosen Prey
Mortal Prey
Naked Prey
Hidden Prey
Broken Prey
Invisible Prey

Dead Watch

Kidd Novels

The Fool's Run
The Empress File
The Devil's Code
The Hanged Man's Song

JOHN SANDFORD
PHANTOM PREY

**SIMON &
SCHUSTER**

London · New York · Sydney · Toronto · New Delhi

A CBS COMPANY

First published in the US by G. P. Putnam's Sons, 2008
A division of the Penguin Group (USA) Inc.
First published in Great Britain by Simon & Schuster UK Ltd, 2008
This edition published by Pocket Books, 2009
An imprint of Simon & Schuster UK Ltd
A CBS COMPANY

3 5 7 9 10 8 6 4 2

Simon & Schuster UK Ltd
1st Floor
222 Gray's Inn Road
London WC1X 8HB

www.simonandschuster.co.uk

Simon & Schuster Australia, Sydney
Simon & Schuster India, New Delhi

A CIP catalogue record for this book is available
from the British Library

ISBN 978-1-47111-094-8

Book design by Nicole Laroche

Printed and bound by CPI Group (UK) Ltd, Croydon, CR0 4YY

PHANTOM PREY

1

SOMETHING WRONG HERE, a cold whisper of evil.

The house was a modernist relic, glass and stone and redwood, sixty years old and gone creaky; not all haunted houses were Victorian. Sometimes at night, when she was alone, she'd feel a sudden coolness, as though somebody, or some *thing*, had just slipped by. This was different. She couldn't pin it down, but it was palpable.

She thought about stepping back into the garage.

"Who's there?" she called. She got nothing back but an echo.

THE HOUSE WAS DARK, except for desk lamps in the front room and in the study, which were triggered by photocells at dusk. She could hear the furnace running. Nothing else—but the hair on her forearms and the back of her neck stood upright. Some atavistic sense was picking up a threat.

She looked to her right. The arming light on the security panel was steady, so the security system had been disarmed. That was decisive. The house should be empty, the security system should be armed.

She stepped back, moving quickly, around the nose of the Jaguar to the Mercedes. She yanked open the driver's-side door, reached under the front seat to the storage bin, popped the lid, and lifted out the Ladysmith .38.

Stood listening again, the gun cool in her hand, and heavy. Couldn't even hear the furnace, now. The Mercedes's engine pinged, cooling down. The overhead garage lights were still on and she watched the door to the house. Something wrong, but the house felt empty.

Her nose twitched. She could smell exhaust from the car, but when she'd stepped through the door to the house, there'd been something else. A subtle stink that shouldn't have been there. Not sweat, not body odor, not perfume, not flatulence, but something organic. Meat?

She had her purse over her shoulder, her cell phone right there. Call the police? What would she tell them? That something was not right? That something smelled a little funky? They'd think she was crazy.

She put her purse on the hood of the Jag, held the gun in front of her, like the handgun instructor had shown her. She was an athlete, and a professional athlete at that: swimming, dance, martial arts, weights, Pilates, yoga. The hard stuff: her body control was nearly perfect. She'd shot the eyes out of the gun-instructor's bad-guy target.

He'd been mildly impressed, but only mildly. A cop for most of his life, he'd told her that every shooting he'd ever seen had been a screwup.

"The question is not whether you can hit something at seven yards. The question is whether you can sort out all the problems, when you've got a loaded gun in your hand," he'd said, a rehearsed speech that might have been written on a 3x5 card. "You have no time, but you have to figure out what's happening—what's going on. To shoot or not to shoot: it all comes down to a tenth of a second, in the dark. You don't want to shoot your kid or a neighbor. You don't want to *not* shoot a junkie with a butcher knife coming for your throat."

THERE WOULDN'T BE a neighbor in the house. The neighborhood was private, standoffish. People drew their friends from their businesses, from their schools, not from the street. The housekeeper was long gone.

Her daughter? Frances had the security code but she always called ahead.

She called out: "Francie?"

No response.

Again, louder. "Fran? Are you there?"

Starting to feel foolish, now. Then she remembered what the gun instructor had told her. "About the time you start to feel like an idiot, that's when they'll get you. If you're scared enough to have the gun out, then the situation is serious enough that you can't be *abashed*."

She remembered the word. Abashed. Was she abashed?

SHE WAS BACK at the door. Kept the muzzle of the gun pointing straight ahead, called out, "Frances, I've got a gun, because I'm scared. Don't jump out, if this is a joke. Frances?"

She let go of the gun with her left hand, reached around the doorjamb and flicked on the lights. The entry was clear, and as far as she could see, the kitchen. She was inside now, the house still giving off the empty feel. Edged forward.

The hair on her arms was up again and she reached inside the kitchen door and hit another block of lights. They came on all at once, three circuits' worth, fifteen lights in all, the kitchen as brightly lit as a stage. She glanced behind her, at the garage, then back toward the dark door beyond the kitchen.

Not right; a few lizard-brain cells were screaming at her. *Not right.*

"Frances? Fran? Are you there? Helen? Are you still here, Helen?" Helen was the housekeeper.

No answer. She let the gun drop to her side. Then, remembering what the cop said, brought it back up, and let the muzzle lead her through the house. Halfway through, she knew she was alone. There was no tension in the air, no vibration. She cleared the last bedroom, exhaled, smiled at her own foolishness.

This hadn't happened before. There was something . . . She got to the kitchen, sniffed, and looked around. Put the gun on the counter, opened the refrigerator, pulled out the bag of pre-cut celery sticks, took out two and crunched them.

Huh.

*

3

ALYSSA AUSTIN LEANED against the counter, a small woman, blond, fair-complected, but not delicate: she had a physical density to her face and hands that suggested the martial arts, or an extreme level of exercise. She looked at the gun on the counter, and half-smiled; it was dark and curved and weighted with presence, like a successful work of art.

She was finishing the second celery stick when she noticed the dark streaks on the wallpaper at the edge of the hall that led from the kitchen to the dining room. The streaks were broom-straw-length and breadth, splaying out from a center, dark but not black, like flower petals, or a slash from a watercolor brush. Not knowing exactly why, she stepped over and touched them—and felt the tackiness under her finger.

Pulled her finger back and found a spot of crimson. She knew instantly and without a doubt that it was blood, and relatively fresh. Saw a small, thinner streak farther down the wall. Backed away . . .

SCARED NOW. Picked up the gun, backed into the kitchen, groped for the phone, punched in 9-1-1. She did it with a bloody finger, not realizing, leaving red dots on the keys.

The operator, an efficient-sounding woman, asked, "Is this an emergency?"

"There's blood in my house," she said.

"Are you in danger?" the operator asked.

"No, I don't . . . I don't . . ."

"Is this Mrs. Austin?"

"Yes." She didn't know how the operator had gotten her name, didn't think about it. "I just came home."

"Go someplace safe, close by."

"I need the police."

"We are already on the way," the operator said. "Officers will be there in about a minute. Are you safe?"

"I uh . . . don't know." She thought, *The police. I should put the gun away.* "Tell them . . . Tell them I'm going to the garage. I'm going to lock myself in the car. The garage door is up."

"Okay. That would be good," the operator said. "Don't hang up. Just drop the phone and go to the car. We should be there in less than a minute now."

She dropped the phone and backed toward the garage.

She could hear sirens in the distance—and not another thing.

THE COPS WENT in with guns in their hands, cleared the house, looked at the blood and called for a crime-scene crew.

Alyssa went looking for her housekeeper, and found her. Helen was utterly confused by the blood; it hadn't been there when she left.

The crime-scene crew, from the Minnesota Bureau of Criminal Apprehension, spent two days in the house. They found more signs of blood, on the tiles in the kitchen and hallway, enough that it had apparently been mopped up. Alyssa and the cops spent the next two days looking for Frances. They found her car, found her last grocery list, but they never could find her. Then the blood tests came back from the lab: it was Frances's blood, all right.

According to the lab techs, there'd been a pool of blood on the floor, which had been cleaned up with a product called Scrubbing Bubbles bathroom cleaner and paper towels—there were little spit-ball, or blood-ball, remnants from the towels stuck in the cracks of the Mexican tiles. The blood spatters on the wall had simply been missed by the killer or killers, who hadn't noticed the thin sprays of blood entwined in the floral pattern of the wall-paper.

Frances was gone, and probably dead, and they all knew it.

Alyssa cried, sporadically and unpredictably, for four weeks, caught in the bureaucracy of mysterious death, a slow-motion nightmare.

No body, just the blood—and the cops coming around, and the reporters, and the cameras, and then the lawyers and the accountants, trying to work through the law. What to do about Frances's car? *I'm sorry to have to ask at a time like this but Frances's belongings are still in the apartment, and if she's not going to be able to pay the rent next month we have a young couple who are looking . . .*

WHEN HER HUSBAND, Hunter, had been killed, he'd managed to die with his typical neatness. Trusts in order, will in place, lists of assets and debts, a file of real estate holdings, careful records of stock-purchase dates, garnished with instructions for everybody. He'd been a control freak right to the end. He'd probably never felt a thing, his silly seaplane dropping like a rock into the Ontario woods, witnesses all around.

When he'd died, she'd been stricken, but had recovered, and knew even on the day of his death that she would recover. They were married, but they'd been psychologically split for years, living separate lives in separate rooms; with a little sex now and then.

FRANCES, THOUGH, was different.

She hadn't had her life yet; she hadn't died—if she were dead— doing something voluntarily. And she was Alyssa's blood. Whatever their conflicts—and they'd mostly concerned the father and husband, Hunter—they would have been worked through. They only needed time, and they hadn't gotten it.

So Alyssa cried, short violent jags at unexpected moments. And she looked for her daughter, the only ways she knew: she called people, politicians, who called the cops, who whispered back that *something was going on here . . .* The politicians apologized and temporized and shuffled away. She'd become a liability.

And she looked in the stars. She did her astrological charts, using the latest software, she talked with a master on the East Coast, who wondered aloud if Frances might still be *alive*. His chart for the girl showed a passage of darkness, but not death. Nothing that big.

"Alive?"

"It's a possibility that has to be examined," he said, in tones portentous even for a wizard of the Zodiac. "I see an instability, a hovering, a waiting . . ."

The cards said the same thing. Alyssa had picked up the Tarot as a teenager, believed in the cards, used them at all-important business junctures—and she'd done so well. So well.

And though the cards and the stars agreed that Frances, or some part of her, remained in this sphere, there was never a sign of her.

THE BURDEN, the insanity of it all, was crushing. Alyssa lived on Xanax and, at night, on Ambien. Then she began to take Xanax to lay down a base for the Ambien; and then a glass of wine as a base for the Xanax, as a base for the Ambien; and still she didn't sleep.

She rolled and turned and her mind cranked twenty-four hours a day, a long circle of jangled thoughts. Sometimes, during the day, from the corner of her eye, she'd see Frances sitting on a couch. She'd come downstairs in the middle of the night, having heard Fran's music playing on the stereo, only to have it fade as she came closer.

She felt cool breezes where there should be no drafts, as though someone had walked past her. And she saw omens. Crows on a fence, symbols of death, staring at her unafraid, but mute. A fire-ball in the sky, when she happened to be thinking of Frances. Fran's face in crowds, always turning away from her, and gone when she hurried to them.

Was Frances alive? Or dead?

Or somewhere in between?

FAIRY HAD SOME of the answers, or believed she did.

Alyssa was a blond, good-hearted, New Age modern woman. Fairy was dark, obsessive, Pre-Raphaelite—and where Alyssa floundered, trying to comprehend, Fairy knew in a moment what had happened to Frances, and focused on revenge.

Fairy stepped out of the shower, toweled off as she walked into the bedroom. When she was dry, she threw the towel on the bed and chose Obsession from the row of perfume bottles on the dressing table. She touched the bottle to her neck and the top of her breasts, judging herself in the dressing mirror as she did.

She didn't call herself Fairy; others did. But it fit—with a pair of gossamer wings, she could have been Tinker Bell's evil twin.

Then Loren appeared. "Looking good. Really, really good. Your ass is . . ."

"I don't have time to fool around, I've got to get dressed," Fairy said. "But you can watch me."

"I know, time to go," Loren said. "I'll watch you undress, later."

She looked straight into his hungry dark eyes, patted her breasts with the flats of her fingers, fluffing up her nipples, and got dressed: black panty hose, a light thermal vest for warmth, a soft black skirt, a black silk blouse threaded with scarlet, tight over the vest. Back to the mirror, she painted on the lipstick, dark as raw liver, penciled her eyebrows, touched up her lashes; smacked her lips like women do, adjusting everything. Arranged the fall of the hair: like a black waterfall around her shoulders.

"Wonderful."

"Thank you."

"That's what you get, when you sleep with an aesthete."

Fairy walked back to the dressing closet and took out the short black leather jacket, pulled it on: the jacket gave her shoulders, and a stance. Two-inch black heels gave her height. Ready now.

"The knife?" Loren asked.

"Here." She touched the breast pocket on the jacket; could feel it in there, new from Target, hard black plastic and soft gray steel, sharpened to a razor's edge.

"Then—let's go." Loren smiled, teeth flashing, his face a white oval above his dark clothing, and Fairy reached out, took his hand, and they went.

Loren was the one who'd found Frances's killers; together they'd scoured her laptop, her photographs—thousands of them, taken with a cell phone and a point-and-shoot Nikon, some of them stored electronically, but hundreds of them printed out, stacked in baskets, stuck to the front of her refrigerator, piled in drawers: a record of her life, from which the killers emerged.

There were three: "I can actually feel her hand on their shoulders," he told her. "These are the people who did it."

The three were scattered through the stacks of photos, but they were all together in one of them. The photo had been taken at a party of some kind, the three people peering at the camera, laughing.

"You're sure?" Fairy asked.

"Never more. Blood on their hands, missus," he said.

"I want them," she said

"Revenge," he said. He smacked his lips. "It's so sweet; revenge tastes like orange juice and champagne."

Fairy laughed at the metaphor and said, "Everything with you goes back to the senses, doesn't it? Sight, sound, touch, taste, smell . . ."

"That's all there is, missus . . ."

THEY BOUGHT A CAR to hunt from—bought it at a roadside person-to-person sales spot, along Highway 36. Gave the seller an envelope full of cash, drove away in the car, an aging Honda Prelude. Never registered the change, never bought insurance; kept it out of sight.

They began to scout, to make schedules, to watch. Early on, it became apparent that the bartender was at the center of the plot—the fulcrum of Frances's Goth world. He took in people, places, events, and plans, and passed them on. He knew what was happening, knew the history.

Fairy talked to him three times: once on the sidewalk, when he passed her, looking her over, and she passed by and then turned and called, "Excuse me, are you Mr. Ford?"

He walked back to her and grinned, shoulders up, hands tucked in his jeans pockets. A charmer. "Yeah. Have I seen you around?"

"I was over at the A1 a few weeks ago with Frances Austin," Fairy said. "Did you hear about her?"

"I did. There's been a lot of talk."

"I can't imagine what happened," Fairy said, shaking her head. "Some people say drugs, some people say she must have had a secret lover."

"She used to smoke a little, I know that," Ford said. "But . . . I'm not sure she even had her own dealer. She didn't smoke that much. I can't believe it was drugs. Must've been something else."

"The police think . . . I don't know. Because she was one of us"—Fairy patted her black blouse—"that maybe somebody sent her to the other side, to see . . . what would happen."

"Well, that's scary," Ford said. "What's your name?"

She made up the name on the spot: "Mary. Janson. Mary Janson." They shook hands. "Some of the people have tried to get in touch with her. On the other side."

Ford's eyebrows went up, and he smiled. "No luck, huh?"

"You don't believe?"

"Oh, you know. I used to, I guess. Used to talk about it, anyway. With me, it's more of a hang-out thing," he said. He looked away. "I used to listen to the people talk about . . . you know. Life, death, crossing over. It's interesting, but, I don't know. Too depressing, if you do it for a long time."

Fairy shook her head again, the black hair swirling around her shoulders: "It bothers me so much. If I could find out why she's gone, what happened to her, I'd be fine. I could sleep."

Ford leaned closer to her: "If you want my opinion, it was a money deal."

"A money deal?"

"You knew her pretty well?" Ford asked.

"I did," Fairy said.

"Then you gotta know she was rich."

"I knew she was well-off."

"Rich," Ford insisted. "She told me that when her father was killed, she inherited, like, two million. She already had money from trusts her parents set up when she was small. She said they put in, like, ten thousand each, every year; during all those big stock market boom times in the nineties, she had a million of her own, before she inherited. So I know she had that much."

"A lot more than I knew," Fairy said.

"We joked about starting a club," Ford said. His eyes drifted away, seeing another reality. "She'd back it, I'd run it. We'd bring in some dark music; change the scene around here. It would have been a moneymaker."

"Sounds wonderful," Fairy said.

A rueful smile: "Yeah: she gets killed, and my life flashes in front of my eyes." Ford looked at his watch: "Shoot. I gotta go, I'm late for work. Are you going to be around? Mary Janson?"

"I'll be around," Fairy said.

He leaned closer again. "You smell wonderful."

She twiddled her fingers at him, and went on her way. "I'll see you at the A1."

LOREN HAD BEEN leaning against an old elm, listening. He caught Fairy down the sidewalk and said, "You smell wonderful."

"I do."

"You heard what he said."

"Money," she said. They seemed, now, to pick things out of each other's minds.

"She must've talked it around," Loren said. "You know how she liked to talk—and so, what happened is, she got some of these people all cranked up about starting a club, a new scene, but you know how conservative she *really* was; so it comes to the moment when she has to produce the cash, and she backs away."

Fairy frowned: "How do you know so much about her?"

"Why, from you," Loren said. "All you do is talk about her. All day, all the time."

BACK HOME, in bed, they made love in his cold, frantic way. Loren's fingernails were an inch long, left scratches on her rib cage and thighs. And afterward, she said, "Ford knows."

11

"Yes, he does. We should see him again; and some of the others. Patricia . . ."

"I don't think she'd be involved," Fairy said, tentatively.

"She's involved," Loren said, sitting up, the sheets falling to his waist, showing off his rib cage. His body was slender as a rake. "I can feel it. She was jealous of Frances. Her parents broke up, they don't care whether she lives or dies. She's over there by herself, nothing to do, no place to go. Frances had two parents who loved her, *and* the money. So the fat girl gets involved in this club thing, she's going to be cool, she's going to be a club owner, or operator, hang out with the bands . . . and Frances finally says she can't have it. Can't have any of it. Jealousy and hate."

"Maybe."

"For sure," Loren said. "As far as I'm concerned, she's on the list."

"We have more scouting," Fairy said. "We have Dick Ford, we have Roy Carter, and Patty . . ."

"So we take a week, and think. Then we move again. If we don't, the energy will fritter away. Just fritter away."

SHE TALKED TO Ford again, for ten minutes, at the A1, passing through. And finally, a third time, just at closing. Went to the bar, drank a beer, and he touched her hand, and touched it again, and the knife was like the Sword of Freya in her belt. When she finished the beer, as Ford was calling to the patrons to "Drink up and go home," she drifted out the back door and looked back, caught his eyes with hers.

THE ALLEY WAS paved with red bricks, covered with the grime of a century of wear; she wanted to lean on something while she waited, but everything was dirty, so instead, she wandered in little circles, rocked back and forth, hoping that nobody else would come through the door.

A thought: *I could leave right now*. She could leave, and nothing would happen. She could sell the car—or not, who'd care?—and be done with it.

She toyed with the thought, then let it drift away. Dropped her hand to the knife. She'd spent some time with it, sharpening the edge until it was like a razor. She yawned: nervous.

Then Ford came through the door. He might have worked on his smile, inside, in the restroom mirror, because it was perfect—an effort to generate a bit of wry charm, in an uncertain situation with a good-looking woman. "So, what's up?"

He was wearing a leather jacket, unzipped, which was good, and beneath it, a canvas shirt. She got close and let him feel her smallness, her cuddliness, while her right hand slid along the handle of the knife. "I can't stay away from the Frances Austin thing," she said. "I thought you . . . could tell me about it."

"Frances Austin?" He frowned: not what he expected. "You're sort of stuck on that, huh?"

There was one light in the alley, and they were almost beneath it. She caught a corner of his jacket sleeve, and tugged him closer to the open end of the alley, toward the street, but deeper into the dark. Turned him, set him up against the wall, pressed into him, said, "You were her friend. You must have some ideas about what happened."

"No, I really don't . . . Not so much."

She whispered, "Don't give me that bullshit," and she jammed the knife into his gut, just about at the navel, and then, as she'd imagined it, pulled it up toward his heart, the blade cutting more easily than she'd expected, and she put all her muscle into it, up on her tiptoes, using both hands on the knife handle. Ford swung his arms at her, but they were soft and straight, like zombie arms, uncoordinated, shock with pain, and she moved around them and pulled on the knife, pulled it up to his breastbone, and then out.

He slumped back against the dirty wall, staring at her, made gargling sounds, his hands stretching down toward the earth, and then he slumped over sideways and fell on his side, and spewed blood.

She squatted, listened to him die, then wiped the knife on his shirt and spit on him: "That's for Frances," she said.

She walked away, down the empty alley, carrying the knife. Got in the car, drove six blocks in silence, until Loren said, "He's gone. I felt him go."

"Yes."

"Pull over."

"Why?" But she pulled over.

"Because I'm gonna fuck you," Loren said.

And he did, and when the orgasm washed over her, it smelled purely of fresh blood.

2

THE DAY WAS slipping from gray into dark, the sun going down to the southwest over the Mississippi, and the rain kept coming— a cold, driving torrent that pounded the windows.

Lucas Davenport sat at a desk, in a dim room, staring at the laptop screen and listening to Tom Waits, the sound tumbling out of a nineties boom box. Waits was working through "Christmas Card from a Hooker in Minneapolis," and the bluesy piano fit with Lucas's mood.

Across the street, a woman tiptoed into her bedroom, stopped to look into a baby bed. Smiled silently; then unbuttoned her blouse, slipped it off her narrow shoulders, hung it on a chair, then reached back between her shoulder blades to pop her brassiere.

A pair of Canon image-stabilized binoculars sat on the desk next to Lucas's laptop. Lucas picked them up and watched as she dug through a chest of drawers. Must be cool in the apartment; her nipples were nicely erect. She was a brown-haired girl, of the brown-eyed tribe, with a long supple back that showed every vertebrae down to the notch of her butt. She'd kept herself in shape.

She came up with a T-shirt and then a heavy blue sweatshirt and pulled them over her head. Her pregnancy was progressing well, Lucas observed. She must be about four months along now, and was faithful about her biweekly visits to the obstetrician.

Bummer. If she was putting on a sweatshirt, no bra, she wasn't going out. Heather was intensely fashion-conscious, a woman who wore high heels to Starbucks. Neither was she tarting herself up, so Siggy was not on his way over.

Sigitas Toms, Siggy to his pals and the cops, had been the Twin Cities's largest-volume cocaine dealer, pushing the stuff through his contacts in the real estate, stockbroking, and used-car businesses. He'd been netting two million a year, tax free, at the end, with money stashed all over the United States and Europe.

When he was busted by the Bureau of Criminal Apprehension and St. Paul police, he'd told the arresting officers that he wouldn't be going to prison. They all had a good laugh at that, Siggy included. He was the affable sort, right up to the time he pulled your dick off with a pair of wire cutters.

Two hours after he bailed out of jail, he vanished.

He'd been under a loose two-man surveillance at the time, one BCA guy and one St. Paul detective. From the jail, he'd gone home to a warm front-porch greeting from Heather. An hour later, hair still wet from what the cops assumed was a postcoital shower, he'd emerged from the house, carrying a slip of paper—a shopping list. Pampers, baby powder. He climbed into his Lexus and drove to the Woodbury Target store.

The watchers weren't too worried when they lost him in the bed and bath department, pushing his cherry red cart between the high stacks of towels and bath mats and sheets, because there's only one way out of a Target, the front, and that was covered, right?

Besides, you'd naturally lose a guy for a minute or two in a Target . . . but when they couldn't locate him in a minute or two, they got anxious, and began running up and down, frightening the shoppers—or *guests*, as Target called them in the letter of complaint that they sent to the director of the BCA and the St. Paul chief of police.

Turns out, Target does have a back door, but not for customers. Siggy hadn't had permission to use it, but callously had anyway; a cold-blooded criminal, for sure.

He'd had a car waiting and nobody had ever seen him again.

Well. *Somebody* had seen him, just not the cops.

HIS WIFE, HEATHER, née Anderson, pled ignorance of everything. She thought Siggy was a humble car salesman, she said from the steps of their highly leveraged two-point-eight-million-dollar teal-and-coffee-painted McMansion. Doesn't everybody have a house like this? The house had been part of Siggy's three-million-dollar bond. When he skipped, the court found out, there was an unremarked second mortgage, and with the slump in housing prices, the two mortgages were underwater. Or, as they say in California, upside down. If the court foreclosed, it'd mostly be foreclosing on air.

So there was Heather, twisting her hands in regret. There was the Ramsey County attorney, mumbling into his torts. And somewhere, was Siggy—a tear for poor Siggy, growing a beard in Mexico or Paraguay or Belize, drinking salty margaritas and cerveza blanca and watching the tourists walk hand in hand down the beach in flip-flops, pining for the old homestead in Woodbury, with its driveway ring of hosta plants, basketball net to the side, its legal writs.

HEATHER WAS PUSHED out of the house eight months after Siggy disappeared. A buyer was found, a radiologist, but the radiologist backed out at the last minute, pleading that he'd received a phone call from a man who told him that if his family moved in, his children would be taken from their grade schools, and their eyes would be put out with a red-hot poker.

So the house sat there, empty, while Heather moved to a second-floor apartment on Snelling Avenue in St. Paul. Her mother lived in the apartment next door, rolling around on a powered chair with a tank of oxygen. Heather's mom was dying of congestive heart failure and wouldn't make it through the year. She might not even make it through the month.

When the old lady croaked, Lucas suspected, Heather and the child would be off to a warmer climate, like Zihuatanejo, or Monaco, where nobody would care about Siggy and his cocaine business in the Twin Cities.

THE BCA HAD taken an apartment above a drugstore across the street from Heather's and, for three months, kept up a regular watch. Then priorities changed, and the watch became sporadic. Lucas and Del took it over, as a hobby. The drugstore apartment was quiet, and Lucas could work there, and the couch was soft, and Del sometimes came by for a nap.

Lucas's group had broken the Toms case, and had made the arrests; had argued, through the prosecutor, that no bail should be allowed, that Toms was a flight risk.

They'd lost the argument, and then Toms had bitch-slapped the BCA and the St. Paul cops at the Target store.

THEN THERE WAS ANTSY.

Siggy's brother, Antanas—Antsy Toms—had been at loose ends since his brother vanished. The cops believed that Siggy had been the brains and the driving force behind the organization. Antsy was . . . his brother. What could anyone say?

Antsy had a tattoo of the Statue of Liberty on one arm, and "US SEAL" on the other, with a dagger with blood dripping off it, though he'd never been in the military. He probably did have a dagger, though, and it probably did have blood dripping off it, from time to time.

When God was passing out the brains, Siggy had been at the head of the line. Antsy, in the meantime, had been off getting F-U-C-K Y-O-U—! tattooed on the knuckles of his hands, upside down and backward from his point of view, but forward and right side up when he was sitting across a table from a cop.

Antsy had done some enforcement work for Siggy, but hadn't been arrested because he really, really didn't know anything. *Anything.* When Siggy split, Antsy had taken up bouncing as a career, and methamphetamine as a hobby.

Most recently, he'd drubbed the bejesus out of two St. Paul cops, one of whom was the daughter of a BCA agent stationed upstate in Bemidji. Antsy, like his brother, was still on the run, but the word was, he didn't have the cash to go far.

Antsy was still around; and he might also be calling on the beauteous Heather, looking for a little cash money—another reason to keep the surveillance going.

SO, HERE LUCAS WAS, observing the often-semi-naked or even fully naked Mrs. Toms every day or two, walking around in front of her open windows, one of the least body-conscious women Lucas had ever done surveillance on, waiting for the family to show up.

He picked up the pregnancy in the third month, the baby bump under her upscale Pea in the Pod maternity clothing.

Nobody had ever seen a boyfriend—so Siggy had been back, Lucas thought, and they'd missed him.

In addition to a salesman's natural affability, and his willingness to use wire cutters on slow-pay retail dealers, Siggy had been a genuine family man. He'd be back again.

Just not today.

LUCAS LOOKED DOWN at the laptop, where he'd been wrestling with bureaucratic ratshit. He was late with the annual personnel evaluations, and some time-serving wretch, deep in the bowels of the bureaucracy, whose life work involved collecting evaluation forms, was torturing him with e-mails and phone messages.

And what, really, could he say about Del? Or about Virgil? Or about Jenkins and Shrake?

The questionnaire asked if Del presented himself in a manner that conformed to standards of good practice as outlined in

Minnesota state regulations. In fact, the last time Lucas had seen Del, he's been unshaven, hungover, three months late for a haircut, and was wearing torn jeans, worn sneaks, and a sweatshirt that said, *underwear not included*.

Virgil, Lucas knew, drove around the state pulling a boat and trailer and almost daily went fishing or hunting on state time, the better to focus investigative vibrations—a technique that seemed to work.

Jenkins and Shrake carried leather-wrapped saps. Jenkins called his the Hillary-Whacker, in case, he said, he should ever encounter the junior senator from New York.

Should all of this go into a file?

LUCAS SIGHED, stood up, put his hands in his pockets, and looked out the window. The last of the snow was being washed out by the rain, and only a few hard lumps of ice remained behind the curbs, where the snowplow piles had been. If the rain continued, the ice would be gone by morning. On the other hand, if the temps had been ten degrees lower, the storm would have produced twenty inches of snow, instead of two inches of rain.

He didn't need that. He was done with winter.

Until the middle of February, it seemed that the snow would keep coming forever. Not much at one time, but an inch or two, every third day, enough that he had to fire up the snowblower and clear off the driveway before his wife drove on the snow and packed it down.

In mid-February, it got warm. Two rainy weeks in the forties and fifties, and the snow was gone. That's when the end-of-winter blues got him. March was a tough month in the Cities. Dress warm, and the day got warm and you sweated. Dress cool, and the day turned cold, and you froze. Cars were rolling lumps of dirt, impossible to keep clean. Everybody was fat and slow, and crabby.

*

LUCAS HAD BEEN playing winter ball in a cops-and-bureaucrats league at the St. Paul YMCA. Some of the bureaucrats were wolverines—hesitate on a shot and they'd have two fingers up your nose and one hand in your shorts. So he was in shape, the theory being that you wouldn't get the winter blues if you worked out a lot.

But that was theory, and mostly wrong. He needed the sun, and for more than a week in Cancun.

LUCAS HAD jet-black hair salted with streaks of gray, and his face was pale with the winter. He had strong shoulders and a hawk's beak nose, blue eyes, and a couple of notable scars on his face and neck. Traces of the job.

His paternal ancestors, somewhere back through the centuries, had paddled wild fur out of the North Woods, mink and beaver and otter and martin and fisher, across Superior and the lesser Great Lakes, down the St. Lawrence. A bunch of mean Frenchmen; and finally one of them said, "Screw this Canadian bullshit," and moved to the States.

When that happened was not exactly clear, but Lucas's father had suggested that when it did, the immigrant might have had a case of blended whiskey on his shoulder . . .

His mother's side was Irish and Welsh, and a bit of German; but Lucas wasn't a genealogist and mostly didn't care who'd done what back when.

HE PICKED UP the glasses and looked through the window across the street at Heather Toms, who was in the kitchen making a smoothie, and doing a little dance step at the same time. She'd done her exercises every day, and while she'd once smoked the occasional cigarette, or maybe a doobie—always on the balcony, so the first baby wouldn't get secondhand smoke—she'd quit with the pregnancy.

Lucas quite approved of the way she was conducting herself, aside from the aiding and abetting of her murderous husband and drug-psycho brother-in-law.

Nothing was going to happen, he thought. Time to go home . . .

LUCAS LIVED ten minutes from Heather's apartment, west across St. Paul's Highland district, in a new house on Mississippi River Boulevard, which wasn't a boulevard. He and his wife, Weather, had designed and built the home themselves, to fit them. They'd done well, he thought, with a rambling two-story structure and ample garage, of stone and cedar shingles, and climbing ivy stretching up the siding.

He'd been home for fifteen minutes, yawning, listening to the rain in the quiet of the house, picking through a copy of *Musky Hunter*, when he felt, rather than heard, the garage doors going up. Weather.

He checked his watch: she was early.

He ambled through the house and met her coming through the door carrying two grocery sacks. She looked around and asked, "Where is everybody?," meaning their toddler son and the live-in housekeeper. Their ward, Letty, was at school.

"Same place you were, I guess—went to the supermarket."

"Well, poop," Weather said. She plopped the bags down on the food-prep island. "We're gonna wind up with about thirty bananas."

Lucas snuggled up behind her and kissed her on the neck and she relaxed back against him, hair damp from the supermarket parking lot. She smelled like woman-hair and Chanel. She wiggled her butt once for his benefit, and then gave him an elbow and said, "We've got to talk."

"Uh-oh."

"I SAW ALYSSA TODAY," Weather said, turning around. She was a Finn, through and through. A surgeon, a small woman with pale watchful eyes who saw herself as Management, and Lucas as Labor; or possibly saw herself as a Carpenter, and Lucas as Raw Lumber. "Actually, I didn't so much see her, as she came to see me when I was working out. About you."

"Ah . . ." He shook his head. "Nothing new on her kid?"

"Nothing new—but it's not that. Did you see the story about the murder in Minneapolis, night before last?"

"The bartender," Lucas said.

There'd been two murders in Minnesota that day. Since one of the victims had been young, blond and female, with large, firm breasts, the bartender had gotten short shrift from television, even though his had been the more interesting crime, in Lucas's opinion, and the blonde had been inconveniently placed in Lake Superior.

"He was a Goth," Weather said. "He ran with the same group as Frances. Alyssa says the Minneapolis cops don't have a clue, but came to talk to her because of the similarity of the killings. She said there was so much blood with Frances—"

"We're not sure about that," Lucas said. He looked in the sack of groceries, saw the white pastry bag, peeked inside. Cinnamon rolls. The small, tasty, piecrust kind. He took one out and popped it in his mouth. "Could have been a little bit of blood, but widely smeared."

"But no viscera or skin," Weather said. "Just blood."

"Wouldn't have much if she were stabbed in the heart through her blouse. The blouse works like a strainer," he mumbled through the crumbs.

"Not the case with the bartender," Weather said. A surgeon, she was familiar with the ways of blood. "I walked over and talked to Feeney. He says the guy was really ripped. Big, heavy knife with a long blade—could have been a hunting knife, but more likely was a butcher knife. Extremely sharp. Went in at the navel, was pulled up and out, and sliced right through the aortal artery. Also dumped out some of the contents of the stomach. The person who did it was strong, and close. To get that kind of a pull, even with a sharp knife, you'd need to be right up against the victim, so you could get the biceps into it. Be like lifting a dumbbell. So Feeney says."

Feeney was a Hennepin County assistant medical examiner and worked just down the street from the Hennepin County Medical Center, where Weather did most of her work.

"So what are we talking about?" Lucas asked.

"Alyssa would like you to take a look," Weather said. "So would I."

"I took a look," Lucas said.

"You read some reports," Weather said. "I'm talking about a serious look. She didn't come straight to you, because she knows what you think."

"She's a fuckin' wack job," Lucas said.

"Lucas: she believes in you," Weather said, taking one of his hands, looking into his eyes, manipulating like crazy. "That you can find her daughter."

He pulled away, held his hands up: helpless, hopeless. "Weather: Alyssa believes her daughter was killed because her Pluto was in her House of Donald Duck. Because of the stars and the moon. That we can find her if we hire the appropriate psychic. I can't talk to the woman. Twenty minutes and I want to strangle her."

"Then give her fifteen minutes," Weather said.

"Weather . . ."

"She looks dreadful," Weather said, pressing. "She loses her husband, she loses her daughter. All she wants is a little help, and all she gets is a bunch of flatfeet."

"Minneapolis guys are pretty good," Lucas said. He popped another cinnamon roll. "They only *look* like a bunch of flatfeet."

"But Minneapolis isn't working her case," Weather said. "They only came to see her because of this dead bartender's connection to Frances—some other Goth told them about the connection."

"So . . ."

"But she says they think it's a waste of time," Weather said. "She could tell by the way they asked the questions. And then . . ."

"What?"

"She says your investigator thinks *she* may be involved. With whatever happened to Frances. She says that's all they can think of. They don't have any real suspects, so they suspect her, and they stopped looking for the real killer."

"Another reason you shouldn't go around casting horoscopes," Lucas said. "People tend to think you're nuts."

"You think she could have done it?" Weather asked.

"No." He thought about it for a moment, then said into the silence, "Hell, I don't know."

Weather took a cinnamon roll, popped it in her mouth, chewed twice, put her hands on her hips, and said, "Mmm. Mega-fat calories. So: will you see her, or will I have to nag you into it?"

"Aw, for Christ sakes," Lucas said.

"Tomorrow?"

"I'm pretty tied up. Maybe—"

"Lucas. You haven't done a thing for a month, except sit around and watch Heather Toms take her clothes off," Weather said. "You always have this slump at the end of the winter. The only way out is work. So find the time."

"If I go along, could you provide me with a few sexual favors?" He wasn't really doing much. And he *was* bummed. Sexual favors would help, and asking for them, as payment, felt agreeably sleazy; and might drain the excess testosterone he'd worked up watching the lovely Mrs. Toms dress and undress.

"Maybe," she said.

"So I'll talk to her," Lucas said.

"Excellent. I'll call her and confirm it," Weather said. "Get away from the cinnamon rolls."

"At her house," Lucas said. "I'll see her at her house."

Weather went to make the call and Lucas popped a third roll. They were about as wide as a fifty-cent piece and three-quarters of an inch thick, a snail of pie dough layered with butter and cinnamon, and baked until they were chewy.

He was modestly pleased with himself. Sexual favors and cinnamon rolls. Like hitting three bells on the Indian slots.

Because, realistically, once Weather had decided that he was going to talk to Austin, there was no way out. If she put her mind to it, she could nag the paint off a garage. But, if he went to Austin's house, he could always leave. No kicking, no screaming, no weeping, no people down the hall wondering what the hell was going on in Davenport's office. He could simply leave.

He thought about a fourth cinnamon roll.

He was in good shape; he'd been working out. He couldn't even pinch a half an inch. How many calories could a cinnamon roll have, anyway?

3

THE RAIN CONTINUED through the night—the better for the sexual favors, which were hottest in a flickering candlelight, with freshets of water pouring through the gutters and downspouts—but was beginning to ease by the time he'd finished breakfast. He drove into the office, made a series of morning calls, checking on his agents, then made the ten o'clock meeting at the planning center, where the BCA director, Rose Marie Roux, chaired the security committee for the Republican National Convention.

Lucas had reported to Roux for years, first when she was the Minneapolis chief of police, later when she was named the director of the BCA, and he'd followed her over. She'd always been political—a street cop for a couple of years, then an office cop while she went to law school, then a state representative, a state senator, Minneapolis chief, and over to the BCA.

She was smitten by the convention job. Lucas thought she was behaving like a starstruck teenager, hanging out with the guys in black suits and ear bugs, who spoke into their cuff links and cut their hair ranger-style.

Smitten was bad.

The security for the convention was going to be inadequate, because the Twin Cities area didn't have the police resources, and the feds weren't coming through with enough extra. None of the big shots would get hurt, of course, because they'd be blanketed by gun-toting Secret Service thugs, but the town, in Lucas's opinion, was toast. Whoever'd had the bright idea of inviting the convention to St. Paul, he thought, should have had his head X-rayed until it smoked.

He slipped out before the meeting was done and before he might be tempted to take out his gun and shoot someone. He went downstairs and called the governor's chief weasel, up on Capitol Hill, and got three minutes alone with the great man.

The governor was at his desk, with a stack of outstate weekly newspapers by his left hand. The sun was shining through a crack in the clouds, in through the window behind the governor's head, and bathed him in holy nimbus. Then the cloud-cut closed, and the nimbus went away.

"What?" the governor asked, when Lucas shut the door.

"Got a favor to ask."

The governor was a thin man, sleek, his hair lacquered in place, with delicate cheekbones and an aristocratic lip. He'd been reading the real estate ads in one of the weeklies, his stocking feet up on a mahogany file cabinet. The governor was the scion of one of Minnesota's bigger fortunes, originally considered to be the runt of the litter, and now pretty much running the state and the family. Some said he thought they were the same thing . . .

His socks, Lucas observed, were a pale lavender with the thinnest of scarlet clocks. The governor cocked an eye at him and asked, "Is this gonna cause me trouble? Whatever it is?"

"Probably the least amount of trouble of anything you've done today," Lucas said, as he dropped into a leather armchair. "If you get assassinated this week, can I have those socks?"

"No. We pass these down through the generations, to the oldest sons."

"C'mon. Where'd you get them?"

"Ferragamo." The governor folded the paper, dropped it in a wastebasket, and said, "The shit is about to hit the fan. The question is, will it hit before the next election?"

"What shit?" Lucas asked. For one crazy moment, he thought the governor might be concerned about convention security.

"The ethanol market is gonna drop dead," the governor said. "Capacity is outrunning demand, and the big energy companies are moving up to the trough. A whole bunch of farmers who mortgaged the farm to build all these small plants, they're gonna lose their shirts. Then they'll want to know what I'm going to do about it."

Lucas shrugged. "That's your problem. And the farmers'. Though it's not your biggest problem."

"What's my biggest problem?" The governor's eyebrows went up.

"The convention," Lucas said. "The protesters are gonna trash the place, right down the hill from your office. If we quadrupled the security we're planning, it wouldn't be a quarter of what we need."

The governor frowned: "I don't know. This is a pretty lefty state."

"The people causing the trouble aren't lefties," Lucas said, rapping his knuckles on the rosewood desk. "They're vandals. Petty criminals. Jerkoffs. They wouldn't care if the Blessed Virgin Mary showed up holding hands with Karl Marx. This is their Super Bowl, and it's sixty-forty that they're gonna tear us a new asshole."

The governor looked mildly impatient. "Is that what you came to tell me?"

"No, no. Nobody listens anyway," Lucas said, discouraged. "The planners believe we can count on the goodwill of the people; like the vandals are just another caucus. Fuckin' morons."

"The people? Or the planners?"

"The planners."

"Anyway . . ." The governor didn't pay any more attention than anyone else, and his eyes strayed back to the stack of newspapers.

"Anyway," Lucas said, leaning forward, "this is something different. Do you know Alyssa Austin, Hunter Austin's wife? Or widow, I guess?"

"Yes." The governor straightened around, picked a pair of black loafers off the floor, and slipped his feet into them, wiggling his toes. "I read about her kid. That's awful. She's dead, right?"

"Ninety-nine percent," Lucas said. "We cover Sunfish Lake on homicides, and we've got a new guy looking into it. He isn't getting much. I'd like to be able to tell people that the governor asked me to poke around, as a personal favor, and that I had no choice but to say yes."

"So you won't piss off the new guy. Or Rose Marie," the governor said. The runt of the litter, but no dummy.

"That's right," Lucas said.

"Go ahead; I'll cover for you," the governor said. "I'll be raising money there this summer, in Sunfish. Probably know half the people in town. So if you could settle it before then, that'd be good."

"Not a problem," Lucas said.

"Let them know that you're out there at my suggestion," the governor added. "Especially if you catch the killers."

Lucas nodded. "Ferragamo," he said, and stood up. The audience was over.

"Yup. You want a fashion tip?" The governor picked up another paper and checked the front page before turning back to the classifieds.

"I always listen to fashion tips," Lucas said. That was true; he did. He didn't always follow them, but the governor had excellent taste.

"You always want your socks and your pajamas to be slightly gay," the governor said. "Not *too* gay, but slightly."

Lucas thought about it for a second, and said, "You're right. I knew that, but I never explicitly formulated it."

"Of course I'm right." The governor glanced at his solid-gold Patek Philippe. "Get out of here."

BACK AT HIS office, Lucas left a message with Rose Marie's secretary about the governor's request, made it clear that the message wasn't too important, then found Jim Benson sitting in his cubicle, fingers knitted behind his head, looking at a whiteboard with a lot of names and arrows. Lucas knocked on the door frame and Benson swiveled, said, "Hey, Lucas, what's up?"

"The governor called me in this morning, man. He raises a lot of money over in Sunfish Lake, and he's asked me to take a personal look at the Austin case."

Benson sat up: "I thought I had the bases pretty well covered."

Lucas said, "You probably do, but old lady Austin and the governor are pals, and she's one of his big backers . . . Nothing personal, man."

"I hate that kind of goddamn politics," Benson said. "Favoritism for the rich, that's what it is."

"Shhh," Lucas said. "For Christ's sakes, you don't know who can hear you."

GETTING THE FILES out of Benson was like pulling a tooth; nasty. But Lucas got them, for a couple of hours, anyway. Told Benson he'd just skim the paper, talk to a few people, kick over a couple of rocks so when the governor asked . . .

He'd already read the preliminary reports. Now he spent an hour looking at the paper, then gave the file to his secretary and told her to xerox it and return it to Benson, as quickly as possible. "It'd be nice if he thought I just glanced at it. Don't mention that you made a copy."

"Ah, screwin' the new guy, huh?" Carol said.

By early afternoon, the storm had cleared. Splashing through the leftover puddles, Lucas took the Porsche off Robert Street south of St. Paul, and poked into the bare winter forest that was Sunfish Lake.

The Twin Cities have no really exclusive suburbs, except those that are exclusively rich or poor. No social barriers: if you had the cash or could get the mortgage, you could live there, whatever your race, color, creed, or national origin. Sunfish Lake was one of those.

The first fifty feet of the Austin driveway were gravel, as if to say, *We may be rich, but we're really country.* The last three hundred feet were blacktop, which said, *We may be country, but we're not stupid.*

The driveway ran slightly uphill, then over a crest and down to the house. The house had three sections that he could see—a center/main section, of stone and redwood, with barren flower beds under the white-painted window trim; and a cedar-shingled wing on each end, bending away from him, toward the lake. The four-car garage was in the right wing.

The house was buried in oaks and spruce, snuggled into the slope, surrounded by a patch of grass that faded into the forest. From the crest of the hill, Lucas could see a broad flagstone path meandering down to the lake. A wheeled dock had been pulled out of the water, next to the path, and a finger of snow hunkered beneath it. More snow hid out in the woods, where it had been protected from the rain.

Lucas parked the Porsche, and got out into the smell of wet old leaves, late-winter woods, and the faintest stink of rotting fish. He walked up to the door, rang the doorbell, and grinned at his reflection in the glass panel beside the door.

He was wearing jeans, a white shirt, Mephisto black-leather athletic shoes, a black leather jacket, and aviator sunglasses. He was packing heat, he thought, and also carried a gun.

Austin glanced at him through the glass, pulled the door open, and said, "I've already got a vacuum cleaner."

"Well, shoot, another wasted trip," Lucas said.

She smiled then, but a sad smile, the kind of smile he might have a month after one of his kids was killed. She said, "Lucas— you look like a rich cop."

He took her hand, which was cool and muscular and dry. "Alyssa. How are you?"

"Not good," she said. "Or you wouldn't be here. Come in."

She was a small woman and slender. She'd been a swimmer in college, and after marrying Hunter Austin, had started a chain of high-end athletic clubs for wealthy women. The clubs—Weather belonged to one—were quiet, discreet, luxurious, efficient, expensive, and successful.

Alyssa Austin dabbled with several kinds of therapies, as well as astrology and tarot. On the functioning side of her brain, she had degrees in management and accounting.

Lucas could see the swimmer in her, the athlete, as he followed her through the entry, down the high-ceiling hall to the living room. Her ass was like a rock, and interesting to look at. His taste in women was catholic, but she fit into a particularly interesting small-tough-blonde slot, the same slot occupied by Weather.

". . . couldn't think of what else to do, so finally I talked to Weather. I know that makes you unhappy," she was saying.

"No, no, I'm happy to do it," he lied. Great ass or not, she was goofy. The thought brought to mind the punch line of the old Mickey Mouse–Minnie Mouse joke—"I didn't say you were crazy, I said you were fuckin' Goofy."

He smiled to himself, then hid the smile.

The living room was done as two partial-hemispheres of glass, looking out toward the lake, almost like the cups of a brassiere. A Steinway grand piano sat in one of the cups, while a circle of overstuffed furniture was arranged as a conversation group in the other. She took him there. "Coffee? Beer? Pepsi? I've got some great coffee."

"That'd be fine," Lucas said.

"Be right back."

She disappeared down another hall, and he could hear her speaking to someone, and a reply. A minute later she was back, trailed by a dark-haired young woman carrying a ceramic tray that held two cups of coffee, a ceramic pot, and a pile of butter cookies.

"Thanks, Helen. Are you off now?"

"Unless you need me," the woman said.

"Take off. Say hello to Ricky for me."

The housekeeper looked uncertainly at Lucas and then said,

"I'd be happy to stay awhile longer . . ." She had an Ole and Lena accent from Northern Minnesota, but had dark eyes and hair that seemed more Middle Eastern than Nordic.

"Mr. Davenport is a policeman. We're discussing Frances," Austin said. "I'm safe—his wife would kill him if he attacked me."

The housekeeper rattled around in the kitchen for another minute or two, as Lucas and Austin chatted about the view over the lake, and about a six-foot-long oil painting that perfectly captured the bluffs over the Mississippi, south of St. Paul's downtown, in a rainstorm.

"It's a Kidd landscape. We were lucky enough to buy it while they were still affordable," Austin said. "Do you know his work?"

"Actually, I know Kidd," Lucas said. "He just got married a year or so ago—he's got a new son."

"Mmm," Austin said. "Too bad. If nothing romantic came along, I was thinking of looking him up."

"You might have gotten along," Lucas said.

"Why? Is he fuckin' goofy, too?"

Lucas's mouth nearly dropped open: she'd snatched the words right out of his head. Instead, he laughed and said, "Actually, he's a pretty nice guy. Used to be a wrestler in college, same time I was skating."

The housekeeper ducked her head into the living room to say that there were more cookies in the jar, and that she was leaving. A moment later, they heard the garage-access door close, and they were alone.

Austin sat on an oversized leather easy chair, and pulled her feet up to sit cross-legged, yoga-style. "How do you want to do this? You want me to talk?"

Lucas took a cup of coffee, leaned back in his chair and crossed his legs, looking at her over the cup. "I've read the file on your case and I checked the Minneapolis homicide guys on Dick Ford. I looked at some of the crime-scene photos on Ford. I can see a superficial similarity in the . . ." He paused, groping for a better phrase, couldn't find one: ". . . blood trail. I know about the Goth connection. That's what I know."

She nodded, and took a cup of coffee, and a sip. "Okay. So you know the basics. Now, you should also know—I don't know if this kind of thing would be in their reports—but your investigating agent, this James Benson, thinks I may have had something to do with whatever happened to Frances."

She paused, looking for a reaction, but Lucas just nodded: let her go on. "There are some reasons that they think that. By their lights. You know, statistics: that most murders like this involve friends or relatives. But Frances didn't have a boyfriend at the moment, and her last two, going back five years, both had alibis. She was careful; she was quite aware of who she was, and how rich she was. Also, if she were murdered here, how did the people come and go? Nobody saw a car."

Lucas held up a finger: "There must have been one, right? If she was killed, and her body isn't here, then it must have been moved." He turned his head and looked out at the lake: "Did they check the lake?"

"No. It was completely iced up, and there was snow, and there were no footprints in the snow. There was unbroken snow around the whole house. So, you're right. There must have been a car."

She'd been gone all day, she said. Helen, the housekeeper, had been there until four, and Frances hadn't shown up by that time. Crime-scene analysis suggested that the blood was a couple hours old by the time Austin got home, shortly before seven o'clock. The cops had taken a close look at Helen, and while she had no specific alibi, she had a bunch of the small ratshit stuff—an ATM receipt, a cash register receipt from a Target—that suggested that she'd been gone before the murder took place.

"Before we get too far, I need to tell you one more thing," Austin said. "Frances and I . . . Wait, to start at the beginning— Hunter and I had problems. Marital problems. Whether we would have worked them out, I don't know."

Lucas uncrossed his legs and leaned toward her. "When you say problems—you mean infidelity problems, political disagreements, what?"

"Oh . . . who knows, really?" She smiled briefly, a quick flash and gone. "He was eight years older than I am. I don't know exactly what it was, male menopause, or maybe he just got tired of my act. As he got older—he was fifty-one when he died—he got more and more *macho*. Hanging out at the airport, working on his plane. Bought a Harley and an Indian and something else. An old Vincent Black, something like that? Didn't pay much attention to me anymore. Hung out with the guys all the time. I thought of it as . . . boy problems."

"Boy problems."

"You know, *is this all there is?* He might have been boinking his assistant, but . . . boys will be boys. Anyway, Frances picked up on the tension, didn't understand what was going on, and took her father's side. When he was killed, she was really torn up. I was, too, actually. We'd been married for twenty-three years; that wasn't nothing. So, after the memorial service, Frances and I began to have disagreements. She'd pick fights with me; go out of her way to do it. We were the coexecutors of Hunter's will, and she hired her own outside attorney and accountant because she thought I might try to do something funny about the money . . . cut her out."

"You didn't do that?" Lucas asked.

"Of course not," Austin said. "There was way more money than either of us needed, for the rest of our lives." She lifted her hands toward the ceiling, to indicate the richness of the house. "Way more than enough."

Way more than enough. Still, she admitted, she'd be the one who'd inherit from Frances, after the estate tax was paid to the state of Minnesota.

"Estate tax makes me laugh," she said. "When Hunter died, Frances had to pay sixty-six thousand dollars in estate tax to Minnesota to get her inheritance. Then she died, if she did die, and I'm going to have to pay another sixty thousand, out of the same money, to inherit from her."

Lucas, watching as she talked, realized—he'd noticed, but hadn't *realized*—how dressed up she was. The pants and jersey together cost two thousand dollars, he'd bet; and her hairdo, done in what Lucas thought of as an ice-skater cut, probably cost five hundred. She'd dressed up for him, something he doubted that she often did, in the daytime, in the winter. She was being formal; she was pleading.

He said, "When women kill, they often do it with a knife. Not because they plan to, but because they do it close to the kitchen, and there are knives handy, and they're familiar with them. They do it in a moment of passion, the heat of an argument. You had a daughter, with whom you'd been having disagreements, a large amount of money was involved, there was a substantial blood trail but no signs of a shot or impact trauma, so if she was killed . . . it's very likely it could have been done with a knife. And you told the police that you think a knife might be missing."

She nodded again: "To summarize the Benson position."

"And you didn't do it."

"No. Not only did I not do it, I can't get the investigation I want, either," Austin said.

She wanted the cops to push the investigation as hard as possible, to include investigating *her*, if they thought it necessary. They'd be wasting their time on her, she said, but go ahead—as long as they looked in other directions, as well. "If Frances was killed, she came here with someone she knew—the alarm system had been turned off. So that's the critical thing: Who would she come here with? Somebody must know. *Somebody must know.*"

"Why aren't you absolutely sure the knife is missing?" Lucas asked.

"Because I don't inventory knives. Do you? I thought not," she snapped. More quietly, "It was a small knife. The kind you use to pare apples. Wooden handle, from Chicago Cutlery. We didn't keep it in the cutting block. It was—at one time—in the end

35

drawer in the kitchen. Actually, it's possible that Frances took it with her when she got an apartment, and then, in one of her moves, she left it with somebody. But the police asked me to inventory the knives, and I couldn't find that one. I know I had it, at one time."

"Mmm."

"What, mmm?"

"The bartender in Minneapolis was killed with a much bigger knife, a butcher knife or a hunting knife, even," Lucas said. "Not an apple-parer."

"Still . . . maybe the killer learned from experience." Her fingertips went to her mouth. "Oh, God. What'd I just say?" Tears glistened at the corners of her eyes.

He sat there watching her as she went through a crying jag, pressing her knuckles into her mouth, but unable to stop for a minute or two. When she finally reined herself in, he said, "I'm sorry, if I touched that off."

"Naw, it's not you. I do that every once in a while," she said. "I talked to my shrink, and he said that releasing the emotion would make me feel better. But you know what? It doesn't. It makes me feel worse."

She started again, cried for ten seconds, then cut it off, wiped her eyes with the heels of her hands.

"You're going to have to fix your makeup," Lucas said. "You've got a smear of eyeliner."

"Yes. I've gotten used to that, too."

AUSTIN HAD MADE a list of Frances's friends—she hopped out of her chair, walked over to the ebony Steinway, got a notebook, slipped out a piece of paper and handed it to Lucas: high-school friends, college friends, a couple of Goths, ten names and addresses, neatly computer-printed on cream-colored stationery. Lucas asked, "Why would you suspect a Goth? Did any of them ever . . . say anything, or do anything?"

She sat down again. "I hardly knew them. When I came, they

left. But I've read about them, they worship darkness, they're fascinated by death, by . . . you know, they're crazy."

"Frances was crazy?"

"No. She was young. She was experimental. Like I was, when I went to school," she said. "Except my experiments weren't like hers. Mine felt outrageous and my parents were outraged, but I wasn't unsafe. I've got a tattoo around my belly button, I smoked some pot, I made out with another woman. I didn't sit around in cemeteries with guys in skirts and white-face, talking about what's on the Other Side. Other Side meaning *death*."

Lucas tried to suppress a sigh, but sighed anyway. She heard it: "What?"

"Let me come back to this thing about your marital problems," Lucas said. "You say your husband might have been . . . I think you said 'boinking' his assistant. That means he was sleeping with her?"

"Possibly," Austin said.

"Possibly? Weren't you a little upset by that?"

Her forehead wrinkled, and she thought about it, shook her head and said, "I suppose. But not too much. It wasn't like she was a threat. If we'd gotten divorced, it'd have been because our partnership wasn't working anymore. But that part—the partnership—was okay. We had the same interests, the same friends, we both got a lot of pleasure out of our work and our home. If he was having an affair, that was just . . . part of this thing he was going through. It was serious, but not critical, if you know what I mean."

"I don't," Lucas said. "If Weather had an affair . . ."

He trailed off, and she jumped in: "You'd what? Shoot her? Beat her up?"

"No . . ."

"Of course not. You're civilized," Austin said. "So you'd shout at her and go storming out of the house. If you were deadly serious, you'd hire some Nazi attorney and pound her in the divorce. But . . . what if you didn't care about sleeping with her anymore,

37

but you still liked her, and you saw it all coming on? Then you might wind up like Hunter and I did. The sex didn't completely stop; it just wasn't central anymore."

"What was his assistant's name?" Lucas asked.

"Martina Trenoff."

"Smart? Pretty?"

"Smart, pretty, big boobs, hustled all the time. Available twenty-four/seven. She did a lot of his work for him, I think, toward the end. She was a junior-level exec when he took her as his assistant. MBA from St. Thomas. She knew some stuff. And he groomed her."

"I'm not all that clear on what your husband manufactured," Lucas said.

"High-tech machine parts. Essentially, a tool-and-die place that also made one-off final products. They have a lot of defense work."

"You still own it?"

"We controlled it until we had to liquidate to pay the taxes—we owned about thirty-two percent of the stock," Austin said. "When he died, five percent went to charity, we got the rest, and when the feds and the state were finished with us, we had lots of money and no stock."

"How about Martina?" Lucas asked. "What happened to her after Austin died?"

"She kept working there, at least for a while. She was there when we cashed out, but I didn't track her," Austin said. "She wasn't too popular, by the time he died. She was telling the other top execs what Austin wanted done, and sometimes, what *she* wanted done. So they may have parted ways."

"Okay. So: the affair wasn't too important," Lucas said.

"Well—important, but not critical."

They sat there for a moment, and he thought, *It'd be critical to me*, and then he slapped his open hands on his knees and said, "I'll talk to some people."

"You'll really make an effort?" She showed her skepticism, as he'd showed the sigh.

"I can't promise unlimited time—and I could get pulled for another job," Lucas said. "We've got the Republican convention coming and I'm on the security committee. But I'll talk to some people."

She snarled at him, "Fuck a bunch of Republicans. Find my daughter."

4

THE INTERVIEW, he thought as he rolled back out the driveway, hadn't been as bad as he feared. No talk of planets, no cards, no chicken guts. And the problem was interesting. Rich people, infidelity, missing knives. Blood on the wall.

He got back on the highway and headed north through St. Paul, and then west to Minneapolis, splashing through the dwindling puddles, whistling as he went, thinking it over. Tiniest of cracks in the winter gloom, he thought—not in the climate, but in his own.

THE MINNEAPOLIS CITY HALL is not a pretty building. A pile of red granite, a sullen nineteenth-century Romanesque lump, it squats amid the glittering glass-and-steel towers of the loop like a wart poking through a diamond necklace.

Lucas had spent half of his career going in and out of the place. He'd been sworn in as a street cop there, had moved up through the ranks, and wound up as a politically appointed deputy chief; and he still walked through every few weeks, for meetings, to visit with friends, to hang out.

He found a cops-only parking spot at the curb and put the BCA tag under the windshield; but enough cops would recognize the Porsche that he hardly needed the tag. Inside, he walked along to homicide, as he had five thousand times before, except that nothing smelled like nicotine anymore. A guy coming out let him in: "Hey, dude."

Harold Anson was sitting at his desk, synchronizing an MP3 player with a laptop, deeply involved, unaware that Lucas was coming up behind him.

Lucas said, "I didn't know there were that many polkas."

Anson jumped, turned, clapped his hand to his heart, and said, "Jesus Christ, man, don't sneak up on me."

"You look guilty," Lucas said. "You stealing that stuff?"

"Of course not," Anson said. "I could be investigated by the FBI."

They both laughed, and Lucas asked, "You're working the Ford murder?"

Anson perked up a bit, punched the computer out, swiveled his chair around. "Yeah. What's up?"

"The governor is a friend of Alyssa Austin's," Lucas said. He propped himself on an empty desk. "He's squeezing me to talk to a couple of people. I don't want to step on your toes."

"No skin off my butt," Anson said, yawning and stretching. "You oughta mention it to Whistler."

Whistler was the lieutenant in charge of homicide.

"I called him, he said it's no skin off his butt, but I should run it past you," Lucas said.

Anson shrugged: "So—no butt skin. Welcome to the big time. We copied everything over to Jim Benson."

"I took a look at it," Lucas said. "He's dead in the water, on Austin. He's not even sure the kid is dead."

"She's dead," Anson said flatly. "You only think she's *not* dead if you think about it too much."

Lucas agreed. Frances Austin was dead. "You guys got nothing on Ford?"

"We're not oversupplied with clues," Anson agreed. "We're still talking."

"I'm going to talk behind you," Lucas said, pushing off the desk. "If I get anything, I'll give you a call."

"Do that," Anson said. "Listen, how much do you think Benson makes over there?"

"I don't know. Maybe seventy-five in an average year," Lucas said.

"Yeah? He doesn't seem like the sharpest knife in the dishwasher."

"He's okay," Lucas said.

"So what would a guy have to do . . . ?"

They bullshitted about job openings for a while. Anson was coming up on twenty-two years with Minneapolis and was looking to double-dip on a pension. "Unfortunately, my only expertise is in street proctology."

MACY'S WAS A ten-minute walk from homicide, through the underground tunnel to the government center, up to the Skyways, and through the maze of bridges and hallways to the heart of the shopping district. Lucas stopped and bought an ice-cream cone, stopped again to talk to a couple of uniforms who were frog-marching a shoplifter down to a squad car.

The shoplifter was dressed exactly like a movie shoplifter, in wrinkled gray-cotton slacks and stained parka, set off with a five-day beard and fuzzy, aging Rasta braids. Half-hanging from the arms of the cops, who were wearing yellow rubber gloves, he said, "Hey . . . Davenport."

"That you, Louis?" Louis didn't look so good. His weight was down fifty pounds, and maybe more, since the last time Lucas had seen him.

"It's me," Louis said.

"You look sort of fucked up," Lucas said, licking the cone.

"Got the AIDS, man." His eyes turned up to Lucas, and Lucas could see that the whites were going yellow.

"Ah, Jesus, Louis."

"Gonna get you sooner or later," Louis said. Louis wasn't exactly gay, but he *was* for sale.

"Don't plead out. Take the jail time," Lucas said.

41

Louis was insulted: "Hey, whacha think I'm doin' getting caught?"

Lucas said, "Don't pass it on, man. You get in there, you sleep on your back."

Louis's eyes turned back to the floor: "What's gonna happen, gonna happen. What it is, is what it is."

"We'll talk to the sheriff's guys," one of the uniforms said.

Lucas nodded and ambled on, looking in store windows, said hello to a salesman at the Hubert White men's store, let himself get pulled inside to look at an Italian summer suit, a steal at $2,495, and then crossed Nicollett Mall on the skyway bridge to Macy's, and found cosmetics. A woman in a white jacket, behind the Dior counter, was staring into space. He walked through the space and she didn't blink. "Charlene Mobry?"

Now she blinked, took him in, sighed, and turned and looked down the counter at another woman in a white jacket, who was rearranging a shelf of eau de cologne bottles. She called, "Charlene? You got a customer."

Charlene Mobry was dishwater-blond, thirty pounds too heavy, puffy lips, green eyes, and small fat hands with tiny polished nails and rings on each thumb. She said, "Help you?"

Lucas took out his ID and unfolded it on the counter. "I'd like to talk to you for a few minutes, about Dick Ford."

"Ohh . . ." Her lower lip trembled and she looked sideways, as though she might run for it. Then she came back to him, with her eyes, and he realized how deeply sad she was. "Did you find . . . who did it?"

"I'm with the state," Lucas said, as he shook his head. "We're doing a parallel investigation: we really want to get this guy. Whoever it is. Don't have him yet."

Mobry nodded and called to the spaced-out woman to whom Lucas had first spoken. "Mary. This guy's a policeman. I've got to go talk to him about Dick."

"Okay," Mary said.

Mobry led the way across the store, behind a counter into a

stockroom, steel racks filled with shoe boxes. A couple of plastic chairs were pushed into a corner; the shelf next to the chairs held an old radio, unplugged, and an ashtray with four snubbed-out filter-cigarette butts. They sat down and Lucas took a notebook out of his breast pocket and asked, "You were dating Mr. Ford?"

"We hung out," she said. "Like we'd go to dinner. We weren't a hundred percent a couple, but we sorta were."

"You told the Minneapolis police that you didn't have any ideas at all about who might have done this," Lucas said.

"An asshole," she said.

"Have you heard anything at all, since you talked to Minneapolis? Any thoughts about Mr. Ford? Anything?"

"Just gossip. Everybody says the Goths must've done it, but I know quite a few of them, and most of them are pretty nice. I never met a Goth who'd have done it."

"You're not a Goth?"

"Do I look like one?" she asked.

"Well, after work . . ."

"No, I'm not. It used to make me laugh. It's too dramatic."

"But Mr. Ford was a Goth."

"Sort of. Yeah, he was. But you know, it comes and goes. Like it was pretty big twenty years ago, and ten years ago, and now here it comes again . . . Dick was really into it ten years ago, but then not so much, and he wasn't so into it this time. He changed. He stopped smoking dope, he stopped drinking, he started saving money, he was taking a class in bookkeeping. He wanted to start his own club, and I think . . ." Her voice went squeaky: ". . . I think he might have done it, if some asshole hadn't killed him."

Lucas paused, waited for her to pull back together; the smell of the old cigarette butts closed in around them. "You saw him the night he was killed. At the A1."

"Yes." Her head bobbed and she bit her lower lip, holding it together. "I went over after work. I had a beer and a cheeseburger, and we talked for a couple of minutes, but it was pretty busy, so I went home. We were going to a play the next night, over at Loring

Park. I never saw him again . . . I went out of the bar and I turned around and waved and he waved back and that was the last I saw of him forever."

"That's tough," Lucas said.

"Yeah."

"You said there was more gossip . . ."

She looked away, then back. "A friend of Dick's, named Karl, said there was a Goth girl around, a fairy . . ." As she talked about it, her voice rose in pitch, and became squeaky with grief. ". . . and she was talking to Dick before closing. Not that there was anything going on, but nobody knew her."

Lucas asked, "Did you tell the Minneapolis police about this?"

"No . . . Karl was supposed to."

Lucas hadn't seen anyone named Karl in the Minneapolis paper. "What's Karl's last name?"

"Lageson." She spelled it, and added, "Karl with a K. He lives in Uptown. I don't know where, exactly."

Lucas noted it down, and asked, "So what's a fairy look like?"

"Oh, you know. Skinny, small, big eyes, dark hair. Short skirts, long legs, ripped stockings. Everything black. Black nail polish, crimson lipstick. Black hair. I mean, not all fairies have black hair, but she did."

"I don't think Karl told anybody," Lucas said.

"Oh, shit. He should have. He's the one who saw her. Or says he did. But he's sort of . . ." She put a finger up at her temple and made a few circles. "He's smoked too much weed. He might have just thought it up. Or gotten it from one of his Goth comics."

"Anybody else see her?" Lucas asked.

"I don't know. If you go down to the A1, they'll be talking about it, if anybody saw her. I mean some hot fairy mysterious Goth chick, everybody would be talking. Goths gossip a lot."

"A few weeks ago, a young woman, a Goth, named Frances Austin disappeared," Lucas said.

"I know about it," she said, nodding. "The blood in the hall. She and Dick knew each other. You probably knew that."

44

"Did you know her?"

Her gaze fixed on him, but lost focus, as she considered the question. "I'm not sure. I saw her picture in the paper, and on TV, and people at the A1 were talking about it, because she'd been there the day before she disappeared. But I don't know if I really remember her, or just remember the pictures on TV. I mean, I didn't *know* her, but I might have seen her."

"What was the nature of her relationship with Mr. Ford?"

"Well, he wasn't sleeping with her, if that's what you're wondering," Mobry said. "It was more like, a bartender with a regular who's an okay person, and they shared some things like the gothic. A person who doesn't start trouble and is friendly and leaves a tip."

"Did you and Mr. Ford . . ."

"Call him Dick. Mr. Ford sounds really . . . dead."

"Did you and Dick talk about her?" Lucas asked.

"Oh, sure, right after she disappeared. The police came and talked to Dick, and he told them what he knew. Which was hardly anything. She came in and got fish 'n chips the day before she disappeared. She was with a couple of other Goths—the police have their names, I don't remember them. But then the day she disappeared, she didn't come in. I think it was in the paper that she and a friend had lunch that day somewhere else, like a bagel place."

"That's right," Lucas said.

"So not at the A1. Anyway, she and Dick weren't intimate—and I don't mean sex. I mean, they didn't share life stories. Dick was a bartender, so you know, he was a professional bullshitter. He didn't even have any good bullshit about her."

"Huh." Lucas rubbed his nose. Goddamn stale cigarettes.

"Do you think the same person who killed Dick killed Frances?" Mobry asked.

"I don't know. We don't even know if she's dead," Lucas said.

She sat with her hands in her lap: "You sound like you're stuck."

"I just started," Lucas said. "I'm trying to get something going."

"Why don't you do some of that magic DNA stuff like you see on TV?"

"We did," Lucas said. "The problem is, it's not magic. Most of the time, you wind up proving that people who already said they were there, were there."

"That doesn't help," she said.

They sat among the boxes, staring at each other for a moment, then Lucas asked, "Neither of you, you or Dick, had any bad vibrations from people, felt like somebody knew something, something was being held back?"

She shook her head. "Nothing. I've got nothing. I don't even have a body. His parents came and got him and took him back to Rochester. The funeral's Friday."

He stood up. "All right. I'm really sorry for your loss. Dick sounds like an okay guy."

"He *was* a good guy," Mobry said, and the tears started again. "Are you going to find the fairy Goth?"

"Yeah, I am. Any ideas?"

"If she's real, somebody at the A1 knows her. Some of the guys would have been following her around, if she looks like what she sounds like."

"Anything else? Anything?"

She shrugged, wiped tears away with her fingertips, said, "Do the Austins have a butler? Maybe the butler did it."

Then she cried, and Lucas patted her on the shoulder and asked if she'd be all right, and she said, "Yeah, I'd just like to sit here awhile," and Lucas left.

She hadn't had anything to do with the murder, he thought. In Lucas's experience, women who killed their boyfriends suffered either from too much intensity or too much innocence; Mobry didn't have either quality.

Like Austin, she was overwhelmed with sadness; all the sadness was getting him down.

5

BACK OUT INTO the skyways, getting-out-of-the-office time, crowds jostling through to the parking ramps, a few of the younger women showing some pre-spring skin, the teen guys flashing tattoos over health-club muscles, their elders often with the competitive, fixed, dead-eyed, and querulous stare of people who were not getting far enough, fast enough, making enough, hustling all the time, working all the time, no time for an evening's *paseo*, no time even for half-fast food. Scuttling people.

By the time Lucas got back to his car, the streets were snarled with evening rush-hour traffic, muttering along in a stink of exhaust and wet asphalt. He edged out into it, went around the block and down a few, to Washington Avenue, took the left, crawled a few more blocks, took the right turn across the Mississippi.

Lucas thought: Goths, mysterious fairies, dead bartenders ripped through their abdominal aortas—much better than a dead woman with a beer-bottle-cracked skull and a boyfriend who claimed he'd been out driving around; or paperwork; or political chores.

So he was whistling as he crossed the Hennepin Avenue bridge. He cheerfully chopped the nose off a Sprinter van, took the finger from the woman who was driving it, beat a red light by minus-fifteen feet, and dumped the car in a supermarket parking lot, leaving the BCA card on the dash.

The A1 was a block away, a brick building painted white, the paint gone dingy and gray, with a miniature theater-style marquee hanging over the door. The marquee said *Surf & Turf, $9.99* and *Happy Hour, 5–*, which was either supposed to be cute, or the second number had fallen off.

Lucas ambled down the sidewalk, looking in the restaurant windows, checking the people on the street corners. The A1, when he came to it, looked respectably seedy; not a place where you'd go to start a fight, but not a place you'd propose to your girlfriend, either.

Inside, the purple carpet felt damp and spongy under his shoes. An anonymous jazz-piano tune was scratching its way out of overhead speakers, and a dim yellow light drizzled from red-shaded lamps running down the wall on his left, over a row of booths. Four of the booths were occupied by couples, and one by a single guy trying to read a newspaper. Two more men sat at the bar, with beers, an empty stool between them.

The bartender, a slope-shouldered, balding man with a rust-colored beard, was stacking wet glasses. Lucas leaned across the bar and asked, "Is Tom Harris in?"

The bartender yanked a couple of paper towels off a roll and wiped his hands. "Nope. He should be in later tonight. Eight, nine, like that." He cocked his head. "You a cop?"

Lucas nodded. "I'm trying to get a line on a Goth woman. She supposedly was seen with Dick Ford the night he was killed."

"You think she did it?"

"I'd just like to find her," Lucas said. "Got any ideas?"

The bartender shook his head. "I wasn't here that night. Thank God. Might've been me."

"Anybody say anything about her . . . ?"

"Yeah, you know. Bar talk. There's some confusion, about whether she was somebody we know, or somebody we've never seen."

Lucas said, "Run that by me again."

"There were three or four Goth women here that night," the bartender said, leaning forward, forearms on the bar. "That's not unusual. You guys already checked them out."

"I'm with the state, not Minneapolis," Lucas said. "I haven't checked out anybody."

"Then you oughta talk to Minneapolis," the bartender said. "They figured out who the Goths were. People knew them. Then this rumor starts that there was another one. But we don't know if there really was, or if somebody's confused, and the rumor's running on its own."

"Huh," Lucas said.

"All sounds like bullshit to me," said one of the guys at the bar. He looked like a failing insurance man, in a brown suit with a green nylon necktie rolled up at the tip. He'd had a few.

Lucas turned his head and said, "Yeah?"

"The more I hear about it, the hotter this chick gets," the guy said. He hip-yanked his barstool around to face Lucas. "When you heard about her yesterday, nobody was sure who they were talking about. Now you talk to somebody, and she's like what's-her-name—the movie star with the big lips."

"She's got big lips?"

"That was just an example," the barfly said. He took a calculated sip of beer, handling the glass carefully.

The other man at the bar said, "Nobody said anything about her lips. They *did* say she had a terrific ass. They were sure about that."

"I heard that, too," the bartender said.

"That narrows it down," Lucas said.

"Shit, if this was Wisconsin, it'd be a positive ID," said the second barfly.

"When did the rumor start?" Lucas asked.

"I heard it yesterday afternoon, from the noon crew," the bartender said.

"Me, too," the first barfly said, and the other one said, "Yup."

Lucas looked around, at the people in the booths. "Doesn't look like a Goth hangout."

"Things change about seven o'clock," the bartender said. "The business guys get out and night people start showing up."

"Oooo, scary," said the second barfly. He burped.

"Could you tell me even one name of somebody who actually thinks they saw her?" Lucas asked.

The bartender sighed and said, "You really ought to talk to Tom."

The first barfly said, "Jesus Christ, Jerry. Dick got *killed*." To

Lucas, he said, "There's a guy named Roy. He works at a liquor store over by Dinkytown. People say Roy talked to her."

Lucas took out his notebook, jotted it down. "Roy, liquor store in Dinkytown."

"Mike's," the bartender added.

"Mike's on Fourteenth?"

"I don't know, I've never been there," the bartender said. "I just know that Roy works at Mike's."

"I've been there," the second barfly said. "I don't know the street, but it's a hole-in-the-wall, kitty-corner from a Burger King."

"Got it," Lucas said. He knew the place, but had never been inside. "How about a guy named Karl Lageson?"

The bartender shook his head. "I don't know that name."

"I think that's Lurch," the first barfly said to the bartender. To Lucas: "Big tall pale white guy. Deep eyes, big forehead. Looks like he ought to have a bolt in his neck. Don't know about him, though."

"I've seen him with Roy," the second barfly said. "If Lurch is the guy you're looking for."

"Getting back to this Goth with the good ass," the bartender said. "I know the Goths that the Minneapolis cops talked to. None of them have got what you'd call an amazing ass. I mean, not so you'd go around saying what an amazing ass she had."

"So she might be new," Lucas suggested. "The other Goth."

"Could be," the bartender said. "Or maybe she's just a figment of somebody's imagination."

"A Fig Newton of the imagination; the little cookie that nobody knew," the first barfly said.

The second barfly burped again, scratched some cash out of his pocket, and said, "Gimme one more. Then cut me off. I gotta drive."

Lucas chatted with the three of them for another five minutes, noted their names, and headed out into the failing daylight, fishing his cell phone from his pocket, calling home. "Go ahead and eat without me," he told Weather. "I'll grab a sandwich. I'm doing some running around on Alyssa Austin."

"Anything I should know?" Weather asked.

"There's a mystery woman," Lucas said.

"That's always good," she said.

"I'll tell you about it tonight."

He stopped at a sandwich shop across the street from the supermarket. He got a free newspaper on the way in; from order to delivery, through eating and reading, a half hour drained away. When he walked across the street to his car, it was fully dark. Mike's was ten minutes away. He got tangled up around a minor traffic accident, and another ten minutes disappeared.

Mike's was a wedge-shaped store stuck into the corner of a 1920s building with fake brown-brick siding made of tar shingles, neon beer signs in the windows, bars under the glass. A young woman was sitting on a stool behind the counter, talking on her cell phone, a pudgy salon-blonde with a thumbprint-sized bruise under one eye, a scattering of acne across her nose. She took the phone away from her face for a moment and asked, "D'you need help?"

Lucas held up his ID. "Need to talk to you about Roy."

She said into the phone, "I've got a cop here. I don't know, it's about Roy . . . I don't know, hang on." To Lucas, with the phone on her shoulder: "What about Roy?"

"Could you get off the phone for a minute?" Lucas asked.

To the phone: "He wants me to get off the phone? Yeah, he is." Lucas thought he'd heard a tinny "asshole" from the phone, and he rubbed his forehead. She picked that up and said, "Call you back." Hung up and said, "Yeah?"

"I'm looking for an employee of yours named Roy," Lucas said.

"He went home."

"You got a phone number for him?" Lucas asked.

"I'm not allowed to give that out."

"I'm a cop. You're allowed to give it to me," Lucas said.

She rolled her eyes, as though she were being tried by the feeble-minded. "I'm not allowed to give to *anybody*."

"You want to stop giving me a hard time here?"

"Me? You're the asshole."

Lucas looked at her for a moment; she was enjoying herself, jerking around a cop. He contemplated her for a second, then took out his cell phone, hit a speed-dial number, waited for a second, then said, "This is Lucas Davenport, with the BCA . . . Yeah, hi, Rog. Look, could you send a squad around to Mike's Liquor on Fourteenth, over in Dinkytown? I'm working that Ford murder thing, I got a witness giving me a hard time. I'd like to get the name and a number for the owner, I might want to pick him up later. Yeah, thanks. Just probably transport her downtown, give her some time in the tank to think about it. Yeah. Yeah. Talk to you."

He hung up the phone and she shouted, "Transport *me*?" Lucas turned away, walked over to the door and looked out. She shouted, "Wait a minute. Transport me? What the fuck are you talking about?"

Lucas crossed his arms, looked down the street.

"Hey, fuckhead. Are you talking about me?"

He was getting a headache, but turned toward her. "When did Roy leave?"

Her eyes were bulging, her face the color of a Coke can, but she gave it up: "Half an hour ago."

A squad car pulled into the curb and a cop got out. "How do I get in touch with him?"

"You can't," she snarled. "He's on a date."

"Where's he going?"

"How'n the fuck should I know?" she asked. "I'm not his mother."

"Where does he live?"

She rolled her eyes again and Lucas resisted the impulse to jump over the counter and slap the shit out of her. "I don't know. In Uptown."

"So what's his phone number?"

"I'm not allowed to give it out," she said.

The Minneapolis cop came through the door, nodded at Lucas and asked, "What's up?"

"Ah, for Christ's sakes," the woman said. Lucas held a finger up to the cop, as she pulled a clipboard out from under the counter, looked down a list, and read off the phone number.

Lucas had his notebook ready and jotted it down. "What's his last name?"

"Carter."

Lucas wrote it down, said to the cop, "We're good to go. Madonna here was giving me a raft of shit."

They stepped toward the door and she shouted, "Fuck you again."

They both flinched and the cop said, "Jesus," and they were out on the sidewalk.

"Sorry about this," Lucas said. "She had me whipped. I was just trying to get a number for a guy whose name I didn't know."

They heard a last "fuck you," faintly, through the closed door, and the cop said, "She definitely needs to take a couple aspirin," and, as he walked around the nose of his squad, "Have a nice day."

Lucas called Roy Carter from the car, hoping that the number would go to a cell phone; but the phone rang twenty times with no answer. He took fifteen minutes getting across Minneapolis, found Carter's apartment in a big old house that had been cut into four crappy apartments. He went up the central hall to the second floor, saw light under Carter's door. He knocked on the door, which rattled in the frame, knocked again, knocked a third time. Felt empty; not even a creaking floorboard.

Back at the car, he thought about heading home; then took out the list of names that Alyssa Austin had given him and scanned down it. The first time he looked, he'd noticed some addresses in Uptown, and the man mentioned by Mobry, Karl Lageson, also lived around there.

He glanced at his watch. Still early.

Lucas got Lageson's address from the duty guy at the BCA, found it, a redbrick apartment house with a rack of bicycles outside, knocked on the door, was a little surprised when it popped open.

Lageson was a tall pale man with a black ponytail, probably thirty, and did look a little like a Lurch. He was cooking chunks of white fish in a cast-iron skillet; the fish sizzling in the background when he opened the door. He pulled Lucas inside so he could attend the skillet, and he seemed to know what he was doing, expertly wielding a pair of stainless tongs as he shuffled the fish in and out of the hot oil.

"I didn't talk to the police about her—the fairy girl—but I suppose I should have," he said as he worked, licking hot grease from his thumb. "I mean, Dick was a big guy and this woman was really small. If she'd tried to stab him he would have thrown her in the river . . . but, I should have mentioned it. It just seemed ridiculous. I could get somebody in trouble and she was just such a . . . a harmless thing."

"You'd never seen her before?" Lucas asked.

Lageson stooped to look in his oven window, then stood up and said, "No, I would have paid attention. She looked really nice."

"How old?"

"Early twenties? Looked like a dancer. Moved like a dancer. Dressed like a dancer, when I think about it. All black, but not drab, you know? Likes clothes. Got some money. She was laughing at Dick's jokes . . . but then, and this is why I never got around to calling your men—she was gone before Dick got off. Like an hour before closing time."

"You didn't talk to her?"

"No. Didn't have a chance," he said.

"You talk to Dick about her?"

"No, I had some friends there . . . you know, this whole thing with the fairy, it lasted about ten minutes. That was it. Never saw her before, never saw her again." He opened the cover again, and the odor of baking bread suffused the room. "You like French bread?"

"Well, yeah, I do," Lucas said.

They ate hot French bread with real butter, and drank fresh-ground coffee, and Lageson ate his fish; the place smelled wonderfully of good food, all over a background of old marijuana smoke. Lageson knew Frances Austin, he said, may have seen her the night before she disappeared. "We tended to go to the same places, you know, and I chatted with her. She seemed like a nice person. No electricity, though. Between us, I mean."

"Did she have anything going on with *anybody?*"

Lageson hesitated and Lucas saw it. He said, "C'mon. You didn't tell us about the fairy girl. You owe us."

"I just don't like . . ."

"Cops?"

"Not that," he said. He pushed a saltshaker around with his index finger. "I don't like to feel like a rat. Get somebody in trouble when I have no idea of whether they deserve it."

"We're trying to catch a cold-blooded killer," Lucas said, snaffling another piece of bread off the plate between them. "I wouldn't hang that on anyone who's not guilty. On the other hand, I wouldn't want you to throw a red herring out there, either—piss on somebody you don't like by siccing me on them."

Lageson watched Lucas butter the bread, then said, "I wouldn't do that."

"Good. So what do you got?" Lucas asked. "You got something."

"I saw her and Denise Robinson running around a lot together—in a busy way, like they were up to something. Denise's boyfriend was in there, too. Mark McGuire. I don't know what they were up to, but they were hanging out."

"Thank you," Lucas said. Lageson had given him a red linen napkin, and he dabbed his lips with it, wiping away the butter. "You don't know what it was?"

"No idea. Maybe nothing. But they were hanging out."

"In a busy way."

LAGESON, LUCAS DECIDED, as he was leaving, was a pretty good guy, though he might have smoked too much dope; Lucas met a surprising number of good guys while he was running around chasing crooks. They usually weren't as interesting as the assholes, he thought.

PATRICIA SHOCKLEY.

He spotted the address and found a parking space two blocks away, strolled back. The night was getting cool, and he walked with his head down, hands in his pockets. Up ahead, the pale faces of a young couple bobbing toward him, the woman prodding her escort, and they crossed the street before Lucas got to them. Jesus, he looked like a thug? In the dark, with the jeans and the black leather jacket . . . Maybe.

Patricia Shockley's apartment was in another of the converted houses, bigger than the house that Carter lived in, and better kept. The front door was locked, and he pushed a doorbell with a label that said Shockley/Price. A woman's voice from a doorside speaker: "Who is it?"

"Lucas Davenport, Bureau of Criminal Apprehension," he said. "I'm a state investigator, looking into the Ford and Austin murders. I need to talk to Patricia Shockley."

After a moment's hesitation, "Where did you get my name?"

"Alyssa Austin. It was also in the state file, from an interview with Agent Benson."

"I'll buzz you in."

The lock buzzed and slipped, and Lucas pushed through the door into the hallway. A Persian carpet covered the wooden floor inside, and a wide oaken staircase twisted up to the second floor. Like a sorority house, he thought. A woman came to the landing and said, "Up here."

Patricia Shockley was in full Goth: black leggings, black blouse, black-dyed hair, badly chewed black nails. Late twenties. She led him down the hallway to her apartment. Another Goth woman, this one wearing a sixties-style black sheath over black leggings, perched on a stool at a dinner bar off the kitchen, legs crossed.

Shockley said, "My roommate. Leigh Price."

Price smiled and licked a knife with peanut butter on it. "Cop," she said. Price was a fairy, if he understood the concept: short, slight, dark, pretty. Maybe thirty. Shockley was thicker, wider; a University of Minnesota basketball player.

"You always work at night?" Shockley asked.

"I'm looking for a guy," Lucas said. "Do either of you know Roy Carter?"

The two women glanced at each other, then they both looked back at Lucas and shook their heads. Price said, "Nooo . . . I don't think so. Who is he?"

"He works at Mike's liquors? Hangs out at the A1?"

Price shook her head: "Not our scene. Why are you asking?"

"I'm trying to put some of Frances Austin's friends together," Lucas said.

"I wasn't one of Frances's friends," Price said.

"I was, all the way back to school," Shockley said. "She was really nice, once you got to know her—but Leigh thought she was stuck-up."

"Stuck-up rich prig. But I didn't think that enough to kill her," Price said. Her dark eyes caught Lucas's eyes as she dug in a peanut butter jar with the knife. Lucas felt a little *thrum*, and it didn't have anything to do with murder.

Lucas said to Price, "Would people call you a fairy?"

Her eyebrows went up, and she said, "Maybe."

"Oh, poop," Shockley said. "You're a fairy."

"You're just as much a fairy as I am," Price said to her room-mate.

Shockley rolled her eyes. "Right." To Lucas: "She's Tinker Bell the Fairy, I'm Clarabelle the Cow."

"Not fair," Price said; but there was a spark in her eye; she knew it was the truth.

Shockley and Frances Austin had gone to Blake Academy from

57

kindergarten through graduation, and then on to separate colleges.

"We didn't date together or anything—we just knew each other for a long time," Shockley said. "We went to each other's birthday parties. I didn't see her much when we were in college, but then . . . we'd hook up for lunch or go out and have drinks a couple times a year. And we were both interested in the gothic, but from different directions. She came in from women's studies and I came in from literature."

"I came in from witchcraft," Price said.

"So you don't really know who she was hanging out with?" Lucas asked.

"She hung out with a lot of students, at night. She was on-again off-again in graduate studies, but there weren't any jobs in her area and she was thinking about changing direction into something more practical. I'm working, I have to get going early, so I don't hang out at night."

"What do you do?"

"Commercial real estate," Shockley said. "Probably start law school in a year or two. My dad says he'll supply the bucks."

Price said, "I'm a chemical engineer. I work at 3M in medical products."

Neither of the women had seen Austin in the two weeks before she'd died. Shockley thought she'd seen her on a Monday afternoon or a Tuesday afternoon, two weeks before, but it had been an accidental encounter in a Macy's store, and they'd gone and gotten cinnamon pretzels and chatted for a while.

"She wasn't worried about anything, except about what she was going to do," Shockley said.

"Did she say anything about her mother?" Lucas asked.

"She was always talking about her mom. She really admired her—her mom's sort of a free spirit, but she also runs a good business, and she's smart, and she's on boards and stuff."

"Her mother thinks that there was a little stress between them, since her father died," Lucas said.

"She was broken up about her father," Shockley agreed. "She said a couple of things about her mom being hard on him, but . . . she wasn't really mad at her mom. It was just a hard time. She was one of the executors of his estate, and she took it really seriously."

"Okay." Lucas looked at his notebook: "Do either of you know a couple, uh, Denise Robinson and Mark McGuire?"

The two women looked at each other and Price said, "Well, sure. Denise and Mark."

"What do they do?"

"They're Web people—they're trying to set up a commercial website. Something to do with video advertisements . . . I'm not too clear about it. Mark has a day job at, uh, some truck thing. Computers and trucks, I don't know what it is."

"I've been told that they were really tight with Frances before she was killed," Lucas said.

"I don't know what that'd be about," Shockley said, and Price shook her head.

"Okay," Lucas said. "I need names . . . I need to run along a rosary of names until I find something."

Shockley suggested three people that he might contact, and had numbers for two of them, and said each of the two would have a phone number for the third. He took the names down, recognized two of them from Alyssa Austin's list.

"Are any of the three fairies?" Lucas asked.

"You know, we don't really call ourselves that," Price said. "I mean, it's not like people go around pointing them out and saying fairy-fairy-fairy."

"Yes, they do. You even dress like that. The waif look," Shockley said. She added, "They call them Lolis, too. Loli is short for Lolita."

"Also lollipop," Price said.

"I'm looking for a woman; and I've been told that she is one," Lucas said.

"Like me," Price said.

"That's what I've been told," Lucas said.

Shockley jumped in. "Karen Slade could be. She's thin enough."

"She's kind of tall," Price said.

Lucas put a check next to Slade's name. "Thanks. I'll call if I think of anything else."

"Do that," Price said.

OUTSIDE, HE LOOKED at his watch. It had been a half hour since he'd left Roy Carter's; might be worth checking back. Or, he could go home.

Got in the car, thought about it; what the hell, he could swing by. Five minutes, found a good parking space, only two houses down from Carter's place. Up the stairs, knock on the door, still no response. But when he was turning away from the door, another door, sideways down the hall, popped open, and a woman stuck her head out.

"Looking for Roy?"

"Yup." He took her in: a round-faced woman, unnaturally pale, with lipstick that looked almost black in the dim light of the hallway. She was dressed in a loose, black, ankle-length dress. Another one; he'd tapped into Goth Central.

"He won't be back until late," she said. "He's out."

"I'm a cop," Lucas said. "I'm going to stick a card under the door. If you hear him come in, could you ask him to call me? Whatever time it is?"

"Okay, but I'm going out myself," she said.

"If you hear him . . ."

"Is this about that guy getting murdered at that bar?" She leaned in the door frame.

"Yup. He might've talked to somebody that we'd like to find," Lucas said.

"Not that little fairy, is it?"

Lucas's eyebrows went up. "Yes, it is. You know her?"

"No. But that's where Roy is. She called him up."

60

"What?"

"They're hooking up tonight."

CARTER HAD STOPPED back at his apartment after work—probably while Lucas was arguing with the woman behind the liquor store counter—had changed clothes, and was gone, hurrying down the steps. He met his neighbor, the Goth woman, whose name was Jean Brandt, on the way down, said, "Hey: that fairy called me. We're going out," and then he rattled on down the stairs and out the door.

Lucas asked her, "You know where he goes? Where he might take her? What does he look like?"

"I've got a picture of him," she said, a worry-crinkle creasing her forehead. She went back into her apartment, came back to the door with a snapshot; Brandt and two men, in a park somewhere. "Roy's on the right." Lucas tilted the photo under the hall light: Roy was a tall man, six-four, thin, red-haired, pale eyes, bony shoulders, and big hands. Even in the park, he was dressed from head to foot in black. He had a silver earring piercing the upper ring of the only ear that Lucas could see.

"You think he's in trouble?" Jean asked.

"I don't know—I'd just like to talk to this woman," Lucas said. "She's apparently the last person to see Dick Ford alive."

"Well, knowing Roy—he's always been a little retarded around women—I'd say he's going to take her to the place he thinks will impress her the most. That's probably November."

Lucas looked up: "November on Lyndale? I thought it closed."

"New management, but they kept the name," she said. "Or he might go to Candy's, but Candy's is big on dancing and Roy doesn't dance so much. And it's loud. I think he wants to talk."

"Thanks," Lucas said, and he turned back to the stairs.

"If you want, I'll ride along," she offered. "If he's not at November, maybe I could ask people that we know. *Somebody* will be there."

"Let's go," Lucas said.

In the car, Brandt said, "Roy is really sweet, but, you know, he doesn't get so far with women. I don't know why, he's really a nice guy. So this one sort of hit on him the other night, actually got his work number. He's been shaky about it ever since. Hoping she'd call."

"Didn't have a name?"

"He didn't tell it to me, if he did," Jean said.

"Did he know a young woman named Frances Austin? She was killed, it was in the papers? She was Goth, or somewhat Goth, hung out at A1."

"I don't know. Roy hung out at A1 and he's Goth. So probably," Brandt said.

"Did you know her?"

"Not as far as I know. My friends are more from, you know, the south side and over toward Edina. Roy's friends were more the university group."

"Do you know Patricia Shockley or Leigh Price?" Lucas asked.

She looked over at him in the dark, her moon face almost luminescent. "Well, yeah. I do. Are they involved?"

He explained about Frances Austin, and she said, "Okay. If you hook up with a Goth, and they talk to you, you can follow a chain around to all the Goths in the Cities, and probably all over the country. So I know Leigh and Pat one way, and I know Roy another way, but if they know each other . . . I don't know."

NOVEMBER WAS A charcoal-colored concrete-block building with a long scrawling *November* above the doors in red neon. The parking lot had two dozen cars in it. Worried about getting parked in, Lucas left the Porsche on the street, a block away. Jean led the way back, and as they passed the parking lot, said, "That's Roy's car." She pointed at an aging red Camry parked at the back of the lot.

"Excellent," Lucas said.

Inside the door, they stopped to scan the main room—black leatherette booths, around a U-shaped bar with subdued light, a harsh black-and-white six-foot photo enlargement of Edvard

Munch's *The Scream* on the wall above the back bar. Jean turned to Lucas and said, "This way," and headed for a booth with two couples, all Goth.

She asked one of the men, "Have you seen Roy?"

The Goth looked around, "Yeah, he's here."

"Is his friend with him?"

"Yeah. They're right here." He sat up a bit and craned his neck, looking toward the back room. "Maybe they went in the back?"

They went into the back, found more booths, scattered around a twenty-by-twenty dance floor, no music yet, and only three couples in the booths. Jean went to one of the couples and asked, "Did you see Roy?"

"He was just here," the man said. The woman flicked her finger toward a hall on one side. "Restroom. Just a minute ago."

Lucas said, "Thanks," to Jean, and headed toward the hall that led to the restrooms. The men's room was empty; Jean saw him back out and said, "Let me look," and went into the women's restroom. A second later, she was back. "Only one person, and it's not her."

"You're sure?"

She said, "Roy called her a fairy. This woman"—she tipped a finger at the restroom door—"is a plus size. Maybe two-plus."

The hall went on past the restroom, and Lucas followed it out, thinking it might lead outside; but it was a loop, leading back to the main room, at the front. They stood there for a moment, peering at the tables, then one of the men they'd first spoken to saw them and pointed at the door.

They stepped over to the booth, and he said, "You talk to them? They just went out. Just now."

There were only two people on the street, both guys, ambling down toward them, apparently heading for the club. Lucas looked in the parking lot, around to the side. The Camry was still there. He walked down to the corner, a hundred feet away, looked up and down the street. There were people about, no odd couple, no tall redheaded guy with a diminutive fairy girl.

Where in the hell had they gone?

6

FAIRY AND LOREN took the Honda, a five-year-old black Prelude SH with a stick shift and some engine work. Small, what car nuts called a q-ship: mildlooking but with a serious bite, put together by some nice Asian boys from St. Paul. With its high-revving engine and tight suspension, it felt, under Fairy's butt, like the Batmobile.

They went west on I—494, up 35E, west on I—94, and off on Nicollet, cutting through back streets, driving with the stick, braking with the engine, spotting a street-parking spot under an elm tree. As she backed into the parking place, Loren said, "I bet he's early. He's eager."

"Can you still feel Frances on him?"

"I can," he said. "I can feel her spirit, her hand on his shoulder."

Fairy looked in the rearview mirror, saw the lights from a car turning into the November parking lot. A moment later, Roy Carter walked out of the lot, slowly, combing his hair, patting it down with one hand, straightening his shirt, tucking it in. "There he is."

"Then, let's go."

She popped the door, got out, shook out her skirt. Her purse had once been an art deco silver-and-onyx cigarette case, and held her driver's license, two credit cards, four fifty-dollar bills and a twenty. The size of a clamshell, she held it in one hand, and it was so cool that other Goth women looked more at her purse than her face.

She crossed the street, as smooth as a leopard, the knife beating in her jacket pocket like a second heart. She paused inside the door, looked left and right, letting the black hair flip, and then Roy called, "Honey."

She looked left and smiled at the name; he was standing next to a table with two other couples. She twiddled her fingers at them, cocked her head at Roy, pulled him in. He was a smooth-faced boy, maybe twenty-four, a few adolescent blemishes still spotting up one cheek. Light brown eyes, he'd have grown to be a light brown man, working wistfully unhappy in some service industry, behind a desk, with a name tag—that is, if he'd had a chance to do it. She said, "Why don't we find a place in back?"

Away from witnesses.

"Sure. Want a wine?"

"Let's see if we can find a place."

They went into the back, and as they walked, she snagged the fingers of his right hand in her left, letting him lead by a step. She knew she was running about 440 volts through him, that the thing with the hand-holding would pull him through.

She looked in a mirror; would Francie be looking out at her? Would Francie have her hand on Roy's shoulder? Nothing.

They got to a booth and she turned to sit down and happened to look back toward the front door and froze for a moment, then unfroze with the thought: *Move.*

Fairy turned her face up to Roy and said, "Just believe in me for two minutes. For two minutes. Come on. Hurry. Come on." She pulled his hand and they went left down a hallway to the restroom and which, she hoped, went to a back door. But it didn't—it led back to the main room. She peeked out. Wait, wait, wait . . .

"What?" Roy whispered.

Then: "Hurry," tugging at his fingers, and they scampered across the room and out the front door. In the cold air, she laughed and said, "Run."

He followed behind, across the street, into the car. She fired it up, cranked the wheel, and they were off down the street: she took the first right, playing with the clutch, rolling, rolling, and she lifted her foot and the clutch engaged and they rolled silently into the dark.

Roy asked, "What was that?"

"An old, old friend who I never want to see again," she said. "Let's find someplace to walk for a while. He'll be gone, we can go back."

65

"I know another place," Roy said. "On the other side of town—across the river. Not so nice as November, though."

"What's it called?"

"A1."

"I know that place," she said. "Sounds like a barbeque sauce."

They parked along the riverfront, because, she told him, she still needed to walk. "I'm cooped up all day. Work, work, work. It's the crisis of American life, huh? We need time to think. Time to brood."

"I get up, I go to work," Roy said, shyly. "I'd like to be a writer. I've got some ideas, but I never have the time. It's like you said—time to think. If I could get away, someplace . . ." He scuffed his feet, head down a little, hands in his pocket, and he said, "Well, fuck it."

She took his hand, pulled him into the strip of grass along the river, under a cottonwood, and said, "If you don't do it, the time can run out on you."

"I know, but . . . I've still got time. I read about writers, you know. A lot of them had lots of experiences, lots of jobs, before they got published. That's what I'm doing now. I'm getting experience. I thought about going into the army, but I've . . ."

"What?"

"Nothing. Nothing serious."

They stopped under the tree and she stepped close to him and looked up and said, "This place we're going—wasn't there a murder there? It just struck me."

"Yeah, the bartender," Roy said. "Dick. He . . . I don't know."

"Did you know him?" Fairy asked.

"Yeah. He was a nice guy. I don't know what happened."

"I saw the story in the *Pioneer Press*," she said. "They said he had some connection with this girl who disappeared. What was her name?"

"Frances. Austin. I knew her, too," Roy said. "It gives me the creeps. I've never even seen a *dead* guy, and now I used to know two people who were murdered."

"The girl . . . they don't know she's dead."

"Well, they think she is," Roy said. "I mean, if you read the papers, I guess her house was full of blood, and they know it was hers, so . . . I assume she's dead."

"How well did you know her?"

"I'd see her around. She was like us, you know, gothic. I'd say hello. We went over to her apartment one time, a bunch of us, got some pizza and played some games."

"God. So you really knew her."

"Yeah, I guess." He shrugged.

She made her move, moving another inch closer to him. "How do you think she died? The girl? Any idea?"

"What?"

"Frances Austin. Have you heard anything? Rumors, or . . . Somebody's got to know. These people are still out there. With two Goths dead . . . I mean, you probably know the killers yourself."

The ambient light came from the condos, a bar, a couple of streetlights, the cars on the bridge; not much, but enough to see his eyes widen. He stepped back from her. "You know, they say Dick . . ."

"Dick . . . ?"

"Dick was talking to a fairy Goth before he was killed."

"A fairy Goth?"

"You know . . ." He smiled, defensive, glanced back toward the bar. "Like you."

"Me."

"It doesn't mean anything," he said. "But you know . . . was it you?"

She let her shoulders slump and she looked up at him, her smile gone and she said, "You're asking me . . ."

"You know, just because you seem interested in the murders . . ."

"Is she dead? Or alive?"

"For God's sakes, how would I know?" There was a note of irritation in his voice now, and maybe fear. He was thinking about her, about how close she was, about how the darkness was almost palpable. Running, screaming, wouldn't be manly, would it? And if she was innocent, he was blowing a shot at the highestquality pussy ever to step out with him . . . He looked down at her, saw something in her eyes; and she saw him seeing it.

She sighed and said, "Uh-oh," and slipped her hand into her coat and felt the dry wooden handle on the knife.

"What?" he asked. He was looking around again, but they were alone. "Maybe we should go . . ."

The knife slipped in so easily. Soft and easy, like it'd slip into the breast meat of a roasted chicken, just out of the oven. She looked up at his eyes, now wider, feeling it, not sure what it was.

She had the handle in one hand, the other hand supporting the first, and she ripped him and he went "Ah!" and tried to run, his legs going all wobbly. He banged into a bench and went over it, and down. She stepped up next to him, knelt, and wiped the knife on his shirt. Sat and watched. He never looked at her, his eyelids simply batted for a while and then stopped.

He was gone.

She stood up, put the knife back into the jacket. Looked around at the lights; and Loren whispered from somewhere nearby, *Time to go; but don't run.*

Back in the car, Loren's eyes were in the rearview mirror. He asked, "Did you enjoy it?"

"A little," she said. Then, "No, not really." And, a moment later, "I wish he'd told us where she is. *How* she is."

"Hovering," Loren said. "We can bring her back, if we can find her. I can sense her, but we need more information. It would help if we knew where she was on the material plane, so we could lay our hands on her."

"Oh, God."

"We still have another possibility, another suspect," Loren said.

"One more," she said. "But maybe we could wait a day or two or three. This one hurt me. The first one, Ford, didn't hurt me. This one did."

"Okay."

Down through the city in the Batmobile. After a while, she said, "I lied. It did feel good. I can't deny it. But it felt good and hurt me at the same time. I had more control, this time, though. I can wait until I get home to fuck you. Last time, I couldn't."

His eyes in the mirror: "I know. You're growing."

"But I need to find out about Frances," Fairy said. "I need to find everybody involved—I need to end this."

7

INSIDE NOVEMBER, Lucas talked with the two Goth couples about Roy and the woman. Both of the male Goths were tall and thin, dressed in black from head to toe: Greg and Dave. Dave seemed to be wearing a skirt, but it may have been a jacket tied around his waist. Both of the women were short and chunky: Sharon and Wanda, who was called Wolfie; both with black fingernail polish and scarlet lipstick.

"They were being flirty," Sharon said. "Cute with each other. She was holding his hand. There was something going on."

"He doesn't have another friend?" Lucas asked.

"Roy? No. Not recently."

"An odd couple," Greg said, pensively.

"Why odd?" Lucas asked.

"Well, she's pretty hot," Greg said. He snapped a sideways glance at his girlfriend and then said, "Roy . . . I've never heard a woman call *him* hot."

"He doesn't ring a lot of bells," Wolfie agreed.

"Tell me about the woman."

The fairy woman was short, lithe, dark-haired, pale-complected, probably in her early twenties. Well-dressed, in the Goth style. Leather jacket, with what Sharon said was a "really nice top. Her skirt was cheapish, though. It looked cheap. Too short."

"Nice shoes," said Wolfie.

"Older than early twenties," Sharon said. "Too self-possessed. Knows what she wants, and making friends isn't one of them."

Dave grinned and said, "She had an early-twenties ass."

"Where does Roy get off running around with a chick like that?" Greg asked. He seemed offended. "I mean, she *is* somewhat out of his league, don't you think?"

The Goths all nodded at one another.

"Too good," Dave said. "Why's somebody that good hanging with Roy?"

"He's actually a good guy," Jean said.

"Yeah, but good like Charlie Brown . . ."

They were still talking when Shockley and Price, the Goths whom Lucas had interviewed earlier, came through the door with a long-haired man in a field jacket and blue jeans bloused over combat boots. Lucas asked one of the Goths, "See the fairy over there? Does she look like the one with Roy?"

"Leigh? Oh . . . she's over in that direction, but it wasn't Leigh. I mean . . ." He raised his voice. "Hey! Leigh!"

Price turned their way, spotted Lucas, came over: "Find her?"

"Just missed her," Lucas said.

"She was here with Roy," one of the Goths in the booth said.

Price shook her head: "I don't know him."

"The guy who started the chicken dance."

Price smiled: "Okay." To Lucas: "I know who he is now. But I don't know him."

"Chicken dance?" Jean asked.

"At the Halloween party. He started people doing the chicken dance. That's not something that Goths do every day."

ON THE WAY out with Jean, Price hooked him by the elbow and pulled him aside, and asked, "So what do you do when you're not copping?"

He felt a little ridiculous when he said it, but he said it anyway: "Taking care of my wife and kids."

"Don't cops have rocky marriages?"

"Some do." He smiled. "I could introduce you to some, if you want. I got this guy Virgil . . ."

"Virgil Flowers?" Her face lit up. "You know Virgil? I knew he was a cop."

Lucas smiled, stepped back. "He works for me."

"Well, shoot. If you see him, tell him that Leigh says hi."

"He's been married so often that he's got a 'Just hitched' sign in his closet," Lucas said.

"I don't want to *marry* him," she said. "He's just a really . . . interesting guy."

Lucas nodded, said, as though jilted, "Well. Maybe see you around," and headed out the door.

"What was that all about?" Jean asked, as she trailed behind.

"Just this guy," Lucas said. "That fuckin' Flowers."

Lucas left Jean at her apartment. She said she'd stay up until Roy got back.

"I'll be up late. When he comes in, call my cell," Lucas said, as he scribbled the number on the back of one of his business cards. "So. Call me."

"You think Roy's all right?"

"I wish they hadn't disappeared like that," Lucas said. "It was so quick, it was like they were running. I wish she hadn't been too good for Roy. That worries me."

"That kind of judgment . . ."

". . . Is almost always right," Lucas said. "Not fair, but right."

WEATHER WAS STILL awake when he got home, sitting in the kitchen, public radio playing around her as she sorted through a box of junk mail. As a physician, she got fifty pieces a week, and there was no way to turn it off. When Lucas came in, she looked up and asked, "Do any good?"

Before he could answer, the phone rang, and they both turned to look at it: late for a phone call, and that was hardly ever good. Lucas picked it up and said, "Hello?"

Harold Anson, the Minneapolis homicide cop, said, "We got another one. I'm headed over there—down on the riverfront, two blocks from the last one."

"If you tell me it's a guy named Roy Carter, I'm gonna shoot myself."

There was five seconds' silence, then Anson said, "Step away from the gun, big guy."

"Motherfucker," Lucas said. "*Motherfucker.* I'll be there in ten minutes."

Weather asked, *"What?"*

"Motherfucker . . ."

He took the truck, heading up the river and across to Minneapolis on I—94, into the loop, then back across the river; Tom Petty was singing about Mary Jane's last dance as he crossed over.

He kept thinking about the time he'd lost when he started looking for Carter. Time getting a sandwich, time getting around a minor traffic accident. Getting to November a minute too late . . .

The previous summer, a bridge on Interstate 35 had fallen into the Mississippi River in downtown Minneapolis. It hadn't gotten creaky and shaky and slowly slumped into the water—it had simply snapped, toward the end of a weekday rush hour, going down in an instant. Thirteen people died.

A new bridge was going up in a hurry. Crews worked late into the night, and Lucas could see the flickering white flares of their welders. And up ahead, the flashing lights of the cop cars on the riverfront, and Petty started on "Something in the Air."

ANSON WAS WEARING a knee-length trench coat and a fedora, which sat back on his head, the brim snapped down over his scalp. He was talking to a cop, stopped when he saw Lucas. "You want to look?"

"Sure."

Roy Carter was lying on his side, mouth and eyes open, his hair flattened, his shirtfront soaked with drying blood. He'd been tall, and almost gaunt, with reddish hair that looked blue in the streetlights, and freckles that looked black, the skin taut around his skull and cheekbones. The bottom arm, his right, was thrown out on the sidewalk; the top arm clutched at his gut and, like his shirt, was covered with blood.

"Same deal," Anson said. "Stuck him, ripped him. It's like a hara-kiri, almost, except that the rip is up."

"Goddamnit, I was looking for him tonight. I missed him by thirty seconds," Lucas said, turning away from the body. "He was with a Goth. They call her a fairy, just like the one who was talking with Dick Ford."

"Ford? What fairy?"

Lucas explained it, taking it step-by-step. When he finished, Anson said, "So the fairy did it."

"We need to talk to her," Lucas said. "We need to find her. Really bad."

"I'll need the names of everybody who knows her," Anson said.

"I'll e-mail them to you tonight, before I go to bed," Lucas said. "You've got some witnesses . . . and somebody told me that the fairy girl had called Carter. I don't know whether it was at work, or at home, or on a cell, or what."

"But there ought to be a number we can get at."

"Should be," Lucas said. "And a photo kit from the people who've seen her. Get it out to the media. Put some pressure on her."

There was nothing for Lucas to do at the crime scene, except stand around with his hands in his pockets and bullshit with the uniforms. As the crime-scene people and the ME's investigators worked over the body, Anson took a call, walking along the river with a finger in one ear, the phone to the other. He rang off and told Lucas that Carter had come from Little America, and that his parents were being notified. "Bad day out in the countryside. His parents both work for the post office," he said. "If this happened to one of my kids, I'd jump off a bridge."

"After you killed the guy who did it," Lucas said, looking back at the body.

Anson nodded: "We don't talk about that."

LUCAS WENT HOME; confirmed the murder to Weather, who was shocked: "We didn't set this off, did we?"

"Nah. I've been working on the case for half a day," Lucas said. "This guy's been a target for longer than that."

"Then how did you miss them at the nightclub? It sounds like they were trying to avoid you—and that'd mean . . ."

". . . that they'd have to know who I was. Or, maybe, she just wanted to get him out of there, away from people who could look at her. Nobody really talked to her—she kept him moving. My guess is, she moved him away from the people in the front room, then went into the back room, the dance floor, and he had more friends back there, so she moved him out of there, too. We just . . . passed each other."

She shook her head. "Too neat. There's something going on that we don't know about."

"Gonna have to think about it," Lucas said.

"Have to think by yourself," she said. "I'm doing a palate tomorrow and it's a bad one. I need to be out of here by five, so I'm going to bed."

"See you tomorrow then." He kissed her goodnight, and moved to the den, where he read again through the paper generated by the Minneapolis guys and his own BCA. Lucas had worked for both, and had his prejudices: the BCA guys worked a couple of murders a year, maybe, and they were often hard ones.

But Minneapolis—a lead Minneapolis investigator might catch as many killings in a couple of years as a BCA agent saw in a career. They were a bunch of flatfeet, but their paper was very good, full of the kind of intuitive detail that caught a guy's eye after ten years on the street and another ten doing violent crime.

At eleven o'clock, Lucas stopped. His brain was getting clogged up. He thought about calling Del. No chance he'd be asleep; the guy was like a bat. His old lady was another matter. He worked through the equities for a minute, then dialed.

Del picked up on the second ring: "What'd ya want?"

"I don't want to interrupt anything," Lucas said.

"I wish you were."

"Where's your old lady?"

"In bed," Del said. "She's been feeling kinda rocky. What's up?"

"Meet you at the apartment?"

"Fifteen minutes."

THE ALLEY BEHIND the drugstore was dark and cold, and something—a raccoon?—was banging around inside the dumpster. Lucas fumbled for the key to the back door, got inside, turned on the stairway light and went up. The apartment was quiet and cold. He pushed the thermostat higher, in the light coming through the front window, and tuned the boom box to a golden oldies station, playing low; picked up the glasses and looked across the street at Heather Toms's apartment.

Toms was in, watching TV in the middle of the three rooms he could see. She was drinking something from a can, a beer or a Pepsi, he thought. Probably a Pepsi, because of the baby. He couldn't quite pick out the logo in the flickering light of the television.

Del showed up a couple of minutes later, trudging up the stairs. Lucas heard the key in the lock, and Del stepped inside, bringing along the odor of hot coffee. He handed Lucas a paper cup and Lucas said thanks, and took a sip. The coffee had never seen Seattle, or even heard of it. But it was okay. Free cop coffee.

Del tipped his head at the boom box: "Clarence Carter—'Slip Away.'" The golden oldie slipped through the room and they sipped along for a moment and then Del took the glasses from Lucas's hand and looked across the street and said, "She's got her shirt on."

"Yup. Took it off last time, though."

"She still looking healthy?"

"Starting to bulk up with the new baby," Lucas said.

"Nipples still point up?"

"So far."

"Wonder if she knows whether it's a boy or a girl?"

"You could call and ask . . ."

DEL WAS WEARING jeans, a gray sweatshirt, and a cracked-leather Goodwill jacket with a fake-sheepskin collar. "Who's dead?" he asked.

"Guy named Roy Carter," Lucas said. "Also a guy named Dick Ford and a girl named Frances Austin."

"Know about Ford and Austin." Del handed the glasses back to Lucas. "I didn't hear about Carter."

"He was just a couple of hours ago," Lucas said. He took two minutes to tell the story, then asked, "What do you think?"

"Well, there's a lot of choices. You think the fairy did it?"

"She knows about it," Lucas said, looking out into the night.

"So she's at least an accomplice."

"I think so."

"From what you say, Frances sounds like she was playing Goth, but was gonna wind up as an executive somewhere. Not really into the poverty lifestyle. So if you don't find a fairy, or if she didn't do it, you've really got to think about the possibility that you've got two separate things going on here. Austin, and the others."

"Be easier if it was all one thing," Lucas said.

"The world isn't easy," Del said. He finished his coffee and pitched the cup toward an oversized plastic wastebasket, and missed. Clarence Carter went away and Jefferson Airplane came up, "Plastic Fantastic Lover."

"It's not two things," Lucas said, after a while. "They're connected. We don't have Frances's body, but the lab says there was a lot of blood. Just like Ford and Carter. They could have yelled, their throats weren't cut, but nobody heard them yell because, probably, by the time they thought of it, they were already going."

"Unless the knife went up into the diaphragm," Del said. "Jesus, though, that'd take some expertise—a doctor or something."

"There's that."

"And from what you say, there's other big differences," Del said. "When they killed Frances, they went to all the risk of moving the body and getting rid of it. Since it hasn't popped up yet, they did a pretty good job. But Ford and Carter, they leave out on the street, like calling cards. Right out there in public, like advertisements."

"Advertisements for what?"

"You're the detective," Del said.

Lucas slurped on the coffee, which tasted sort of brown, like a cross between real coffee and the paper sack it came in. "If they're advertisements, there'll be more of them. And now that you brought it up, another question about Frances. People were going to miss her pretty quickly, so why bother to move the body at all?"

Del shrugged. "Don't know. Maybe to shift time, to give themselves an alibi. Maybe to shift the place, so you wouldn't look at people who had keys to the Austin house. But then, if you're right, and the cases are connected, why does the fairy let herself be seen now? Doesn't she care? There are probably what, a half-dozen people who'd recognize her now?"

"Maybe she just doesn't give a shit," Lucas said.

"You know what it adds up to?" Del said. "Either you've got two separate things, or she's nuts. She lets herself be seen, then she runs and hides. It's like a game to her."

Across the street, Heather got up, stretched, loafed into the kitchen, got something out of a cupboard—black corn chips, Lucas thought, and a bottle of salsa. They watched her carefully fixing the snack. "Is salt okay at this point? In the pregnancy?" Del asked. "Those chips have got a lot of sodium."

"Dunno."

Lucas said, after another moment, "There's something else going on, too. Austin—Alyssa—says her husband might have been sleeping with his assistant. Smart, pretty, big boobs; that's Alyssa's description. Alyssa said she didn't care too much."

"Bullshit," Del said.

". . . because on other levels, the marriage was still okay. They had a solid partnership."

"Wasn't okay. Another woman gets to her husband in a way she can't? That's never okay," Del said. "If she tells you that, she's lying."

Lucas shrugged. "All I can do is tell you what she said."

"Did you check the plane crash?"

"Not personally. I read some paper on it. Supposedly, he's at a fly-in fishing place up in Canada. He'd been there before, had gone up by himself, meeting some pals. On the day he's scheduled to leave, he takes off, had a power problem when he's a hundred feet up, tries to turn back down the lake, dead stalls, and goes straight into the ground. The Canadian investigators didn't find anything particularly suspicious. Happens a few times a year up there. This was an old rebuilt plane, a Beaver. And boom. Alyssa was back here; the daughter was back here."

"What about the guys up there? His pals? Alyssa didn't have anything going with any of them?"

"You're a suspicious motherfucker," Lucas said. And, "I'll check that."

"Wup-wup-wup . . ." Del said, pointing across the street.

Toms was running toward the kitchen and Lucas put the glasses on her. "Phone call," he said. He looked at his watch and noted the time. She spoke for ten seconds then hung up.

"Quick call," Del said. "Setting up a meet?"

"Dunno." Toms walked back through the visible rooms, then disappeared down a hall that led only to the door. "Somebody coming up?"

"Didn't see anybody going in the front."

"I think somebody called her from the door."

They sat cocked forward on the folding chairs, tensed up; Toms was gone for another ten seconds, then reappeared, pushing an old woman in a wheelchair. "Ah, shit," Lucas said. "It's her mom."

"You know anything about Goths?" Lucas asked.

Del did. He'd even dated a couple of them, twenty years earlier, during their initial efflorescence. Much of the Gothic trip was a deliberate, ironic, self-conscious pose, along with a genuine interest in the subject of decadence and the transcendent. Most of the Goths he knew, Del said, were smart. If they'd had a scientific bent, instead of a literary bent, they'd have become geeks.

"I've always been more on the industrial side myself," Del said, "but there were crossover clubs that had both things going at the same time. Sort of Gotho-Industrial."

"I understand all the words you just said, but none of the concepts," Lucas said.

Del said, "Yeah. See, there's this alternative non-jock universe that you wouldn't know anything about . . ."

THEY TALKED ABOUT Goth for another fifteen minutes and came back to the murders only at the end. "How much money did Frances get?" Del asked.

"According to her mother, a little more than two million. Some carefully calculated amount that she could get without anybody paying taxes. I don't understand all the ins and outs of it."

"Okay. Two mil," Del said. "Lots of people have been killed for a hell of a lot less. Maybe Mom's a money freak."

"She says she doesn't care about the money."

"Oh, bullshit. How many rich people you know who don't care about money?" Del asked. "How about you? You're rich. What would you do if somebody said, 'Uh, shit, we just lost all your money in the market'?"

Lucas grinned. "Well, hell . . . it'd be a shock."

"Yeah. You like your money."

"Alyssa may like the money, but she didn't kill the kid," Lucas said. "If you'd seen her, Alyssa, you'd know how this whole thing has gotten on top of her. She is seriously fucked up."

"So she didn't kill the kid."

"I don't believe so," Lucas said. "She could be a psycho killer, and then it's all up for grabs. But to me, she just looks like a hippie chick who did good for herself. And then everybody around her went and got killed."

"A quick nasty argument about Daddy—maybe the kid found out something?—one of them picks up a knife, there's a struggle, the kid gets stuck . . ."

Lucas shrugged: "Anything's possible. But if that's what it is, why is Alyssa campaigning to get more cops on the case? The whole case was dead in the water. And if she killed the kid, and if I'm right about all three being killed the same way, by the same person, then why did she kill the other two?"

"Maybe somebody else figured out the connection?"

"Aw, come on, man. A bartender and a twenty-something Goth?"

Del nodded. "Okay. But I'll tell you what, I don't have that much experience with your basic upper-class crime."

"Being pretty much a proletarian yourself," Lucas said.

"A working man."

"A horny-handed son of the soil."

"You got me on the horny," Del said. "Anyway, I don't have that much experience with the upper classes, but I don't think I've ever heard of a crime where there was millions of dollars floating around, where the money didn't have *something* to do with the murder; especially if there was philately going on."

"That'd be philandering," Lucas said. "Philately is stamp-collecting."

"That's what I meant—stamp-collecting."

Lucas scrubbed an index finger across his philtrum, then said, "You're right about the money and fucking. And when you're right, you're right."

Lucas said, "Are they arguing?"

Del looked across the street, where the old lady was jabbing her finger at Heather.

"Looks like it." Heather laughed and said something, and the old lady laughed. "On the other hand, maybe not."

Lucas said, "You've been grousing about your old lady. Everything okay?"

"Ah, everything's okay, but she's been sick for a couple of

weeks," Del said. "Not enough to go to the doctor, but, you know. Doesn't want to walk around much: her stomach is upset."

"Jeez, man, a couple of weeks? That could be something serious. You gotta get her to a doc."

"There are two kinds of nurses," Del said; his wife was a nurse. "There's the kind who think the sun shines out of a doctor's asshole, and the kind that think most doctors are running a long-term hustle, and who don't trust them any further than they could throw them. I got one of the second kind."

He turned his head to the window: "Old lady's leaving," he said. "Looks like it's bedtime."

"She'll be changing into her nightgown," Lucas said.

"Can I borrow the glasses?"

"Get your own fuckin' glasses."

Eric Clapton: "Willie & the Hand Jive."

AFTER A RESTLESS night—disturbed a last time by Weather getting ready for work—Lucas had breakfast with the kids, talked to Letty about hip-hop music, stuffed creamed corn and whipped ham into Sam's mouth, and argued with the housekeeper about the lawn service, which wanted, too early in the year, in Lucas's opinion, to schedule a winter cleanup. At eight o'clock, he was on the phone to Alyssa Austin.

"I was wondering—have you begun organizing the financial records for Frances's estate?"

"Not yet, really—there's an accountant and a lawyer, but they're not pushing too hard," Austin said. "Not yet, anyway."

"Would it be possible for me to look at her financial records? Checkbook and investment records? All that?"

"Of course, if you think there might be something in there."

He hesitated for a moment, then said, "There was another Goth killing last night."

"Oh, no!" Her voice was a groan. "Who was it?"

"A kid named Roy Carter," Lucas said. "Middle twenties, I guess, worked in a liquor store and hung out at the A1 and

November, at least some of the time. Did Frances ever mention the name?"

"Not that I remember. She had friends I didn't know, but he wasn't one of the long-term ones. What'd he look like?"

"Tall, pale, red hair, thin—bony, almost," Lucas said.

"That doesn't sound familiar . . . Does he have a family?"

"Yeah, his parents are postal workers, I guess. Out in the countryside, somewhere."

"That's awful for them. That's awful," Austin said.

"So I can get that stuff?"

"Yes. I'll put it all out for you. I've got a board meeting today, but Helen will be here. I'll stack it up in the front room. You're welcome to stay as long you want. Helen can get you Cokes and coffee and sandwiches."

"One more thing. Have you heard of a couple . . ." He looked in his notebook again. ' . . . named Denise Robinson and Mark McGuire?"

"Sure. They were friends of Francie's. I should have given you their names, but I didn't think of them," she said. "They came by with her a couple of times after Hunter was killed, last fall sometime."

"What does Robinson look like?"

"Mmm, tall, gawky, blondish hair—sandy, maybe—wears big plastic-rimmed glasses. She's a marathoner. Bony shoulders, drinking-straw arms. She told me that she ran it under three, which means she's pretty serious about it. Why?"

"Just a couple names I picked up," he said. "I'm pushing all of Frances's friends for names."

And Robinson didn't sound like a fairy, he thought after he'd rung off.

HE CALLED ANSON, the Minneapolis detective, from the car, on the way to Austin's house. Anson was sleepy: he'd gotten six hours the night before. "And I gotta have eight, or I'm just not worth shit." They both yawned together, into their phones, and

82

Anson added, "We got the ID last night, it's confirmed. I got our guys to make up a mug shot of the fairy—I'm going to run it around this morning, talk to all those people on your list."

"Let me know what you get," Lucas said. "I'm on the way over to Alyssa Austin's to look at her daughter's financial records."

If nothing came up sooner, they agreed to talk at noon, to compare notes.

LUCAS FOUND four boxes of records waiting for him at Austin's. The housekeeper met him at the door, took him into the living room, said, "Mrs. Austin said to try to keep all the folders together, because there's really a lot of paper and if it gets confused, they might not ever get it straight again."

Austin had been right about the paper. There were two intersecting sets of records: Hunter Austin's estate, two million of which went to Frances, while the rest went to Alyssa; and then Frances's estate, which included not only the two million from Hunter Austin's estate, but another half-million that she had apparently accumulated earlier, presumably through gifts and investments made on her behalf.

Hunter Austin's estate was still mostly intact, because the estate return had only recently been accepted by the IRS; and all of his investment, banking, and retirement accounts and trusts were still operating. That produced dozens of checks coming and going each year, on top of money coming in from his investments.

Frances Austin had had two major accounts of her own, one with Wells Fargo investment services, and one with Fidelity Investments. As money came in from one or the other—about a quarter of her accounts were in bonds that produced regular income that she apparently used for living expenses—it was deposited in her checking account, which was also at Wells Fargo.

The totality was confusing. At eleven o'clock, though, his neck and back muscles starting to cramp, he had what could be a breakthrough. In December, Fidelity had issued a check for fifty thousand dollars to Frances. There was no check form where the other check forms were, and there was no record of the fifty thousand going into her checking account.

Where had the money gone? Had she simply endorsed it to somebody? Had she walked it into a bank and gotten cash—not all that easy to do, in these days of drug awareness and terrorism alerts. What had she spent it on?

Del had been right, the night before, when he said that people had been killed for a lot less than two million dollars; and a lot less than fifty thousand dollars, too.

He stood up, stretched, went into the kitchen for another diet Coke, found the housekeeper unstacking the dishwasher. "Do you have a cell phone number for Mrs. Austin?"

"There's a list," she said. She went to a cupboard near the wall phone and opened the door: on the back of it was a list of fifteen or twenty phone numbers: plumber, appliance repairmen, lawn and pool services, Mercedes and Jaguar dealerships, and three different numbers for Alyssa Austin: Office, 1Cell, and 2Cell.

"Her personal phone is 2Cell; 1Cell is the business cell," the housekeeper said.

Lucas called her on the personal phone: she answered on the third ring. "Sorry to bother you," Lucas said. "I have a question. Frances took fifty thousand dollars out of Fidelity in December, but there's no record of it going into her checking account. Do you remember anything like that? Did she sign it over to somebody for a car or something, or put a down payment on a condo?"

There was a long pause, and then Austin said, "Fifty thousand? I don't know anything about that, at all. I would have known—if she was thinking about spending fifty thousand dollars on something, she would have mentioned it."

"She didn't say anything?"

"Nothing at all," Austin said.

"I'm going to leave some documentation in a folder on your dining table," Lucas said. "Could you take a look at it, and the other expenses she had at the time? See if anything rings a bell."

"I'll look as soon as I get home—I'll come back as soon as this meeting is done."

"Good. Let me give you my cell number. Call me anytime."

When he got off the line, he took out his book and found Anson's number. "Get anything?" he asked, when Anson came up.

"I took that photo kit of the fairy woman around to the people who saw her," Anson said. "And to Frances's friends. One of her friends said the fairy looked like . . . guess who?"

"I don't know. Lana Turner?"

"Close, but no cigar. They said it looked like Frances Austin."

8

A SLAP in the face.

"Frances Austin's dead," Lucas said.

"You know that and I know that," Anson said. "The question is, does Frances Austin know that?"

"Man . . . the blood at Austin's. You've seen the lab reports?"

"I'm just telling you what I was told. We really don't know how much blood there was at Austin's place, whether it was a little that got smeared around or a lot that got mopped up. But here's a question for you. What if the fairy is Alyssa Austin? She looks a little like Frances."

Lucas had to think it over. Why not? "You're thinking outside the box," he said finally.

"She gets a wig, she gets some black clothes . . ."

"She's forty-five, or something like that. Everybody says the fairy is in her early twenties," Lucas said.

"Yeah, that's a question," Anson said. "Still, I wouldn't mind getting a peek in her wig drawer."

Lucas thought, *I'm right there.* He glanced sideways. The

housekeeper was twenty feet away, poking a coat-hanger wire down the drain on the left side of the two-basin kitchen sink, her lips moving, as though she were trying to talk it into the garbage disposal. Paying no attention.

But how was he going to get into the bedroom? The housekeeper wouldn't be leaving for hours. And if he found anything, could he tell Anson? It'd be an illegal search and he didn't know Anson that well. "We'd need something," he said. "To get a warrant."

"Think of something," Anson said. Disappointed? "Did you get anything?"

Lucas told him about the missing fifty thousand dollars. "Looks like she just cashed the check, or signed it over to somebody. Or something. Anyway, it doesn't pop up in any of her accounts that I can find."

There was a silence of several seconds, then Anson said, "Fifty grand?"

"Yeah. The question is, what would she use it for? She doesn't seem like a gambler. Cocaine? Doesn't seem like that kind, either. Maybe . . . who knows, maybe she was buying photography equipment or computers or something. But Alyssa says *she* doesn't know, and she thinks that she would."

"So now what?"

"I'll get my financial guys to look into it. Maybe go back to the A1 tonight. People knew her there. See if she was throwing any money around, talking about anything."

"What about the photo kit?"

"Gotta think about that. Fax one to me, will you? I'll look at it later."

LUCAS HEADED BACK to the BCA, with copies of the Fidelity documents made on Alyssa Austin's home-office copier. Give them to the accountants, he thought, and let them figure it out.

He'd parked, was out of the car, walking toward the door, head down, when Jenkins and Shrake came hustling out of the building, carrying vests.

He stopped. "Where're you going?"

"Antsy Toms is back in town," Shrake said.

"I'm coming," Lucas said. "Let me get my vest."

He ran inside, up the stairs, down to his office, threw the copies at his secretary, Carol, and blurted, "Give these to Dan Hall, find out who cashed the fifty-thousand-dollar check." She said, "What?" and he pulled his vest out from behind his file cabinets, shouted, "Dan Hall, find out about the check, the fifty grand."

"Where're you going?"

"Antsy Toms is back in town," he said, and he ran past her, down the hall and back down the stairs. Shrake was at the wheel of his personal Crown Vic, waiting in the street. Lucas climbed in the back.

"Where is he?"

"At his mom's house in Frogtown," Jenkins said, as Shrake jumped on the gas. "We own the guy who lives across the street. He's on his second continuance on coke charges. He's been going down to the cathedral, lighting candles, hoping that Antsy would show up so he could turn him in."

"He wouldn't be shittin' you?" Lucas asked.

Jenkins snorted. "He ain't gettin' a third continuance."

"Gotta stay cool," Lucas said. "Antsy's got more muscle than *Rocky II*."

"And he's more fucked up than Rocky the Flying Squirrel," Shrake said. "I'm just praying he hasn't left."

"Is St. Paul on the way?" Lucas asked.

Long pause. Then Jenkins said, "I guess we forgot to call them."

"You morons," Lucas said.

Jenkins struggled, turned in his seat, and looked at Lucas: "Call them if you want, you yellow motherfucker."

They looked at each other for a minute, then Lucas said, "Whatever."

Shrake busted a red light turning onto University, and the

Crown Vic took about three turns that the road didn't, and Lucas said, "I can't believe you went out and bought this piece of shit."

"Couldn't help myself," Shrake said. "The seats fit my ass."

"The experts rated it on Microsoft Network," Jenkins said over his shoulder.

"How'd they rate it?"

"Six out of ten," Jenkins said. Then he made a laugh sound that went like "bwa-hahahah," and Shrake said, "Fuck you," and then, "We're four blocks out."

"Put it at the Taco Shed," Jenkins suggested.

"Somebody'll steal the tires," Shrake said.

"Not when they see us getting out of the car," Jenkins said. He reached between his legs and swung up a pump shotgun.

"Maybe we could rob the Taco Shed before we take Antsy," Lucas said.

"Not a bad idea," Jenkins said, "except that it's daylight."

A block from the Taco Shed, Jenkins called St. Paul and identified himself: "We've got a semi-confirmed tip that Antsy Toms is at his mother's house."

He gave them the details, and help was on the way. It'd get there only a minute or so too late, Lucas thought: as planned.

The Taco Shed was two houses sideways from Toms's mother's place. In addition to being Siggy's stupid younger brother, and occasional cocaine runner, Toms was a weight guy, a lifter, a bouncer, a steroid freak, and a meth enthusiast. Three weeks earlier, stoned out of his mind, and tired of constant cop probes about his brother, he'd beaten a St. Paul cop unconscious, then pinned him on the floor and methodically kicked his balls until they turned to ravioli.

The cop's partner, a twenty-four-year-old woman named Les Cooper, had gotten into it, and Toms had picked her up by the short hair at the back of her head and whacked her face twice against a mahogany bar, crushing the bones around her eye sockets. She was the niece of a BCA agent who worked out of the Bemidji office.

Toms had always been a cruel, racist, child-beating, dope-taking freak, and had always walked . . . until now. He'd been hiding out ever since he'd beaten up the cops, but had been seen a couple times in western Wisconsin and north of the Twin Cities in St. Cloud, so they knew he was still around.

His real name, Lucas had once been told, was Antanas. From there, Antsy was a natural: maybe the name had made him what he was. Like Bugsy . . .

They made the Taco Shed parking lot and climbed out of the car, three large men wearing bulletproof vests. Shrake hit the locks and the car beeped at them and they ran across the lawn of the first house and then up the porch steps of the second house and Shrake kicked the door and they were inside and there was Antsy, standing in the middle of the living room with an old-fashioned princess phone in his hand.

Jenkins pointed the shotgun at him and screamed, "On the floor, you piece of shit," and Antsy threw the phone at Jenkins's head and spun and ran for the stairs. Jenkins ducked and pointed the shotgun, but shook his head and screamed, "Stop . . . wait, wait."

Antsy's mother, a large woman in blue Nike workout sweats, appeared in the kitchen doorway carrying a cutting board as though it were a Ping-Pong paddle and she threw it overhand at Lucas, who ducked, and then Shrake was on the stairs going after Antsy and they heard a rumble and Antsy's mom yelled, "Not the organ," and an old Hammond electric organ flew down the stairs like a freight train and Shrake jumped down just in front of it.

As it crashed at the bottom of the stairs, they heard windows breaking upstairs and Lucas yelled, "He's going out the window," and Jenkins yelled, "I'm going up, you guys go out," and he pushed the shotgun out in front of him and took the stairs.

Shrake ran toward the front door and Lucas toward the back of the house, through the kitchen. Antsy's mom had run back into the kitchen after the organ crashed, and she pulled a butcher

89

knife out of a drawer and blocked Lucas's route past the kitchen counter.

Lucas got in close, then punched her with a good right hand and she flew ass-over-teakettle under the breakfast table. Lucas went out the back door and around to the side, where he saw Shrake coming toward him. Antsy, appropriately dressed in a wife-beater shirt, jeans, and socks, with no shoes, had climbed out of a dormer window, hesitated on the edge of the roof, just above the gutter, thinking about jumping, twelve feet up.

Then the barrel of Jenkins's shotgun poked through a broken window and hit him between the shoulder blades, hard, and he tipped forward, tried to catch himself, swinging his hands in little circles, said, "Shit," and jumped off the roof and landed in the neighbor's hedge.

Shaken and maybe hurt, he rolled onto his stomach and Shrake ran up and screamed, "Look out, look out," and punted Antsy in the teeth. Antsy was flopped over on his hands and knees, still in the hedge, which seemed to be some kind of prickly stuff, roses, maybe, and Shrake took the opportunity to kick him in the balls, hard, with a steel-toed brogan.

Antsy groaned and scrambled straight ahead, still tangled in the hedge, and Lucas vaulted the low chain-link fence around the neighbor's backyard and ran up as Antsy finally staggered to his feet, clutching at his crotch, blood bubbling out of his mouth, around his broken teeth. Lucas hit him as hard as he could right between the eyes.

Antsy went back in the hedge and this time didn't move. Jenkins came running out of the house and said, "Goddamnit, you didn't wait for me."

"He's a violent man," Lucas said, breathing hard, shaking out his hand.

But the movie wasn't over, quite.

Antsy's mom came out of the house, screaming, fat, Lithuanian, they'd heard, from the Old Country, hard lard, not soft, waving the butcher knife. "His mother made him what he is,"

Jenkins said, quoting a country song. Mom had fixed on Shrake, and charged him, and Jenkins swatted her in the face with the butt of the shotgun and she went down.

There were sirens, had been sirens, and then a uniformed St. Paul cop looked back around the house, saw them, ran up and said, "Whoa. Resisting arrest," and kicked Antsy in the ribs hard enough to knock him back out of the hedge. More steel-toed shoes.

St. Paul arrived in force, and they dragged Antsy out of the hedge and propped up his old lady, who started crying, and Antsy said, "You motherfuckers are gonna pay for this. We got more goddamn guns than you do and Siggy's coming back, you motherfuckers. You beat up our mom, you motherfuckers."

"I hope he's coming back," Jenkins said through his teeth. "That cocksucker will look good on the end of my shotgun."

Antsy spit blood at him, but missed, and the St. Paul cop said, "Maybe we oughta put a spit shield on him."

"What a buttwipe," Shrake said.

"Problem with a spit shield is, sometimes it covers their eyes so much that they can't see the car roof when they're getting in, and they just knock the shit out of themselves," Jenkins said.

"Siggy's gonna fix your asses," Antsy said, but he didn't spit again.

His mom said, "I didn't know Antsy was coming home, I didn't know, not my fault . . ."

Antsy said, "Shut the fuck up."

His mother was bleeding heavily from her nose, and the cops helped her up and started her toward the car. "You criminals," she mumbled. "You criminals . . ."

LUCAS DIDN'T GET back to the office until four-thirty. Carol, his secretary, looked at him and said, "You've been taking some exercise."

"Yeah." He felt pretty good, in fact, except that his right hand hurt.

The Tomses were both at Regions hospital in guarded

condition, with a few broken bones and blunt trauma between them, and Antsy also had about a million tiny thorns sticking in him. "Don't know what we can do about that," a doc said. "Let them work their way out, I guess. Gonna itch like fire, though."

"We'll have to find a way to live with it," Shrake said.

"I GOT THAT stuff from Dan Hall," Carol said. "He faxed a subpoena to Fidelity and they sent back a fax of the canceled check. Frances Austin had a checking account at Riverside State Bank."

"Huh." The Antsy episode had temporarily kicked the Austin case out of Lucas's frontal lobes. He wanted to go around and punch walls, and talk about the bust, and maybe have a couple of beers and kick cans down the street and laugh out loud.

"I got you a subpoena for her Riverside records," she said, and handed him a piece of paper with his own signature at the bottom. "They close at five. The records will be ready when you serve the subpoena."

Lucas looked at the paper, felt the high leaking out. "I think I should have been there . . . you know, to sign it?"

"You were, in spirit," she said.

The Riverside State Bank was not on the side of the river, but in one of St. Paul's downtown skyways, an obscure bank, one that you didn't think about. Lucas left his car on the street, got a bag of popcorn, and wound his way through the skyways, replaying the Antsy Toms fight in his head.

How did some people grow up to be pieces of shit? They didn't have to be—they just were. They liked it. What was the Kid Rock song? "Low Life"? Like that.

The bank was painted in tints and shades of brown; if you didn't look at it carefully, it might not have been there—in a fantasy novel, it would have been the gate to an alternate reality.

The vice president in charge of the branch, a tall, balding man with weasel-like teeth, took the subpoena and produced a piece of paper, an account file.

"This is it?" Lucas asked, turning it over. "One side of a piece of paper?"

"An unusual account," the vice president said. "What do you think she's up to?"

Lucas shook his head. "She's dead."

The vice president's hand went to his lips. "Not . . . She wasn't withdrawing . . . Somebody wasn't taking out . . . ?"

"No, no. She was killed after the last withdrawal. A month or so afterwards. And this is still open, right?" He held the paper up. "Nobody's gotten in touch about an estate?"

"No. There's nothing in her file at all. No notations. We did issue a check-cashing card."

"And it's open."

"It's still open, but only has a hundred dollars in it. The fifty-thousand-dollar deposit was withdrawn in cash, starting two weeks after it was deposited. Then nothing more."

"Hmm."

"That's what I thought, when I saw it," the vice president said. "Of course, this is all automated, and it's not big enough to draw any particular attention. But, look here . . ."

He reached out for the file, and Lucas let it go, and the vice president put it on the desktop, upside down from himself, so Lucas could read it, and used a pen to point out the individual lines of the withdrawal records.

"We have five branches: this one, plus one at Maplewood, one at Signal Hills, one in Woodbury, and one down at Midway. The money was taken out twenty-five hundred dollars at a time, in cash. Twenty withdrawals, one a day. Look at this code—this tells you the branch where the withdrawal was made. The first was taken out here, the next in Maplewood, the next at Midway, the next at Signal Hills. And so on. Every week for four weeks."

"Why would they do that?"

"My thought was, she didn't want to be seen taking out too much money at once," the vice president said. "I looked in my computer records, and I can tell you that she never saw any teller twice. Since we only have two or three working at a time, that doesn't work out statistically."

"So she was avoiding the tellers she'd seen before," Lucas said.

"That's my idea," the vice president said.

"Thank you," Lucas said. He started away, then turned back. "The fifty thousand wasn't the first deposit?"

"That's on the paper," the vice president said. "The account was opened with five hundred dollars. There were two one-hundred-dollar withdrawals on the check card, then nothing for two months, then the big check, then nothing for two weeks, then four weeks of daily withdrawals."

Fifty grand. What had she been buying? Maybe nothing. Maybe she was putting together some case money, a stash. Shit, maybe she was a terrorist. A rich Caucasian Goth terrorist, buying RPGs. Maybe she was going to war against the Republicans. Lucas smiled to himself: maybe not.

So what had she been buying? Or why would she need case money? He couldn't remember the names, looked in his notebook: Denise Robinson, Mark McGuire. Hung out with her, might have wanted to start a business. Wanted her for the money? Something to push.

HE WENT HOME for dinner, the kitchen warm and smelling good, like potatoes and salmon, Sam making a hash of his hash, Letty working on algebra while she ate ("If a train is going sixty-five miles an hour to the east, and another train is going forty-five miles an hour to the west . . ."), and took time out to grouse about not getting a cell phone, because everybody else had one, and Weather, quiet, amused, and at the same time, tired from a seven-hour-long operation, talking about going to bed early. A happy moment: if he'd ever thought of commissioning a painting of his family, that would be the moment.

"I've got to run out," Lucas said, when things had settled down to coffee. "Down to the A1, see if I can catch a few of Frances's friends, people we haven't touched yet. There's some weird stuff coming out."

"You could have another piece of pie," Weather said. "A small piece."

Felt so good, in a quiet way.

He left at eight, feeling a tug back toward the brightly lit windows, but going on into the dark, in the Porsche, around the corner, and then up Cretin to I—94.

HE FOUND A place in the street to park the car, under a streetlight.

The A1 had changed, just as the bartender had said it would. The lights had been turned down, and the crowd was younger and quieter and dressed in black. The bartender was the same guy: Jerry. Lucas nodded at him and asked, "Can you point me at anybody who knew Frances Austin?"

The bartender asked, "What kind of beer do you drink?"

"Leinie's?"

The bartender nodded and pulled a bottle of Honey Weiss out of a cooler and said, quietly, "Take a drink and then turn and look around, but not like I told you. There's a guy over there with a black cowboy-like hat. He knew her. But don't go right over."

Lucas took a sip of the beer and nodded, and the bartender went down the bar, to the only other customer sitting on a stool. Lucas took another sip, then turned and looked at the rooms, clusters of black-garbed Goths on their night out, mostly wine with a little beer here and there, quiet enough. The guy picked out by Jerry wasn't wearing anything like a cowboy hat, Lucas thought; it was the kind of hat you'd wear with a cape, or with a pencil-thin mustache. Lucas turned back around, took another sip, and the bartender laughed with the other guy down the bar. Good time to move . . .

Lucas stepped over to the booth where the hat guy was, with two other Goths, one male and one female, and took out his ID and said, "I'm an agent with the Bureau of Criminal

Apprehension." He held out the ID, and the three of them looked at it doubtfully, and he said, "Some of you knew Frances Austin, and I'm trying to figure out what happened there. I've got a photo kit . . . Could you tell me if this is Frances?"

The girl said, "I didn't know her," but the two guys did, and they shared the photo kit, and both shook their heads. "It looks a little like her, but the hair's wrong, and this woman is skinnier than Frances. She had a little heft to her. Not fat, but she wasn't this small."

The hat guy looked over the back of the booth and said, "Hey, Darrell, look at this."

In a couple of minutes, a half-dozen Goths had checked the photo kit, and asked why he didn't have a regular photograph, and then one of them said, "This isn't Frances. This is the fairy Goth. I heard you guys were looking for her."

Lucas nodded. "The fairy Goth. You sure?"

"Yeah. I saw her," the guy said. "In this picture she looks a little like Frances, but she doesn't look like her in real life. She's smaller and skinnier and darker."

"You know both of them."

He shook his head. "I don't know the fairy, I just saw her one night. I didn't know anybody was looking for her until tonight." He glanced at the bartender. "Jerry told me. Anyway, they are definitely different people."

"Well, shoot," Lucas said. But he'd known that. Frances Austin was dead. He spent a couple of minutes taking down names.

Then, an odd event.

A dark-haired man, with a funny fuzzy mustache, in sunglasses and a leather jacket, stepped through the back door and looked directly at Lucas, held his eyes until he saw Lucas look up at him, held them for another beat, then backed out through the door.

Wanted to talk privately?

Lucas said, "Excuse me," and went after him.

The alley behind the building, where Dick Ford had been killed, was illuminated by a single electric lamp above the A1 door, and by a streetlight down at the end of the alley. The mustachioed man was down there, at the end of the alley, looking at the door when Lucas came through, and behind him a slender dark-haired woman who darted out of sight. Lucas took a step that way, aware of the litter and the Coke can to his left, the uneven brick surface, and then the man made a gesture with his right hand, and everything seemed to go sideways.

In the first millisecond, Lucas continued with the step he was halfway into; in the second millisecond he recognized the gesture; and in the third millisecond he may have thought, Gun . . . and his hand started moving toward the pistol on his hip. Then the man opened fire, white sparkles and firecracker bangs and Lucas caught the closing steel door with his hand and lurched back behind it, feeling pain in his left leg, and he sagged against the wall, fumbling his pistol out.

He was hurt and bleeding, he thought, and he peeked, heard people shouting in the club, and he saw the man running out of the alley. There was something wrong with him, fire in his leg, but Lucas lurched that way, and he thought about getting hit in the groin and all the arteries down there and he followed his pistol down the alley, limping, hopping, hurting, then he was at the corner and he heard a car accelerating hard, around the corner, a half-block away, out of sight, and then he thought, *Hope it didn't hit me in the balls hope it didn't hit me in the balls* . . .

And the pain came in a wave.

He lurched back to the bar and the crowd growing around the door, waving his pistol with one hand, and he groaned, "I got shot," and he sat down in the alley just outside the door, under the light, and people were shouting about ambulances and cops, and one of the Goth women said, "I'm a nurse, let me look at it," and she and one of the Goth guys got his jeans down and they looked at his bloody thigh.

"No artery," she said, looking up at him. "You're bleeding. We've got to get you to the hospital, but it's not pumping, it's not pumping, it's through-and-through." She shouted over her shoulder, "Ask Jerry if he's got a first-aid kit." And to Lucas: "We gotta get some pressure on it. Get some pressure on it."

Jerry shouted, "Cops are on the way, ambulance on the way."

The cops were there in one minute: a red-faced blond and his black partner, who looked down and said, "Holy shit, Davenport, man, what happened?"

"Motherfucker mustache guy shot me," Lucas said.

The Goth nurse was pressing an antique gauze pad, from a thirty-year-old first-aid kit, against the hole in his thigh. "I'm working the Austin case, ahhh . . . and the Dick Ford case, with Harry Anson," Lucas told the cop. The leg was on fire, was burning up. He grunted to the nurse, "Goddamn, that hurts. That hurts." And to the cop again, "Call Anson. Guy ambushed me. Middle height, black hair, mustache, black leather jacket, had a car parked around the corner. Might have a limp. Jesus, that hurts."

The ambulance was there a minute later and they put him on a gurney and ran him out, and the EMT started running down his list, asking about aspirin and street drugs and heart medications, and Lucas answered and then got his cell phone out and the EMT said, "You can't use that here," and Lucas said, "Bullshit. I'm gonna call my wife before anybody else does."

He did and it was confusing, but she was coming. Because his mind was still operating in some cold not-quite-shocked mode, he made one more call, almost fumbling the phone as he worked down through his call list. But he got it, finally, and Alyssa Austin answered the phone. He hung up without saying anything: but Austin was at home. If the woman he saw running away was the fairy, and it could have been, then Austin was not her.

The ambulance made a swooping move and one of the EMTs said something he didn't understand, and then the doors were popping open: the hospital. He'd been there before, rolling down a hallway looking up at the passing lights, talking to the docs in their scrubs. One of the docs said, "Sir, you understand me? Sir? It's more than a couple of stitches, you've got a hole there and I'm going to have to clean it out? Do you understand that, sir?"

They were pulling his pants off as they talked and Lucas asked, "What'd it hit?"

"Your leg; I'm going to have to clean it out, okay? We have your permission to clean it out?"

"Yeah, yeah, go ahead."

"Do you take a heart aspirin or Plavix or Coumadin, any drugs that you think might affect . . ."

Some time passed; he didn't know exactly how much, and then he was moving again. He was out of his clothing and there was something cold and wet on his leg and belly and nurses were pushing and pulling on him, transferring him to an operating table, and a masked man looked down at him and then he went away for a while . . .

Weather was sitting white-faced in a chair next to the bed when he came back. He was in a recovery room, and she must've gotten in on her physician's ID. He groaned, "Ah, man," and she stood up clutching a purse to her chest and she began to weep and said, "Oh, God you scared me, goddamn, you scared me . . ."

Lucas said, "I'm gonna kill that motherfucker."

9

AT THE SURGEON'S INSISTENCE—backed up by a brook-no-argument Weather—Lucas stayed in the hospital overnight, all the next day and the next night, forced to sleep on his back, which he never did. By the end of it, he had a crippling ache at the juncture of his back and butt.

Before that, though, he'd been heavily fussed over.

The morning after the shooting, at first light, the surgeon

showed up. End of his shift. He looked at the wound and said, "I do good work."

"Everybody keeps saying, 'It wasn't much,'" Lucas said.

"It really wasn't," the surgeon agreed. He was a small, compact, swarthy man in good shape; looked like a handball player. "But man, it should have been. One inch to the left, it would have taken out your femoral artery. You'd have been forty-sixty getting to the hospital before you bled out. Two inches to the right, and we have massive genital involvement. You'd still be on the table, with the microsurgeons trying to sort out the pieces."

"Ah, jeez."

"Yeah. Anyway, we're gonna keep you here today at least, overnight, and maybe tomorrow, depending," the doc said. "There was some crap in the wound, material from your jeans. I got it pretty clean, but we want to watch it."

"Is it gonna hurt?"

"On a scale of one to ten, about a five, to start, then going to a three, and then fading away," the surgeon said. "But it'll go away pretty quick. You'll be good as new in a couple of weeks. Or three or four. Depending."

Weather showed up. She'd gone home when Lucas had been given a sleeping aid the night before, mostly to comfort the kids, and hustled back in as the surgeon was leaving. They talked for two minutes, out of Lucas's earshot, and he heard them laughing, and then Weather came in and said, "You stay in bed all day, and all night, pee in a bottle like a good boy, and maybe go home tomorrow."

"What were you laughing about?" Lucas asked.

"Ah, nothing."

"What?"

"Ah, it's pretty funny."

"What's funny?"

"Well, they didn't know what they were going to have to do to you last night, so when they put you on the table, they scrubbed you up and . . . shaved. You got what we call a winky cut."

"Aww . . ." Lucas pulled the robe apart and looked. A nether Mohawk, actually, both sides shaved, with a strip left up the middle. "Awww, man . . ."

They gave him Egg Beaters and a muffin for breakfast, which the breakfast lady said was heart-healthy, but seemed to Lucas to be nutrition-deadly. There couldn't have been more than fifty calories in it.

"Quit complaining," Weather said. "There are little children starving in Texas."

Anson showed up at eight o'clock, as Weather was gathering up her purse to leave. She stayed to listen.

Lucas told the story again, in minute detail and gave Anson his car keys, and Anson said he'd have a cop drive the Porsche over to Lucas's place. "He might want to take a dogleg through Milwaukee, first. He's kind of a motorhead," he said, and Lucas said, "He probably shouldn't; I'm not in that good a mood."

"You saw the shooter."

"Yeah, but I couldn't positively identify him if I saw him again," Lucas said. "I saw him twice, once when he stuck his head in the door, and once in the alley. He had a mustache and sunglasses, and the sunglasses should have tipped me off . . . In the alley, I only got to look at him for half a second before I started tap-dancing."

And he remembered: "By the way, about two minutes after I got shot, in the ambulance, I called Alyssa Austin. She was at home."

"So she's not the fairy," Anson said.

"She could be, but then the woman in the alley wasn't. And I have no idea who else she'd be, or the guy with the mustache, or why they'd want to shoot at me. I'll tell you something else: I think the mustache might have been a Halloween mustache. I'm thinking about it, I'm thinking about when he looked at me in the bar, and there was something wrong with it."

Anson had heard about the raid on Antsy Toms and wondered if the shooter might have been a Lithuanian crazy, getting some payback. But they couldn't figure out how one of Antsy's pals would know that Lucas would be at the A1.

"One of the Goths might have called the shooter when I came in—and it's possible that they thought that I was you," Lucas told Anson. "You were walking around talking to all those guys today . . . you might want to take it a little easy."

"I'll think about that," Anson said.

"So what'd you get out of the alley?"

"No shells, so the guy was using a revolver. A .38. We've got three slugs, two of them pretty bad ricochets—he seemed to be shooting way low, we've got at least one hit right about where your feet would have been. The third one was higher and went into a nice soft wood two-by-four at the corner of the door. It's in pretty good shape, so if we can find the pistol, we can match it up."

"Excellent," Lucas said.

"And we got a half-assed witness," Anson said. "A guy walking back home with a sandwich heard the shots, and he looked back down the street and saw two people running, one tall and one short, man and a woman. Just what you saw. He also saw their vehicle. He doesn't know what kind, but it was a pickup."

"That's something," Lucas said. "But not much."

When Anson was gone, Weather asked, "Antsy Toms? What was that?"

But Lucas had drifted away from her, rerunning the shooting in his head. The shooter had been too far from him—too far for accurate shooting. Probably sixty or seventy feet. Lucas could see him jerking at the trigger with each shot, the gun barrel all over the place.

And in that mind's-eye image, Lucas counted off the shots: he'd been shot at, he thought, six times, and hit once. He might have been hit in the head or the heart or he might not have been hit at all—the shooter was a fuckin' amateur, and he'd been nervous and probably scared and maybe desperate.

What had Lucas done to make anybody desperate?

102

"Antsy Toms," Weather repeated. "Isn't he the guy who beat up those officers?"

HIS BOSS, Rose Marie Roux, came by for a look: "Jesus, Lucas, you're supposed to be the brains of the operation. You're not supposed to get shot in alleys. Not any more. Those days are over."

"Hey, I didn't go looking for it." He got the flash again: the guy's hand pumping out the bullets. How long? A second and a half?

"Then what were you doing in the alley?"

"Working. And this isn't much—shit, I've been hurt worse than this doing home repair," he said.

The governor's chief hatchet man called, and Carol, his secretary, called, crying, and then Del stopped by, and the governor himself called.

Del wanted to look at the bullet hole, but was satisfied by looking at the bruising. "Nasty. But remember that time Gutmann got shot through both cheeks of his ass . . . ?"

Alyssa Austin called, and wanted to come see him, but he told her he was too tired.

LUCAS SPENT MUCH of the day watching TV and reading the papers, saw pictures of himself on all the nightly newscasts—top story on two stations—and tried to think about the case, but found himself sleeping, instead. The photo kit of the fairy was featured as the possible Female Assassin, and a Goth, interviewed at the shooting site behind the A1, described her as gorgeous, and the TV guy inflated that to "mysterious raven-haired beauty."

Weather came and went. Sometimes, her chair was empty, and he'd close his eyes for just a second, and when he opened them, she'd be there.

After a second restless night, the surgeon came in at the end of his shift, looked at the wound, pronounced it not bad, and told him that he could go home, but he'd still have to be signed off by the medicine guy, who'd given him a couple of prescriptions for pain pills. The wound itself was a harsh line of stitches, purple and black, and around it, a bruise the size of his hand, and growing.

He had Egg Beaters again, and read stories about himself in the *Pioneer Press* and the *Star Tribune*. Ruffe, the crime reporter, had taken care of him, but the editorial page had done a snide, "Davenport, Again" story, which recalled that Lucas had once beaten up a pimp and had had to leave the Minneapolis police force for a while. The paper did not mention that the pimp had church-keyed one of Lucas's street sources.

Weather showed up and said, "They redid that story about me doing the tracheotomy."

"Yeah, I saw." The story about him getting shot in the throat by a little girl, his life saved with a pocketknife . . . Hardly ever thought about that anymore, but when he touched his throat, he could still feel the scar that Weather had left behind. She asked him once if he'd married her because of it, and he'd grinned and said, "No, but if you hadn't done it, I wouldn't have married you."

"What?"

"Think about it."

HE FINALLY GOT out at 11 A.M., wheeled to Weather's car in a wheelchair, given a crutch for the last four feet. In the car, as he settled down, she said, "If you were a little smarter, I'd worry about post-traumatic shock." Her eyes caught his when she said it.

"That's no way to talk to a patient," he said.

The fact was, he hurt more this second morning than he had the first morning-after. His leg now felt as though he'd been hit with a baseball bat, rather than a pointer. He was grateful for the painkillers.

He stayed home for the day, and made the housekeeper lie for him: when the phone rang, and it was media, she told them he was at work. He first lay in bed and then on the couch in the living room, and read a book called *The Seasons of Tulul,* by Egon Lass, about living with Bedouins, and a cop novel, *Death Comes for the Fat Man,* by Reginald Hill.

HE COULDN'T GET comfortable with the leg, and the house-keeper bothered him with food, as though she were feeding a favored canary. The pain in the leg seemed to be diminishing when he made two trips to the bathroom, but flared up again late in the day.

They all ate dinner together, and Letty talked about bullet wounds she'd seen, which were numerous, considering her age, and compared his current wound to a hangnail.

He snapped at her: "It might be a hangnail, but it hurts like hell," and she suddenly got teary, and pushed away from the table and stalked out of the room and when he called, "Hey," she called back, "I was just trying to cheer you up."

Weather said, "Ah, jeez," and Sam exhaled and looked suddenly sad.

"Better tomorrow," Lucas said.

Another restless night, but this time, thinking about Letty and Sam.

The third morning after the shooting, the pain was still there, but more of an ache, like a bruise, than a cutting pain; like the pain you get forty-five seconds after being hit by a fastball. Weather redressed the wound and pronounced him improved. The wound had sealed, with no obvious inflammation showing, and she said that it was superficial and shouldn't be dangerous.

"Good. I'm going downtown."

"Take the truck," she said. "You won't want to use a clutch."

Letty made a point of kissing him on the forehead before she left, which really did make him feel better, if elderly. Sam ran into a wall and creased an eyebrow and thought not much of it. Sam ran into things a lot and called the subsequent wounds "bimps."

Before he left, he read the *Star Tribune*'s second-day story about the shooting, which was a rewrite of the first day's, leaving out the history, and adding only that the police had learned nothing more.

The *Star-Tribune* had asked the governor for a comment, and he'd said, "Sometimes, in these matters, we have to take risks, and sometimes we get hurt. I'm told Lucas is already on his feet, and I expect he'll get right back out there and nail this guy." The governor sounded as though he'd been behind Lucas's left shoulder, with a gun in his hand.

He got the crutch and went out to the truck.

LUCAS LIMPED into the office and Carol asked, "Oh my *God*, what are you *doing* here?"

"Working."

"That crutch looks like a waste of time."

He looked at it. "Yeah."

He called Austin: "I've got to see you, the earlier the better. Where are you?"

"In my car, I'm almost at the Wanderwood location, it's up by North Oaks. I'll be here for a couple of hours, if you could stop by there?"

"Sure. Half an hour, probably."

When he left, Carol was coming back up the hallway carrying an old-fashioned wooden cane. She gave it to him and said, "Try this."

"Ah, for Christ's sakes, I'm not elderly."

"Try it."

He tried it, and it helped. "What a pain in the ass," he said. "If it'll make you happy . . ."

He strolled down to the elevator, twirling it like a baton, but after he got downstairs, used it to walk out to the car. It took a few pounds off the leg, and that helped. A lot.

Fuckin' women.

WANDERWOOD WAS A well-kept, yellow-painted concrete-block building that shared a parking lot with a Caribou Coffee shop. He left the cane in the truck, thinking that he could suppress the urge to limp, took two steps, and went back for the cane. Inside, a receptionist looked him over and said, "You're not here about the mirrors."

"No. I'm here to see Alyssa Austin. She's expecting me."

"Hang on one second," the receptionist said, and disappeared down a tiled hallway. Lucas looked around: there was just the faintest tang of sweat about the place, but it might have come from a spray bottle. Otherwise, it smelled like Chanel, or some other kind of French perfume.

Expensive-looking easy chairs were arranged around a tree-trunk coffee table, very ecological-looking, in the waiting area. The table held an apricot-colored orchid in a plain terra-cotta pot, and a stack of appropriate magazines: *In Style, Vanity Fair, Fitness, Marie Claire, Allure, Vogue.* Nothing with a car on the cover, or even a suggestion that a car existed.

He paged through *Fitness* for a moment, then the receptionist reappeared and said, "Come on back."

She took him past a small open workout area, where a half-dozen women rode bikes or ran on treadmills, to a private workout room where Austin was working with a trainer, doing Pilates. She was flat on her stomach doing foot-and-hand lifts with light weights in her hands, sweating like a dog, but when she finished, she did a kind of snap push-up that bounced her to her feet. The trainer nodded and said, "Not too bad, but you have to start finishing the routine."

"How many times have I missed?"

The trainer, a woman a bit taller than Austin but just as fit, bones showing in her face, said, "Week before last, you only got halfway through."

"I'm doing good; if I only miss one in six, I'm doing good," Austin said, and then, to the trainer, "Take a break. I've got to talk to this guy."

"You're pretty hard-core," Lucas said, letting his eyes walk around her body.

"I can't believe *you're* walking around," she said.

"Ah, I've been hurt worse doing home repair." He'd been using the line frequently, because he thought it was pretty good.

Austin stepped over to a barre and pulled a towel off, mopped her face and her neck. "I'm a jock, I've always liked to sweat," she said. "My problem is, I tend to work too much, and eat too little. Then my ass disappears. The people who come here definitely don't want to see an assless CEO."

"You're holding your own," Lucas said. He quickly added, lest she misinterpret a comment that he intended as purely aesthetic, "That fifty thousand bucks that Frances took out . . . there's something strange going on there. We need to find out where it went. She took it all in cash, and the way she did it . . ."

He told her about his visit to the bank and she said, "I've no idea what that was about. I've never had fifty thousand in cash, myself, in my entire life. I mean, you can't buy anything with it. Anything legal."

"We were wondering about that ourselves," Lucas said. "Drugs . . . or maybe some kind of political thing. We're trying to think of stuff."

She crossed her arms and looked down at the floor, tapping one foot, as though trying to work through it, then said, "Frances did this Goth thing, but you know what? She was really a pretty mainstream kid. She wasn't a big risk-taker. She was a little risk-taker . . . and why would she finance something like drugs? She had all the money she needed. I assume you're not suggesting that she *used* fifty thousand dollars' worth of drugs."

"Could be done, but you'd see it."

"I never saw her loaded," Austin said. "Never. Fifty thousand in cash, she would have had to be involved in distribution or something. And I can't see that. Not at all. If you knew her, you'd know how crazy it seems."

"She wouldn't have had to use it all at once," Lucas said. "She could have been running on credit for a while, until she got her money, and then paid off her dealer."

"She *wasn't* a druggie," Austin said. "She just wasn't."

"Do you know what a druggie looks like?" Lucas asked.

"I do. We have women here, well-off people, who got involved with cocaine or pills, they come out of rehab and straight into here because the doctors tell them to. Sometimes it helps and sometimes it doesn't, but I get a sense of what druggies are like and Frances wasn't like that. She may have smoked a joint on occasion, but who hasn't?"

Lucas noticed that Austin's daughter was now in the past tense, but didn't mention it.

"She didn't gamble."

"No."

"So where did the money go?"

"I don't know. It's just not right. It's *just not right.*"

Lucas limped over to the barre and leaned his butt against it. Austin said, "You got shot in the same bar where Dick Ford was murdered. Near where this other boy was killed."

"Yup."

"So there must be something there."

"That's what I think." He felt a twinge from his groin, and winced a little.

"*Why* are you walking around?" Austin said. "Your face just went white as a sheet of paper."

"Because I'm bored and I wasn't hurt that bad. And I'm interested: you know a guy, a friend of Frances's, middle height, maybe five-eleven or so, black hair, black leather jacket, jeans, cheap sunglasses, a crooked mustache but maybe not, a hip-looking guy?"

She cocked her head to one side. "Like a wannabe biker?"

"Yeah. Sort of a broken-ass wannabe biker."

"God. He sounds like . . . quite a while back, I only saw him once, there was a guy named Larry," she said. She held her hands to her lips. "No, that's not right. It was an L name, but like a woman's name . . . Lauren? Loren? Loren, I think. It sounds like him."

"Loren."

"Yes. I'm sure of it. When I saw him, he was wearing a white T-shirt with the black jacket and black jeans and black hair, and I thought, you know, Here's a guy who could manipulate his way into a young girl's pants, and he'd be pretty heartless about it. But I don't think she was seeing him. I don't think they had any kind of physical relationship. At least, not at the time I saw him. They didn't have that . . . intimacy about them."

"Loren," Lucas said. "No last name?"

"No. I only saw him that one time, they came by the house in Frances's car, but . . ."

"He came by the house?" Lucas asked.

"Yes, just for a while," she said.

"Did he look it over?"

"Well, they carried some things from Frances's room down to her car . . . but you know, I don't really remember him that well. As it turns out, I never saw him again. He didn't seem like Frances's type. That's why I remember him at all, because . . . he seemed like somebody to be wary of."

"How old?" Lucas asked.

"Late twenties, probably. Early thirties at the most," she said.

"Get the feeling that he was local?"

"I didn't get any feeling for that." Her forehead wrinkled, and then she said, "I didn't notice an accent. So probably local."

"That's something."

She looked up at him and said, "I never would have remembered to tell you about him. It was too long ago, and I only saw him that one time. All I've got left is a kind of ghost image."

10

HE'D GOTTEN NO further on the fifty thousand dollars, but he had a name: Loren. Back at the office, he ran the name through the DMV computer and found, unexpectedly, that there were hundreds of Lorens in Minnesota. He called out to his secretary, "Hey, Carol—where's Sandy?"

Carol came to the door: "She doesn't work today. She's got classes in the morning . . . you might be able to get her on her cell phone."

He got the number and dialed, and Sandy came up in a few seconds. He explained the problem. "Get all the Lorens, filter them for age twenty-five to middle thirties, then look at the ID photos and get me dark hair."

"Maybe I should look at the university records, too," Sandy suggested. "If she was going to school, could have been an out-of-state school friend."

"You've got access?" Lucas asked.

"I do, but you can't tell," she said.

"How long?"

"I've got a link at home now . . . an hour?"

"We gotta pay you more," he said.

When he was off the line, he walked down and got a can of diet Coke, stretching his leg, ran into Shrake, who said, "What the hell happened?" So he had to tell Shrake about it, and then Jenkins showed up and said, "You got in the papers again, you goddamn publicity dog."

"I was badly wounded," Lucas said.

"You didn't shoot anybody," Jenkins said. "You didn't even *try* to shoot anybody."

"The guy was gone before I got my gun out," Lucas said. "I was doing a two-step around the incoming."

"You should have shot *somebody*," Jenkins said. "Anybody. This makes us look bad. Like pussies."

Shrake closed one eye and said to Jenkins, "Maybe you oughta let up. Our boy don't look that happy."

Jenkins: "So what? Fuck him. If you don't kick a guy when he's down, you're stupid."

Shrake asked Lucas, "You okay?"

"I don't know," Lucas said. "He missed my balls by two inches, and if it'd been an inch the other way, he'd have blown out my femoral artery. I have no idea who he is, what he wants. But he goddamn near killed me."

"He's a nimrod," Shrake said. "He gave you everything he had and just nicked you."

"That makes it worse, almost," Lucas said. "I was almost killed by a fuck-up."

"Not worse," Jenkins said, shaking a finger. "If he comes back for you, you'll get him. If he'd been a pro, or a cop, or anybody who knows about guns, he'd have waited right outside that door for you, and he would've shot you from two feet and you'd be dead now. He was scared of you. He was standing back far enough to run away."

"Does this involve the Austin thing?" Shrake asked.

"Christ, I hope so," Lucas said. "If it's not that, I've got no idea what it would be."

Jenkins to Shrake: "Maybe we ought to see if Antsy has another brother. Or a special Lithuanian pal."

Lucas shook his head: "Any pal of Antsy would have been better at it. This guy was a total fuckin' amateur. I don't think he'd ever shot a gun before. He held it low, with his wrist cocked, like that picture of Elvis Presley in the cowboy suit. He had no idea where the bullets were going."

Jenkins slapped him on the shoulder. "Well, I gotta say, I'm glad he didn't kill you. God knows who we would've got in your job. Probably some bureaucratic motherfucker."

Back in his office, Lucas stared at his computer screen for a while. His leg was itching, a painful itch, like poison ivy, so he took half a pain pill, took a peek at the bandage, didn't see any leakage.

And thought about the fifty thousand, *It's not enough for anything.*

Not enough for anything that would be important to her, financially. Even if she bought fifty thousand in dope, wholesale, she wouldn't make enough back to justify any risk—the profit, even from a dope deal, would have been a drop in the bucket compared to what she already had.

And after what Austin had said, the prospect of a dope deal seemed thin, although it was one explanation that would put Frances close to somebody who might kill her.

The key thing was, she took it in cash.

That meant that she didn't want it traced—couldn't be any other reason to take that much out at once. Of course, she could have planned to loan it to someone who didn't want the IRS to know about it, who didn't want a paper trail; or, even more unlikely, she might have planned to pass it along to some extremist political group, and she didn't want the ties to show up.

But it all seemed like bullshit. The explanation, when it came, would probably be simpler than any of that, Lucas thought. Shit, maybe she bought a Ferrari from somebody who didn't take checks.

Then why the secrecy about the withdrawals . . . ?

He took out his notebook, noted "Mark McGuire, Denise Robinson," looked them up in the license bureau's database, and then the phone companies'.

Robinson answered the phone. Lucas identified himself and said, "I'd like to run out to see you. About Frances Austin. You and Mr. McGuire."

"Mark won't be here for half an hour or so . . ."

"Neither will I," Lucas said. He got his jacket and the cane and said to Carol, "I'm gonna run out."

"Where're you going?"

"Out to Maplewood. This couple Denise Robinson and Mark McGuire, friends of Frances Austin," he said.

"Maybe you ought to take Del with you."

"Nah. I'm okay; this is just a check," Lucas said.

"What you really ought to do is go home and go to bed," she said. "You don't look that good."

On the way to Maplewood, Sandy rang on his cell phone: "I've got eighteen Lorens for you."

113

"God bless you."

"It's an old-fashioned name: there are more of them in their fifties and sixties than in their twenties and thirties. Anyway, I pulled the .jpgs out of the DMV folder and I'm sending them right . . . *now* . . . to your office e-mail."

"Okay. Run them through the NCIC, will you? Get back to me."

"I'll put the returns in your e-mail. But I'm going out tonight, so this'll be the last thing I can do today."

"Got a date?"

"Yes, I do," she said.

ROBINSON AND MCGUIRE might be characterized as "Not-Goths," Lucas thought when he saw them. They lived in a nondescript robin's-egg-blue, fifty-year-old split-level house in a nondescript baby-boomer neighborhood that once probably had about a million kids running around in the streets, and now was full of old people.

Denise Robinson was just as Alyssa Austin had described her: tall, gawky, short sandy hair, big glasses, about thirty. She met him at the door, invited him in, said, "Pay no attention to the living room; it's the way we live now."

The house smelled of coffee and pizza, and the living room was an office, stuffed full of computer equipment, file cabinets, two desks, and a cat-torn couch pushed against the farthest wall, with a red-striped cat perched on the back. McGuire was sitting at a computer, head bent toward the monitor screen, curly dark hair, shorter than Robinson, wearing jeans and a sweatshirt, maybe a year or two older than she was. A pair of dirty white Nikes sat in the foot well.

Still, when he turned to Lucas, Lucas thought, *Huh*. Dress him up a bit, and he could have been the shooter. McGuire reluctantly signed off what he was doing and turned toward Lucas without getting up.

Robinson said, "So what's going on?"

Lucas stepped over and scratched the cat between the ears, and it sniffed his hand and produced a perfunctory purr. Lucas said, "I've been compiling all the information I can find on Frances Austin, and I understand you three were close."

Robinson opened her mouth to answer but McGuire got there first: "We were friends. We don't know what happened to her."

"Do you think she's dead?" Lucas asked.

This time McGuire looked at Robinson, who said, "We think so. Not because we know anything, but just because . . . people usually are, when they're gone this long. We talked to her the day before she disappeared, and there wasn't any sign that she was going anywhere, that she had anything planned."

"Probably kidnapped—her old lady has all the money in the world," McGuire said.

"Were the three of you in business together?"

A line of wrinkles appeared in McGuire's forehead: "Where'd you hear that?"

"Just from . . . friends."

"We talked about it," Robinson said.

Looking for a little shock: "Did she give you fifty thousand dollars?"

Robinson: *"No way."*

McGuire, almost angry: "She didn't give us a fuckin' nickel."

Lucas went in again. "She didn't give you fifty thousand dollars in cash, mostly fifties and hundreds?"

"No. She didn't," McGuire snapped. "What the hell is this?"

"Trying to find out what happened to the money," Lucas said. "We heard you were trying to build a website. A website takes money. This"—he gestured around the living room, at the computers and servers and cable lines—"takes a lot of money."

"Takes thirty thousand, and we busted our butts getting it," McGuire said. "If we went national, we'd be looking for more money to set up an office and buy more equipment, and we talked to her about it, but she disappeared before we did anything. And we weren't asking for fifty thousand. Fifty thousand wasn't enough—we were looking for a quarter million, and even then, I'd have to keep working."

Not enough money, Lucas thought. He asked, "Where do you work?"

McGuire worked at Inter-Load Systems, a company that tracked mixed heavy freight and matched it with space available on over-the-road trucks. The company was a new start-up, and McGuire worked on the mathematical models that worked out delivery routes and times.

"Sounds complicated."

"It is," McGuire said. He was surly, and he looked tired; more than tired. Exhausted.

Lucas asked where he was the night of the shooting. "Working here," McGuire said.

"Any witnesses?"

"Well—Denise. I mean, it was the middle of the night, where'd you expect me to be?"

"Out clubbing, maybe," Lucas said.

McGuire snorted. "I don't have time to take a leak. The last time I went to a club, the Beastie Boys were big."

Lucas peered at him for a moment, then asked, "So what does this new website do? The one you were working on with Frances?"

"Tries to get people to make free advertisements. Then we test them for online reception, and try to sell them to the companies that they advertise," McGuire said.

"What?"

Robinson stepped up. "Suppose you're, like, Coca-Cola, and you keep putting out those crappy old Coke ads that no kid would ever watch, because they're so lame. So we solicit ads from guys with video cameras—high-quality stuff, not your home video—and when they come in, we test them, and then we pitch them to Coke. Coke gets a really out-there ad, something the kids will watch, really cheap—even if they reshoot it—and we get a cut."

"Is that going to work?" Lucas asked, genuinely curious.

"Not unless we can come up with a quarter-million bucks in the next few months. Word's getting out, and we're not moving fast enough," McGuire said. "We get four or five guys doing this, only one's going to make it. He'll make a hundred million bucks, everybody else goes broke."

"Well, shit," Lucas said. He scratched his head. "If advertisements are so expensive to make, why would anyone make one for free?"

"The model's already there," McGuire said. "It's publishing. When Stephen King was starting out, nobody paid him a nickel for all the work he was doing. Eventually, he sells a book, and then the big money arrives. But the publishing companies didn't put up a penny until he had something good.

"So you've got all these guys with cameras and they've been to film school and they know models and young actresses—they can put out a video for a few hundred bucks. Get some experience, get some attention, and maybe, if they're lucky, they get a whole bunch of money. It's like publishing, and we're like the agents."

"Huh," Lucas said. "That could work."

"I sure as shit hope so," McGuire said.

"So you see why we're missing Frances," Robinson said. "There was a possibility that she could round up some money. Her, her friends, maybe her mom and her mom's friends."

"Some of those people could drop a quarter-million dollars on the ground and not miss it," McGuire said. "Frances's dad joined a golf club out in Palm Springs a few years ago, and the admission fee was a quarter-million dollars. For a *golf club*. And here we've got this idea, and we . . . just . . . can't . . . get it done."

Showing anger again. Frustration. Interesting.

Lucas asked more questions about Frances: was she angry, lonely, addicted, scared, vague? No, they said, she wasn't any of those things. Robinson said at the end, "It was like one of those things where somebody's killed in a car wreck after the senior prom. Everybody's happy and then bam! Everybody's dead. I didn't see anything in Frances that I didn't see every day—she expected to see us, to call us, and maybe to get in the business someday."

"It wouldn't have pissed you off if she'd said 'no'? Sounds like she sort of led you on," Lucas said.

"Would have pissed me off—but I think she was sold on the idea," McGuire said. "I really thought she was going with us. When she disappeared, I thought I was going crazy. I kept trying to find out what happened, and nobody had anything to say."

"You talk to her mother?" Lucas asked.

"I did once . . . right after Frances disappeared," Robinson said. "Just seeing if anybody knew where she was. Mrs. Austin seemed really confused. Out of it. Like she was losing her grip. I felt so sorry for her."

"Do you have any idea why she might have disappeared?"

McGuire said, "Well, you've been all over it: money. She was smart, but not brilliant or anything. She looked okay, but she wasn't super pretty, like she might have a stalker or something. She was . . . nice. And she had money."

There wasn't much more. McGuire stood up when he left, and Lucas looked at him, standing, tried to imagine him with a gun in his hand. Still possible, he thought.

At the door, McGuire asked, "You don't have anything to do with Davenport Simulations, do you? There was a cop involved in that."

Lucas turned. "I started it, with a friend. He bought me out, when it got over my head. I'm out of it now."

McGuire's head bobbed: "I'm officially impressed. You probably know what I'm going through right now."

"Fun at the time," Lucas said.

"That's because you made it," McGuire said. "If you'd been wiped out by a competitor, it might not have been so much fun."

"There were no competitors," Lucas said.

"The olden days, when the world was new," McGuire said.

"I'm not that ancient," Lucas said.

"About six generations down the road, computer time,"

McGuire said. "I mean, you probably once used cameras with *film.*"

McGuire stayed in the doorway, and as Lucas got to his car, he called, "If you want to make another butt-load of money, all we need is a quarter million."

Lucas paused with one hand on the car-door handle: "Gimme a week to think about it and talk to some friends. Maybe . . ."

"I'll call you," McGuire said. "I'll call you."

BACK AT THE OFFICE, Lucas pulled up e-mail from Sandy. One had NCIC data on the Lorens, the other had photos. He looked at the pictures—and ran into the eyewitness problem: the eighteen were all between twenty-two and thirty-five, with dark hair, and most of them could have been the guy who shot at him. Most of them, in fact, could have been McGuire, but weren't. He couldn't pick one out.

He got on the phone and called Alyssa Austin on her cell. "Where are you?"

"At our Edina site," she said.

"Do you have access to a computer, where you could get e-mail?"

"Of course. Right here in the office—I can access my account."

"I'm forwarding eighteen digital photos to you. All Lorens. Stay on the phone, take a look at them."

"Hang on."

Lucas hung on for a minute, two minutes, then heard her pick up the phone and she said, "Lucas, I'm sorry. I just don't remember. It could be any of them. Or none of them. Except the two guys with the receding hairlines. It wasn't them."

"All right. I had the same problem—I couldn't identify any of them as the guy who shot me. We've got some more digging to do."

HIS LEG WAS hurting again, a continuing ache that occasionally flared into a streak of pain that shot down his leg to his foot. He sat at his computer, ignoring it, working the list of Lorens through the DMV, looking for pickup trucks. There were four—four out of eighteen—about average for Minnesota men, he suspected. Cut the list anyway, although he cut it to three, rather than four: one of the four just didn't look right.

The leg would no longer be ignored, and he finally got the cane and told Carol that he was going home, and limped down to the car.

He was, he thought, caught in a loop.

Frances's disappearance led to Dick Ford's murder. Dick Ford's murder led to the fairy. He investigated the fairy girl and got shot at by a dark-haired stranger. And the stranger—Loren X?—goes back to Frances. Maybe?

THE HOUSE WAS empty when he got home, the housekeeper off somewhere with Sam, Weather still at work, Letty at school. With no need to use the car for a while, he took a full pain pill and went back to a computer, and called up Sandy's e-mail on the NCIC files.

One of the Lorens who owned a pickup had had a minor drug bust—personal use marijuana—in Minneapolis. Another had been arrested and convicted of theft from a Wal-Mart warehouse and had made restitution. The Wal-Mart guy didn't sound like he'd be the type to hang around with Frances. The third guy lived in Fertile, and that was too far away.

The doper was a possibility. 2002 Toyota pickup. Huh. He called Del.

"You got a little time?"

"What's up?" Del asked.

"I want to talk to a guy on the Austin case, but I've taken a couple of pain pills."

"You need a designated driver."

"Yeah."

"I've never been one," Del said. "I'll be there in a couple of minutes."

★

LOREN WHITESIDE O'KEEFE lived in a nice-enough, but not too nice, apartment complex in Woodbury, east of downtown St. Paul. They pressured an assistant manager into letting them through the locked outer doors, and took the elevator up to three. Identical blond-wood doors were spaced evenly down long blank corridors, the medium-blue carpet the indoor-outdoor stuff that looked good for a year.

"Place will be a slum in ten years," Del said. "Walls look like they're made out of cardboard."

"Owners'll pay it off in ten, though," Lucas said. "Then it's all gravy."

"If you don't mind being a slumlord," Del said.

Lucas was limping, and Del asked, "You all right?"

"Yeah, I'm terrific." The pain had definitely backed off, but every once in a while, a muscle spasm took him by surprise.

O'Keefe was in 355. They heard music, knocked, and a pudgy, big-headed, rosy-cheeked man opened the door. "Eh?"

"Loren O'Keefe?"

"Ya. Who're you?"

He had dark hair, a big head, and sloping shoulders. The man who'd shot at Lucas had square shoulders and a small head. Couldn't see that in the driver's-license photograph. The photo also didn't mention that O'Keefe had a slight but distinct Irish accent. Austin had said specifically that her Loren sounded local.

"Minnesota Bureau of Criminal Apprehension." They showed O'Keefe their IDs.

"So what's up?" he asked. The TV behind him was tuned to an Oprah rerun.

With the sure sense that he was wasting everybody's time, Lucas said, "We're looking for a Loren who dated a girl named Frances Austin."

O'Keefe looked at them blankly. "I'm sorry. That's not me."

"Ever hang out with any Goths?" Del asked.

"I've had a couple in my classes."

"You're a teacher?" Lucas asked.

"At Augsburg," he said. "I teach drama."

"Huh. You had a bust for marijuana."

"Yup. Two fat boys," he said cheerfully. "Jaesus, I bought three, only had time for one. Why couldn't I be one of the guys who's arrested for three seeds? No, they gotta get me with two-thirds of the weekly allotment."

Lucas looked at Del, and tipped his head toward the corridor. "Okay. Well, I think you're not the guy we're looking for."

"What? Already? You can't leave me hanging," O'Keefe said. "C'mon and have a cuppa tea and tell me about it."

If his leg hadn't hurt, Lucas wouldn't have done it. He said, half to O'Keefe, and half to Del, "I've dinged up my leg. I wouldn't mind sitting down for a minute."

"Oho! Are you that copper that got shot?" O'Keefe was delighted. "Your name rings a bell."

Lucas nodded: "That's me."

"You're chasing a ripper, like good old Jack. Damnit, what good luck. Come in, come in."

He'd had a pot of tea going, and had it ready in two minutes, fussing around like an old lady, with a tray and cup, and offered them milk to put in it. They both declined, while he took some; he had them sitting in a conversation group, two easy chairs and a love seat.

"So it's this bartender and this liquor store clerk you're investigating, then," O'Keefe said. "How did my name come up?"

Lucas gave him a short version of the investigation, O'Keefe manically stirring his tea as he listened, his bright blue eyes like cornflowers in his pink face. He asked questions, and winkled more out of Lucas than Lucas had intended to give.

When Lucas finished, O'Keefe took a sip and said, "You shouldn't be chasing Lorens, then. You should be putting pressure on the Austin woman. You should be . . . reenacting the crime. Right at the scene of the murder."

"There's a surprise," Del said. "A drama teacher who wants to reenact."

"Ah, but I have a reason," O'Keefe said. He shook a finger at them, like a professor might. "You have only two things. You have a motive: money. And you have a scene of a crime and it's the first crime. Would I be wrong in assuming that the first crime of a series is probably the key crime?"

"Sometimes it is," Lucas said, mildly amused. "There have been cases where a first murder was done to set up a second one, so that it would look like a series killing."

"About as often as you've seen a leprechaun, I would expect," O'Keefe said. He went on without waiting for an answer. "You have a motive and a crime scene. If you go back and reenact the crime as you believe it happened, you will see much more deeply into it, I guarantee it. I'm a playwright, as well as a teacher, and when you're writing a play, you always go and look at the scene of the crime. Or whatever scene. You go to the actual place. When you're in the actual place, you can work out possibilities and discard impossibilities. You can see the idio-syncrasies that make a scene come alive. I would urge you to reenact."

"Maybe I will," Lucas said. "Maybe—"

"And then, of course, there's the obvious question. Often comes up in drama . . . in fact, it'd be a cliché, I'm sure you've already checked it out thoroughly."

Lucas spread his hands. "What's the obvious question?"

O'Keefe leaned forward, his trigger finger still crooked through the cup handle: "Mistaken identity." He wiggled his eyebrows. "The daughter comes home, it's dark, she turns off the security system, and the killer strikes! But, ho! To his or her horror, he finds that he has struck at the wrong person. Hoping to recover, some-how, he bundles up the body and cleans up the crime scene. Since the daughter doesn't live there, perhaps nobody will tumble to her disappearance for a day or two. Or three or four. Give him a chance to cover his tracks—or to strike again at his real target! The Austin woman!"

At some point during the recitation, O'Keefe had gone on

stage, and Lucas and Del both bought it. When he snapped, "The Austin woman!" they both jerked away.

O'Keefe smiled: "But you've thought of that."

They argued about it for a bit, as they finished their tea, and Del told O'Keefe about working undercover, which was something of an acting job.

"Fascinating! Fascinating!" O'Keefe said. "Have you ever thought about collaborating on a play? I think there could be great potential in a play about an undercover man: it's so *right* for the stage; it combines friendship and treachery and a modern existential angst. Should you destroy your friend for the sake of The Man? There are so many ways we could take it. It's just fantastic material!"

AS THEY TOOK the elevator down, Del asked, "You gonna reenact?"

"No," Lucas said, with a Valley-girl inflection. "Jesus Christ, Del."

"The guy might be on to something," Del said.

"You gonna collaborate on a fuckin' play?"

Del didn't say anything for a moment, then shrugged. "Maybe."

Limping across the parking lot, Lucas asked, "Mistaken identity?"

"Never occurred to me," Del said. "It's got a funky logic to it."

"Funky being the key word." Lucas nibbled on the corner of his lower lip, then laughed and said, "Reenact. Reenact, my big white ass."

"Like we were talking about what-if the other night, at the diner," Del said. "What if Alyssa Austin was screwing somebody, like her husband was. What if this guy knocks off her husband to get at her? He thinks he might marry somebody with a billion bucks, or whatever she's got. What if she begins to suspect? What if he decided he had to get rid of her and her suspicions, and he goes after her. But instead of getting Alyssa Austin, he gets the daughter. Female, looks about the same, she shows up in the dark and knows the security system . . ."

"I'll think about it, but it sounds overcooked," Lucas said.

"A little overcooked," Del agreed.

BACK AT HOME, Lucas walked around the house for a bit, working the leg, kneading it, took another pain pill, found his thinking was a little fuzzy, and went to take a nap.

Weather woke him at dinnertime: "Leg hurts?"

"It has been." He rolled a bit, flexed it, tried it out: better. "Not so bad, now."

Weather knelt next to the bed, pulled the bedside lamp over. "Let me see it." She pulled the tape and the dressing, her fingers stroking the bruises. "No new bleeding—but you're pushing too hard. I want you immobile for the rest of the evening. And tomorrow, take it easy."

"All right."

She sat back on her heels. "You agreed too fast. It must hurt more than you're telling me."

Lucas said, "It's not that—it's fucked me up this time. Getting shot at. I've been thinking about it, all those shots. Could have hit me in the heart as well as the leg—and no more you, no more Sam, no more Letty."

She'd gotten the gauze and tape and a tube of disinfectant ointment out of the bedstand, and folded the gauze and laid it over the wound, and said, "Last time you got shot at, you were on your own. No responsibilities."

"It's not responsibilities," he said. "You guys would get along without me. It's *me*. I wouldn't get to see the kids grow up, I wouldn't get to jump your bones . . . I'd miss too much."

"Talk to the governor," she said. "Get an office job."

"Be nice if it were that easy," he said. "Just make one change, and life becomes simple."

She finished taping him up, put the medical kit back in the bedstand drawer, touched his cheek. "I've got no advice. Except, c'mon and eat."

He sighed and sat up. "Gotta call Alyssa."

"You're not quitting?"

"No. I need to go back over to her house," he said. "Get in there alone."

"You're gonna sneak something?"

"No. I'm gonna reenact the crime," Lucas said.

"Attaboy," she said.

11

AUSTIN MET HIM at the door, the bright sunlight breaking around her, barefoot, in a woolen top and straight long skirt. She smiled and at the same time looked sad, too sad. "You're going to reenact?"

"Yeah. I got some advice that I might as well take," Lucas said. "Also: when I was reading the case file, there was an inventory of Frances's apartment, and a note that you were going to move her things and close the apartment. Did you do that?"

"Yes. Everything was brought back here. It's all up in her room," she said.

"I would like to take a look," Lucas said. "When you're gone."

"Absolutely. C'mon, I'll show you where." He followed her up a curving stairs, all polished maple, down a long hall that, at the very end, appeared, through a half-closed door, to open into a bedroom the size of a basketball court. She stopped short of that room, opened a different door, flipped a light.

Frances's room was full of cardboard boxes. "I never unpacked. I haven't been able to look at her stuff, yet," she said. She touched one of the boxes. "The big ones are clothes. The small ones are personal effects. Books and jewelry and letters and notes and all that."

"I'll start with the acting," he said. "It'd be better if I were alone."

"And I've got work to do," she said. "I've got so many meetings I might as well be a politician."

"Before you go," he said as they went down the stairs, "I was kicking this whole thing around with another guy. This idea came up—what if there was somebody here, waiting for you? And they attacked Frances by mistake. As I understand it, neither you nor anybody else expected Frances to come home. You told the crime-scene people that there hadn't been a burglary, you weren't missing anything, so it probably wasn't a burglar. Is there anyone who would be interested in hurting you? Is there anything going on in your life? An angry boyfriend, a relative who'd benefit from *your* death, a business competitor . . . though that's a bit far-fetched."

"A mistake?" She was shocked, an open hand going to her breastbone. "Somebody coming for me?"

"It's thin . . . but is there anybody?"

"Well, I have relatives. My parents. Hunter's mother died years ago, but his father's still alive, out in LA. He'd get some money, but he doesn't really need it. There are some specific bequests in our wills. You think . . . the Bach and Beethoven Society would put out a contract on me?"

That made him laugh; but he said, "I'm a little serious. Is there a boyfriend?"

"No, not yet," she said.

"Was there a boyfriend? When Hunter was alive?"

"No. There was not." Some frost, now. "No girlfriends, either."

"Hey—I'm not trying to insult you, I'm trying to figure this out," Lucas said. "Any businesspeople who were pissed at you? Did you or Hunter screw somebody to the point where they might come looking for revenge? Or maybe a stalker—some deluded guy who thought he'd been screwed . . ."

She'd softened up after he snapped back at her: "Lucas, we've got money, but we're really pretty ordinary people. Nobody stalks us, nobody cares. Hunter had a nice company, but it wasn't General Motors. We had disgruntled employees, but nobody dangerous, as far as I know. They didn't know me, anyway. And Hunter was dead. Why would they come after me?"

"Think about it," Lucas said. "If you think of *anything*, let me know."

She left him standing in the kitchen. He heard the Mercedes come to life, and then the garage door rolling up and down. They'd pushed the housekeeper out of the main wing, and he could hear the faint sound of vacuuming somewhere down the endless hallways. Other than that, he was alone.

Okay. According to the crime-scene analysts, the murder—or whatever it had been—occurred where a hallway exited the kitchen, leading down to the living room on the right, with the dining room right around the corner to the left

But wait.

He wasn't reenacting, he was just thinking about it, simply buying the crime-scene report. Start over. He walked back to the garage, out into it, then turned and came back.

It was dark. Huh. Austin had come in from the garage, but would Frances? Why would she? Two spaces were taken up by Austin's cars, a third space by the housekeeper's, although the housekeeper's space would have been empty. Still, Frances would probably park in front and enter through the front door. Wouldn't she?

He had Austin on speed dial, caught her a mile or two out, still in her car. "When your daughter came over, did she park in the garage, or out front?"

"Out front."

"Thanks." Click. Outside, to the front door. Okay, the kid comes in through the front door. She can go straight ahead to the kitchen, left, to the family room / entertainment wing, or right into a public space, a greeting room. No reason to do that.

So she disarms the alarm system, walks straight ahead, into the kitchen. Now what? He stood there, at the corner of the kitchen. The reenactment was already breaking down, because there were too many possible branches. Two possibilities right here, or maybe three.

—She argues with somebody who came with her.

—She argues with somebody already in the house.

—She encounters somebody in the dark—all right, give the credit to O'Keefe—who was waiting for Alyssa Austin, but who attacks Frances by mistake.

But did it happen right after she came in? Might not be able to tell without her coat—if the coat was cut through, then she'd still have had it on.

He struggled with it for a bit, then thought, *Let it go.*

Anyway, Frances is attacked. Does the killer already have the weapon, or does he get it from the drawer? If the killing was carefully planned, why would he do it with a paring knife?

Lucas looked back down the kitchen counter from the death scene. If he wanted to use a bigger blade, there were plenty of them fifteen feet away, sticking out of a knife block. Heavy knives, easier to handle, deadlier.

And if he came to the house intending to kill, why hadn't he brought a weapon of his own? A club, maybe. Quiet, effective, less likely to leave blood all around.

Lucas formed a little tent with his hands, folded them over his nose, working through it. The guy *would* have brought a weapon. If given a chance, once determined to kill, he *would* have used a bigger knife.

Therefore: the killing was spontaneous.

If he took the knife from a drawer, had he known it was there? Was he intimately familiar with the kitchen? Or had the knife been left on the counter? Maybe somebody was cutting up an apple, or a chunk of cheese. Have to look at the crime-scene photos.

He considered the possibility of a burglar. But why would a burglar take the body, and clean up? Burglars got in and out, fast. Most of them got nervous if they spent more than two or three minutes inside a house. He might have taken the body to obscure some crime, though Lucas couldn't think what the crime might have been, to have gone undetected this long.

Maybe he'd come in to steal, knew that he'd left behind some fingerprints . . .

No, no, no. Wrong direction.

THE KILLING, done for whatever reason—maybe the fifty thousand, but maybe not—was spontaneous, but then, after it was done, the killer had thought about it, at least for a couple of minutes. Had to have thought about it—and then, he'd moved the body. Why? To obscure the time of the murder, or the place?

If there hadn't been a small spatter of blood, that Austin had spotted among the tangled flowers of the wallpaper, if they'd cleaned that up . . . nobody might ever have discovered that the murder had taken place at the Austin house.

Given the tendency of erratic young Minnesota girls to run off to more romantic places, far away from January in Minnesota . . . the cops might not be looking for her, even now. Not too hard, anyway. Not yet. And the date of her disappearance might be stated as several days too late.

So the killer had thought about it. He'd taken the body out to his car, had cleaned up—had missed a couple of small spatters, but had gotten the rest of it, enough so that only a clued-in crime-scene team could find the signs.

Once the body was in the car, he'd wanted to get rid of it. Cold, snowy January. Impossible to dig a grave, without heavy equipment. So much snow that he wouldn't be able to get back into the woods, on a trail.

Lucas went to the phone, called the office: "Carol. Something to do right now. I want all the local sheriff's deputies and highway patrolmen alerted to the possibility that there's a body out there in the ditches, where the snow's melting. Also, in parks that were open at night, or anyplace that was cleared by snowplows. I want them to check any bags that might be large enough, anything that looks anomalous."

"Frances Austin?"

"Yeah. She's out there," Lucas said. "And not too far from Sunfish Lake."

A chance they'd find it, he thought, when he'd hung up. On the other hand, if the killer had hauled the body down into an overgrown gully somewhere, or into a still-standing cornfield, it might not be found for months.

He was standing there, working it out, when the housekeeper came down the hall, pulling on an ankle-length loden-green coat that made her look like an East German cop. Or what Lucas imagined an East German cop had once looked like. "I have to go to the supermarket with Mrs. Austin's list," she said. "I'll be gone an hour; will you still be here?"

"Probably."

"If you have to go, could you set the security system? Mrs. Austin is very particular about that." She showed him how to do it: a one-button press-and-hold. "Then you have thirty seconds to get out."

When she was gone, he thought about the thirty seconds. Why had the alarm system been off when Austin came home? Because the bad guy didn't know how to reset it? Or because it would take more than thirty seconds to get the body out the door? But he could have come back.

Hmm. Either the killer didn't know how to reset it, or Lucas was making too much of the alarm. The stress of the murder, he might simply have forgotten.

Of course it had been turned off—so had the killer arrived with Frances? It seemed so. Or perhaps shortly after her.

But if he'd arrived separately, there would have been two cars, and Frances's had been found back by her apartment, had been examined minutely, and there was no blood in the interior.

Had two people come together, and then left separately, one driving Frances's car, one driving the car with the body? Two killers? He worked on it for a minute, and found only one handy solution: either the killer had arrived with Frances, or there were two killers.

He gave the housekeeper five minutes to drive toward the supermarket, went out by the front door, and watched the driveway for another two or three.

If she hadn't come back by then, he thought, having forgotten something, she probably wouldn't. After a last long look out at the driveway, he hurried up the stairs, down the hall to the big bedroom he'd seen earlier. The door was open three inches. He pressed it open with a knuckle—no prints—and stepped inside.

Checked a closet: women's clothes. Alyssa Austin's bedroom.

She was tidy, which wasn't good. He'd have to be careful. He checked a dressing room, lined with closets and drawers, found what must have been two hundred pairs of shoes and at least a dozen suits and a hundred other outfits, all neatly arrayed on wooden clothes hangers, by type: blouses, skirts, business dresses, gowns. Most of the clothing was sealed in plastic dry-cleaner's bags. No wigs. Opened drawers and cabinet doors, one after the other. Obvious spots to store a wig, if she had one, but nothing there. No fairy clothes, either.

Back in the bedroom, he checked the bedside end tables, found nothing of note.

Looked at photos on the wall: people he didn't recognize, for the most part, and shots of Alyssa Austin with Frances and Hunter Austin.

Two large chests of drawers. He ran through them quickly, found fifty pounds of lingerie and underwear, and a battery-operated vibrator.

Of course it's battery operated; what else would it be operated by, a fuckin' windmill?

That was it. But the vibrator made him curious. The bedroom was distinctly feminine, with a careful, cheerful paint job, and light, graceful furnishings. He walked down the hall, opening doors, and found another bedroom, smaller than Austin's, but still large, that was distinctly masculine, right down to the antique airplane prop over the bed, the solid dark-mahogany bureaus, the ranks of beaten-up books in built-in bookcases. He picked one at random: *Scaramouche, A Romance of the French Revolution,* by Rafael Sabatini.

Had to be Hunter's bedroom. Austin had said that she and Hunter had marital problems, but implied that they might have worked through them, had he lived. But if they slept in different bedrooms, each decorated with some thought and expense, then their arrangement must have been long-standing. The troubles were more serious than she'd led him to believe.

Huh.

He went back to Austin's room, closed the door to the exact degree that it had been closed when he came upstairs, and walked down to Frances's room.

Twenty-two cardboard moving boxes, all open at the top. He went through them quickly, found clothes and bedding and shoes and books and jewelry and a dozen bottles of flavored water and, in one of them, envelopes full of photographs.

He set them aside as he went through the other paper he'd found, but he found no scribbled notes about fifty thousand dollars, no love letters, nothing but the typical detritus of a young life.

He went through the photographs, which apparently went back to her high-school days. The envelopes had dates, and being a fussy kid, she always ordered duplicates, and there were a lot of reprints, people doing high-school stuff like plays and dances and proms with guys in tin man, lion, and scarecrow costumes from a production of *The Wizard of Oz,* in which Frances apparently played one of the witches.

He was going through them at a hundred miles an hour, like a guy playing cards, Frances's life flashing before his eyes, high school and college and after-college and on-the-job and then some Goths, and he slowed down, and then in the very last pack of photos, a shot showing a bunch of Goths at a Halloween party at November, and there in a photo with Frances was Roy Carter, and looking over his shoulder, Dick Ford, and a half dozen other Goths, three men and three women . . .

Doing the chicken dance. He took the photo to a window, looked closer. Two of the women were none other than Leigh Price, the fairy girl who'd twanged Lucas's magic twanger, and her roommate, Patricia Shockley.

He looked at the rest of the photos, found two more of the November party, but couldn't pick Frances out of them—it must have been her camera. She took the shots, except in the single photo. He put it in his pocket, whistling, headed down the stairs to the kitchen, got out his book, found Shockley's cell number—he hadn't taken Price's, but remembered that she worked at 3M, and 3M wasn't too far away.

Shockley answered on the second ring, and he identified himself and said, "I need your roommate's number."

"Uh-huh," she said. A taste of cynicism: "Some marital problems cropping up?"

He had to think about it for a second, then said, "No, no. I've found a photograph. You and she are both in it, along with Frances Austin and the two men who were killed, Ford and Carter. All three murdered people in one shot. She's close, you're not. I want to identify all the people in the photo."

"Are you serious?" Fascinated, not frightened.

"Absolutely. Do you have her number?"

"I've got two. Her cell number . . ."

Lucas jotted them in his book, a cell number and an office phone. "Now listen," he said. "Do not talk to any fairy women. Do not do that, not when you're alone. If a fairy tries to get you alone, get into a crowd and call me. Okay?"

"Oh, God. You think . . . ?" Worried now.

"I don't know. But do not get alone with a fairy."

"I won't. Oh . . . Jesus."

Lucas tried Price's cell first, got her on the third ring.

"Leigh Price." She sounded busy. Un-Goth-like.

Lucas said, "This is Davenport, the state cop who talked to you a couple nights ago. I've got a photograph that I need you to look at right away. Like now."

"At the lab, at 3M. My office."

"Tell me where."

SHE WAS AT the main 3M campus, straight up a limited-access highway from Sunfish Lake. There was really no hurry getting there, but it was spring, the roads were dry, he had the Porsche. He clipped a great new red-LED flasher on the roof, a six-hundred-dollar light cheerfully paid for by Minnesota taxpayers, and made his way out to the highway.

He was careful on the gravel roads—a Porsche paint job was not something you fucked with lightly—but once on Highway 52, he let it about three-quarters of the way out, and blew the shorts off a top-down, cherry-red '65 Corvette Roadster. In the rearview mirror, it dwindled like a poppy seed that you drop off a bagel.

When he cut into the 3M parking lot, he thought, he unquestionably held the Sunfish-to—3M land-speed record, and it would probably last forever.

Price's office looked like the office of a university professor—bookcases stuffed with publications and stacks of paper held together with clamps or rubber bands, a fake-wood-grained desk, an impressive-looking computer workstation, a half-dozen plants that all seemed to be dying, but not quite dead, lots of xeroxed *Far Side* cartoons, a rubber chicken hanging by its neck, a steel sheet with dozens of magnetized words, one of those poetry boards; a few of the words had been arranged to say, "The ugly gristle of morning smears a dry bone landscape down the flawless tapestry of night."

Price was sitting in an Aeron chair, her feet up on her desk, peering at a scholarly publication through oversized black-rimmed glasses. When Lucas stuck his head in the door, she said, "There you are." She patted the seat of a visitor's chair that sat beside her desk.

Price gave off a certain wavelength of fuck-me vibrations. Many women did that, Lucas believed, but they were only received by men who were tuned to the right wavelength, which was determined by birth or accident, perhaps, but not by choice.

Weather was one of them, and she broadcast on Lucas's frequency, and he'd begun picking them up before he could even see her face -(she'd been wrapped in a parka when they met). Price broadcast on the same frequency; and she knew that Lucas was a receiver.

She smiled and said, "So what's the big deal?"

He took the picture out of his pocket and passed it to her. "This was taken at a Halloween party at November. I need to know the names of the people in it."

She took the photo—looked at his face, as though she hadn't really believed that there'd be one—and said, "Oh, God. This is the Roy guy, isn't it"—she touched Roy's face—"and this guy is named Richard Trane . . . Richard, not Dick or Rich. And this guy . . ." She closed one eye, thinking, then said, "Brad. Brad something, I don't know his last name, but Judy would, they went out." She touched the unknown woman. "This is Judy McBride."

She knew Frances, but not Roy Carter or Dick Ford. "I do remember that Karen Slade took the photograph, she was having like a brain-fart or something, she couldn't push the right button, she tried like ten times." She had Slade's phone number, but no numbers or addresses for anybody else.

She told him all this in a blast of words, wide eyes behind the glasses, her body small and close and soft and round, and when she was done, Lucas had decided that, circumstances being different, he would happily have locked the door, pushed the magazines and all the other crap off her desk, and banged her brains loose right there—the other circumstances being that he was happily married and pathetically loyal.

Instead, he stood up and said, "You've got to be careful. Do *not* go off to dark corners with women you don't know—or men, for that matter."

She stepped close and put a hand on his jacket sleeve. "You really think . . . there could be a problem?"

136

Yeah. There could be a problem. You could find your shorts down around your ankles about five seconds from now. "Yes. Obviously." He stepped away. "You really have to be careful. And while you're being careful, you've got to watch people around you. This fairy woman *lures* people to places where she can kill them. If you get that vibration from anyone, anyone at all, that they're trying to pull you off somewhere . . . call me."

He took her cell phone and programmed his cell phone number into it, and she walked him out to the door and he rambled through all the warnings again, and she waved goodbye and watched him cross the parking lot to the car, and when he got inside, he twiddled his fingers at her, and realized that for the first time in several days, his leg didn't hurt.

LUCAS HAD LEARNED to recognize when criminal cases come to tipping points, when the clues and the facts begin to coalesce, and that was happening. He was getting the breaks, he'd picked up momentum, the case was turning his way.

He was wrong about that.

For the next three days, nothing at all happened, except that his leg started hurting again. He tracked down each of the people in the photograph, asked about approaches, quizzed them about their relationship with Frances, or about men named Loren. He got nothing about Loren, but was given more names, more possibilities, and spent his days driving around the metro area, finding people, looking in their eyes, running their names and DOBs through the NCIC.

One of the men, Brad Francetta, knew Roy Carter and said, "Roy knew who the Austin chick was, he'd talked to her, but he didn't know her that well. I mean, I knew Roy pretty well, and he'd get excited about . . . possibilities with women, and if he'd done anything with Austin, he would have told me. Are you sure you've got this right? With the photo? Maybe they were just in it by accident."

"I don't know," Lucas said. "But two people in the photo are dead for sure, and another almost for sure. I'm telling you to be careful. Don't get in a dark corner with some new fairy chick that you haven't seen before. Especially if she's coming on to you hard, wants to take you for a ride."

"I can handle myself," Francetta said.

Lucas nodded: "I don't doubt it. But the rule with cops is, if a guy with a knife gets within ten feet of you, you're gonna get stuck. Doesn't make any difference if you have a gun, or even if you shoot him—you're gonna get stuck. So you think you can handle yourself, what're you gonna do, beat her up first and then check her for a knife? Or are you gonna let her get inside ten feet? Don't mess around, man: the dead people'd tell you it's not a joke."

"But it can't be just the photo," Francetta said, looking at it. "It's just a bunch of people doing the chicken dance. Did something else happen that night? Maybe somebody shouldn't have been there? Or is that too TV?"

Lucas frowned. "I don't know. That's part of what I'm trying to find out."

HE DIDN'T FIND it out.

"Not a thing," he told Del. They were listening to Bob Seger's "Night Moves" on the boom box, watching Heather Toms across the street as Heather watched television. She'd gotten a new wide-screen LCD job, and Lucas suspected she'd gotten an envelope from her old man. "I been running my ass off. I've been asking the right questions—Albert Einstein would be proud of me. I got nothing."

Del said, "In a harsh sidelight, do you think the lines in my face would make me look old?"

Lucas thought about the question for a second, parsing out the reasons Del might have asked something that stupid, and then said, "Oh my God. You're hanging out with O'Keefe."

Del curled his hand in front of his face, his voice trembled, and he said, slowly, with a sandy grind in his voice, "Out, out, brief candle. Life's but a walking shadow, a poor player that struts and frets his hour upon the stage, and then is heard no more; it is a tale told by an idiot, full of sound and fury, signifying nothing."

"Ah, fuck me," Lucas said.

"The other woman," Del said, back in his own rat-fucker persona. "Go for the other woman."

Lucas went for the other woman.

AUS/TECH, Hunter Austin's company, was located in a tech zone northwest of Minneapolis. Lucas got an appointment with a woman named Ann Coates, head of the Human Resources Department, though he was told on the phone that Martina Trenoff, the other woman, no longer worked for the company.

The AUS/Tech building was a block square, with a narrow strip of grass along the sides, and a Wal-Mart-sized parking lot in the back; and was built of concrete panels, without a single window, except in the front, where a cluster of small fixed glass panels hung like afterthoughts around the steel-and-glass shed of the main entrance, and on the west side, where an identical steel shed marked the employee entrance off the parking lot. Rust-colored steel emergency exit doors were spotted at twenty-yard intervals along the sides, with no sign they'd ever been used.

There were no visitors' slots near the building, and Lucas had to park at the back of the lot: two hundred yards, and he was limping again by the time he got there, thought about the cane, which he'd left at the office. Goddamn leg.

The AUS/Tech entrance area was as spare as the exterior: hard blue carpet, pale walls hung with poster-sized black-and-white photos of unsmiling men standing next to unidentifiable machines, and a steel-and-composite counter. The two older women behind the counter watched him through the door, gave him a name tag, and turned him over to Coates, who walked him back to a conference room.

Coates was a tall woman with dark hair, closely cut; steel-rimmed eyeglasses; high cheekbones and thin lips; and her navy blue suit appeared to have been chosen for its social invisibility. "One of our vice presidents would like to sit in with us," Coates said.

"Just a couple of questions," Lucas said. "I was hoping to talk to somebody who was friendly with Ms. Trenoff."

"Tara and I knew her about as well as anyone," Coates said. "Tara Laughlin, she's our vice president for legal affairs."

"Ah. A lawyer."

THE LAWYER KEPT them waiting for about four seconds, and Coates seemed surprised by the delay. When Laughlin arrived, she nodded at Lucas, took a seat at the head of the conference room table, and leaned back in her chair. Like Coates, she was a tall woman with dark hair and glasses, but her suit cost a couple hundred dollars more, and was a slightly more fashionable black-and-white check.

She put a file folder on the table in front of her and asked, "What exactly is the nature of this inquiry?"

"I'm investigating the murder of Frances Austin."

"I didn't know that she'd been definitively identified as a murder victim," Laughlin said.

"I have done that," Lucas said. "And I am authorized to do that. So. As part of the investigation, we are looking at people who may have had antagonistic relationships with the Austins, including Ms. Trenoff."

"You're not going to record this?" Laughlin asked.

"No." Lucas raised his hands above the table. "Nothing up my sleeves, no secret microphones. I was hoping to have a completely informal, off-the-record conversation about Ms. Trenoff's relationship with Mr. Austin, before I approach Ms. Trenoff herself."

"We are concerned about possible lawsuits involving slander and possible damage to reputation."

The bullshit dance continued for a couple minutes, Lucas assuring them that there'd be no record of the conversation, and that if no legal charges came from it, there'd never be an official reference to it. "I'm looking for background. If we need a formal record, I'll bring a subpoena."

Once the walls were broken down, the two women relaxed and brought out the knives. "Hunter gave her a lot of jewelry. I saw some of it—she was quite open about their relationship—and I'd have to say that this was not mistress jewelry. This was serious stuff," Coates said. She had a habit of pushing her glasses up her nose with her middle finger; Lucas suppressed a smile.

"How serious?" he asked. "Five thousand, ten thousand . . . ?"

"More than that," Coates said. She was talking to Laughlin now: "I saw one of those singleton diamonds, you know, like the Forever diamonds, that must have been six or seven carats." Back to Lucas: "It looked like an acorn. And she had quite a bit of it. She would go on business trips with him, but Hunter always got a suite and she always got the cheapest room available, and she wasn't the kind to stay in a cheap room."

"So they were staying together," Lucas said.

"Of course," Coates said.

"And it was a sexual relationship."

Laughlin nodded. "It was more or less explicit. We had a deal in San Francisco, a contract meeting, and we got together in Austin's suite the morning of the meeting. I happened to glance in the back bathroom and the Viagra was right there—like the quart-jar size."

"Do you think any promises had been made?" Lucas asked. "About a permanent relationship? Marriage?"

"I think she expected it," Laughlin said. She pulled her lips back and showed a well-developed set of eyeteeth. "She behaved that way, as though she were the spouse, an owner. She became quite preemptory."

"Did you see any signs of conflict between Mrs. Trenoff and Mrs. Austin?"

"You wouldn't see them together very often, and when I did, they didn't talk—they didn't really acknowledge each other," Laughlin said.

Coates added, "Mrs. Austin didn't come around much in the last few years. She had her own business interests. We'd see her on business-social occasions, and then Marty would stay in the background."

Laughlin leaned forward, one elbow on the table, and dropped her voice: "I saw her watching Alyssa once. It was like a fox watching a chicken. Alyssa seemed unaware of her, though I'm sure she wasn't."

"Of course she wasn't," Coates agreed.

"Sounds like it'd be a good mud-wrestling match," Lucas volunteered.

The two women looked at each other, and then at Lucas. Neither smiled.

He said, "So. When did you get rid of her?"

"It wasn't quite like that," Coates said. "When Hunter died, well, she was his private assistant. The job no longer existed. She finished up her work here, transferring files over to the new leadership, and then she . . . moved on."

"To General Mills?"

Coates nodded. "Yes."

"With a good recommendation?"

"The best," Coates said.

"A good severance?"

"Very good," Coates said. Now *she* showed some teeth in a tight smile. They were the wolves, and they'd run the other woman down like a sheep. "We were very generous. Considering."

"Considering what?"

"Considering what a mammoth pain in the ass she'd been," Laughlin said.

"When are you going to interview her?" Coates asked.

"Probably Monday," Lucas said. "I haven't called her yet—I wanted to talk to you guys first."

"Off the record," Laughlin said.

"Yeah, except for the microphone down my pant leg," Lucas said.

"You had me fooled," Laughlin said. Her lips may have twitched, a smile? "I thought it was a Chapstick."

"Hey . . ."

Coates said, "When you see her, say 'Hi,' for us."

THEN ON SUNDAY, as Lucas and Weather and the kids were about to sit down to dinner with his old friend Elle, he took a call from the Dakota County sheriff's office.

"We got your bulletin about Frances Austin. We've got a dead female, appears to have been stabbed, though we haven't moved her yet," the deputy said. He was standing in a ditch, talking on his cell phone. "Body's in a ditch, about ten miles south of Sunfish Lake. She's got a charm bracelet on her wrist and one charm says, 'Frances.'"

"Don't move," Lucas said. "I'll be there in fifteen minutes."

Weather looked at him in dismay, the roast and the potatoes and the fresh hot bread right there, steaming, and she said, "Oh, Lucas," but he shook his head and said, "Your fault—you got me into it."

"What?"

"It's Frances."

12

AT THIS POINT in his life, Lucas had no idea how many times he'd done it: stood by the side of a road, cops parked at weird angles and tilts, white faces in passing cars, maybe a Coke or foam cup of convenience-store coffee in his hand, looking at a tarp-covered body in a ditch. He didn't know how many times, but it was a lot.

When he got to the scene, driving his truck, he introduced himself to the deputy in charge, who walked him over to the body.

Frances was faceup, her face old and wrinkled like a monkey's, her lips shriveled to show her teeth, but still mostly intact, protected by the frost in the earth, and the slow snowmelt. She wasn't actually in the bottom of the ditch, through which a trickle of water was now flowing, but partway up the far side.

The ditch had probably been mowed in August, and the grass had regrown to mid-calf length. The body was curled in a translucent plastic painter's drip sheet, which had been partly torn away at the hip and around the head. From the roadside, it looked like somebody's garbage, or flotsam from a passing truck.

Lucas knelt next to the face and took a photo out of his pocket. He knew already, but he showed it to the cop, and the cop nodded and said, "That's her."

Lucas could see paper towels wrapped inside the plastic, apparently soaked with blood—they must have been used in the cleanup. He pointed them out to the cop and said, "It might be possible that the lab could recover prints or hair or something there. We want to save everything—everything. This is gonna be a big deal, okay? We don't want to screw anything up."

"Should we go ahead and notify?"

"I'll do it," Lucas said. "My wife is a friend of her mother's—I'll get her to go along with me."

The cop nodded, said, "Good enough," and he seemed competent enough, so Lucas went on down the road and called Weather. "I don't know any other of Alyssa's friends, so it'd be good if you could come along with me," he said.

"Yes, sure," she said. "You want me to meet you there, or . . ."

They agreed to meet on the edge of Sunfish Lake: that'd save time.

When he got off the phone with Weather, he called the BCA agent originally assigned to the case, Jim Benson, got him on his cell phone as he was walking out of a WalMart. "Dakota County found Frances Austin."

Benson was a little miffed at not being called first, but Lucas was far enough up the hierarchy that he didn't whine too much;

and he was a new guy, so a certain amount of oppression was a way of life. He was happy enough that Lucas would do the notification. "I'll get down to the scene," Benson said. "Hope they're keeping everything together."

"Do keep a close eye on that," Lucas said, giving him something to do. "She's wrapped in plastic, and we might get something useful out of there."

LUCAS GOT TO the rendezvous first, went on into Sunfish, saw lights in the Austin house, turned back to the rendezvous, pulled off, wished he had something to drink or read, something to do other than stare into the dark, but he didn't, so he stared, and saw Frances's face, not as it had been, but in that gray feral snarl of death.

Weather arrived five minutes later and he rolled down the driver's-side window on the truck and said, "Follow me in."

She followed him down to the Austin driveway and he parked, with Weather behind him, and saw a shadow on a curtain on the second floor, and he got out and walked to the front door and rang the bell. Weather, before she'd moved down to the Cities to take a microsurgery residency, had been a general surgeon in a small hospital in northern Wisconsin, where she'd occasionally served as a coroner in noncontroversial deaths; she'd done notifications before.

She came up behind him and took his coat sleeve and said, "I can hear her feet."

Austin came to the door, turned on the porch light, peeked out through a glass pane in the wall to the right, opened the door, looked at them for a moment, and then began to back away and said "No no no no no . . ." but smiling as she said it, a kind of placating smile that asked for good news but Lucas stepped inside and he said, "We found her down south of here, the Dakota County deputies . . ."

Her face spasmed and she began to weep, and wrapped her arms around Lucas's waist, and Weather wrapped an arm around her shoulders and they stood like that for a moment, then Weather pried her free of Lucas and said, "C'mon, c'mon, let's go sit down."

AUSTIN'S PARENTS LIVED in Minnetonka, on the far side of the Cities. When she was able, she called them with the news. "They're coming," she said. She was drained, perched on the couch with her hands between her knees: demanded the details of the discovery. Lucas made it as simple as he could, obscuring details.

"There isn't any doubt, though."

"I saw her face . . . the snow . . . you know. She's still intact. She was wearing a charm bracelet."

"The charm said 'Frances.'" Lucas nodded and she said, "She got it from her father when she was twelve," and she started crying again.

Her parents showed up in an hour, gray-haired, shocked, late sixties or seventies in cloth coats, her father clicking his tongue as he tried to comfort his daughter, her mother weeping with her; and after a few minutes, when Austin said they'd be okay, Lucas and Weather left.

Weather said, on the way to her car, "I never, ever want to go through that. Never ever." And, "Catch the guys who did it."

"Doesn't really help much," Lucas said. "Won't help her."

"Maybe not, but it'll help the rest of us," she said. "Put those assholes in a cage."

ON THE WAY HOME, following Weather, Lucas called Ruffe Ignace, the crime reporter at the *Star Tribune*, at home. "Has the paper bought out your job, yet?"

"No. I asked them to, but they said they valued my talents," Ignace said.

"Miserable motherfuckers."

"No kidding," Ignace said. "They give me fifty grand, I'd be working in Manhattan tomorrow."

"Some kind of cabaret, waiting tables?"

"Fuck a bunch of cabarets. I'm talking the *New York Times*. I get up every morning and practice my liberal clichés in the mirror," Ignace said. "Wanna hear one?"

"Maybe one," Lucas said.

"Income disparity in this country hasn't been so high since before the Great Depression," he said.

"Not bad," Lucas said.

"I got a hundred more, and I can say them with a straight face," Ignace said. "So what's up?"

"I owe you one half of a favor, I think, from the other night," Lucas said. "So—Frances Austin's body was found a couple of hours ago in a ditch out in Dakota County."

Lucas gave him a few details, including the name of the deputy in charge. "You heard nothing from me."

"Of course not. Any chance of art?"

Art was what newspaper reporters called a photograph of a dead body; or anything else, for that matter. "I don't know, but they'll be on the scene for a while. If you could jack a guy up and get him out there."

"Talk to you later," Ignace said. "I'll go do some jacking."

The rest of the way home, Lucas thought about the sad scene at the Austins', the loss of a daughter and a granddaughter, and the effect it'd had on his wife, and the fact that he'd just peddled the information to a newspaper reporter, for some future consideration.

At a stoplight, he looked out the window and into the car to his right, where a young woman was laughing as she talked to the driver, whom Lucas couldn't see; and how happy she looked and how miserable Austin and her parents must be. And how he felt bad that he didn't feel worse about talking to Ignace.

That night, Weather looked at his leg, shook her head. "The persistence of the bruise bothers me," she said. "There might still be a little bleeding going on—not serious, but something."

"Ah, shit," he said. "You don't think they'll have to go back in?"

"No, you'd know that, if it happened. You'd have a lump like a golf ball, if there was a big problem. It's not hard to the touch . . . so . . . it'll just take a while. The sutures look okay, everything feels fine, smells fine."

"There's some science for you," he said. "Smells fine."

"Don't ever let anyone tell you that medicine is a science," she said. "It's always been an art, and it still is. Look at the training: we're artists, not scientists."

IN THE MORNING, he popped a couple of Aleve, and then, working without inspiration, he called Dakota County and talked to an investigator named Pratt, who'd already talked to Jim Benson. "Jim and I are sort of running in parallel," Lucas said.

"Okay—well, I can tell you she was stabbed eight times in the stomach and chest."

"Ripped open? Or stuck?"

"Stuck," Pratt said. "In and out. Short weapon, thin blade. A little tearing, but not like a positive effort to rip. More like the victim was twisting away from the knife. Benson told me that you guys were thinking about a paring knife. The wounds are consistent with that."

"But no knife."

"No. We walked the ditches with metal detectors, but everything seems to be contained within the plastic sheet. The killer drove along until there were no cars coming, threw her body in the ditch, and drove away. The plastic sheet is the stuff you can get at Lowe's or Home Depot or anyplace else. And, this could be important, there was some oil in there, that we think came with plastic. It's not regular oil, it's transmission fluid."

"You got that back from the lab?"

"No—one of our guys looked at it and sniffed it, but I believe him," Pratt said. "What I'm thinking is, maybe she was transported, wrapped in the plastic, in a work truck or a pickup, where you might have some tools or other gear. Engine parts. From talking to

Benson, I got the impression that the killers were in a hurry to get out of the house. And he checked with Mrs. Austin, and she said they hadn't had any painting done recently. So I'm thinking that the killers had the plastic with them. So maybe a painter's truck? Or somebody else who'd have a plastic sheet in their truck. Anyway, if we can find the truck, we might be able to match the transmission fluid. That stuff is sticky, and it's hard to clean up."

"That's something," Lucas said, and it was. "Any other debris with it? Leaves, or anything organic, or paint? Carpet fibers? Something we could put with the transmission fluid to triangulate on the truck, when we find it?"

"Don't know yet," Pratt said. "The lab stuff won't be back for a while—we're pushing it, but you know: it takes time. We're going over the plastic sheet with a microscope. I'll tell you, the transmission fluid was sticky as hell, so if anything else was floating around in the truck, it probably picked it up."

"That's good; that's good," Lucas said. "What else?"

"Well, she had a coat wrapped around her legs and there are no holes in the coat, so she wasn't wearing it when she got stabbed. I don't know if that means anything."

It did, Lucas thought, going back to his reenactment. It meant that she'd had time to take off her coat in the house, which probably meant that she wasn't ambushed in the dark. "They were trying to cover up the killing, probably just threw it in," Lucas said. "But get Mrs. Austin to ID it."

"Yup. And there was about a half-roll of paper towels soaked in blood, and you can see where somebody held them, squinched them, and one of our guys thinks we might be able to get something out of there. Prints. I have my doubts."

"Sounds unlikely."

"You gotta know the guy," Pratt says. "He watches all the science shows."

"Anything else?"

"If you mean, did she scratch 'John did it' on her palm—she didn't."

"Okay. Get me all the paper on it, will you? I'm trying to pile up as much stuff as I can . . . copy everything that you send to Jim."

"I'll do that," Pratt said. "One more thing. The ME says there's so much damage that she bled out in a minute or two. So the murder was done in Sunfish. You guys still got the case."

LUCAS GOT BENSON on the phone and asked, "Have you talked to Alyssa Austin this morning?"

"No, I haven't. You want me to?"

"I'll go. You got any ideas?"

"I'm just watching you, man—you're the guy who got shot, so there's gotta be something there. I'll take care of the lab stuff."

AUSTIN WAS ON the phone when the housekeeper let Lucas in, and her mother was still there, fussing around the kitchen, and gave Lucas a cup of coffee. She said her husband was at the funeral home, making financial arrangements, and that Austin was turning her business over to her Number Two. She still hadn't been told when Dakota County would release the body, but it could yet be several days, she said.

When Austin got off the phone, she came to him with a smile and gave him a hug, but she looked pale and thin and dry, and felt that way when she squeezed him: "Thank you for finding her," she said.

"I just . . . uh. I just talked to the Dakota County cops," Lucas said. "I don't know what they told you about what happened to Frances."

"Hardly anything."

"I can tell you some of it, if you want to hear it."

"I do. Absolutely," she said.

"Your mother said you were turning your business over to an assistant?"

"Not an assistant—she's a vice president and does our finances," Austin said. "She does the hard part of running the place. I told her I'd be away for a few weeks. No big deal. She's done it before, when I ran off to Europe or China."

They sat in the living room with coffee. Lucas knew from experience that relatives wanted to know what had happened to their loved one, not every brutal note, but the substance of it, and that plain talk was valued over euphemism. "She was stabbed to death. She died quickly. I think the Dakota cops told you that she was wrapped in a plastic sheet."

"A painter's sheet," Austin said. "A drop cloth. We last had painters here four or five years ago. I could look it up, but they were older men. Fifties, anyway. I wouldn't think that they'd fit a profile for this kind of thing."

"When we had our house painted—we built our house a few years ago—I don't think the painters used that plastic," Lucas said. "I think that's what you get when you're painting one room, one time, on your own. Our painters used regular canvas cloths."

Austin frowned, and her eyes shifted away, and then came back. "I think you're right. That's what ours did. I remember they had a lot of tape."

"So did ours. The Dakota guys didn't say anything about painter's tape. I don't know. Looking for painters might be going in the wrong direction, but we'll check—I'll have Jim Benson run them down."

"Was there any . . . I mean, you know, on TV . . . Did she have any skin or anything under her fingernails . . . ?"

"I don't know. They're going over the plastic with a microscope. Literally—with a microscope. If there's any blood there, or skin, or anything that would nail a killer, the lab will find it."

"I had another thought," Austin said. "I don't know whether you had it or not. But if they wrapped her in plastic, is it possible that they brought the plastic to wrap her with? That they came here knowing that they were going to kill her?"

Lucas scratched his jaw: "I didn't have that thought. When I did my little reenactment, I decided that it was spontaneous. The evidence is consistent with her having been stabbed with that little knife, the one that's missing. If somebody came here planning to kill her, and then to cover up, why did he do it that way? There are other ways to have done it that wouldn't have left any blood."

"She *must* have come here with him," Austin said. "Her car was back at her apartment. So she knew him."

"I don't know. I just don't know," Lucas said. "But I'm gonna find out."

AUSTIN HAD GONE off in a new direction. "Is the autopsy done?"

"I'm not sure; I know they at least did a preliminary."

"Did they check to see if she was pregnant?"

"Huh. I'm sure they would have . . . and they would have said something. Why?"

"I just keep wondering about it; about the whole scene, about the attack. Spontaneous, violent, had to be very emotional. What would set somebody off that way, somebody that she knew well?"

Lucas shook a finger at her: "That's something. That's what I'll push next. She had money, maybe she'd hooked up with somebody, some thug, who had his eye on the money. Then something happened here and she blew him off."

"And you're going to find out who it was."

"Oh, yeah. Yeah. Count on it."

Austin leaned forward from her spot on the couch and touched Lucas on the knee: "You think it's the money? And not the Goth thing? The dark culture?"

"Could be both; could be the killer is wiping out the people who he knows talked with Frances. Maybe he's afraid she told them something that would identify him."

She shook her head: "The Goths. It has to be in that circle, somewhere. I mean, look what happened to you. You talk to Goths and you get shot."

"Yeah, yeah." He shifted around in his seat and looked out

toward the lake, trying to piece it together. He said, "I spoke to some people at your husband's company, about Martina Trenoff. She works at General Mills now."

Austin nodded: "They got rid of her."

"They did. What if she had a key to this house? She goes psycho, she comes here to confront you, she's angry, she's lost her job. She's waiting in the kitchen, Frances comes in . . ."

"Martina has a flinty soul," Austin said. "But she's very controlled—I can't see her murdering somebody."

But Lucas was building it: "She could be a sociopath. They're typically intelligent and well-controlled. She uses your husband to promote herself in the company, has a plan that nobody is allowed to interfere with. Then it all goes to hell and she winds up on the outside. She feels like Hunter owes her something, or the Austins, and convinces herself that she should come here to collect it."

"Criminals think like that?"

"Exactly like that."

"Huh. A sociopath. I think . . . she is a sociopath, of course, but, you know, I suspect that she'd find herself in this situation, and she'd run the numbers, and she'd see that the risk of murdering somebody wouldn't pay off. So she wouldn't do it. That's what I think."

Lucas's eyebrows went up. "Of course? She's a sociopath, *of course*?"

Austin nodded. "I have a personal theory that 'mental illness' is just an extreme version of a common tendency. I'm a little bipolar. Not too much, but a little. Everybody knows people who are a little paranoid—not enough to be crazy, but that way. A lot of creative people are a little schizophrenic, with other worlds that are very clear to them. Most successful businesspeople are sociopathic—they don't let a lot get in their way. Anyone who's built a business has hurt people. You should know that. You were Davenport Simulations."

"I didn't build it," Lucas said. "I couldn't. I didn't know how. So

I got a guy to do it for me, and when I started getting in his way, I took the money and got out."

"Not sociopathic enough," she said.

"Maybe not," Lucas said.

"When you left, did you feel the other guy's hands in your back, pushing?"

"A little."

"See? He's a sociopath," Austin said. "Cutting you off from your baby. And probably felt good about it."

"Okay," Lucas said. It was all true.

"So if you're not a sociopath, what are you?" Austin asked. "Obsessive-compulsive?"

"Or like you, bipolar, maybe," Lucas said. "Maybe a little obsessive."

"And you'll use it to get this guy."

"I *am* going to get him," Lucas said.

"And maybe a little egomaniacal? Lucas?"

He'd drifted away for a split second. He came back and said, "I bet Martina's small and dark and athletic."

Austin shrugged: "Not athletic by my standards. I'd say, *trim*. She'll have a satchel butt by the time she's forty-five, if she doesn't watch out. Dark brown hair, taller than me, but . . . I'm short. She's on the short side of medium height."

Lucas said, "I gotta go see her. Like right now."

"An epiphany?"

"A stupidity. Why haven't I talked to her? Why is that?"

THE MEETING TOOK an hour to organize—forty-five minutes to batter through the General Mills bureaucracy, fourteen minutes of phone calls to pin down her actual working location, one minute to set up the meeting: she was cool, efficient, and had been expecting the call.

They met at a Caribou Coffee shop in the Minneapolis Skyway: she'd told him on the phone that she didn't want him coming to her office at General Mills. "We could shut the door," Lucas said.

"My office doesn't have a door," she said. She sounded, Lucas thought, like a wounded animal.

He picked her out as she walked along the skyway. Moving quickly, swerving through the crowd, carrying an expensive-looking black-leather woman's briefcase; a bit nerdy for a woman, in a slightly masculine navy blue suit, low practical shoes, and steel-rimmed glasses. She could be the fairy, Lucas thought, though nobody who'd seen the fairy mentioned glasses.

She walked into the shop, looked around, spotted him, came over and said, "Mr. Davenport." Not a question.

He stood as she came up, and she put out her hand and he shook it, and she said, "Sit down while I get a coffee. Watch my case, please."

He watched her in line, three back, then two, rocking on her feet, impatient, looking at her watch: a Rolex or a good copy. No; it wouldn't be a copy.

The woman in front of her wanted to know about available flavors and Lucas could see Trenoff's jaw working impatiently; high stress, a pusher. She got a large cup of coffee, spilled in some cream, got several napkins, and carried it quickly to the table and sat down.

"You said you were expecting the call," Lucas said, and he took a hit on his diet Coke.

"I couldn't imagine why you hadn't called sooner—or somebody," she said. "Everybody knew about my relationship with Hunter, and that I'd been fired, and sooner or later, it had to occur to somebody that I might have cracked and decided to take my revenge on Alyssa." She took a tentative sip of coffee and her eyes came up to Lucas, over the rim of the cup. "Mistaken identity . . . says something for the state's lack of efficiency that it took this long."

"What can I tell you?" Lucas asked. "We should have talked to you sooner."

"Of course, limping around like you've been, I'm surprised it's you at all," she said.

"You knew I was shot?" Lucas asked.

"Saw it on TV," she said. "I'm very interested in the Austin case. Very interested. Another year, I would have been Frances's stepmother."

"Did you have a key to the house?" Lucas asked.

She shook her head. "No. Hunter had a key to mine. People knew about us, but it's not like we were down in the next bedroom."

"Had Hunter asked you to marry him?" Lucas asked.

"No. But he would have," she said. "We'd talked, and I think he went up to Canada to think about it. He would have decided that it was the thing to do. A matter of time."

"You're sure," Lucas said.

"I'm sure. I don't think Alyssa would believe that—but the fact is, Hunter really did need an emotional relationship with somebody, some warmth," she said. "He didn't get it from her. They'd signed off on that. They slept in separate bedrooms, led separate lives."

"Excuse the expression," Lucas said. "But uh, why should he buy the calf if he's already getting the milk?"

The question made her laugh, sputtering in her coffee. "God, if that weren't so offensive, it'd really be offensive."

"Sorry."

"No, you're not. You're trying to provoke me. Give me a moment." She stared down at her coffee cup for a moment, as if saying grace over it, then looked up again. "See, many men and women need more than sex. They like to sit at dinner and talk about what happened that day—all the inane moments in daily life, who said what to whom, why so-and-so always wears blue suits, what happened to the Beaver's aileron. It's called 'having a life.' Hunter and Alyssa didn't have one. We did."

Lucas said, "Huh." They looked at each other for a moment, over their drinks, and then Lucas asked, "I don't want to sound too much like a TV show, but where were you the night Frances was killed?"

"Working," she said. "I'd been one week at General Mills and I needed to get up to speed."

"Witnesses?"

She cocked her head: "People came in and out . . . I work in a big bay, with cubicles. If you pressed, you might find people who saw me that night, but couldn't vouch for the fact that I'd been there the whole time. If anybody remembered at all. The story didn't get out until the next day, so it was just another working night. Or, come to think of it, there are cameras around, so there might be videotapes, if you asked GM security."

"So the short answer would be, 'No—probably no witnesses,'" Lucas said.

"Something like that, but not that short," she said. "Maybe, no witnesses, but videotapes."

"How often were you at the Austin house?"

She had to think, her lips moving, her eyes up toward the ceiling: "Three times. Or, let me see. I've got a feeling there might have been another time, a fourth, but I can't remember what for. All business-social."

"Did you help with the food?" Lucas asked.

"I don't help with food," she said. "I don't know where they kept the knives."

"In a drawer in the kitchen."

"There's a surprise," she said.

"What kind of name is Trenoff?"

Her forehead wrinkled: "What kind do you think?"

"Russian?"

She exhaled and said, "Your mind is a steel trap."

That made Lucas smile: "Not first generation."

"About fifth. What difference would it make?"

"Just making conversation, to prove that I'm human and to loosen you up for the killer questions," Lucas said.

"Well, here I am, all loose," she said. "Wheel those bitches out."

He laughed again and confessed, "I don't have any, I'm afraid. Do you like your new job?"

"I hate it," she said. "I'm at the bottom of the heap again. I took it because I needed to bring my marketing skills up to par. I went from a junior position at AUS to the top of the company, and now I need to sharpen up and get back into it. I've got a job interview, I won't say who with, but a company bigger than General Mills, in two weeks. I *will* get the job. And my office *will* have a door on it."

"So you're a little bitter," Lucas suggested.

"Oh, no. I couldn't stay at AUS. I knew that—I couldn't have stayed if Hunter and I had married. I was on my way out one way or another." Now her chin trembled and a tear popped out; she took off her glasses to wipe it away. "We were going to have kids. He wanted a son. Alyssa didn't like stretch marks, she didn't like being pregnant, I don't think she liked Frances that much. Maybe I'm not being fair."

"I think she loved Frances," Lucas said. "Maybe in a WASP way. As opposed to the Russian."

"That's about right," she agreed.

They chatted about smaller matters, but she was getting impatient. She had nice teeth, and a nice smile, and if he dropped his eyelids a bit, blurred her out, he could see her as the fairy. Some lipstick, some makeup, some clothes . . .

"What do you know about Goth?" he asked.

"Goth? What do you mean, Goth?" she asked. "Gothic? Like the cathedral at Chartres?"

"Where?" Now *he* was confused. "Cathedral?"

"Chartres. France," she said. "Like, the country."

He shook his head. "No—I mean, like the people who walk around in black clothes."

The forehead wrinkle again: "Oh. Well. Nothing."

"I GOT NOTHING else," he said, at the end of it.

"Hmm," she said. "I'd expected one more thing."

"About what?"

"About Alyssa's affairs," she said.

"She had affairs?"

"Several. Maybe not several, but two or three. Dancer kind of guys. Hunter was really straight—you know, navy flier, hard work, even church, sometimes. He carried a little too much weight. He looked like a *man*. Alyssa was one of those women who . . . she thought she was Madonna. She always had the taste for the well-turned male butt."

"Dancer kind of guys," Lucas said.

"Yes."

"So what are you telling me?" Lucas asked.

"I don't think she had anything to do with Frances," Trenoff said. "But what if there *was* a mistaken identity, but it was one of these guys?"

"Do you know any of them?"

"Frank Willett. W-i-l-l-e-t-t. Write it down," she said.

Lucas wrote it down. "Who is he?"

"He worked as a trainer at one of her clubs. Karate guy, you know. Model. Bicycle racer, rock climber, surfer, ski-racer. One of those guys you can't figure out how they make a living."

"When was this? The affair?"

"Well, they were going at it a year ago," she said. "Hunter told me about it."

"So he knew."

"She didn't tell him, but he knew. And they *did* do it at her house."

They sat in silence for a moment, and then she said, "Awful, isn't it? People selling each other out?"

"Trying to catch a killer," Lucas said.

"Well, if your online biography is right, you're pretty good at it."

"Not bad," he said. He stood up, and she stood up, and they shook hands again.

"Good luck with the new job."

She clutched the briefcase to her breast, looked out over it and said, "Luck is not a factor. I'll get the job and then I'll work harder than anyone they've ever hired."

He watched her going off down the skyway, weaving through the crowd, looking at her Rolex.

She would always be in a hurry, he thought, right up until she dropped dead.

Could be the fairy. Physically, anyway.

But if she was the fairy, what was she doing with the guy who shot at Lucas? She seemed to have nothing but disdain for Austin's lover. And, if Lucas could judge by a one-second look, and he thought he could, the guy who shot at him would be one much like Frank Willett.

One of those guys who you can't figure out how they make a living.

He looked at his notebook: Maybe get a look at Willett, huh?

13

FAIRY WAS in the kitchen when he called to her; out the window over the sink, the moon was rising behind the bare branches of the winter oaks.

"Hello? Hell-o-o-o?" Loren said. He walked in, wearing another new outfit, this one with a ruffle at his neck, with a green velvet coat that was cut long, as though he'd been traveling in the nineteenth century. He brought her hand to his mouth and kissed it. His lips were cold and dry. Then he stepped back and, looking down, said, "Those shorts aren't particularly becoming."

He was not trying to be offensive: he said it with the detached professional tone of a hairdresser about to suggest a change of style.

"I've been moving furniture," Fairy said.

He cut her off: "Just an observation," he said. He cocked his head and grinned, a practiced gesture that might have been made by a French fop in a romantic novel. But something caught in her throat, and she suspected he knew it. He was still holding her hand, and she could feel the edges of his fingernails in her palm, like claws. "Pale women have a problem with thighs," he said. "Their paleness, which can be very attractive, also makes them look a little heavy. A soft dress, on the other hand, something in a cool green, or a mint, would be stunning. Black would be good, in the evenings; ivory would be fine, too—but of course, you know all this."

"Now you're a fashion maven?" Fairy asked.

"I have an interest in costume," Loren said, not quite dismissively. Before she could say anything else, he turned to the piano and hit a chord.

"You talk about the piano, but you never play," she said. "You *do* play?"

"Yeah, sure. I've seen your sheet music here, the 'Moonlight' . . ."

With a glance at a wall mirror, to check his look, Loren settled on the piano bench and played a long run from the final movement of Beethoven's "Moonlight Sonata" missed a few notes, shook his head, tried again, missed again, and banged out a few loud chords. "My problem has always been, I think about it—if you think about it, you can't do it . . . At least, I can't."

"Stupidity, a piano method by Loren Doyle," she said, pulling his last name from thin air, not knowing where it came from.

"Doyle," he said, looking over his shoulder at her, "It means 'dark stranger.' How about that?"

"You certainly fit the name," she said.

Loren threw back his head and laughed, his longish hair flipping back to his shoulders. "One thing you've got to remember about Beethoven," he said, picking out the theme of the 'Moonlight', "is that he's dead. On the other hand, Bob Seger is still alive."

Loren launched into "Old Time Rock & Roll," pounding it out, his right hand bouncing up and down the keyboard in a chord-claw, and Fairy began to laugh . . . and laugh.

And Loren stopped playing, stood up, and gripped the hair at the base of her skull in his left hand, and turned her face to his and said, "I need somebody to laugh for me." He kissed her on the mouth.

She let go, closed her eyes, opened her lips. His tongue was cold and she shivered, but she let it go.

UP AND INTO the bedroom: sex came first. She hungered for it, needed it, hung on to him. He said, "I'm very cold."

"Please," she said. "Please help me here."

"I was thinking . . . a hot shower?" One cool fingertip traced the line of her throat from chin to collarbone, then down, along the line of her blouse to the first button, popped it, and then another, and slipped inside to her breasts. He didn't seem intrusive: but it did seem practiced.

"All right," she said, half turning away, not meeting his eye. "All right."

He always wanted heat, any way he could get it, from a shower, from her. Heat.

"YOU HAVE very nice breasts," he said. The water coursed down her chest and across her stomach to her thighs. He traced it with his knuckles, between her breasts, her stomach, over her navel, then to the side, just inside the line of her hipbone, to her thigh. "The first night that I watched you—that's the first thing I thought."

"I should shave my legs," she said nervously, stretching for something prosaic to right herself. "I'm like barbed wire."

"Do I feel cold to you?"

"Yes . . . but not so much as before."

"I don't think it's the water."

"No . . ."

"I think it's *you*. You bring me heat," he said. "Would you like me to shave your legs?"

"No, I'll . . . I don't . . ." Confused.

162

"Here. Let me." He stepped out of the shower, opened the medicine cabinet, probed it.

"No razor?"

"In the basket behind the cupboard on the left."

He opened the cupboard under the sink counter, took out a wicker basket, rattled the contents, took out a pink-plastic throw-away razor, started to put the basket back and then said, "What's this?"

A straight razor. He flicked the blade open.

"It belonged to my husband," she said. "Put it back; you can hurt somebody with it, if you don't know what you're doing."

He grinned at her and flipped his hair in the practiced way: "Yes, you can; but I do know what I'm doing."

"No . . ."

"It feels good," he promised. He pushed her back into the stream of hot water. "I've done this before . . ."

"With who?" she blurted.

"Before," he said. His left hand stayed with her body, trailing gently down her hip all the way to her ankle, as he knelt down.

"I, ah, jeez," she said shakily.

"Shut up for a minute," he said. Looking down, she saw him set the razor aside on the floor with his right hand, which moved to her groin. His fingertips probed lightly in her pubic hair, as though he were combing it. "Open here, just a little," he said. "Your legs."

His hands were gently, but insistently, prying.

"No, c'mon," she said, but her legs opened, just a bit, the warm water running down between her breasts, her head thrown back. His hand moved between her legs and she felt him opening her.

"Very warm," he said. He leaned forward, the water from the shower splashing onto his wet dark hair, and the most exquisite, soft-sexual thrill climbed through her as he stroked her clitoris with his tongue.

"Oh, God . . ." She put her hand in his hair, on the back of his head, and let the weight of it press his face into her.

After a moment, he picked up the razor. She stepped back,

leaned against the cool wall. The steel of the razor touched her at the point of her hip, then moved along the outside of her left thigh all the way to her ankle in a single rasping stroke.

"Feel that?" he asked.

"Feels . . ." she said.

Another long stroke, and another; a dozen of them, then small, quick gestures, touching up.

"Done here," he said. He started on the right leg, moving quickly, adept with the edge, cutting, rinsing, patting, cutting. And then, "All done."

She looked down at him, and his dark eyes were on her face. "Except for this," he said.

He laid the tip of the razor at the top of her thigh, under his thumb, and traced a sinuous curve down her quadriceps. Her leg tingled, as though a hot nail file had been drawn down it. Loren was kneeling, expectantly, looking at her leg, and then the blood appeared, seeping out of the nearly invisible cut, a crimson curve.

"An L," she said.

"For Loren," he said, nodding. He bent to her knee and his long tongue came out, and he licked and traced the bloody curve with the tip of it. He did it once, twice, three times, and then the blood had stopped. "Barely broke the skin," he said, grinning up at her through the spray. A trickle of blood ran from the corner of his mouth, pink in the flow of the shower.

She started to bleed again as Loren dried her with a rough terry-cloth towel. He did her legs first, before the blood surfaced again, and she watched it bead along the line of the cut.

"That's so . . . I've never . . ." She didn't know what to say. Loren turned her and did her back and buttocks.

"You're ready now."

"You're right," she said.

LATER, IN the Prelude, cutting through the night. "Hunting is better than sex," Loren said. "Don't you think?"

"They're almost the same," Fairy said. "I can't explain it."

Loren reached across in the dark, stroked the side of her face. His hands had gone cold again, an hour out of the shower, a half hour out of the bed. "I know what you mean. Exactly what you mean."

They flashed over the LaFayette Bridge into St. Paul, the city brilliant on the bluff above the Mississippi; they took the wrap-around exit onto I—94 and headed west toward Minneapolis. "You're sure?"

"I'm sure. She was involved."

THE APARTMENT was dark. They sat in the street, waiting, their breath steaming the windows. They had been here four times; and three of those times, Patricia Shockley came back early, while Price stayed out late. Price was the lover and the dancer and the socializer. Shockley was the intellectual, the loner, who always left early and ostentatiously.

Fairy rubbed a circle in a steamed spot, watching. "Freak me out if she didn't come." Loren reached out and touched the radio dial, a golden-oldie station, and Roger Waters jumped out, Pink Floyd, wailing "One of My Turns."

And after a while, six or eight or ten more songs, there she was, alone, wobbling along, a little drunk.

"Wait until she's up; she's going to have to buzz you in anyway, and we can see if anybody's coming along behind. If Price is coming," Loren said.

"My bigger worry is that Price is up there entertaining," Fairy said, looking up at the dark windows.

Shockley turned into her house, fumbled out a key, pushed through; Loren watching her with lycanthropic eyes. "Ready?"

Fairy bobbed her head. "Talk is done with. Talking time is over."

Loren said, "Go."

SHE PUSHED the button, and Shockley came back on the inter-com: "Who is it?"

"Patricia, this is . . . this is . . ." She had to grope for the name;

so far down that she could barely recall it. "This is Alyssa Austin. I need to talk to you. I've just been talking to Lucas Davenport, and he told me some things . . . We need to talk."

"Mrs. Austin . . . let me buzz you in."

She climbed the stairs, turning the knife in her hand. The talk was done. Strike and get out. Loren touched her on the back, just next to her spine, urging her on.

She knocked on Shockley's door, heard soft footsteps inside, as though Shockley had taken off her shoes. The door latch turned, and the door opened four inches, a heavy chain across the gap. Shockley peered out, smiled.

"Mrs. Austin. Alyssa," she said. "Let me get the chain."

SHE WAS still Fairy, and paid no attention to the words coming out of Shockley's mouth. She simply smiled and when the door opened, walked through, dropped the knife from her jacket sleeve into her hand. The knife had a wooden handle, dry and warm. Shockley was talking, but she wasn't listening, wasn't hearing the words, nodding and smiling as Shockley closed the door and fixed the chain, then turned and Fairy stepped toward her and the knife drove up and into Shockley's belly.

And Shockley flinched away at the last second, her eyes widening, and the point of the knife hit something hard and went sideways instead of in. Shockley said a syllable of some kind, a *gahh* or an *unhh*, but Fairy couldn't hear it; she sensed it but didn't hear it, and then Shockley swung something, a purse? A small black hand-sized purse? Fairy leaned outside the arc of the swing and went back in with the knife, but Shockley was a big woman with good reflexes and she swung again with one of her ham-hands and hit Fairy on the forehead, staggering her.

Fairy went in again, Shockley tripping backward and going down on her butt and screaming, once, loud, and Fairy tried to grab her hair and Shockley hit at her legs and Fairy went down as Shockley tried to roll over and get up, and the knife finally went in and went in and went in, Fairy riding her back and Shockley making an audible sound now, an *ung-ung-ung,* and then Fairy stood up and looked down and Shockley opened her mouth and said, "But I loved her. I loved Francie."

The words threw Fairy out of herself, and Alyssa looked down at the dying woman and the first words through her mind were, *Oh, my God, she's hurt.* She looked down at herself: she was wearing a black jacket over a blue wool jersey and black pants, and the jersey was dappled in black that when she brushed at it, came off in her hand as crimson—blood, in fact.

Then Fairy was back, like a blink, and she knelt and said, "You didn't love her, I loved her," and she drove the knife in under Shockley's chin, and there was more blood and Shockley's blue eyes rolled up and she was gone.

Fairy stood up and looked around and called, "Loren?" But Loren was gone, and Fairy felt herself fading, dropped the knife, picked it up, staggered back away from the dead woman, realized that the blood on her hands was showing, but she didn't care; she went to the door, took a handkerchief from her jacket pocket and pulled the chain and opened the door and closed it behind her and ran down the steps and out.

Across the street to the car, got in the car: "Loren? Loren, where are you?" And she continued to fade, and this time she went: Alyssa found herself sitting behind the wheel of a strange car, and she shook her head, tried to understand it, fumbled in her pocket for a key, felt the dampness of the fresh blood, could smell it, got the key in the ignition and set off.

Then Fairy surged back, and with it the killing heat, and she hammered the little car down the street and out to I—94, blood on her hands and face, racing down the highway, looking for sanctuary.

14

THE USUAL SCRUM of official cars were parked outside Shockley's house, along with two remote TV crews. Lucas parked off a fire hydrant on a side street, tossed his ID card on the dash, and walked back in the dark, zipping his leather jacket against the cold night air. His leg hurt. Not the fire, anymore, but an ache, as if one of his thigh muscles were clenching into a fist. He ignored it.

He knew the uniform working the sidewalk, who said, "Hey, man," and Lucas said, "Hey, Jerry." The flash from a strobe reached out across the street at them, and Lucas blinked it away and said, "Looks like we got media."

"Yeah. They're asking about the other ones, too. Ford and Carter, like the presidents."

"Shit."

There was a high-pitched whistle from across the street, the kind a movie New Yorker might use to hail a movie Yellow Cab. Lucas looked that way, and saw the *Star Tribune* crime reporter, Ruffe Ignace, drifting down the opposite sidewalk, looking at him, his cell phone to his ear.

Lucas turned away and asked the cop, "Is Harry Anson up there?"

"Yup. And the usual bunch."

On the way up the stairs, his cell phone rang and he took it out of his pocket and looked at the caller ID: Weather. She said, "Ruffe called here one minute ago, and said he saw you going into this woman's house, and he wants to know if the three stabbings are related to Frances Austin."

"Ah, poop. What'd you tell him?"

"I told him I was going to bed and not to call back," Weather said.

"But he's figured it out."

"Yes, he has. And good luck and good night."

ANSON WAS leaning on a second-floor banister, overlooking the stairwell, talking to an ME's investigator. He saw Lucas coming and said, "Help!"

"What the fuck happened?"

"Patricia Shockley, stabbed eight or ten times, bled out in place. Probably two hours ago. Found by her roommate . . . Leigh . . ." He flipped a page in his notebook.

". . . Price," Lucas said.

"Price. Who is now next door." He pointed down the hall with his pencil.

Lucas climbed the last couple of steps. "Eight or ten times. So she was killed like Frances Austin. Not like the others."

Anson nodded. "Except that the body wasn't moved. Other than that, and from looking at the Austin photos, I'd say they're almost exactly alike. Bigger knife this time, but it looks like there was a struggle. Some blood got thrown around. Take a look."

The apartment was being processed, and Shockley's body, still uncovered, lay spread-eagled on the floor six feet from the door. "Ah, Jesus," Lucas said.

"This will get in the papers and on television, and people will become extremely upset," Anson said. He was pretending to be funny, but his voice wasn't funny, and his eyes weren't. 'Why didn't the police warn the people of the Twin Cities that a serial killer was roaming loose?' I'm working out the answer in my little notebook."

"The answer is, because it wouldn't do any fuckin' good," Lucas said. "We got the fairy's face out there, looking for help . . ."

"Not the same."

"Ah, fuck it. What have you got?"

Anson said, "We have a witness who lives here, a Bob George, who looked out his window and saw an unfamiliar woman walking away from the house about the time of the murder. He'd heard a noise, but didn't know what it was—he thinks now that it might have been a muffled scream. He lives downstairs from here, says he only heard the sound once, and so he didn't look to see what it was. He's heard other sounds like it, and wasn't even sure it was in the house."

"Did she look like the fairy? The woman he saw leaving?"

"No. He couldn't see much of her, but she appeared to have lighter hair. Anyway, not black, or dark brown," Anson said. "Something between blond and medium brown, but the lights aren't so good outside, so he's not sure. Just an impression."

"Body style?" Lucas asked.

"Hard to tell. He was up here, the angle was bad."

"Gotta be the fairy. She's changing her look."

Lucas was pissed and washed with sorrow for the young woman on the floor. He took in the scene, as much as he could with the administration of murder going on around him, and then he headed down the hall to talk to Price.

PRICE WAS dressed in mourning black, as she'd been the first time he'd seen her, with the little phony Raggedy Ann rips and tatters. Tonight, though, she had dark rings under her eyes, and a trembling disbelief in her lip. An older woman, a dyed-redhead in jeans, was sitting with her when Lucas stepped past a uniformed cop into the living room.

"Ah, God," she said, and she stood up and stepped over to him and wrapped her arms around his waist, her head on his chest, and she started weeping. The uniform cop watched with interest, and Lucas let it go for a few seconds then pried her loose and said, "Easy. You better sit down. Really, you better sit down."

"She was just . . . she was just trying, *trying*, to get on with her life," Price groaned.

"Did she give you any idea . . ."

"She was going to go to *law school*," Price wailed. "She was practicing the LSATs. She was going on a *diet*. Jesus Christ, what's wrong with everybody?"

"Why would the person who killed Frances, come and kill Pat?" Lucas asked. "Why? There must be something that ties them together."

170

"I don't knowwww . . ."

"Frances took fifty thousand dollars in cash out of her bank account. Could she and Patricia have been involved in some kind of business deal? In something, in . . . in . . ."

But he didn't know what, and she looked at him with a stupefied frown, as if he were speaking Norwegian or something, and finally asked, "What? Fifty thousand dollars?"

"Were they involved in . . . What would they do with fifty thousand dollars in cash?"

"I don't know," Price said. "They hardly ever talked to each other. Why would they . . . ? Fifty thousand? What can you do with fifty thousand? You couldn't start a pop stand with fifty thousand dollars. I mean, *I've* got fifty thousand dollars."

"I thought . . . I don't know. Drugs? Gambling? Politics?"

Price's lips trembled again. "You don't know what's going on here—you just don't *know*. Drugs and gambling, that's crazy. There was no fifty thousand dollars. I would have known about that . . ."

When he had no more questions, Price asked, "Is this fairy coming after me? If I'd been here, it would have been me that was dead, wouldn't it be? You're looking for a fairy and I would have seen . . . Oh." Her fingers went to her lips.

"Oh, what?"

"She always kept the chain on the door," she said. "Patty. Always. The door wasn't bashed in or anything, was it? I didn't see anything like that."

"I don't think so," Lucas said.

"Then she had to *know* the guy," Price said, eyes wide. "She *never* took the chain off. When I was out late, she'd wait up until I got in, so she could get the chain. If she went to sleep, I'd have to pound on the door until she got up, because the chain was on."

"The chain wasn't on when you got home tonight?"

"No . . . and . . . I mean, she was right there, dead, when I pushed the door open, but I was already worried a little bit when

I saw the chain wasn't on, I was about to call her. I knew she was supposed to be there, because I saw her leaving the club."

BACK IN Shockley's apartment, Lucas checked the door; the door was fine. Anson came over and asked, "What?" and Lucas told him about the chain.

"Well, that's something," Anson said. "She let her in. If it's a her."

"And Price says she wouldn't have let a stranger in the door. Not even a woman, since this shit started."

"So who is it?"

"Dunno," Lucas said. "But I should." He thought about that for a moment, and then said, "You're tearing the place apart?"

"Naturally."

"I want to know about money. I want to know how much she had, and where it went, and if she got new money, or if she spent a lot recently. That fifty grand plagues me—it's all over my ass."

15

ALYSSA AUSTIN felt not confused, but broken—as though a wire had come loose somewhere in the circuitry of her brain, that her mind was full of static. Felt as though the picture tube was about to blow up, or that a thunderstorm was overhead, ruining reception.

Once in the car, she could feel Loren, there behind her, as surely as if she'd had a pumpkin in the backseat: and at the same time—*at exactly the same time*—she knew that Loren didn't exist, that Loren was a flaw in the wetware. The woman, the nightmare, the horror that Davenport called the Fairy—*she* was the Fairy.

And the Fairy struggled to come back, did come back, fading in and out, as though Alyssa were getting alternating shots of Xanax and cocaine.

She sliced across St. Paul on I—94, headed south across the Lafayette Bridge and down Highway 52, then cut east to the South St. Paul municipal airport; all on remote control, as though she were getting directions from a comic book, frame by frame.

Hunter Austin had a condo-hangar, not yet sold. She used her card-key to get through the gate, wound through the clutter of dark hangars, picked up the garage-door opener off the front seat, punched up the hangar door, and when it had opened, pulled the car inside.

Her Benz was crouched there, waiting, and she shifted to the bigger car, hurrying, forgot to get the garage-door opener, and after she'd backed out, had to jump out of the car and go back and get it. *Hope nobody sees me, hope . . .* The hangar area was dark as a coal sack, cold. Not another living thing, only Alyssa, scurrying in and out of her car's headlights, at Hunter Austin's hangar.

From there, it was ten minutes home. Loren's face blinked in the mirrors and the windows and the glass panels around the house, but she ignored him: programming errors, nothing more. Once she thought she heard him cry out to her; thought she felt him plucking at her jacket. She ignored the cry, the touch, hurried up the stairs to her bedroom, to the bathroom, to soak her face in cold water, to take a shower . . .

Flicked on the light, and stopped, staring, agog. She was covered with blood. Her face, her chest . . . she touched her blouse, found it sticky, soaked with still-wet blood. "Oh, God . . ."

She peeled off the clothes, ripping them away from herself, staggered into the shower, turned it on, scrubbed at herself, the stains resisting the body wash, giving way to a loofah. When she got out of the shower, shivering, not with cold, but with fear, and regret, and astonishment . . . she raised a washcloth to her face and saw the black new moons of blood under her fingernails.

She would have pulled the nails with pliers, if she'd had some pliers; frantic, she dug through her travel kit and came up with some blade-ended tweezers and used a blade to scrape deep under the nails. "Get it out," she moaned, digging. "Get it out."

Finally clean, she picked up her clothes, and saw blood on the floor. Her clothes were soaked in it. She wrapped them in a towel, used another towel to clean up the blood on the floor, carried the bundle down to the laundry, shoved them into the washer, poured in a cup, then another, of Tide.

Put the bottle down, saw the flecks of blood on her forearms, began to weep, backed away from the washer, ran back up the stairs, to the bathroom, watched her frantic, harried eyes in the mirror as she washed off this last insult. Looked in the mirror and then touched her hair, and felt the thickness, and took her fingers down and found more blood . . .

Weeping, back in the shower, soaking her hair, pouring on the shampoo, scrubbing until she thought her scalp would come loose; and then finally, stepping out, finding a new towel, wrapping herself in it.

My God, the car. Both cars. If anybody looked in the car in the hangar . . . there must be blood everywhere.

Loren flicked in the mirror, his mouth open, but she put out a hand and brushed him away, wiping the slate. Loren wasn't real, she was. And one car was surely soaked in blood, and the other would have at least traces.

With that, something clicked behind her eyes.

She looked at herself again. She was standing there, with a towel on her shoulders. She liked her body, normally, but now it all looked blue and cold and slumped, and her hair hung off her head in tangled wet strands, as though she'd just survived a ship-wreck.

Okay. Manage it. *Manage it.*

She'd killed a woman. Had she killed anyone else? She must have—why else would she have that little car?

It was all in there, in her mind, but again, it was like black-and-white panels in a newspaper cartoon. She had killed three people. She had killed them under the guidance of Loren Doyle, a man who'd come from nowhere, and convinced her that Frances had been murdered, and that she was the only possible instrument of retribution.

Innocent people. Crazy. Insane. But there it was. She didn't feel crazy now . . .

She stared at herself: *Manage it.*

Had anyone seen her? Davenport was investigating the murders, but had no idea who'd done them.

Frances? Oh, God, no. Had she killed Frances?

She closed her eyes, held on to the bathroom counter, and flipped back through the comic-book images, the last time she'd seen Frances . . .

Nothing there. She opened her eyes, relieved and puzzled. *She* hadn't killed Frances.

She looked at the towel in her hand, draped it through a rack, wandered to the dressing room. Pulled on clean underpants and a soft bra, a tracksuit, soft woolen socks, and running shoes. Warm and comfortable.

My God, she'd killed three people. With a knife. Where was the knife? *Where was it?* Still in the little car. On the floor, under the front seat. Have to get rid of the car. Clean it up, get rid of it.

She went out into the bedroom, turned off the ceiling lights, lay on the bed in the dim light coming from the bathroom, and thought through it.

She hadn't gone to Shockley's place as Fairy, because Shockley wouldn't have let Fairy in the door, not with Davenport roaming around, asking people about her. And *shit,* she had to get rid of the Fairy stuff.

She started to roll off the bed, but then thought, *Wait, wait, slow down. Think it through. Manage it.*

She hadn't gone to Shockley's as Fairy, so if anyone had seen her, they might be able to identify her. If they had, or if they would, she was gone. She hadn't seen anybody, but she hadn't covered her face, and people did watch the street from windows, lonely people, curious people . . .

But it had been dark, and she'd been moving; and nobody inside the house had seen her.

If they suspected, though—and Benson, the first BCA agent, suspected that she had something to do with Frances's death, even though she didn't—if they suspected, they'd go through the house. They'd eventually find the Fairy stuff, and probably blood and hair on that, DNA stuff, and she'd be done.

They'd look at her car, and if there was blood on the car, they'd find it, and they'd match it to Shockley's, and she'd be done.

If they learned about the hangar, they'd search it and find the car, and that surely had blood in it, and she'd be done.

If they looked in Fairy's purse, they'd find the photo that Fairy had used to track Frances's friends, and she'd be done.

Manage it.

LOREN CALLED HER: "Alyssa, please, please help me. I'm fading."

"Fuck you," she said.

"Dragging me down, Alyssa. They're dragging me down . . ."

"Fuck you. Go," Alyssa shouted, but his words were as loud as her own.

THE FIRST TIME she'd seen him, a month after Frances's murder, she'd run into the night, had called the police from a neighbor's house. The police were at her house in a minute, more coming in behind, just as they'd come in the first time, when Frances was killed. Again, they went through the house inch by inch, pistols drawn.

As they hunted for the intruder, it came to Fairy's mind that the intruder wasn't so much *reflected* in the mirror, as he was *inside* the mirror.

The police found no one, but didn't doubt her. Not at first. They were back the next day, in the daylight, to interview her.

The intruder, they believed, must know her—must know the house, to get out of sight and out of town so quickly. Or perhaps was a resident. The woods were thick enough that somebody dressed in black, as the intruder had been, could come and go at will, if he was careful and familiar with the terrain.

But he hadn't looked like a neighbor. The neighbors were sometimes eccentric, but the intruder had been theatrical, in the old sense of the word, the Oscar Wilde sense, loose silk shirts and tight butt-hugging pants, side-zip boots.

That, the neighbors weren't.

He came back; not all at once, but with hints, a few piano notes here, a figure at the corner of the eye. He frightened her at first, and then not so much. Late one night, he was simply *there,* in her dressing-room mirror.

"Who the hell are you?" Fairy asked.

"I'm a ghost," he said.

"A ghost."

"That's right. Not many people can see us, though we can see you. We're dead, and mirrors are our windows into your world."

"Why are you showing up now?"

"I've always been around," he said. "Around somewhere. I drift around the city, watching people. You couldn't see me; but now you can! I'm amazed. Nobody can see me."

"Really . . ."

"Really."

"What do you want?" Fairy asked.

He smiled: "Not much. A little time, a little conversation. A little piano playing, a sing-along."

"I'm crazy, aren't I?"

"You have to be a little crazy to see me, but you're not insane, if that's what you mean. I'm really here."

"I'm insane," she said, and she turned away from him.

"No, no," he said, the anxiety high in his voice. "Don't go away. Don't go. I can help you . . ."

He told her about death. About rising up from his own body, then losing sight of it. He'd been in water, he thought, with other people around, but he couldn't see them after he died. He'd been wandering in a fog forever, it seemed like, coming upon little shafts and rectangles of light, and looking through them, realized that he was looking out of mirrors. All over St. Paul, all over the whole area . . . He'd been inches from living people, but they'd never seen him.

And then he'd seen Alyssa, first drawn by her body. Then one day, he'd played a few notes on the piano that was in the mirror with him, a reflection of the piano in Alyssa's music room.

And he'd seen her *react*.

"I can't tell you how excited I was. You *heard* me."

HE KNEW about Frances. Knew she was dead. Could feel her there, on the dead side of things.

"She's gone for good, isn't she?" she asked.

"Not yet from this plane," he said. "She's restless, she wants to move on—but can't, not yet. She can't find peace."

"Could you find her for me?"

"No. I can't see anybody else here. It's like night, like a foggy night . . ."

"Maybe she'll come to me," Alyssa said.

"Finding the way is . . . hard," Loren said. "From here, you can't see anything but lights from the mirrors, and other shiny things, little threads of light here and there, and rectangles and circles of it, the mirrors. I found your mirror, at random. The mirrors look like campfires around a lake. When I go back, during the day, I sit there, waiting for night to come, so I can see the mirror again. And the light. I'm afraid sometimes that night will come and your mirror will be gone and I'll be wandering, crazy, looking for it, seeing all those people on the other side, eating and fucking and playing music, and all I get are shadows . . ." He was running on, and he shuddered.

★

HE SAID, "Frances can't leave here until she has justice. She can't go on."

"Go on to what?"

"To heaven. To rebirth. To whatever it is—I don't know myself."

"Why haven't you gone?"

"I don't know. I just can't . . . I can't . . ."

"LET ME help you find justice," he said.

She was skeptical: "How will you do that, mirror-man?"

"We can work this through. We can explore it. We can get . . . documents. Talk to people."

"People will talk to a ghost?"

"No, but I can advise you. I can come with you when you hunt them . . . you can pull me through."

"Pull you through," she said. She stepped back, out of reach.

"Pull me through," he said. He couldn't hide the eagerness in his voice. "Take my fingers, pull me through. I can't stay, I fade when the sun comes around, but for a few hours I can be with you."

"You'll hurt me," Fairy said.

"No, no." His eyes widened, and his hands spread, palms up, in supplication. "I could never hurt you. You're the only person who can see me—you're the only person I can talk to. Without you, I'm alone."

"You have a cruel lip; I can see the cruelty in it."

"No, no . . ."

THE RELATIONSHIP took time.

She walked away from him the first night, heard him crying as she left the room; and when she came back, he wasn't there, nor was he there the next night. The third night, he was back again and she walked away. She walked away for three, four nights.

"You almost ruined it," he said, almost choking on the words, the words tumbling in his rush to get them out. "You didn't believe in yourself, you thought I was imaginary. I'm not imaginary, I'm right here. I'm *human*."

On the fifth night, she pulled him through. The night after that, he touched her; and the night after that, they made love, though that wasn't exactly what it was.

Loren was cold as ice. He didn't really want sex; he wanted heat.

And as they lay side by side, talking of Frances and justice, he told her about the other side, the underworld, the dark and dim place where he spent his days. "I know—I just know, I can't tell you how—that other people move on. I haven't. Maybe I was made to stay here to help you find Frances. I don't know."

"You don't even see them when they go? When their spirits move over?"

"No. They're here, I think, but we can't see each other—the dead. Sometimes, though, I'd wake up and find myself outside, along the Mississippi in St. Paul. Nobody else on the streets. Dark, foggy, wet. Streetlights—I could never see the lights, but there'd be these cones of light coming down to me. Then I'd come to a bluff, and I'd see a riverboat down there. Casting off, pulling away. As though I were just too late to make it . . . Going somewhere."

"You've never run down to catch it?"

"I can't get there," he said. "It's like one of those dreams where you can't find a classroom, or you can't find a locker, and every time you think you're getting close, you take a wrong turn. The boat would be down there, and I could see the street going down the hill, but I'd always take the wrong turn and wind up somewhere else."

AND AFTER the sex they'd gone hunting.

NOW THAT was done.

She was a killer and Loren Doyle, the fault in the wetware, the bad cells, still called to her from the mirrors.

*

HAD TO manage this. Had to manage it, right through whatever shreds of insanity were left, whatever came back to haunt her, she had to manage it.

SHE LAY there for a few more moments, thinking about it, then launched herself from the bed. First thing: rubber gloves and garbage bags.

She walked down to the kitchen, her mind clear now, not a flicker of Loren. Opened the utility closet and looked at the supplies: it'd been a while since she'd done this. She was pleased to see that Helen kept the place stocked. She took a fresh pair of rubber household gloves and a tie-top garbage sack.

Climbing the stairs again, she turned away from the master bedroom, walked past Hunter's bedroom, past the last guest room, to the door there; opened it and climbed the stairs to the attic.

A plastic storage box from Target, under a pile of old jigsaw puzzles. She pushed the puzzles off to the side, opened the box, took out the Fairy costume and the wig, stuffed them in the garbage bag.

Carried the bag down to the laundry, left it there, got a flashlight, and went out to the car, opened the passenger door, and after a moment of minute examination of the seat and armrests, experienced the warm and holy glow known to people who have had a stroke of the purest luck.

She could not find the smallest spot of blood.

When she'd looked at herself in the mirror, when she turned on the bathroom light, she'd seen blood on her face and hands, and she'd had blood on her blouse and slacks, but only on the front; some of that, undoubtedly, would have rubbed off in the small car. But by the time she'd gotten to the Benz, the blood on her hands had apparently dried, and her back and the back of her legs had been cleaned: so there was no blood on the leather steering wheel, or the seats.

She sat back on her heels, and a smile crept across her face. All right.

And Loren whispered to her, *You see, the Powers wanted it this way. The Powers are on your side, Alyssa. Alyssa, listen to me . . .*

"Fuck you," she said aloud. "You're just a couple of bad brain cells. That's all done now."

A BURDEN off her back, she returned to the house, to silence, and frowned: Should it be this quiet? Ah: the washer.

She went back to the laundry, took the clothes, wet, out of the washer and put them in the dryer, moved into the kitchen and opened the cupboard. She picked a green spider-leg tea from Japan, added just a finger twist of ground rose hip, and brewed a cup; this particular combination was good for centering yourself when you were under stress.

She had to get rid of Fairy's clothes, and, come to think of it, she might as well get rid of the stuff in the dryer. Wouldn't wear them again anyway.

She sat with her tea and thought about it: she could put them in the fireplace, put on a little lighter fluid. But what if the police checked and found residue? The wig was real hair, what if a neighbor smelled burned hair?

The tea calmed her down, redirected her mental energy through a calm space, and when she finished the tea, she had determined the best possible way to dispose of the clothing.

She did the Fairy clothes and the wig, first, then got the clothes from the dryer, before the end of the cycle, still damp.

She was still working when the phone rang.

She looked at the caller ID, Davenport. She knew what he'd say: that there had been a new killing. She licked her lips, drew a breath, picked up the phone: "Oh, no, no, no. Oh, no. Lucas . . ."

He would see her tomorrow, he said.

She'd pulled it off.

AN HOUR LATER, she was at her spa in Highland Park—not far from Davenport's house. He'd be in bed, probably. She'd have to think about Davenport, already regretted inviting him in on the case. He was too smart—he'd have to be dealt with.

How to do that? She'd think about it overnight.

The spa was dark, silent. She went back to the women's locker room, into one of the bathroom stalls, and carefully and slowly fed the shredded wig and the Fairy costume and her clothes from the evening, all carefully scissored into one-inch squares, down the toilet.

There.

Let the police find that.

She gave it a couple of extra flushes to make sure nothing had gotten blocked, and walked out to her car. She wasn't sleepy yet. She remembered the crime-scene crew working in the kitchen after Frances disappeared . . .

Maybe she could go on the Internet and find out if there was anything about destroyed DNA. If there was a cleaning product, she'd take the time to clean out the Benz, even though there was no visible blood. Then, maybe, trade it. She'd been told that a lot of low-mileage traded Mercedeses wound up in Mexico. If that were true, they'd never locate it . . .

Outside, she paused in the parking lot, her hand on the car door. Not a bad night, she thought. The air was cold, but you could smell the spring just around the corner.

Tomorrow, she'd figure out the small car.

And Davenport.

And maybe Fairy.

16

LUCAS GOT UP angry, felt the mood settling in for a stay. Knew it, suppressed it at breakfast, but both the housekeeper and Sam picked it up: he was trailing the anger around like a faint odor of skunk. He called Austin before he left for the office, and she told him that she was at the Highland Park spa. If he could stop on the way to work, she said, she had some thoughts.

"We could use a few thoughts," he said.

"Then I'll see you in ten minutes?"

AUSTIN WAS WEARING a form-fitting bloodred tracksuit, a peculiar shade of red that always looked good on blondes, and that only blondes knew about. She was talking with another client, who patted her on the shoulder, then gave her a squeeze. Lucas recognized the other one's face, but couldn't remember her name. Then Austin looked past her friend and the woman turned, eyebrows went up and she stuck out a hand and said, "Dalles Burger, Stone & Kaufmann. Lucas, how are you?"

"Sure, Dallie"—like he knew who she was all the time, doing a little tap dance while his brain retrieved her file card: lawyer—"I don't think I've seen you since, what, the no-strike committee meeting. Are you going to arbitrate?"

She was flattered that he remembered: "I will. We'll be doing it right on the spot, so it'll be touchy."

"Ah, you'll work it out."

"I've got to talk to Lucas for a moment," Austin told Burger. "He's investigating what happened to my daughter."

"Oh, boy. Let me get out of here," Burger said. And, "I want you to call me. If you need *anything,* just call. I'll run errands, whatever."

"Thanks, Dallie; I'll call."

When Burger was gone, Austin pointed Lucas at a chair and asked, "What was this committee? No-strike? Arbitration?"

"The building trades have agreed to a no-strike provision on the Republican convention work, but they wanted arbitration if there was a disagreement. The governor's people put together an arbitration committee."

"Ah. Politicians." Austin settled back in her own chair.

"They're not all terrible," Lucas said.

"Yes, they are. Every single one of them," Austin said, a little serious behind the smile. "They take property away from people who work to get it, and give it to people they think will vote to keep them in their jobs. It's that raw."

"Then you should be happy to see the Republicans come to town," Lucas said.

"They're just as bad as the other ones," Austin said. "I am seriously disaffected. I believe what's going on in this country is evil. The president is an evil man, and the people who oppose him are evil people. That's what I think."

Lucas shrugged: "All right."

"You think I'm crazy."

"Well . . ." He spread his arms and gave her his most charming smile, and made her laugh.

She leaned back and said, "I was thinking last night, that of all the issues that have come out of these killings, Frances and all the other people, we know one thing for sure, and we also know that you have developed the only worthwhile clue, and only one of them. I don't feel that you're pushing it in the right way."

Lucas said, "Tell me."

"The thing we know for sure, is that all the killings are linked. They have to be. Same style. One group of people is being attacked. Something is going on that got all these people killed—and it seems like it's still going on, whatever it is. Okay?"

Lucas nodded: "Okay. But knowing that doesn't get us far, if we can't break into what's happening."

She held up a finger. "The second thing that happened was that Frances created a secret bank account that was apparently set up simply to get fifty thousand dollars in cash—in currency, in bills."

"I'm pushing that."

"Not hard enough," Austin said firmly. "And that must lead somewhere. Fifty thousand isn't that much in this day and age, but it's not nothing, either. If she spent fifty thousand dollars in a couple of weeks, it'll have to show up somewhere. And there are other odd things about it . . . like the secrecy. So my opinion is, that whatever's going on—the thing that links the killings—must involve the fifty thousand. Somehow. And maybe the bank itself . . . because the bank involvement is odd, when you think about it."

Lucas leaned forward. "What do you mean?"

"When Hunter was alive, we'd go out to Las Vegas every April for a military procurement convention," she said. "It'd still be cool and wet here, but Vegas would be warm and dry and it made a nice vacation. Hunter would talk to his military people, and Francie and I would hang out. Instead of taking a lot of cash with us, Hunter would set up an account at the hotel. When Francie or I needed something, we'd charge it. Or, we'd go get some tokens, if we felt like it, and play the slots."

"Yeah?"

She shook a finger at him. "If you needed to get fifty thousand in cash, from money that you had legally, but you didn't want people to know about the cash aspect, that you were putting together this . . . pot . . . how would you do it?"

"Might be a few ways," Lucas ventured.

"Maybe. But one of them, which Frances knew about, would be to send checks totaling fifty thousand dollars to two or three of the big casinos in Vegas, to set up accounts. Once they were cleared, you simply fly out and lose it. But not really. You buy tokens for the slots on the account, and then cash them in for hundred-dollar bills. Do it for a week: party, lie around the pool, pretend to play the slots, cash the tokens. You could easily do six or eight or ten thousand dollars a day, spread between the casinos, and nobody would know and nobody would care and nobody would remember. Except that the hotels would call you up three times a year with offers of a free room."

They thought about it for a minute, then Lucas said, "The point being, there were easier ways to get this money, even in cash, even anonymously, discreetly, than to set up a secret account."

"Not just that: also, *Frances knew about it.* She didn't have to invent some secret bank method. So she must've gone through the bank for a reason. Maybe she *wanted* to leave tracks. Maybe . . . I don't know. But it's something. I thought about it all night."

"So what would you suggest?" Lucas asked.

She shrugged: "I'm not the famous detective. I've got a funeral to work through. I've got . . . things. But. You have to push the money. That's what people always said in the procurement business, when we went to Vegas. If something smelled bad, look at the money. Always look at the money. Maybe you could go back to the bank . . . push all of her friends about the money. It befuddles me: what would she use it for? What, that she couldn't simply write a check for? That she couldn't get *me* to write a check for?"

Lucas peered at her for a moment, then asked, "That's what you've got?"

"That's what I've got," she said. "Are you going to think about it?"

"Yes. That's what I'll do today," Lucas said. "Think about the money, God help me, and nothing else."

THAT'S WHAT he did.

His secretary, Carol, came and looked at him, and went away, and then came back and looked at him again, and finally asked, "What are you doing?"

"Thinking."

She looked worried. "Huh. Could you take a look at—"

He held a hand palm-out to stop her: "No. I won't look at anything. Go away."

She peeked a couple more times. Once she asked, "How's the leg?"

"Not good," Lucas said. "I need to find a teenage girl to suck on it."

"I'll leave you alone," she said.

Just before noon, as he was sitting reviewing, in his mind, everything that had happened, the obvious occurred to him. He called Austin on her cell and said, "I need pictures of Frances."

"I'm at home, working on the funeral. I'll get a bunch together. Is this about the money?"

187

"Yeah. But I'll tell you what, this would all be a lot easier if she had a loser boyfriend."

He called the vice president at the Riverside State Bank. "Could you get me the name of the banker who opened Frances Austin's account?"

"Sure. Just a minute." More like two minutes. When he came back, he said, "Emily Wau. She's now the manager at the Maplewood branch. I checked, and she's working today."

"Give me her number," Lucas said.

LUCAS RAN down to Sunfish Lake, left the car turning over in the driveway. Austin had a dozen photographs: "I'll get them back to you as soon as I can," he said. "At the funeral?"

"That's okay—she had duplicates of everything."

"Well—I'll get them back."

Emily Wau was of Asian descent, a small, smiling, efficient woman in a conservative gray-green dress. "You want me to look at pictures of Frances Austin, to see if I can remember opening her account?"

"Yes. It would have been only about five months ago. October. You must've spent a little time with her."

"I looked at the paperwork—she opened it with five hundred dollars," Wau said. "So it would not have been a remarkable event."

"Still . . . six months. Not very long ago," Lucas suggested.

"Let me look at the pictures," Wau said.

Lucas passed them over, and she went through them, carefully, one at a time, turning each over, facedown, on her desk as she finished with it. When she was done, she picked them all up, looked at them again, then stared at a monitor camera mounted in one corner of the bank's ceiling, a thinking-about-it stare, then looked back at Lucas and said, "You know, it was several months ago, and I probably talk to twenty people a day, so I can't be sure, but . . . I don't believe I've ever seen this woman."

Lucas said, "I'm not surprised."

AND THERE it was: the case was cracked, though there was some cleaning up to do—like figuring out who the killer was. Lucas left the bank whistling, and on the sidewalk, got on his cell phone and called his secretary: "I need to get Dan Jackson to take some pictures for me."

"I'll see if he's available."

"Do that. I'm going to lunch."

He stopped at a McDonalds, had a Quarter Pounder with cheese, fries, and a strawberry shake, thought about the implications, rolled on into the office. Carol saw him coming and said a couple words into a phone, hung up and said, "Dan'll be up in a minute."

"Excellent."

DAN JACKSON was a middle-sized, middle-weight black man with short, neatly trimmed hair and a tightly, neatly trimmed mustache, and black plastic-rimmed glasses. At work, he wore button-up shirts with collars, and sweaters and khaki slacks and Patagonia jackets. He was, he said, invisible, not only to white people, but to black people as well. "I've been on elevators alone at night with white women and they never knew I was standing there," he'd told Lucas. "When I'm in the uniform, I am fully god-damned invisible."

Now he showed up carrying a Nikon camera with a lens more than a foot long, and Lucas groaned to himself, but smiled and said, "Dan, sit down."

"Got something for me?"

"I need surveillance shots of five women, plus about five more women at random, for a board," he said. "Usual range of sizes and shapes on the random shots—give me a couple of each: blond, sandy hair, dark brown. All white. Get some of our people out in the parking lot if you want, for the dummies, but don't make it obvious—get a bunch of different backgrounds."

"I'm ready to go," Jackson said. He patted the camera. "I got the new D3 with the 200–400 f.4 VR AF-S. Good ISO up to 6400,

I can go to 12800 if I have to, but there'll be some noise. Twelve megapixels so we get plenty of resolution. With this baby, you can really reach out and touch somebody. Brady squealed like a stuck pig when I put in for it—with the police discount, the lens is still better than four grand, and the body's five . . ."

"That's great," Lucas said.

". . . And I've been out shooting a little wildlife, to familiarize myself with the whole system. The white balance and auto-focus is as good as I've seen. I tested it against a 1DsIII, and the D3 is better. The IDs'll give you more resolution, but I'd defy anyone to say which is which when you look at it on a computer monitor, or a sixteen-by-twenty print, for that matter."

"Terrific."

"That fuckin' Flowers is already sniffing around, trying to borrow it," Jackson said. "He's still shooting a D2xs and I told him, - 'You'll have to pry it from my cold stiff fingers.'"

Lucas's head was bobbing: "That's just what we're looking for, and fuck Virgil. Anyway, I got a short list." He pushed it across the desk.

Jackson fondled the Nikon and leaned forward to look at the list. "Who are these people?"

"Suspects in a series of murders, so you've gotta be discreet," Lucas said. "Alyssa Austin; her housekeeper, a woman named Helen Sobotny; Leigh Price—that's L-e-i-g-h—who works up at 3M; Martina Trenoff, works at General Mills; Denise Robinson . . ." He pushed another sheet of paper across the desk. "Here's their home addresses. I need them as quick as I can get them. If you need some cover from somebody, refer them to me. Overtime's not a problem." He filled in the detail, and pulled up Austin's spa website, showed Jackson a photograph of her, and driver's-license photos on Sobotny, Price, and Robinson.

"Nasty pictures—nasty," Jackson said, looking them over.

"Not good enough to be used on a board," Lucas agreed. "We need civilian clothes, no particular background. If you have to shoot Austin coming out of one of her spas, then you'll have to do something to alter the background. Full-face, side views. Full body."

"I could Photoshop them if I had to."

"The problem is, Austin lives in Sunfish Lake and your cloak of invisibility won't work there."

They hashed it out for a few more minutes. "I'll do what I can," Jackson said. "Talk to you tomorrow."

THEN LUCAS was stuck: the next move was to try to identify the person who'd opened the account, without giving anything away. He signed papers for Carol, cleaned up a few more bureaucratic items, then headed for the apartment.

Halfway up the stairs, he could hear the head-banging rock. He opened the door and found Del, with his feet up, watching Toms's apartment with the binoculars, listening to AC/DC's "All Night Long." Del looked back at him and said, "She's running around."

"Like how, running around?"

"Like she's cleaning the place up, and singing a happy tune while she's doing it."

"Gonna be kind of a downer when we bust her old man," Lucas said. Lucas turned the radio off and dragged up a chair and said, "I caught a break on Austin."

"Yeah?"

Lucas told him about it, and then said, "So here's what I'm thinking. Nobody can figure out why Frances needed fifty thousand in cash, or why she took it the way she did. The answer was, she didn't. She didn't take the money, somebody else did. Somebody opened a bank account in her name and got Fidelity to transfer money to it."

"They'd need an ID to open the account. A valid driver's license. Maybe a second form of ID."

"That's true," Lucas said. "Which means, they'd have to find a way to dupe a driver's license, which is not all that easy anymore. How much they cost on the street now?"

Del shrugged: "One that a bartender will take, three hundred. One that'll fool a cop, five hundred. One that'll fool a machine, I don't know."

"But the banker who opened the account didn't run it through a machine," Lucas said. "She probably barely looked at it."

"What about the second form?"

"Suppose Frances Austin, a new millionaire, got a preapproved credit card form, or several forms, in the mail."

"She'd have to be dead not to," Del said. "Even then, she'd get a few."

"Right. So somebody who's right there—a close friend at her apartment, or the housekeeper at the Sunfish Lake house, or somebody we don't know yet, but who had to be close—fills out one of these forms, applies for the card. Has all the information. The card comes back, it's activated, Frances never knows, because it's never used. There's your preferred two forms: driver's license and credit card."

"That'd work," Del said.

Lucas picked up the glasses and looked for Toms, but she wasn't in front of a window and he put them back down. "Damn right it would work. A minor variation on a really old hustle."

"Then they kill her to cover it up."

Lucas said, "I'm not that far, yet. The killing could be spontaneous. Looks spontaneous. Let's say it's the housekeeper. She's just getting ready to leave for the day when Frances shows up, and Frances *knows*. She's actually been tracking her Fidelity account, figures out what happened, and there's an accusation, a confrontation, an argument . . . the knife is there."

"Go pick her up," Del said.

"There's one teeny-weeny little problem," Lucas said. "The housekeeper has a pretty good alibi. And there's this car thing I can't figure out . . . Plus, would somebody really take the chance of identifying herself as Frances Austin, in a St. Paul bank, a few months after Austin's name and photos had been all over the place because of her old man getting killed?"

"Maybe," Del said. "It'd take some balls."

"Lots of balls," Lucas said. And, he added, "Whoa-whoa-whoa . . ."

Del turned and looked across the street; Lucas was using the glasses. Heather Toms had just gone to the front door, opened it, and led a man back inside. He was a tall man, thin, with curly black hair and a saturnine face. When the apartment door was closed, the man pushed Heather against the wall and with one hand on her slightly protrudent baby belly, kissed her hard.

"Sonofabitch," Del said.

Lucas handed him the glasses, and Del watched for two seconds. "If it's Siggy, he's grown six inches . . ."

". . . could be lifts in his shoes . . ." Lucas said.

". . . lost thirty pounds . . ."

". . . that could happen . . ." Lucas said.

". . . got plastic surgery . . ."

"You can do that in Mexico," Lucas said.

"If that's Siggy, I'll kiss your ass," Del said, and handed the glasses back.

Lucas looked: they moved slowly from the hallway through a blind spot and then into the kitchen, where the guy got Heather's butt against the kitchen table and kissed her again, tipping her back, and Lucas said, "Holy shit, he's gonna do her on the kitchen table."

"No way," Del said.

Across the street, Heather righted herself and pushed him off, but she was laughing, and this wasn't the end of it.

"Where did this guy come from?" Lucas asked.

"Who knows," Del said. Sounding pleased, Del added, "Treacherous little minx, isn't she?"

"Siggy is gonna kill her."

"Especially if that little knob on her tummy isn't Siggy's work," Del said.

Lucas handed him the glasses. "If it's not Siggy's, then we're probably wasting our time sitting here. Siggy's never coming back.

She's way too smart to do that to him. He'd kill her with a god-damn chain saw."

"Not a complete waste of time," Del said. "I've never seen any-body get laid on a kitchen table, except in that baseball movie. I don't think it really happens—but if it does, I'd like to see it."

"I meant, waste of time in terms of life, liberty, and the Minnesota way," Lucas said.

"Fuck that," Del said. Talking to the guy across the street: "Go for it, guy."

Lucas asked, "How's your old lady?"

"Better. Must've eaten something that made her sick," Del said. He took the glasses from Lucas and put them up to his eyes. "You can't guilt-trip me outa watching this. This is purely professional."

AT HOME that night, Lucas told Weather about the break.

"It'll lead to something, for sure?" she asked.

"It feels that way in my gut—it'll lead to something," Lucas said. "I need to take a really close look at this housekeeper, and maybe Austin herself, and maybe these two friends of hers, McGuire and Robinson, who wanted to start the Internet site. The guy has contacts in the trucking industry, and that's one place you can for-sure get good fake driver's licenses—and he may have had access to her apartment, and to her computer, since he was a computer guy. So . . . it feels good."

"How's Heather?" she asked.

"Life with Heather is getting complicated," Lucas said. He told her about the new man, and she was enthralled.

"You think he wanted to do it on the kitchen table . . . ?"

"I don't know—they didn't, but they pulled the blinds in the bedroom, which is the first time that's been done, so *something* happened in there."

"Kitchen table would probably hurt your hip bones, your shoul-der blades, the back of your head, your elbows . . ."

"Depends on which way you were facing, I suppose," Lucas

said, and he picked up that morning's *Star Tribune* and turned to the comics pages.

She had to think about it and then said, "Lucas! God!" But, like most women, she valued a little vulgarity from time to time.

DAN JACKSON showed up with the huge camera and a giant Domke photographer's satchel at eleven o'clock the next morning, and sat in Lucas's office until Lucas got back from the convention security coordination committee. Lucas rolled in fifteen minutes later, yanked off his necktie and threw it at a photograph of the BCA Shooters, the Y-League second-place basketball team a year earlier; the tie caught and hung up on the picture frame.

"Should I ask?" Jackson asked.

"Fuckin' morons." Lucas dropped in his chair, shook a finger at Jackson. "They're doing estimates on how much damage we might get from protesters at the convention. They chose 'not much' because that was what they're budgeted for. It's like New Orleans: How big will the hurricane be? Well, not very big, because we can't afford it."

"Be some good photography, though," Jackson ventured.

"Yeah? Talk to the newspaper guys about that," Lucas said. "Most of the trouble takes place at night. Nothing like running around in the nighttime with a goddamn strobe, taking pictures of people committing crimes, with no backup."

"Hmph. I may have to reconsider," Jackson said.

"Reconsider your ass off." Lucas stood up, turned in a full circle, dropped back in the chair, exhaled and said, "Screw it. They know what I think."

"Not necessarily good to be right, when all the big shots are wrong," Jackson observed.

"Yeah, yeah," Lucas said. He leaned forward: "So. You get it?"

Jackson patted the Nikon. "It was a snap." He chuckled. "You get it? It was a *snap*?"

"Dan . . . when can I get the snaps?"

"Right here," Jackson said. He reached into the back flap of the photo bag and pulled out a set of 5x7 color prints. "I got all your women, and five from here in the office. They all look equally candid, I think—shouldn't be any bias toward our gals. None of our people have accounts at the bank, so they shouldn't be contaminated that way."

Lucas thumbed through the prints. Ten women with hair that ranged in color from blond to dark brown, looking generally past the camera, but nearly frontal; and side views as they passed. "These are great. Great. I'll recommend you for the four-to-midnight shift at the convention."

"You're a prince."

EMILY WAU, the banker, was waiting when Lucas came through the door. "More pictures, huh?"

"Yup. A bunch of suspects. Secret camera. Just like on TV. Do you have a conference room?"

They did. Lucas turned on the lights and spread the photos over the conference table, all mixed up. "Just let your eyes roll across them . . . look at all of them before you focus on one," Lucas said. "Then . . . whatever."

Wau took her time: five minutes to look at ten women, including Alyssa Austin, Helen Sobotny, Denise Robinson, Leigh Price, Martina Trenoff, and the BCA dummies. At the end of the five minutes, she touched her lips with her index finger, like a schoolmarm signaling, "Shhh," scanned all of them a last time, and said, "Nope."

"Nope?"

"I don't remember any of them," she said. She said it confidently, and Lucas felt his heart sink.

"Ah, man."

"Something happened the other day, somewhat related, that made me think of you," Wau said. "I was standing by the door, and we've got this thing we do, whenever somebody comes in. We say, 'Welcome to Riverside.' This man came in and he said, 'I remember you, you opened my account.' And I remembered him. I didn't even think—I said, 'You're Jim!' and he said, 'That's right.

I'm flattered.' So we were both happy. Later, you know, thinking about you, I looked up when he opened his account. It was the end of December. Right after Christmas."

"So you do remember the people," Lucas said.

"Well, I remembered *him,* when I saw him," she said. "And he was nobody spectacular, just a guy."

"Poop," Lucas said.

"I'm sorry."

"We're not done, yet," Lucas said.

THEY WEREN'T DONE YET, but where to go? When he'd walked into the bank, he would have given 3–2 odds that they'd get an ID. A thought popped into his head: What if Wau were involved? What if . . . horseshit. It ain't Wau.

He sighed, looked back at the bank, and headed for the car.

Had to be somebody close to Frances. *Had to be.*

SITTING IN THE APARTMENT, looking across the street at Heather Toms's place, listening to the Doors doing "Love Me Two Times." Heather was not in, and Lucas got his feet up, and closed his eyes, and ran back through the faces of the women. Nothing there. Thought about Austin, and what she'd said about insanity, about how it was nothing more than an extreme version of everyday quirks . . .

Good theory, he thought. Lucas had a theory of his own, sociological, rather than psychological.

Some people, he believed, looked at the world and saw a clockwork: events happened and triggered off other events, people did what they were programmed to do, and the results came out the other end: love, hate, war, murder, children, whatever.

Other people, Lucas among them, looked out the window and saw nothing but chaos: accident, chance, stupidity, intelligence, avarice, idealism, all rubbing against one another in an unpredictable stew.

How could Heather Toms, he thought—as Heather came

through the door of her apartment carrying an oversized shopping bag from Neiman Marcus—how could a nice suburban girl like Heather Toms ever expect to wind up as the loving wife of a murderous Lithuanian gangster, mother of his children, secret lover of one of the gangster's underlings?

For Christ's sakes, she'd been a cheerleader at Edina, one of the toniest high schools in the metro area. How could she . . .

The answer, of course, was that she couldn't have predicted any of it. If she'd stopped somewhere for a cappuccino, she might not ever have met Siggy. Now she'd be married to an insurance agent or a cop or a finance guy . . .

The problem with this view of life, this philosophy, was that it suggested that what happened to Frances Austin, and what happened to the other murder victims, was not the result of a cold calculated plan by anybody at all. The whole thing could have been set off by accident, by a bump in the dark, by a burglar . . .

But then . . . three killings?

Nope. It might be chaotic, but there were threads in the chaos. He was just pulling the wrong one.

ACROSS THE STREET, Heather was looking at herself in the mirror, holding up an outfit. Then she turned her head, walked to the door. Her mother was there, said something, and Heather disappeared down the hall, leaving the door open, and was back a moment later with the toddler.

She put him on the floor and went back to posing.

Lucas watched in the binoculars and thought, *Huh*. She supposedly had no money. Her mother supposedly paid half her rent, out of her Social Security and pension.

And that maternity stuff she's looking at cost at least a grand.

A light went on: the guy she'd met at the door, the underling, had delivered more than a good time: he'd brought money from Siggy. Dollars to doughnuts; and Heather was flush again.

There *was* contact.
She wants to look nice.
Bet Siggy is coming . . .

17

THE NEXT MORNING, instead of pushing the Austin file, Lucas sat in Rose Marie Roux's office in the Public Safety building and they shouted at each other about the Republican convention. Roux was working on a matrix of all possible outcomes of the street demonstrations, from minor disturbances to full-blown call-out-the-National-Guard riots—not to determine staffing levels, but to propose differing political postures for the governor and his pals, depending on what happened.

"If we really had a disaster, there'd be some fallout for us, too," she said, solemn as a priest. "Wouldn't just be St. Paul."

"If there's a disaster, another Seattle 'ninety nine, there'll be fallout for everybody," Lucas said. "Forty thousand demonstrators showed up in Seattle and that was for the World Trade Organization. How many people know what the WTO is? And we're gonna get the Republican Party and the most unpopular president since Richard Nixon."

"The biggest horse's ass since Richard Nixon."

"I can't stand it when you guys say that," Lucas said, his voice rising. "Somebody says, 'The black bloc is coming, the anarchists, we're gonna have a riot,' and one of you political guys says, 'The president is a horse's ass,' like that's an answer. Do you think it makes any difference to Gepetto's, if some goddamn ratshit anarchist throws a firebomb through the dining room window, if the president's a horse's ass? Don't tell me about him being a horse's ass, 'cause I don't give a shit. Tell me how you're gonna keep the firebomb from going through the window."

"A giant horse's ass, a horse's ass of biblical proportions." Rose Marie was goading him, and he knew it, and that infuriated him even more.

". . . And that's what Gepetto wants to know, too. He's full every night, he's turning tables as fast as he can push food at people. He doesn't give a shit whether the Republicans come to town. What he wants is police protection . . ."

". . . You're shouting again . . ."

". . . and when Gepetto asks, 'How're you going to protect me?,' all you guys got is, 'The president's a horse's ass.' That's a *really* great answer."

"There is no Gepetto," Rose Marie said. "The place is owned by Tommy Reed."

"I know who it's owned by. Does that make any difference? Do you—"

His cell phone went off, and he pulled it out and looked at the screen: Dakota County sheriff's department: "Yeah? Davenport."

"This is Dick Pratt down in Dakota. A guy walked in the door early this morning with Frances Austin's purse," Pratt said. "No cash, but all of her ID is there. Credit cards, driver's license. He remembered the story, drove it in. He found it in the ditch a couple miles north of the body."

"Anything good?"

"Maybe," Pratt said. "You got a guy named Frank connected to her? Heard that name?"

"Uhhh . . . yeah. Somewhere."

"Figure out where. There was a letter in her purse, handwritten, we think it's her handwriting, with a felt-tip pen. Water got to it, in the ditch. The paper's falling apart and a lot of the note is one big ink stain—but we can read the top part of it. Addressed to Frank, it looks like she was breaking off a relationship."

"That's good," Lucas said, standing up, focusing now. "That could be critical. We were told that she didn't have a boyfriend. You're sure it's her handwriting?"

"Pretty sure. There was another thing in there, a list, and the handwriting looks the same to me. We'll have a handwriting guy give us an opinion. But who else's would it be? That kind of a letter?"

"Goddamnit."

"And you got a Frank?" Pratt asked.

"Someplace in the notes. I'll find it. The letter's in really bad shape?"

"Yeah. Our guys got it flat, and got it dry, but it was in the water too long. Even the part we can read is smeared. 'Frank,' is pretty clear, though. It looks like she folded it and refolded it about a million times, like she hadn't sent it. Like she was thinking about it."

"I'd like to come down and take a look," Lucas said.

"If you want, I can have our guys take a high-res photo of it and e-mail it to you. You could have it in two minutes, save you a trip."

"Let's do it," Lucas said.

He rang off and Rose Marie asked, "Catch a break?"

"Maybe. I've got to get back to the office."

"Nice screaming at you," she said.

HALFWAY BACK to his office, Lucas realized where he'd heard the name Frank. He was so startled by the realization that he pulled the car over and dug out the notebook, to check.

Yes: Martina Trenoff made him write the name down. Frank Willett was a trainer at one of Alyssa's clubs and, she'd said, one of Alyssa's lovers. Karate, she'd said. Model, bicycle racer, rock climber, surfer, one of those guys who you can't figure out how they made a living.

The rest of the way back to the office was a fantasy, a story that Lucas made up as he drove: a guy with no money, fucking both an heiress and the heiress's daughter, who was, come to think of it, also an heiress.

But the mother, in addition to being a little goofy and believing in astrology and probably tea leaves, also had a tougher, business side. In addition, she'd had a number of lovers, and might not have been interested in a long-term relationship with somebody like a bicycle racer/model/ surfer guy.

She might like fucking him, okay, but long-term, she'd want somebody with status in the community, somebody with . . . good shoes. She'd mentioned the artist, Kidd—a perfect match for her. As an artist, he'd certainly be goofy enough, and hell, he was in *museums*. That's what she'd want, not some guy who walked around thinking about his next pair of sunglasses.

The daughter, on the other hand, young, inexperienced, not all that great-looking, might be a bit more influenced by a guy with big muscles and a surfer's outlook.

And if the guy were looking for money . . .

From there, that one thing, that relationship, all kinds of other things might have fallen out.

She tells him she's going to break it off: they argue in the kitchen, there's some pushing, she reaches for a knife, he takes it away from her and sticks her. Wonder what kind of truck he'd have, whether there'd be transmission fluid in the truck bed? No doubt in Lucas's mind that the guy would have a truck, if he was a surfer, a bike-racer, a rock-climber, all that.

Or, how about this: the daughter finds out that he's fucking both her and her mother: goes to Mom with the story, there's an argument that turns violent, one of them yanks out the knife in a fit of passion, or jealousy, or even self-defense and . . . zut.

"Finally," he said aloud. The whole Frank thing made everything clear: this was no big cosmic mystery, it was just some of the same old bullshit. An argument about sex and love, some hysteria, and a murder.

Why were the others killed? Because they knew about the relationship? Was Frank there the night of the chicken dance?

He thought about Austin for a moment.

Not Austin, he decided. She was tough, but unless she was totally nuts, there was no way that she could have produced all the tears that came with Frances's death—and he'd seen her face when

202

they told her that the body had been found. Until that moment, Lucas thought, she'd had some hope that Frances might still be alive.

Not Austin.

At the BCA office, he ran halfway up the stairs, until his bad leg bit back at him, and he nearly fell. Limping into the office, he nodded at Carol, who asked, "What's happening?" and came to stand in the door while he punched up the computer.

"Got a break, maybe," he said. "Found Frances Austin's purse, got a breakup note out of it. Breaking up with a guy named Frank."

"Old-fashioned name, Frank," Carol said. "Don't see many Franks anymore. If they'd gotten married, it would have been Mr. Francis and Mrs. Frances Austin."

Lucas was listening to her prattle and he pulled up the e-mail, then frowned and looked up and asked, "What'd you say?"

She shrugged. "Nothing. I was just going on."

"You said Frances and Francis—are they spelled the same?"

"No, but I don't know which is which."

"I bet no one else does, either," Lucas said. He ran his hands through his hair, said, "Holy shit. Holy shit. Go get me Dan Jackson, on the run, and tell him to bring that big fuckin' camera. Holy shit, the Frances Austin who went to the bank could have been a *man*."

HE TOOK A moment to explain, walking around his desk, then, as Carol went to call the photographer, went back and pulled up the photo of the breakup note. As Pratt had said, the note was badly smeared, but the salutation was clear enough:

Dear Frank,
    I've put off writing this letter for a long time [smudge] *heart I didn't want to believe what I heard. There's no point in* [longer smudge] *hear from you again, really. I also don't want* [smudge]

From there, it was a black stain; maybe the feds could make something out of it, but felt-tips don't make much of a physical indentation on paper, her handwriting was small, and the stains were dark. Still, it was possible that a lab could recover the original.

Not that he needed it to push the investigation. What they had was, for now, good enough.

Lucas frowned: but where would the fairy fit in this scenario?

He thought about it for a moment, and then let it go. If they nailed down Willett, he thought, the fairy would come clear. She was probably another of his lovers—maybe the one who put Willett up to stealing the fifty thousand.

"Carol!"

She popped back in the office: "Dan's on his way."

"We need to get everything on paper that we can about Willett. Run everything you can think of. If we come up with previous addresses, out-of-state, we're gonna want to get their stuff . . ."

Jackson, the photographer, came in a moment later, and Carol called, "We've only got one Frank Willett locally—it's Frank, not Francis, on his driver's license."

"Where's that Willett work? We need an address," Lucas said.

"I'll get into the employment security, hang on . . ."

Jackson, stepping around Carol, asked, "Another rush job?"

"I think we've got something this time," Lucas said.

Carol called, "It's him, he works for A. Austin LLC in Minnetonka. He lives in St. Louis Park."

And she pulled up his driver's-license photo: Willett had long black hair, carefully arranged on his shoulders, an oval face, square white teeth. He looked good, and he knew it, even in a license photograph.

"Ooo," Carol said.

Lucas squinted at the picture, trying to make him as the man in the alley. Couldn't do it; the long hair was distracting. The guy in the alley seemed to have short curly hair, he thought. But if Willett had cut it . . . or maybe even if he'd been wearing a ponytail on the night of the shooting . . . it wasn't impossible, but he couldn't ID him from the photo.

Lucas had Carol call Minnetonka and ask for Willett. When the receptionist transferred the call, Carol hung up.

"I'm going out there," Lucas said.

"Want to ride along in the van?" Jackson asked.

"I'll meet you over there," Lucas said. "I don't want to get stuck if you have to wait awhile; but I'll come and sit for an hour or two."

MINNETONKA WAS ON the far western edge of the metro area, and from the BCA office, took a solid forty-five minutes, west on I—94 and I—394, winding around in the maze of streets at the end of it. Lucas had Jackson on the cell phone, and they cruised the spa, Waterwood, from opposite directions, then hooked up at a strip mall and Lucas transferred into the back of the van.

The GMC had been taken away from a dope dealer. It had nice captain's chairs in the back, tinted windows, a dresser with a mirror, and, if the chairs were moved, space for a narrow memory-foam mattress, which had been stripped out.

Jackson took it back to Waterwood, parked across the street, eased into the back of the van and took the other captain's chair. "Magazines in the chiffonier, diet Coke and raspberry-flavored water in the fridge," he said. "I got the rest of the subscription to Sirius, long as you don't play any country and western."

Lucas settled for a bottle of water and a classic rock channel, checked the magazines: *Blind Spot*, *PhotoPro*, *PDN*, a couple of *Shutterbugs*, *Men's Journal*, a *Playboy*, and an aging *Esquire* with a picture of Charlize Theron on the cover, as the world's sexiest woman.

"You think she's the sexiest woman?" Jackson asked, about Charlize Theron.

"There is no such thing," Lucas said. "That'd be like the best baseball game. You can argue about it a long time, but you'll never agree."

"I think she's the sexiest," Jackson said.

"Angelina Jolie?"

"She's good, she's good," Jackson admitted.

"Michelle Pfeiffer?"

"Ah, Jesus, now you've got me confused," Jackson said. "I like the blondies . . ."

So they talked about sex and tried not to drink too much water, because they'd have to pee, and Jackson had a sack of black-corn chips and some nacho sauce in a plastic cup, and they ate some of that, but not too much, because then one of them might develop gas, and then they talked about the truck for a while, and whether there was any *real* difference between a GMC and a Chevrolet, and they watched women coming and going, and Jackson said, "I wouldn't mind seeing her with her clothes off," and Lucas asked him if he'd ever shot any nudes. Jackson said he dreamed about it, but his wife would kill him, so he didn't.

"You got any nude pictures of your wife?" Lucas asked.

Jackson bit on the oldest baits in history: "No, uh, you know, I . . ."

"Want to buy some?"

They were still laughing about that when Frank Willett came out the door with an old lady. Willett was six feet tall, Lucas thought, narrow shoulders, no hips at all, probably weighed a hundred and sixty pounds, and all of it was muscle: like a snake. He was wearing sweats with a hood folded back on his shoulders, gym shoes, and a black ball cap; round, steel-rimmed glasses; and he dangled a gear bag from his left hand.

Jackson started whaling on the camera the moment they came out the door. The outside walks were made of flagstone, and Willett and the old lady chattered along as they ambled toward the street, and then took a right toward the parking lot. Lucas said to Jackson, "Short hair," but when they turned, he spotted a short ponytail sticking out the back of Willett's ball cap. "Shit. Ponytail."

"Hair's black, though, like you wanted," Jackson grunted. "Suck-ass license photo, it could have been any color."

In the parking lot, Willett patted the old lady on the shoulder and walked across to his car, a gray Land Rover LR3. "Get the plates," Lucas said to Jackson.

Jackson did, but said, "Just as easy to look them up."

"The guy's a personal trainer," Lucas said. "Where does he get money for a Land Rover? It might not be his."

Jackson was shooting: "Well, there's ways . . ."

"And I know one of them," Lucas said. "You take fifty thousand dollars off Frances Austin."

WHEN THEY WERE GONE, Lucas said, "Let's get these back and get some prints. Need them quick."

"You can have them in two minutes, if you want," Jackson said.

"Yeah?"

Jackson pulled open the bottom drawer of the chiffonier, took out a Canon photo printer about the size of a carton of milk, and plugged in his memory card. Lucas picked out four photos on the small LCD screen, and Jackson printed them as 5x7 glossies.

"Christ, this place is like a photographer's dream," Lucas said, as the photos pooped out of the tiny printer.

"And when some asshole tries to take it away from me, I'm counting on you to back me up," Jackson said.

"Absolutely," Lucas said.

THE RUN across town was delayed by construction, and Lucas, pissing on his own shoes for choosing the wrong route, took an hour to get to the Riverside State Bank in Maplewood. As he was pulling into the parking lot, he took a call from Carol:

"Not only does our man have a history, there's an outstanding warrant from San Francisco," she said. "He never showed up for a court date on a sale-sized pot bust, so he is fair game. We can bag his tight little ass anytime we want."

"How much did he have?" Lucas asked. "How do you know he has a tight ass?"

"Six ounces. And Dan got back and showed me some of his shots."

"Well, shit, that's not much of a sale."

"The information out there claims he was providing it to meditation clients to smooth them out," she said. "He was teaching in a program called Action Zen, where you'd jump out of an airplane or climb a cliff, and then smooth out on dope."

"Sounds weird," Lucas said.

"Sounds fun," Carol said. "But the important thing, like I said, is that he's fair game."

EMILY WAU, the banker, looked at the photographs for three minutes, shuffled them around on her desk in different configurations, then said, "No."

"No?"

"I think I would have remembered this one, for sure," she said. "Is he married?"

"Jeez, Emily, give me a break. I'm not a dating service," Lucas said.

"Maybe you should be—you're not doing that well as a cop," she said, but she smiled when she said it.

LUCAS THOUGHT about it for a few minutes, as he drove away from the bank, then put in a call to Alyssa Austin. "I need to talk to you about Frank Willett."

There was a moment of silence, then, "Uh-oh."

"Where are you at?"

"In St. Paul. I can be home in fifteen minutes. If we have to talk about him, I'd rather do it at home, than here."

Somebody was sitting across her desk, Lucas thought. "Half hour," he said.

On the way down, he called the number he had for McGuire and Robinson, the couple who were setting up the website.

Robinson answered, and he identified himself and said, "Did you ever meet a friend of Frances named Frank Willett?"

"Uh . . . maybe."

"Maybe?"

"Yeah. We went out to a place in Stillwater, last summer, a restaurant down on the water."

"The Dock," Lucas said.

"Yes, that's it," Robinson said. "Anyway, she was there with a guy, and she might have said his name was Frank. I don't know what their relationship was—they seemed kind of standoffy, but you know, funny-like. Like maybe they were unhappy about us seeing them together."

"Denise, you didn't mention this when we talked."

"I didn't even remember it until you asked me about Frank," she said. "And I'm not sure the guy was named Frank—we didn't eat with them; they were at a table for two, we just said hi, and we moved along."

"You remember what the guy looked like?" Lucas asked.

"Pretty good-looking. Like a ballet dancer, or something. Thin, big hands."

"Hair color?" Lucas asked.

"Black; with a ponytail. Two-day stubble. And he had a diamond earring."

"Of course he did," Lucas said.

"Yes; of course he did," she said. "What's this all about?"

"We're taking a look at him," Lucas said. "Now, I'm very serious about this. And you tell McGuire, too. If you see this guy again, you get away from him. Especially if you see him on the street, and he comes over to you."

"You think?"

"We can't take the chance," Lucas said. "So if you see him . . ."

He could hear the shiver in her voice: "Get away."

AUSTIN WAS wearing a black velour sweat suit and pink dance shoes. She held the door open, closed it behind him, and said, "So somewhere along the line, you ran into Frank. I've been thinking about it, who you could have talked to, and I'm worried that one of my employees tipped you off."

"Why should that worry you?" Lucas asked.

"Because I wouldn't take that kind of disloyalty," she snapped. "If you heard it from one of my people, I'm going to have to root her out."

Lucas was shaking his head. "Relax. It's not one of your employees."

She nodded: "Then it was Martina, that bitch. I thought Hunter might have figured something out. We were at an event at the Walker, and who should come wandering by, but Frank. I told him to get away from me, but I saw Hunter notice, you know, looking at me and then at Frank, and I was afraid he'd figured it out. And *he* told *her.*"

"*You* should have told me," Lucas said. "For Christ's sakes, your daughter was *murdered.*"

"The relationship was over for six months before Frances was killed," she said, and she started to tear up. "There was no connection. Frank is not a bad guy."

"California wants him on a dope warrant," Lucas said.

"*What?*"

"Not that big a deal, really—but he does have a warrant out," Lucas said. "If he gets stopped on a traffic ticket, and they run him, that could pop up."

"Oh, shit," she said. They had trailed into the living room, and she plopped on a couch. And she shouted, "Helen!"

The housekeeper scurried out of the kitchen.

"Squeeze a couple of oranges for me, will you? Maybe an orange smoothie. Lucas? You want a smoothie?"

"That sounds fine," Lucas said.

When the housekeeper was gone, he said, "I gotta tell you about something, and the way you're talking, I'm not sure you knew about it."

"About what?"

"About Frank and Frances."

"What about Frank and Frances?" Her hand went to her throat, and she half-laughed, but with shock in her eyes, denying it, and said, "You've got to be kidding."

"We think there was something going on there. The Dakota County cops came up with her purse—a guy found it and turned it in. There was a letter . . ." He took the folded print out of his pocket and handed it to her.

She looked at it for a long time, more than a minute, then shook her head and said, "Well. Not much here."

"But it looks to me—"

"Me, too. It's her handwriting, no doubt about it," Austin said.

"Do you have any idea when the relationship might have started?"

"It would have to be after he and I broke it off."

"Why? Why afterwards."

She looked at him, blankly, for a moment, then halfsmiled: "Because he would not have had the energy to be sleeping with her, too. I, uh, needed a lot of attention."

"Okay. So when did you break off?"

"April, the middle of April, right around tax time," Austin said. "I had a lot to do, he started getting a little testy when I put him off . . . and finally I told him that we should end it. And I did. We did. Agreed to."

"Sounds like *you* did," Lucas said.

"Maybe," she conceded.

"And he would have gotten to know Frances through you?" Lucas asked.

"Well, through the spa in Minneapolis, Riverwood. It's right over in St. Anthony Main."

"By the A1," Lucas suggested.

"Oh, God! I never thought of that. I mean, it's several blocks, but it's an easy walk." She turned her face away from him for a moment, thinking, and then back: "But so what? I mean, what would that mean?"

"I don't know. But tell me about how they probably met," Lucas said.

"Well. She was going to the university, off and on, had an apartment over there, and the Riverwood location was the closest one, so she took a locker and would work out over there," Austin said. "Frank works at several of the sites, usually one morning or one afternoon a week, doing tai chi, yoga, Pilates, meditation, whatever the members want."

"Did she know that you were seeing Frank?"

"Not as far as I know. But I'm sure a couple of members could have figured it out and let her know. I wouldn't be surprised if something like that precipitated this letter."

"She apparently hadn't sent it," Lucas said. "It was still in her purse. So they were going on at the time."

"You think that he might have come here?"

"What if she thought you were still sleeping with him? When she was? He denies it, she comes here to confront you, they argue . . . I mean, his job is at stake," Lucas said. "Another thing—that fifty thousand dollars? You may not have noticed it, but your employee is driving a Land Rover. Do you pay him that well?"

Now she blushed, the pale pink tint creeping up her neck to her cheeks. "Actually . . . Look, I wasn't paying him to sleep with me. But I have lots of money, and he was driving around in this old Jeep Cherokee with holes in the floor. I was afraid he was going to gas himself."

"*You* bought him the Land Rover?"

"I helped him with it, yes," she said.

"Shit. I thought it could be the fifty thousand. That would have tied things up just perfectly," Lucas said.

She looked out at the lake, her eyes narrowing, her lips tightening, and she said, "I cannot believe that *asshole.*"

"And he was gone, your affair was done, before Hunter was killed?"

Her face jerked back toward him. "You don't think . . . ?"

"There's nothing to suggest it. But there are a lot of dead people."

She shook her head. "I'll tell you something: Frank knows nothing about mechanical things. I don't see him sabotaging an airplane in such a complicated way that Hunter could fly it all over the place, and then up to Canada, and then have it fail at that one moment when it couldn't, without crashing."

"If it failed anytime up in the air . . ." Lucas began.

"No. If it had failed at five thousand feet, he could have landed it anywhere with water. They even used to practice it—coming in without using the engine."

Lucas shuddered: he did not like airplanes. "You mean, just turn it off?"

"No, it was on, but they'd land without using it, just gliding in. From five thousand feet, in a Beaver, you can glide for miles."

"Huh."

She ticked a finger at him: "The fifty thousand. If he was a drug dealer in California, even if he was small-time—especially if he was small-time—fifty thousand dollars might have meant a lot to him. I mean, what if she just wanted her money back? Found out about him?"

Lucas nodded: "That's something. I'll look into it. Now, the Land Rover: he's had it for at least a year?"

She thought, then nodded. "Maybe thirteen months now."

"So he would have been driving it when Frances was murdered," Lucas said.

"Yes."

"Okay . . . Okay, that's another thing we can check on."

"So what are you going to do?" she asked.

"I'll nail down everything I can, then I'm going to pick him up on the California warrant, and I'm going to squeeze him."

"You want me to wait until then, before I fire his ass?"

A smile flickered on his face. "If you don't mind."

★

SOME OF THE AIR had gone out of the tire, but Willett still looked good, Lucas thought, as he headed back downtown. Anytime a young woman was murdered, with some indication of passion around it, a boyfriend would be a prime suspect.

If the boyfriend had slept first with the mother, then with the daughter, if he looked to lose the possibility of a marriage to a lot of money, if he was a hustler as Willett apparently was, if he was keeping it all a secret, and kept it a secret even after his girlfriend was murdered . . . and that Francis/Frances coincidence might have given him the idea of pulling Frances's money out of the bank. They must have talked about their name similarity.

There was even a possibility that the old movie cliché, the mistaken identity, had been at work—that Willett had come to the house intending to kill Alyssa Austin, and killed Frances instead.

Willett was just too good: half the cops that Lucas knew would simply say, "He did it."

Just a matter of finding the proof.

LUCAS AND DEL sat watching Heather Toms until she packed it up and went to bed.

"I feel like a slimeball," Lucas said.

"So don't watch," Del said. Across the street, Heather, with her back turned, popped her brassiere, took it off, then turned to the window to pull her sleeping T-shirt over her head.

"Has it ever occurred to you that a lot of what we do for a living would be against the law, if we weren't cops?" Lucas asked.

"You mean like stalking people, being Peeping Toms, doing dope deals with them?"

"Yeah."

"Maybe we just don't have the guts to be crooks," Del suggested. "Don't have the instinct for the big score; we like life insurance and health insurance and pensions too much." Heather kissed the baby good night and turned off the bedroom lights, and Del put the glasses down.

"That's not it," Lucas said. "There's lots of ways we're not like crooks. For one thing, we got better hours and make more money. Still . . ."

"Stop worrying," Del said.

"Okay."

"You ready?" Del asked.

"Let's do it."

WILLETT LIVED in a small house in St. Louis Park, an inner-ring suburb west of Minneapolis. There was an attached garage, which meant they wouldn't be able to get at the car. But he also had an evening tai chi class at the Maplewood location; they cruised it, spotted the Land Rover in the back parking lot, with a half-dozen other cars scattered around. The class was twenty minutes under way when they took the first look.

"You're sure this is going to work?" Lucas asked.

"The guy who programmed the key says it'll work perfect," Del said.

"If the car alarm goes off . . ."

"Not a chance," Del said.

They found the closest parking space, left the borrowed BCA Mustang, and walked on down the street, checking windows, porches, side streets. The night was cold and close, with a touch of sleet in the air; not many people outside.

They cut across the spa's parking lot and came up to the Land Rover. Del punched the remote key, the truck lights flashed, and Del said, "Should be open."

Lucas tried the back door; locked. "Punch it twice, maybe . . ."

Del punched it again and the lights flashed twice and Lucas felt and heard the lock pop. Lucas took a flashlight out of his pocket, took a last look around, and turned it on. The back of the truck was neat as a pin, with a long plastic storage box on one side, and a couple of plastic milk crates on the other. No trace of oil, of any kind, on the carpeted floor, no painter's plastic sheets or any painting equipment.

Lucas leaned inside and pulled the latch of the storage box, looked inside. Camping equipment: sleeping bag in a stuff sack, stove kit, nylon pop-up bivy bag, pots and pans in a nylon bag, a bundle of socks, a big Ziploc bag stuffed with fabric, with the word "thermal" written on the outside of the bag with a Sharpie—long underwear. One of the plastic crates held a variety of rubber-soled shoes that might have been climbing shoes; the other held two pairs of hiking boots.

Del had gone in the side door, to look through the various front-end storage bins: "Anything?"

"Nothing that shouldn't be here," Del said. "He's tidy. He's organized."

Lucas took a long look around, said, "Let's go," and they shut the doors quietly and walked away.

"Got to give it to you—the key worked perfectly," Lucas said.

"Except for the fact that we got nothing," Del said.

"Except for that."

18

ALYSSA AUSTIN SAT barefoot in a big black-leather easy chair with her feet pulled up under her, her legs folded to the right, thinking about Frank Willett. Davenport knew that the four murders were linked, but didn't know that they were linked through Alyssa.

If Frank had killed Frances, she thought, he had essentially killed the other three as well, by destabilizing her mind. If he were convicted of one, or of all four, it'd make no difference under Minnesota law. There was no death penalty, but there was a minimum sentence for first-degree murder, of thirty years. He wouldn't get out, in any case. Not until he was almost seventy.

The car, Loren whispered.

"Go away," Alyssa said.

Loren had been flickering in the mirrors around the house, like a weak over-the-air signal on an old television. She'd fought it at first, but had then grown tired of fighting. Let him—or whatever brain cells were misfiring to produce him—do as he wished. At times, he acted as an effective foil for her thoughts.

"I can't go away. You're my only chance," he said. His voice became louder, clearer, whenever she acknowledged him. "I'm having trouble holding myself together—but you need me. You need me to talk to. To plan. You need the Fairy, too."

They'd begun referring to Alyssa's shadow aspect as the Fairy, because that's what Davenport called her. "Why would I need her?" Alyssa asked.

"Because she does some things better than you do," Loren said. "She kills better than you—you can't kill at all. She does it quite easily. She comprises aspects of your real personality that you've repressed over the years. She was there when you were swimming, and winning, but all that mushy New Age shit pushed her under."

"We're all done with the killing," Alyssa said.

Loren was fully formed now, a man all in black, speaking from the mirror above the antique chest where they kept the board games and playing cards. "Maybe, but maybe not," Loren said. "You made a big mistake when you brought Davenport into the picture. Fairy and I had it under control."

"You had *nothing* under control," Alyssa snapped. "You murdered those people; as far as I know, they had nothing to do with Frances."

"Of course they did," Loren shot back. "A spirit on this side pointed at the photograph, and now, I have to *assume,* I *know,* that it must have been *her* spirit. Who else would care? Willett may have killed her, but the others were involved. It was all part of a conspiracy. If only you could let go completely, we might be able to set up a line with Frances, if she's not already gone on the boat."

"Oh, God, go away." She waved him off with the back of her hand.

217

"Wait, wait, wait. We need to talk about Fairy. *You* need to talk about Fairy," he said. "You *are* Fairy. You can let her out. You can free her and then put her back; but she's more than you are, and you need her. Especially now, with the police sniffing around. You've got that car to deal with. You *can't* forget about the car, you *can't* let it go. And you've still got Frank Willett to deal with—what are you going to do about him? Fairy can work that out."

"You want her out, because she'll let you out of the mirror," Alyssa said.

"That's true. She will—you will. If you let her out, if you relate to her, then, I think after a time, you'd integrate. You'd be both Alyssa and Fairy, with no conflict—she'd almost be like a strong mood," Loren said. "Alyssa: you need her."

Alyssa rolled off the chair and walked into the kitchen, got a single-serving can of V8 out of the refrigerator, poured it into a wineglass, added a sprinkling of black pepper. Loren was there, in the kitchen, but only in fragments, in wisps of movements seen in the reflective parts of cabinet knobs and chrome sink fixtures. She looked out the kitchen window at the lake: late afternoon, the sun in the west, and the ice was like a slab of lead. She carried the glasss of juice back to the black chair and closed her eyes and sipped it, and thought:

She had to get rid of the car.

She had to help Davenport get at Willett.

"Let her out," Loren said. "Let Fairy out."

"How?"

No real problem: sit in the big chair, legs crossed, eyes closed, relax. Fairy flowed into her.

"There you are," Loren said.

"Not entirely," Fairy said. "Alyssa's here, too." Fairy reached out to the surface of the mirror, pulled him through. He was wearing black slacks, a black silk shirt with a dark sport coat, and pointed black Italianate shoes. He followed her to the easy chairs and took one, opposite her, as she curled into the chair.

"Ideas?" he asked.

"The car's a problem because it's soaked in blood," Fairy said. "We can't sell it, we can't abandon it—they could find a few of my hairs in there, or something, along with the blood. If they do the DNA, they'll connect us."

"So we have to burn it," Loren said.

"That's my feeling. We've got gas out in the garage. If we splashed five or ten gallons of gas inside it, it would burn right down to the wheels. Alyssa looked it up on Google."

Alyssa flowed back. "As soon as I read about burning it, I tried to figure out ways to do it. But there are all these stupid problems. Like, how do I get home without witnesses?"

How to get home without catching a ride, without a cab-driver? She could, she thought, drop the car someplace where it could sit for a day or two, without being noticed, then drive in, set it on fire, and drive away. Maybe that would obscure a taxi connection. But then, what about surveillance cameras wher-ever she left it? What if somebody noticed it had been parked for a long time, and then checked it. What if she bumped into some-body she knew?

"That sounds like Alyssa talking," Loren said.

"It is," Alyssa said.

Fairy came back, speaking to Alyssa: "You know, honey, there aren't any guarantees—and you're making this way too compli-cated. You think we've got to get the car far away from here, but we don't. If something happens with the car and they can match us to it, then we're finished, no matter where it is. If we burn it completely, and they can't make an ID, then it doesn't make any difference if we do it right down the street."

Alyssa thought about that for a moment, then nodded, sipped the V8. "Okay. But I'd rather not burn it *right* down the street."

"Of course not—but it doesn't have to be in North Dakota, either. I say we move the car out of the hangar during the night, drive it onto one of the construction sites down by the river bridge—that'd mean we'd actually be in the car for only a couple of miles, which would reduce our chances of getting stopped for some reason. We park it, we set it on fire, right then, in the dark, and then we run. Simple, effective. Black jogging suit, scout the way in and out ahead of time, burn it."

"In the dark?" Loren asked. "You don't see a lot of women jogging down there. There are some rough people around there."

"I'll take Hunter's switchblade. It's still there in his bedstand, and I know how to use it," Fairy said.

"Of course," Alyssa said, and she actually smiled.

"If the police get there too fast . . ." Loren began.

"We use a fuse. Soak it in fuel oil and gas, ten feet long, under the car, light it and run," Fairy said. "We'd be a hundred feet away before it got to the car. In a minute, we'd be three blocks, jogging. The police aren't going to get there in a minute. From there, it's probably three or four miles—we can jog home in half an hour."

"A risk."

Alyssa snarled at them: "If you morons hadn't gotten us into this, we wouldn't have to take any risks. If some guy thinks he'd like to sneak a peek at Hunter's hangar, sees that car, looks inside . . . we go to jail. My prints and Patty's blood are all over it. Maybe blood from some of the others, now that I think about it. You weren't all that careful."

"We were a little carried away," Loren said. "The revenge was so . . . tasty."

Fairy: "So we have to do something. We can't *not* do something. I'm in favor of the straight-ahead, burn it and run. No point fucking around with something subtle, that'd leave a trail."

Alyssa: "You may be right."

Fairy: "Of course I'm right."

Loren: "What about Frank Willett?"

"I've got an idea on that," Alyssa said. "The car not only has blood in it, it's got the knife you used on Patty. We lift the knife out of there, clean off the handle so there are no fingerprints, but leave a little blood down where the blade goes into the handle. A few specks, stains. Then we put the knife in Frank's house."

"How do we get in?" Loren asked.

Alyssa said, "I've still got a key to his house, if he hasn't changed the locks since we were dating. I can't believe he's organized enough to do that," she said. "We jog again. Watch until he's out, I go in, I leave the knife, and then we figure out something that triggers Davenport to make a search."

"We scare him. We get him to run away," Fairy said. "We get Frank to make a break for it."

Alyssa: "Not a bad idea. How do we do it?"

Fairy: "I call him. I tell him that I heard that the cops were coming for him on the California dope warrant. I bet he'll run. I bet he will."

Alyssa: "He'll recognize my voice."

Loren, on the opposite chair, shook his head: "No, he won't. You two don't sound much alike. Fairy sounds younger, more perky, like a Valley girl. Her voice is pitched higher. You don't sound much alike at all."

"Really?" Alyssa said.

"Really," Loren said. "So. When do we do all this?"

Alyssa looked at her watch: "Can't do Frank until we've done the car. We've got just enough light to scout that right now."

"Then we could even do it tonight," Fairy said.

THEY TOOK the Benz, and Loren sat in the back, where he could watch Alyssa's eyes through the rearview mirror. "I like the idea of tipping Frank so he runs," he said, as they headed out the driveway. "But if you're the only one that Davenport's told about the warrant, then he'll figure out that you're the one who told Frank."

Alyssa nodded. "Let me think about it."

"Gossip," Fairy said a minute later.

"What?" Alyssa asked.

"You could talk to Gina. She's the worst gossip on the staff, and she goes around to all the spas. You could tell her confidentially about Frank—ask if he's been giving or selling dope to any of the customers. She'll tell other people—it'll be all over the place by the end of the day. Then, if Frank is tipped, it could be any of the staff members, clients, who knows?"

"Excellent," Loren said.

Alyssa said, grudgingly, "It's an idea." And a second later, "That would work."

THE RIVER-BRIDGE area wasn't going to work for burning the car, they decided—the fire would be too visible to too many people on the highway; too many cell phones. It'd be reported within seconds. They gave it up after driving across the Wakota Bridge a couple of times, and instead began probing the area south of I—494, along the Mississippi.

The South St. Paul airport, where the car was hidden in Hunter Austin's hangar, sits on the top level of the Mississippi's western valley wall. Down the hill east of the airport, Concord Street runs parallel to the river, and on the river side of the street, a complex of railroad-to-truck freight terminals are jumbled along dead-end streets between the river and Concord.

"If somebody was planning to burn a car, this would be one place to do it," Loren said, as they probed back into the complex of streets and warehouses. "You'd have to run less than a mile. You'd only be exposed for maybe ten minutes."

"It's better than I thought," Alyssa admitted. "We do it like this: we drive the Benz to the hangar, leave it, drive the little car down here. Right behind that pallet yard, along the fence, where the fire would be hidden from the street by the warehouse. Touch the fire off, and we run straight down the road for what . . . maybe two hundred yards? We hook around that garage, cross Concord, and head up the hill to the airport. If we're lucky, we'll be across the street before anybody sees the fire."

"Unless there are watchmen," Loren said.

"Watchmen would be inside, not out. I'll look for lights . . . can't be out here without lights. We can always revise at the last minute, drive around the block and come back, if we have to."

"You could hurt yourself running in the dark."

"Not if I stay in the middle of the street. There are enough lights around that I should be okay."

They drove the route, and Loren pointed out a couple of potholes left over from winter. "If you step in one of those, you'll sprain your ankle. You could break a leg."

Alyssa looked back along the road. "They're both on the left side. I'll stay on the right."

They followed the approach up the hill to the airport, and the road in. Access to the private hangar area was through a card-controlled electronic gate, no problem to a person on foot, who could simply duck under it. Again, there should be enough ambient light to work with.

"Can't do it in the middle of the night, though," Loren said. "If people see you running then, they *will* notice."

"So, nine o'clock."

"We've got the gas," Fairy said. "Let's do it tonight."

"What about the knife?" Loren asked.

"Soon as we can—before Davenport has too much time to think about everything," Alyssa said. "I asked his wife to get him to investigate because he's smart. Now, I wish he was a little dumber."

"Water under the bridge," Loren said.

". . . but we could place it tonight," Fairy said. "Frank always goes out at night; I doubt that would have changed."

"What if somebody sees us at his house?" Alyssa asked.

"How many times did that happen when we were visiting?" Fairy asked. "One out of five?"

"Still happened once," Alyssa said.

"So, we check it out first. Go in the front door, one step to the left, key in the lock, we're inside. Hide the knife, peek out the window for people on the sidewalk, listen at the door, and we're out. If somebody should pop up by surprise, we go back, get the knife, and throw it in the river."

"Okay. I'm just a little nervous."

"You're about to pee in our pants," Fairy said cheerfully. "Don't do that. I can't stand wet pants."

BACK AT the house, Alyssa looked at the gas cans. The three identical red plastic containers were used to gas up Hunter's home toys: the John Deere lawn tractor and a smaller Lawn-Boy trim mower, a heavy Toro snowblower, a Stihl chain saw, a weed whip, a leaf blower, the limb-trimmer. They had a yard service to do all of that work, and a plow guy to clear the driveway in the winter, but Hunter liked to putter, and he had enough money to putter with what he wanted.

There were probably ten gallons of gas in the three containers. She wouldn't be able to bring the container back with her, so she'd have to leave it in the car. Would Helen notice that one of the gas cans was gone? No matter—Alyssa could go someplace far away and buy another, when she had time.

She filled one of the containers all the way, pouring from the other, then humped it over to the Benz. Damn thing was heavy. As she lifted it in, she thought, This is crazy.

"No, it's not," Fairy said. Fairy was popping up whenever she wished; at the same time, Alyssa no longer worried that she might take over. She now seemed more like a twin sister than an alien being. "It has to be done. *It has to be,*" Fairy continued. "If there's one thing we can chicken out on, it's putting the knife at Frank's place. But we must obliterate any evidence that can be used against us. We have to get rid of the car."

So Alyssa put the can in the trunk of the car, on top of a layer of newspapers, closed the trunk, and looked at her watch. Seven o'clock, and dark. "Might as well do it," Fairy said. "Let's go . . . Can I drive?"

A FEW last things to do. She found an old T-shirt, cut it into strips, made a ten-foot-long soft-cotton fuse, soaked it in gasoline, and put it in a Ziploc bag. She'd string it out when she got there, and the Ziploc bag would keep the odor of gas out of the Benz. Got a bottle of Windex, a role of paper towels, and a pair of yellow plastic kitchen gloves, and put them in the Benz. She'd clean up the Honda's steering wheel and other plastic surfaces, just in case. And finally, she changed into a navy blue tracksuit and running shoes.

"I'd really like to fuck you," Loren said from the bedroom mirror. "Turns my crank when I watch you getting dressed.

"Don't talk to me like that," Alyssa said. She was cold, and frightened. Her life hung on what would happen in the next hour.

"He's talking to *me*," Fairy said.

"Oh, God," Alyssa groaned.

"Listen, you know—maybe it's time for me to drive," Fairy said. "Like, right now. Totally."

THE HANGAR AREA was deserted, dark and cold, and moving the car, for the first five hundred yards, was not a problem. But outside the gate, after she turned down the hill, a cop car came around a corner and fell in behind her.

Fairy was sitting on a plastic sheet; and became so obsessively careful, so slow and purposeful with her turn lights, that she flashed on the possibility that he'd check to see if she were drunk. When she turned the corner at the bottom of the hill, on Concord, he followed after her, and stayed behind. When she turned left, off Concord, though, he went on, apparently never giving her a thought.

She exhaled, and touched her forehead, found cold sweat. Nothing ever goes as planned. Never.

INSTEAD OF DRIVING directly to the site where she planned to burn the car, she did a couple of laps around the neighborhood, checking for police. And she said, "I can feel you there, Alyssa, you're slowing me down."

They had decided to burn the car against a chain-link fence, in a patch of weeds, behind a warehouse wall, where the view to the street would be blocked. If the fire was low enough, it might not be discovered for quite a while, she thought. Nothing was moving along her dirt road behind the place when she pulled in and killed the lights. She sat for a moment, letting her eyes adjust to the gloom, then slipped out of the car.

Cold. Colder than it felt in her driveway, or up at the airport. She shivered, looked around, couldn't see much; security lights down the way. She could hear cars from over on Concord . . . but nothing else.

The gas can was there, on the backseat. After a last look, she reached in and tipped it upside down between the front and back seats. The gas poured onto the floorboards; she got the gas-soaked rag out of the Ziploc bag, stretched it out, ten feet; waited for the gurgling to stop in the back of the car, looked around one last time, stressed, jittery, got a matchbook from her pocket, stood back from the end of the fuse, dropped a match on it, and turned to run.

Match went out: no fire. Went back, lit another match—the thick odor of gasoline flowed around the car—and dropped the match again and started to run. Stopped, almost started back, when she saw the fire start, and then begin working down the fuse.

She ran. She was a hundred feet away when the car went up with a huge WHOOOMMP and she thought *ohmigod* and the fire climbed higher than the roof of the warehouse, a pyramid of smoke and flame probably visible for a mile around, and she dug in and ran, and ran, and crossed the street and ran up the hill and in the distance, heard the sirens . . .

LATER, in the night.

At Frank Willett's house, a snug little ranch, with the incriminating knife in her pocket, she jogged along the street, away from her car, watching, watching, was about to turn in at the front door when she saw a woman walking toward her, on the other side of the street, carrying a grocery sack, and she went on by the house, turning her face away from the woman, jogging and thinking, *Nothing ever goes as planned.*

She jogged back, five minutes later, and this time, made the move.

And it went as planned . . .

Why was that? she wondered.

19

LUCAS SPENT THE morning arranging surveillance on Frank Willett, a loose one-man tag until they could decide whether or not to pick him up. He'd called Austin early and had gotten Willett's work schedule. He was teaching tai chi at one spa and had Pilates classes at two others.

"I've been thinking about Frank," Austin said. "He seems too gentle to kill anyone. But I can't let this go. I've got to check and make sure he's not selling dope in my places."

"Just take it easy for a couple of days, huh?" Lucas asked. "A couple days won't make any difference. We'll make some kind of decision by then."

She said she'd think about it.

AND HE HAD bureaucratic stuff to do, with the Republican convention security committee. After the committee meeting, he stopped at United Hospital to check on a friend who'd had an early-morning angiogram, and had gotten a couple of stents in his heart. After that, dropped down to the United cafeteria for a slice of pepperoni pizza and a bottle of diet Coke, and tried not to think about stents.

Coming up the ramp from the hospital's subterranean first floor, his cell phone rang: Carol. "You've been out of service," she said.

"Can't get anything in the hospital," he said. "What's up?"

"A cop is calling from San Francisco on Willett," she said. "He said he'd be there for another hour—that's a half hour now. I got a number."

LUTHER WANE sounded like a cheerful man, though he had a gravelly smoker's cough. Between hacks, he said, "I talked to the prosecutor and they don't want him. I mean, they'd take him, if it was free, but they don't want to pay to send somebody out there to get him."

"That sorta sucks," Lucas said.

"Yeah, well, they'll probably have to dismiss anyway. Even if they don't, he won't get any time. We got too many people in jail and the budget's all shot in the ass, and a skinny case on a small-time dealer that's six years old . . . they figure it'd cost us ten grand to come get him and they don't want to pay."

"But if he jumped bail . . ." Lucas said. It seemed ridiculous.

"That's another problem," Wane said. "He was bailed out with a court date to come. But the prosecutor in the case got killed and the paper got lost, and we can't prove that he was ever notified of his court date. And his lawyer at that time, a court-appointed guy, moved to New Mexico and is running an ashram or some shit, and . . . you see what I mean? Too much horseshit and not enough money."

"Yeah. Doesn't help me, though," Lucas said.

"You know what I'd do?"

"What?"

"I'd bust him anyway, if I was ready," Wane said. "On the California warrant. It's still good. Then you notify us, and it takes a while for the paper to get through the mill, and then some time to get back to you . . . You could have him inside for probably ten days or two weeks if you picked your weekends right. Bust him on a Friday, notify on a Monday, takes four or five days out here, we decline to prosecute the following Tuesday or Wednesday . . . and we can probably drag our feet a little."

"I might do that," Lucas said. "We only wanted a shot at squeezing him, anyway."

"So if I get some paper from you, I'll know what you're doing."

"Good enough," Lucas said. "The prosecutor—he wasn't stabbed or anything, was he?"

Wane laughed. "No. We got one of those two-story McDonald's here, you know? He takes his Big Mac and his fries upstairs to eat and read his newspaper, and when he finishes, he heads for the stairs, still reading the *New York Times*, trips and falls down the stairs and breaks his neck. He's dead on the scene."

"Jesus," Lucas said. "Anybody get sued?"

Wane laughed a little longer, the laughs interspersed with hacks. "He had an estranged wife. She testified that he'd come over twice a week and spend forty-five minutes trying to work through the estrangement. Doggy-style, for the most part, the rumor is. Anyway, she was still his wife, technically, and she sued for loss of companionship and got three-point-four million from McDonald's. *Then* she married the guy's boss. Heh-heh."

"If there's an afterlife, he's probably got a serious case of the red-ass," Lucas said.

"If there's an afterlife, he's got more problems than that," Wane said. "Nasty little bullet-headed know-it-all fuck."

LUCAS WAS BACK at the office and took a call from Sandy, the researcher: "I've got a Loren who might be interesting." When Lucas didn't immediately respond, she said, "You know—you had me looking up Lorens?"

"Oh, yeah. That didn't come to much," Lucas said.

"You still want this guy?" she asked.

"What's he look like?"

"He fits the general description. Dark hair, anyway. The key thing is, he went to the university at the same time as Frances, and it's likely, but not for sure, until I can check some more, that they were in some of the same classes."

"Jeez," Lucas said. "That might be something. Shoot it over here."

The photo popped up a couple minutes later in his e-mail. He looked at it, called Jackson, the photographer, and asked if he could get a print. "Forward it to me," Jackson said. "By the time you get down here, I'll have it."

Lucas forwarded Sandy's e-mail, got a diet Coke from the machine, and walked downstairs to Jackson's cubbyhole. Jackson said, "I'm doing a little work on it." He had the photo on a computer screen and was touching it up. "A little Photoshop."

A minute or so later, he tapped a couple of keys, got up a response box, clicked his mouse, and the printer churned out a glossy print. "Another piece-of-shit photograph—I wonder why nobody makes an effort to get decent ID shots? They should at least look human."

"Maybe you should start a campaign," Lucas said. He looked at the photo. Could it be the man in the alley? Could be.

He called Austin, who was at home.

"I'm ten minutes away—I want to run down and show you a photograph," he said.

"Of who?"

"I'd rather have you respond to it sort of . . . spontaneously."

AT THE AUSTINS', a man in a jean jacket, jeans, and cowboy boots was putting a cardboard carton in the back of a pickup, where a half-dozen more cartons were already stacked. Austin was at the door, and when Lucas came up, she waved at the pickup driver, who was backing the truck out, and said to Lucas, "Finally pulled the trigger on Frances's clothes. Sent them off to Goodwill."

"That's got to be harsh," he said.

"Had to be done. She's gone," she said. And, "Come in."

He stepped inside and said, "Just need a minute." He had the photo in a manila envelope, slipped it out and handed it to her.

She looked at it, and her face turned white and she blurted, "Oh, my God. It's Loren Doyle."

"This is the guy? The Loren?" Lucas asked.

"Oh my God." Her hand was at her throat. She pushed the photo back at him and said, "That's the guy, but I just remembered, when you handed it to me . . . I mean, I never knew him well, just saw him that once, but now I know why I remembered him."

Lucas spread his hands: "What?"

"He's dead," she said. "He was killed in an awful boat accident on the Mississippi, right below downtown St. Paul. He was in one of those jet boats with a couple of other guys and they hit a barge. I think there were three people and they all got killed."

"Ah, jeez, I remember that," Lucas said. "But that was . . ."

"Way before Frances. I remember now. He was in one of her classes, they were on a project together, a case study for a business class. About General Electric or General Mills or General Motors. And then she told me he was killed. They weren't close, but we were both shocked. You know how people are when it's somebody you just met and was alive and everything?"

"Damnit," Lucas said. He looked at the photo. "I thought we were on to something." He looked at her, still white. "Are you okay?"

"It gave me such a start," she said. "Like he came back from the grave."

LUCAS WAS BACK on the road two minutes later, driving away with the uneasy sense that something had just gotten by him. Was it possible that Loren *wasn't* dead? That Austin was lying about it? But it seemed improbable—it'd be too easy to check. He thought about it, then called Sandy: "I've got something else for you. I need it ASAP. This Loren guy . . ."

He was almost back at the office when he took a call from Cheryl Weiner, the agent watching Frank Willett. "Lucas, this guy is getting ready to run," she said. "He just brought a duffel out to his truck and he seems to be in a sweat. He was supposed to be doing a Pilates class and he skipped it . . . Okay, here he comes again. He's got skis."

"Stick with him," Lucas said. "I'm on the way."

He was halfway to Minneapolis when she called back: "He's in his truck, he's backing out, you want me to block him? Want me to grab him?"

"No, no, no . . . we don't know what he's up to, if he's got a gun. If he's our guy, he's killed four people, he might feel like his back's against the wall. Just tag him. We'll get some help."

She tagged him, staying back. He showed no sign of looking behind him, in his haste to get out, she said. She took him up to I—94 and then north, as Lucas closed in from behind. He called Carol, got piped to the highway patrol district office, and asked for help. Two patrol cars were nearby and available, one north of Willett, and one south. The one on the south blew past Lucas, and Lucas, still on with the patrol's district office, warned them that he was going to fall in behind, and he did.

The car coming down from the north got off, waited for Willett and Weiner to pass, and then fell in behind. When the south car caught up, the two patrolmen moved on him: fell in behind, with lights and sirens, pulled him over, blocked front and back. Lucas and Weiner came in behind, waited for a lull in the traffic, and got out.

Willett didn't resist and was cuffed by the time they were out. He was dressed in loose nylon pants and a sweatshirt. His brown hair was undone and fell almost to his shoulders.

"What?" he asked Lucas.

"We're arresting you on a California warrant for possession of marijuana, and on suspicion of murder in the death of Frances Elaine Austin," Lucas said. "You have the right to remain silent . . ."

Willett's face tightened up: "What? Frances? What're you talking about, man?"

". . . the right to have an attorney present during questioning . . ."

"Man! What are you talking about?" Willett yanked his arms against the highway patrolman, who jerked him backward away from Lucas.

". . . cannot afford an attorney, one will be appointed for you. Do you understand this, Mr. Willett?"

"Yeah, yeah, yeah. What about Frances? I didn't have anything to do with Frances," he said.

"Let's get him off the highway," Lucas said to one of the patrolmen. "If one of you guys can haul his butt down to Ramsey, maybe the other guy could help us pull the car apart."

"Pull my car . . . wait a minute."

"Why'd you decide to run?" Lucas asked. "Somebody tell you about us?"

Willett's eyes strayed away, then came back and he shrugged. "Well—yeah. But I don't know who it was. Some chick. A client, I guess. She heard a rumor about the dope thing, said she'd hate to see me in trouble. Called me on my cell."

"How many people have your cell phone number?"

"About a million," he said. "All my clients. You know, Frances— I didn't have anything to do with Frances, but I think I better have a lawyer. I'm gonna need one, aren't I?"

"You got any money?" Lucas asked.

"A thousand, maybe."

"We'll get you one," Lucas said.

The truck had nothing but clothing and outdoor gear. The highway patrolman would arrange for a tow, and Lucas thanked Weiner and said goodbye, and called Carol. "We need to get a search warrant for Willett's place and a couple crime-scene guys to go through it."

"Probably be a few hours," she said. "Maybe tomorrow?"

"That's okay; I'm going back down to talk to Austin again," he said.

Another dead half hour, going back across town. Austin came to the door, a small frown on her face. "Something more?"

"Who did you tell about us watching Frank Willett?"

She posed for a moment, then said, "Gina Nassif in Human Resources. Oh, shit. What happened?"

"Somebody called Willett and he made a run for it," Lucas said.

"That should tell you something," she said.

"Maybe he didn't want to go back to California," Lucas said. "Anyway, I asked you—"

"I had to talk to Gina. If we have an employee handing out drugs, I could lose my shirt. I asked her to be discreet, but . . ."

"What?"

"She tends to gossip a little bit," Austin said.

"Ahhh . . . You couldn't wait for a couple of days?"

She pushed a lip out. "I'm sorry if it messed something up."

Didn't sound sorry, Lucas thought.

Late afternoon, traffic building: Lucas decided to stop at the drugstore apartment and watch Heather Toms for a while, then head home for dinner. Let Willett stew overnight, search his place first thing in the morning.

The apartment was empty when he got there: Del had been around, leaving behind a foam coffee cup, empty except for a wad of paper. Lucas turned on the boom box, dropped in a Norah Jones disk from a stack of disks on the floor, kicked back in the desk chair and picked up the glasses. Nobody visible in the apartment across the street, but he could see the light of the television flickering on the wall.

He called Weather and she said they'd have center-cut pork chops, sweet potatoes, and corn bread. He said he'd be home at six.

He sat and thought about Willett, and Alyssa Austin, and the others in the Austin case: he'd missed something that day, something about Austin, maybe, and it was right there, almost close enough to touch.

Thought about it, went to the refrigerator, found that somebody had drunk three of the six diet Cokes he'd put inside, took one, twisted off the top, then did a half-dozen toe touches, stretching his bad leg. Damn thing still hurt, but more of an ache, now, than the rippling hot pain that he'd had earlier.

As he did one of the stretches, Heather Toms stood up, just visible at the edge of one of the window frames, pointed a remote at an out-of-sight TV, clicked the TV off. A couple of minutes later, she went to the door, and her mother wheeled in.

Heather was looking pretty good, Lucas thought. She went into the bedroom and dug through her closet, tried on a couple pairs of shoes, and then walked back to the living room, disappeared, reappeared in a dark raincoat, said something to her mother, and headed for the door. Going out. Someplace where she'd wear heels.

Lucas looked at his watch: five o'clock. He had a little time.

WHISTLING AS HE went, he locked the apartment and hurried down the stairs, to the end of the block, and slipped into the Porsche. Heather appeared a moment later, up from the underground parking ramp, in her red Lexus SC 430. Not a hard car to follow, and he stayed back as she turned north on Snelling Avenue, then east on Randolph, and south on I—35. They tracked south and then west of I—494 to the Mall of America. She parked in a ramp at the west end of the complex, looked at her watch, then wandered down into Nordstrom.

Lucas stayed well back; a narrow-eyed saleswoman started tracking him as he cruised the women's clothing, and finally she came over and asked, sharply, as though she were sure she couldn't, "Can I help you find something, sir?"

He took out his ID: "I'm a police officer. I'm working. Go away and don't look at me."

She looked at the ID and then said, "Okay," and walked away.

HEATHER WAS LOOKING at her watch again—it was 5:25 on Lucas's watch—and headed for the store exit that led into the main mall. He followed her, still way back along the north wing of the first floor. At the center exit, she stopped at a bank of telephones and looked at her watch again. Now it was 5:28.

Sonofabitch, Siggy Toms is calling her at 5:30, Lucas thought.

He got on his cell and called Carol, but Carol was gone. Called the duty guy and told him to set up a phone trace, he'd have the number and the time coming. Then, he thought, a phone rang, because Heather turned and picked it up.

Her face didn't look that happy when she was talking. Not a lover's face, he thought, although given her other love interest, maybe Siggy was a problem, rather than a solution.

At that moment, a tall man, thin as a rail, wearing a battered white cowboy hat, a pearl-button shirt, and jeans worn nearly white with weather, stepped out of a store with a shopping bag, looked down toward Lucas, looked the other way, and wandered off.

Something about him, Lucas thought. Where had he seen the guy? What the hell was it? Was he hooked to Heather Toms somehow? But the man went on past Heather without looking at her, bow-legged and clunky in his boots . . .

Thirty feet away, Heather was talking, her face and body animated; an argument? After a minute or so, she hung up, smiled, as if she'd accomplished something, and walked back toward Lucas. Lucas stepped inside a junk store—a store full of useless shit—and watched her walk past, and let her go.

The man with the cowboy hat was gone.

Don't know what that was all about, the cowboy, he thought. Something though.

And Siggy, he thought, as he walked down to check the phone, was coming.

AT THE DINNER TABLE, over the sweet potatoes and pork chops, he told Weather about it. ". . . calling from a pay phone in Chattanooga. That's a long day's drive out of Miami—I bet he's on the way."

"I'd hate to see the baby at risk," she said. "If Siggy comes, do you have to take him at the apartment? With Heather there?"

"We'll take him when we see him," Lucas said. "He is a *bad* guy."

"I'd like to be there," Letty said. "Be a good story for the station."

"You are *not* going to be there," Weather said.

Letty had a half-assed high-school internship at Channel Three, through one of Lucas's former lovers, the mother of his other daughter. She asked him, "What do you think?"

Lucas said, "Over my dead body."

"Jeez Louise . . ."

"When Siggy comes in, we won't be fooling around," Lucas said. "He's been gone a year and more. He thinks he can sneak in here, and back out—he's probably got some cash stashed here, that he couldn't get at. But when we take him, he's gonna know that he won't get back out a second time. He'll be inside for twenty or thirty, and the feds might tack more onto that. He's not gonna be in a mood for any pissing around."

"Boy," Letty said. "I'd give my left nut to be there."

"Forget it," Lucas said, not rising to the "nut" bait.

"You can let the SWAT guys take him," Weather said to Lucas. "You've been shot enough this year."

"Got that right," Lucas said.

20

LUCAS ARRIVED at Willett's house at nine-fifteen, a little later than he'd intended. The crime-scene crew had already gone in with the search warrant and was doing a preliminary walk-through with a dope-sniffing German shepherd. Lucas waited until they finished with the office nook off the kitchen, then got all the paper he could find, and began looking for Frances's fifty thousand dollars.

He didn't find it—no receipts for large purchases, no bank deposits, no new warranties. On the other hand, if the fifty thousand had gone for dope, there wouldn't be any of that—but there should either be a surge of money from somewhere, or there should be some dope. Willett hadn't been carrying anything in the truck, money or dope, and now the mutt couldn't find anything at the house.

When the dope-sniffing dog was gone, the search began in earnest: it would go on for most of the day, but ten minutes after it started, one of the crime-scene guys whistled: "Got a knife."

Lucas got up to look. The crime-scene guy had taken all the clothes out of the bottom drawer of the unpainted bureau in Willett's bedroom. There, in the back, a butcher knife's handle protruded from a rectangle of cardboard—the knife blade had been slipped into the edge of the cardboard, and pushed deep, with the cardboard acting as a scabbard.

As Lucas watched, they took photos of the room with the bureau drawer open; then a medium shot that included only the bureau, with the knife visible in the bottom of the open drawer; and then a close-up of the knife in place, with a scale next to it. Then they repeated the sequence with a second camera, as a backup.

When they were done, the tech lifted the knife out of the drawer with gloved hands, holding it by the edge of the cardboard, put it three inches under his nose, and said, "Huh. I think we've got some blood."

"Let me see."

"Don't touch," the tech said, as he held the blade three inches below Lucas's nose. "Look right where the blade goes into the handle. See that brown crust?"

There wasn't much, but it was there. "Can't believe it's a pork chop," Lucas said.

"We'll find out," the tech said.

Lucas snagged the supervisor: "I want to get the knife back to the lab right away. I want to know whether it's human, and the blood type, if you've got a big enough sample to do that without fucking up the DNA."

The supervisor squinted at the knife, turned it over, made a supervisory decision and eased the blade out of the cardboard by a half-inch, said, "Got a little more on the back . . . should be enough."

"How long on the DNA?" Lucas asked.

"If we pound it . . . thirty-six hours."

"Pound it. We don't care about budget or overtime. Pound it."

NOT MUCH to do until the preliminary results came back, which would be early afternoon. On the way back to St. Paul, thinking about Willett and the knife, he found the car drifting off I—94 and up the Snelling Avenue exit. He rolled past Heather Toms's apartment and around the block: he'd never watched her at midday. When he pulled up to the drugstore, he saw Del's car, and then Del, coming down the street with a sack from a bagel place and a cup of coffee.

"Thought you were tied up this morning," Del said, when they met at the door into the apartment level.

"So'd I," Lucas said.

He told the story about the knife, and Del said, "That's the stupidest goddamn thing I've ever heard. He's running because he thinks he might get hit by the cops, but he leaves behind a knife he's used to kill four people, with blood on the blade? What the fuck was he smokin'?"

"Well, he might have been smokin' something," Lucas said. "He's been into dope, and he might've had that fifty grand to play with."

THE TOMS apartment was empty. Heather had gone someplace and taken the baby. Lucas told Del about the phone call from Chattanooga, and he said, "Wonder if she's running?"

"She'd be leaving a lot behind."

"That's how Siggy punked us the last time," Del said. "Parked his car at Target, walked away from it, never looked back."

"You think Heather would leave the kid's jammies?" He passed the glasses to Del, who took them, did a tour of Heather's apartment as he chewed on one of the bagels, then said, "Probably not."

"She would have taken the jammies," Lucas said. "Unless she's a totally heartless bitch."

"Could be that," Del said. "That guy she was screwing—that was Hilaire Jukos, another Lithuanian, Siggy's left-hand man. I looked him up."

"What's this with Heather and Lithuanians?" Lucas asked.

"Well, they got a reputation, you know—Lithuanians tend to be very well hung, the best in Europe. That could turn the head of a former Edina High School cheerleader."

"I thought the Italians . . ."

Del was shaking his head. "That's getting it up—Italians lead the league in getting it up. Lithuanians are purely size."

"Sounds like you've done your research."

Del shrugged: "I'm a professional detective."

At that moment, a man came out of the apartment building, looked both ways down the sidewalk, zipped up his jacket, and walked away from them, wobbling a bit. Lucas put the glasses on him, the way he walked—was that the cowboy from the mall? No. This guy was shorter, with long hair, and seemed to be younger, but still had that wobbling, pointy-toed walk.

Lucas took the glasses down. "Sonofabitch."

"What?"

"I just had an epiphany," Lucas said.

"You can get some ointment for that."

"No—I'm serious," Lucas said. "I've been seeing all these guys in cowboy boots, and I remember—I told people this at the time—the guy who shot me seemed to have a limp. He didn't have a limp—he was running in cowboy boots."

"Yeah? Is that a big deal?"

"I don't know," Lucas said. He took his cell phone out of his pocket and punched up Austin's cell.

She came up and said, "Hello, Lucas. Are you still mad at me?"

"Yup—but that's not why I'm calling," he said. "The other day when you were loading those cartons of Frances's clothes into the pickup truck for Goodwill—did you hire that driver? Did you know him?"

"That was Ricky Davis, Helen's boyfriend. Why?"

"What's he do?"

"I think, uh, he works nights for a wrecker service in South St. Paul. Then he's got a plow blade for his pickup and he plows snow in the winter. He sells firewood . . . that kind of thing."

"Okay," he said.

"So tell me . . ."

"Nope. Last time I told you, you blabbed. I don't think this is anything, anyway, just that the guy was wearing cowboy boots, and I find that interesting," Lucas said. "But, let me ask you a favor. I don't know how to put this, delicately . . ."

"You don't have to be delicate," Austin said.

"Okay. Could you please keep your fuckin' mouth shut about this? That I asked about Helen's boyfriend? Just keep it shut."

"I swear to God, I will," she said. "Besides, with Frank, I didn't exactly blab—it was business."

"And don't start looking sideways at Helen," Lucas said.

"I promise . . . I sometimes go days without even seeing her. I'll just stay away for a while."

"Do that," Lucas said. "I'll tell you about it tomorrow or the next day."

Del was curious. When Lucas got off the phone, he asked, "Break the case?"

"I don't know," Lucas said. "Something might have happened." He dialed Carol. When she came up, he said, "Hey—we've got another job for Jackson and his camera."

HEATHER CAME into her apartment carrying grocery sacks, as Lucas was on the phone, and then went back out, and came back a minute later with more sacks as Lucas got off, and Del said, "That's a lotta food for Momma and baby."

"I'm telling you, Siggy is coming," Lucas said. "If he was in Chattanooga last night, he'll be in northern Illinois tonight, and up here tomorrow afternoon or evening, depending on how hard he's pushing it. Not too hard, I think, because he wouldn't want to get stopped for speeding."

"He wouldn't be driving under his own ID," Del said.

"Still, he wouldn't speed. He didn't last as long as he did, dealing big-time dope, being careless."

Del, with the glasses, said, "Uh-oh."

"What?"

"She just unloaded a six-pack of Heineken."

Lucas could see the green bottles with his naked eye. "There you go," he said. "She hasn't had a drink since the bump showed up."

"Whoops . . . looks like a bottle of Stoli."

Lucas said, "Siggy-Siggy-Siggy . . . come to Mama."

THE LAB TECH called a little after noon, about the blood on the blade. "It's human and it's A-positive. No prints on the knife. I've started the DNA, we got a good sample, we'll crush it, but it'll be a couple of days."

"Thirty-six hours, I was told," Lucas said.

"That's two days, unless you want the results at midnight," the tech said.

Lucas called Harry Anson, the Minneapolis homicide cop: "We're looking at a guy who was an employee of Alyssa Austin's. Hit his house this morning."

"I heard."

"Yeah, sorry about that, but things were moving. Anyway, we got human blood on the knife, no prints. The blood is A-positive. I don't have the paper right here on the three who were killed in Minneapolis."

"It's Patricia Shockley. A-pos," Anson said. "Sonofabitch. You started the DNA?"

"Thirty-six hours. We got the guy locked up in Ramsey on a California warrant, it's probably good for two weeks."

He explained the California problem and Anson said, "If we can't nail it down in two weeks, we won't get it. Hell, the knife is probably enough. The circumstances, if he was nailing Frances *and* her mother . . . there's plenty of motive in that, somewhere. Get a shrink on the stand . . ."

"We could do that."

"Lucas, I knew there was some reason I liked you," Anson said. "I just couldn't put my finger on it."

"Yeah, well, I'm heading over to Ramsey to squeeze Willett's pointy little head," Lucas said. "You better be there."

"Gimme a time."

WILLETT HAD A public defender named Tony Mose, rhymed with Rose, who met Lucas in the lobby of the Ramsey jail and trailed him back to the interview room, where Willett was already waiting with a deputy. Mose was dressed in a somber black suit and white tie, like a guy going to a funeral. He was not, Lucas thought, a bad attorney.

"You get a chance to talk to him?" Lucas asked Mose on the way back.

"I did. I'll tell you what—this time, for once, I might actually have an innocent guy."

"Nah." Lucas shook his head.

"I'm serious, Lucas, the guy's got that thing about him—he didn't know what in the hell I was talking about when I asked him about the knife," Mose said. "He said *you* must've put it there."

"You hardly ever hear that," Lucas said. "The cops must've did it."

"The difference is, I think he *meant* it," Mose said.

Willett had had a bad night, as Lucas had hoped—his eyes were puffed with fatigue, and when they came in the room, he looked up and said, "Now what?"

Mose laid it out: Lucas had some questions. Mose would stop any questions that were improper, and any questions that Willett didn't feel like answering, he didn't have to answer.

"I didn't do a thing," Willett said. "Wait, I did, you know? I had some bud back in San Francisco, but it was all for personal use. I wasn't dealing or anything. This Frances thing, this is crazy. I had nothing to do with Frannie getting killed."

"Did Frances know that you'd been sleeping with her mother before she was sleeping with you?" Lucas asked.

Mose said, "Keep in mind, you don't have to answer."

"But also keep in mind that sleeping with both of them isn't a crime and we can prove that you were anyway—we'll be giving Mr. Mose a copy of a note we took out of Frances's purse, addressed to you," Lucas said to Willett.

Anson came through the door: "Did I miss anything?"

"Just started," Lucas said. He turned to Willett. "You're in a lot of trouble, Frank. We need to talk about the knife, but we need to talk about this other stuff, too. If you did it, we're going to put your ass in prison. If you didn't, we're your best chance of staying out. Now—did Frances know?"

Willett bobbed his head a couple of times and then said, "I think she found out. I don't know when. But things were going sour at the end. I hadn't even talked to her for a week before she disappeared."

"You didn't exactly hurry up to give the cops whatever information you had, after she disappeared," Anson said.

"What would you have done?" Willett asked. "I didn't know where she went, or why she went. But if a rich girl disappears, and the poor guy she's been hanging out with, it turns out they were breaking up, and if that guy's got a dope thing hanging over his head . . . well, what are the cops going to think?"

He was right about that, Lucas thought: that was what he *did* think.

HIS RELATIONSHIP WITH Frances peaked in the summer, Willett said, then cooled off in the fall, and by December, they'd stopped sleeping together. "I told her right from the start that she couldn't let her mother know. I mean, I knew what would happen if she did—Alyssa would be all over the place. I'd lose my job, Frances would be gone, I'd be back at Snowbird flippin' burgers. When we started breaking it off, I said, 'Please, please, don't tell your mom. She'll fire me.' And Frannie said she wouldn't tell. We didn't hate each other, but she was getting all corporate, and I am . . . what I am. We could see that we weren't going to make it."

"How often were you over at the Austin house?" Lucas asked.

"When I was going with Alyssa, you know, a couple times a week," Willett said. "I never went there with Frannie. I mean, we were afraid that Helen would tell Alyssa, and that'd be it. There wasn't any reason for us to go there. We went to Frannie's place, or mine."

They pushed and pried, with Mose as an umpire, but couldn't get Willett to admit any animus toward either of the Austins. "You know, I think sex is a perfectly natural process, and I've had relationships with quite a few very nice women and I valued all of them and I'm still friends with most of them and some of them still sleep with me sometimes, and that's all cool," Willett said. "It's not like I'm some crazy geek, and when a woman goes away, that's it, my world is over. There are women all over the place, and lots of them are pretty good."

"Good in bed?" Anson asked.

"That's not what I meant—I meant, pretty good. In general," Willett said. "Good people. With a few witches mixed in."

"You a Goth?" Lucas asked.

"Do I look like a Goth? No, I'm not a Goth," he said. "Frances was a Goth for a while, but she was beginning to see that it was all pretty make-believe. She said to me, one time, 'I'd like to meet a Goth who could change a flippin' tire.' So she was pretty much done with that scene, I think. Play-acting."

THE KNIFE.

"We found the knife, Frank."

"You guys—"

"No, and you gotta know that's bullshit," Lucas said. "I was there, we had three crime-scene techs who didn't know this case from a dognapping, and they found it, not me. And they went in before I got there, so nobody planted the knife. And the knife has Patty Shockley's blood on it—it's human blood, and it's her blood type."

"I don't even know Patty Shockley. I don't know any of them besides Frances."

Lucas rode over him: "There's enough blood to get a DNA match, which will be coming. But we're willing to bet, and I'd stake my next year's pay on it, that it's her blood. How'd it get there, Frank?"

Willett slapped both of his hands on the top of his head, face down, and smoothed his hair back with his fingers, dragging at it, and said, "Honest to God, I don't know. I honest to God, I told Mr. Mose . . . I honest to God think that one of you cops put it there. Maybe not one of you, but some cop. I mean, there was no knife there. No knife. No fuckin' knife. It's like I've been dropping acid or something, everything is crazy. I just don't know what happened."

"Have you had any blackouts from the drugs you've used?" Anson asked. "Pot, or acid, or coke or meth or . . ."

"I don't use any of that shit—I smoke a little bud from time to time, but that other shit will kill your body. And I can't afford acid or coke. I wouldn't take meth, that's like sniffing glue, it'll fuck your brain. I just can't figure . . ."

He confessed that he probably had no alibis for the nights of the killings, simply because he hung out at night. "That's what I do. I hang out, couple clubs, tavern, walk around on Hennepin Avenue, whatever. Hang out."

They talked about his relationship with Austin: had that dissolved in anger? "No. Well, you know, maybe you'd have to ask her. But we stopped when she just got busy with taxes, and we didn't start up again. I knew it was just a thing—she knew it, I knew it, it felt good, and about the time it should have started coming apart, it did."

"She gave you that truck," Lucas said.

"She did. She was a sweetie," Willett said. "It wasn't payment, or anything—she gave it to me because I had this old piece of shit that had holes in the floorboards and I just about gassed myself every time I drove it. I had to keep the windows open. So she got me this truck—surprised the shit out of me."

"And it wasn't for the sex, it wasn't to say goodbye."

"Might have been a little bit to say goodbye, but the basic thing is, the Austins have so much money that she just really didn't care how much it cost," Willett said. "The way she thought was, *If I did what he did, rock-climbed and surfed and skied, this is the kind of truck I'd want.* So that's what she got. The money, the money was nothing. A bad day on the stock market, she'd lose ten times what that truck cost."

THEY WORKED HIM, and pushed him, teased him and tried to make him angry, but he only got sadder and more confused. When they were done, they all stood up, and Lucas called the deputy, and Mose said he wanted to talk for a few more minutes, and Lucas and Anson stepped toward the door.

Willett said, from his chair, "Officer Davenport—when you saw that knife, in the drawer, what'd you think?"

Lucas shrugged. "I don't know. I thought, maybe, *There's something.*"

"You didn't think, *That's the stupidest thing I've ever seen in my life?* That a guy would go on the run but leave the bloody knife right in the first place somebody would look, in the bottom drawer of a chest of drawers, under some old underwear? Maybe I should have tacked a sign on the thing that said, 'Knife inside.' 'Murder Weapon Here.' I mean, it's just so *fucking stupid.*"

As Del said—but Lucas dodged. "People who murder other people usually aren't wizards," Lucas said.

"But it's got to be the stupidest thing you've ever heard of."

"No, no," Lucas said. "Not the stupidest. But . . . it's up there."

"Think about that," Willett said. "Think about it."

OUT IN THE HALLWAY, Anson said, "Loser."

Lucas said, "We didn't move him much."

"I'll background him, if you want."

"That'd be good," Lucas said. "There's quite a bit of paper over at his house—we've got his cell phone records, address book. Any kind of a profile . . ."

WHEN LUCAS was alone in his car, he thought about Anson's "loser" label. Lucas had been an excellent college hockey player—second team all-WCHA in his senior year. He wasn't pro level, but he was almost pro level. He could have fooled himself into thinking he was. Could have hooked up with a minor league team, could have hung on to the edges for a few years.

But he hadn't. He'd known he wasn't good enough, so he looked around for something that he'd like, and that he'd be good at. He joined the biggest police department around, with the intention of becoming a homicide cop. He'd done that, and a few other things that came along the way.

If he'd gone the other way—tried for the pros—where would he be now? Flipping burgers in hockey's equivalent of Snowbird? The line between winner and loser was pretty thin, and the paths were pretty crooked.

Willett was smart enough; women seemed to like him; he had some skills, some abilities . . . And he was coming up on forty, had a thousand dollars and a truck given to him by a woman, and at nights he hung out.

Seemed like waiting for death—and yet the line was so thin, and the paths so crooked.

21

ALYSSA COULD FEEL the Fairy, there, behind her own eyes.

The Fairy had been her, when she was a young girl, before Alyssa fell into the hands of the Coach. The Coach had known what Alyssa could do in the water, had seen it when she was eight, had pushed her with a ruthless discipline and determination to do what she, the Coach, hadn't been able to do: win. Win all the time. If she'd come up in the right year, she might have gone to the Olympics, but that was the breaks of the game. As it was, she'd been the best athlete at the University of Minnesota, despite what some of the football players might have thought . . .

But getting there had been brutal, and terminated an otherwise unremarkable childhood.

Her parents hadn't seen the brutality behind the swimming: they'd just seen their kid's name in lights, at the end of the pool, most of the time with a big "1" in front of it. The Coach had buried the Fairy . . . little bits had resurfaced over the years, perhaps, with her playful-yet-serious interest in astrology, and particularly in the tarot, but mostly, the Fairy was buried under purpose and will and discipline.

Which, in the end, was the only thing that would get her through this.

LOREN SAT on a chair turned away from the living room table, while Alyssa lounged in an easy chair, a glass in hand. A bottle of Amon-Ra shiraz from Australia sat on the end table beside her, eighty dollars a bottle, and worth it.

Loren was dressed in a sixties-rocker-look brown-velvet suit, narrow pant legs, and a pinched waist on the jacket, with heavy brown brogans that would have been good for kicking someone to death. Alyssa said, "One thing that's hard for me is to understand why you're here. Are you really here? Are you an external reality, or are you all in my mind? Could I take a picture of you with a camera?"

He shook his head. "I don't know about the camera, but I'm at least as real as Fairy."

She wagged a finger at him. "No, you're not. I know what Fairy is. Would you like to talk to her?"

Her voice pitched up and she giggled: "All right, here I am," Fairy said. "You wanted Fairy. Woman with a knife-edge wit."

Loren said, "Quit messing around, Alyssa. I need you back. We've got to talk."

Alyssa came back, a slack smile playing around her lips: "See, I know what Fairy is. She's me—another piece of me, and I think we'll eventually get back together. We'll heal. Other people have had this disorder—maybe my case is a little different than others, but all cases are a little different than others. Anyway: I understand it. I can look it up on the Internet. I can read stories about people who have gone through it. But you, Loren—the only people who have experiences like you, are total goofs. Crazy people. But you seem so . . . rational. Are you the devil?"

"There is no devil," Loren said.

"Isn't that what the devil would say? You talked me into all these evil things . . . I killed three people—or Fairy did—and you were right there, eating it up, pushing me. If you're not the devil, you're a pretty good mock-up."

Loren looked away: "Well, I'm not the devil. I'm dead and I have a dead person's psychic ability. I could feel the hands of those people on Frances's shoulder, and if Frances were here to talk to you, she would tell you the same thing. Killing them was the right thing to do."

"And Frances is still dead," Alyssa said.

"But she's not gone," Loren said. "I can feel her aura. She's around here, but maybe not for long. She might be getting on the boat, to go over."

Alyssa sighed. She had heard it before. "And over . . . is heaven? Or hell? Or purgatory? Or what?"

"Who's to know who hasn't gone?" Loren said. "When I've seen the boat, sometimes it's all lit up and cheerful, like the *Delta Queen,* with the calliope playing, and sometimes it's this dark little rotten boat with a red stern wheel . . . Who knows where it's going?"

"Whatever," she said, waving him off. "There's nothing to do about it now."

"Unless you see Frances, of course," Loren said. "You have to be prepared."

"Oh . . . bullshit. Bullshit." Now she was angry; wineangry, more wind than real violence to it. "You are nothing more than an illusion. I wonder what Xanax would do to you, if I got rid of a few anxieties for a while?"

Didn't faze him: "You can take what you want, but your problem isn't going away," Loren said. "In fact, your problem has gotten worse. When you let Fairy out the other night, you let her out at exactly the wrong time."

Alyssa leaned forward, elbows on her thighs, an empty wineglass in her hands. "Lucas Davenport," she said.

"Yes." Loren stood up, thrust his hands in his pants pockets, wandered around the room looking at the paintings, stopped in front of the landscape by Kidd. "You know, this landscape. Those are the bluffs over the Mississippi just downstream from St. Paul—right where the river turns."

"That's right," Alyssa said.

"It's odd—it's not completely realistic, but it's completely real. The other odd thing is, *that's* where the riverboats leave from. Oh, a little upstream, by the upper landing, but right there in that stretch of river. Weird that you should have this painting, hanging here."

"Forget the riverboats!" Alyssa snapped. "We need to focus on Davenport. Something's going on with Helen. Why's he looking at Helen? Why's he looking at Ricky?"

Loren walked away from the painting, around the table, sat down again, his eyes sliding past hers. "Maybe he found something. Maybe they had something to do with Frances. If they did, this is a serious problem, Alyssa. Right now, he thinks all four killings were done by the same person. If he decides that Helen or Ricky were involved with Frances . . . then why was that knife in Frank Willett's apartment?"

"I have to think . . ." she said, dropping her face into her hands.

"You have to think as Alyssa—not as Fairy," Loren said. "Fairy is the impetuous one. She's the one who wanted to do the car and knife in the same night. She almost blew herself up with the car."

That made Alyssa smile. It had been one hell of a blast, all right. She'd been both frightened and exhilarated when she got to the top of the hill and ran toward the private plane hangars. "That *was* pretty amazing."

"Amazing," Loren said. "And she got away with it. But there was no need to do the *knife* that same night. If we'd had time to think, we could have directed Davenport at Frank, without giving up the knife. We would have been better with the ambiguity . . . but the knife is a hard fact. There has to be an answer to it."

"Helen," Alyssa said after a while. "Helen knew that I was sleeping with Frank. We used to come here in the afternoons, send her off to the other end of the house. But she knew what was happening."

"Could we set her up if we need to? Point Davenport at Frank?" Loren wondered.

"He's already looking in her direction. If he comes to us for more information—we give it to him," Alyssa said. She refilled the wineglass, shook out the last couple of drops. "We tell him that she knew about Frank Willett. And this fifty thousand dollars that he's been looking for . . . all of Frances's important mail came here. Bank statements. Estate stuff. Who'd be better placed to intercept them than Helen?"

She frowned and asked, "Is Helen that smart?" A little drunk, answered her own question: "Maybe she is."

Then, continuing, "So we can push him at Helen."

Loren said, "We can push him at Helen, but what if he doesn't bite? There's always the question of alibi. If Helen has a hard alibi for even one of the killings, then . . . that's a big problem."

Fairy: "A problem that we can take care of. We take care of Davenport."

ALYSSA: "There's a bad idea. Lucas is good-looking and gentlemanly and all that, but one inch below the surface, there's a thug. And he's also a police officer."

Fairy: "My impression of him is this: he's doing this in his head.

He's running on instinct. He's not filing the paperwork. He doesn't have any paperwork. Paperwork is for other people. If he begins to suspect us and shows it—we pop him. Who could possibly expect that the beautiful Alyssa Austin, heiress and rich woman, could shoot a thug like Lucas Davenport and get away with it? Who'd believe that she could even think of it?"

"Shoot?" Alyssa said.

"A knife won't work," Fairy said. "If he begins to suspect, he won't let us get close enough. And like you said, he's big and tough. He's not some skinny Goth kid."

"How then?"

"The best way would be to watch him and catch him when he's going out at night," Fairy said. "Do the jogger routine again. Shoot him, and run. One shot in the heart. It won't make any difference how tough he is, he won't live through that."

Alyssa closed her eyes: "God, it gives me a headache, thinking about it. We're much better off trying to tie it to Helen."

Loren nodded: "Absolutely. But take Fairy's point, with my point, and put them together—if Helen has a hard alibi, then it doesn't leave a lot of candidates for the other three killings. There are people who have seen you, as Fairy, and he has talked to some of them. Eventually, he may get around to having them look at you. But *he's* the only one who would do that. These other people, the Minneapolis cops, have no idea about you."

"I could do it," Fairy said. "I could do it just like I did the car."

"The car was just a lump of metal—it wasn't big and mean, it wasn't carrying a gun, it wasn't alive," Alyssa said.

"I don't care. I can do it," Fairy said. "I'm not saying we should, I'm just saying that if worse comes to worse, I can do it."

ALYSSA, REALLY feeling the wine now—the last glass had done it—looked at Loren.

"Well, what are you doing?" she asked.

"What do you mean?"

"What are you doing? Right now?"

He caught on, and smiled. "You want to go upstairs?"

"You might talk me into it."

THE SEX wasn't perfect—it never was, in her experience, there was always something not right, and in Loren's case, it was that his body, including his tongue, was cold as ice.

But it was good enough for the moment, for an evening otherwise alone.

An evening where she would, she thought, inevitably have to think about Lucas Davenport. But for now, she didn't think about anything.

For now, she let the pleasure flow.

Davenport was for some other time.

22

INVESTIGATING FRANK WILLETT was like chewing on a bad cheeseburger: the longer you worked at it, the worse the taste became. The crime-scene people pulled Willett's apartment to pieces, and in addition to the knife, came up with one aging pack of High Wire Long hemp rolling papers that might have been there before Willett moved in.

Willett, in fact, had curled his lip at the suggestion: "Wires? We don't need no stinkin' wires," he said, which had made Lucas laugh despite himself.

And that was it. The most worrying thing was that Lucas was sure that they'd find some sign of the fifty thousand dollars, but there hadn't been a thing.

Willett, aside from the occasional stressed-out joke, was suitably desperate, but wasn't giving any ground. He didn't do anything, he didn't know anything.

★

A CALL CAME, from a South St. Paul police officer named Janice Loomis-Smith. She said, "Hi, this is Janice Loomis-Smith, down in South St. Paul? I sat next to you at the symposium on tool mark evidence?"

"Hey, Janice, how are you?" He remembered her as a frizzy-haired piece of leather who'd spent two years in Iraq. Smart. "What's up?"

"We got what you call your anomalous situation. We got this dude named Xai Xiong, street racer guy. His car burned up off Concord Street, this Honda Prelude, burned right down to the ground. Apparently arson—somebody filled it up with gasoline, and it blew; I guess you could see the fire for a mile, all the way across the river. Anyway, we tracked it down through VIN, and went and talked to Xiong. He swears that he sold it a month ago. There's this informal sales lot down off Highway 36 near Stillwater—people park their cars with For Sale signs in them."

"I know where that is," Lucas said patiently. "It's over where that apple orchard used to be."

"Right. Anyway, he said he sold it to a woman who gave him cash, and he signed the papers and she took them and said she'd file them later. She never did—I mean, if he's telling the truth. Anyway, the reason I'm calling . . ."

"Yeah," he said, still patient.

". . . Is that he said the woman was the spitting image of this woman whose face has been in the paper. The fairy woman."

"Far out," Lucas said. Though it sounded weak. "Give me his name again."

THEN JACKSON, the photographer, called and said, "I got your Ricky Davis guy."

"Yeah? Well, I'm sittin' here with my dick in my hand—might as well drag some pictures around town."

"Might want to wash your hands first," Jackson said.

*

EMILY WAU saw him as he walked into the bank and waved cheerfully. "I saw in the paper that you arrested the good-looking guy," she said. "Dating him would have been a mistake, huh?"

"Maybe," Lucas said. "But maybe not."

"You've got another picture?"

"One more—a guy named Ricky Davis."

"I don't remember the name," she said. Lucas handed her the photograph, and she looked at it for a long time, then her dark brown eyes flicked up at him and she said, "I opened an account for him last fall."

Lucas recoiled in surprise, then smiled. "You're sure."

"Yes. I'm sure." She wandered back to her desk and sat down, elbows on the desktop, fingers massaging her temples for a moment. She looked up and said, "I don't think he said his name was Ricky, but I can remember a little bit. I had the impression that he'd never opened a bank account before, or maybe it had been a while, though he's not that old . . . he seemed really unsure about what he was doing. What's important is—I mean, for you—is that I gave him a lot of literature inside one of these folders."

She opened a bottom desk drawer and pulled out a slick-paper folder with a picture of a paddlewheel steamer on it, and "Riverside Banks, the Home-Grown Alternative."

Lucas said, "That's important? Why?"

"Because he seemed interested in all the financing options . . . farm financing, if I remember correctly," Wau said. "I bet he kept it. If he kept it, my fingerprints will be all over it, and then we'll know that he was the one."

"You're a pretty smart cookie," Lucas said. "Thank you."

LUCAS THOUGHT about it as he drove back into town. Del, he thought, was probably at the apartment. If Siggy came in, he'd be running early—but he was coming, and the watch had gone full-time.

Lucas went that way.

DEL WAS sitting at the desk, reading a thin paperback, when Lucas came through the apartment door. He glanced back at Lucas and then said, "Heather is putting stuff in a couple of suitcases."

"Huh."

"Yeah. Those windows bother me, though. Wide open like that. If you're gonna sneak out of town, wouldn't you pull the blinds?"

"I would. I don't think Heather has a modest bone in her body," Lucas said.

"It's not modesty—if she's gonna run, she'd want to keep it a secret," Del said. He fumbled the paperback out of sight, but before it went, Lucas saw the title: *Waiting for Godot*. "She might be perfectly happy hanging her tits out the window, but packing a bag?"

Lucas picked up the binoculars and took a look. "I don't know," he said. "That's weird."

They watched awhile longer, then Del said, "I didn't think you were coming over. What's up?"

"The Austin case may have just solved itself," Lucas said. He explained about Ricky Davis.

". . . so I'm pretty sure he's the guy who opened the Frances Austin account. There's the fifty thousand. His girlfriend, Helen, had all the access she needed. She'd have to figure out a password or something, but they could do that, one way or another. Then, all she had to do was call Fidelity with the password, and have a check sent to the address that Fidelity already had. No reason for them to suspect anything was wrong. Helen intercepts the mail— she's there alone almost every day—and passes it to Ricky, who'd already set up the account."

"Why'd they kill Austin?" Del asked.

"Don't know that yet—maybe Frances figured it out. You want to hear a scenario?"

"Go ahead."

Lucas pulled up another chair, sat, leaned back with his hands behind his head, feet up on the desk. "Frances is at home and decides to get some money from Fidelity. She sits down and makes the call, paying no attention to Helen, who hears her say the password, or maybe a couple of passwords. There it is—the money's just sitting there. And—we'll have to show this—Helen really needs the money. Or Ricky does. For some reason or another. So they come up with this scheme, and it almost works. But Frances, who is no fool, looks at an account statement, maybe a whole month later, if Helen worked it right, and she *remembers* . . . She remembers Helen being there, when she was on the phone to Fidelity."

He continued: "But she's not sure, so she goes to the house to confront Helen. They argue, it gets physical, there's a knife, and Helen sticks her. Freak outs, calls Ricky, who comes in his truck, one of his trucks, and they move the body. Helen drives Frances's car back to her apartment, and then . . . I don't know. She takes a cab, or Ricky picks her up, they go back and get her car. Or Ricky parks someplace, after dumping the body, and walks in and moves her car. Anyway . . ."

"They work something out," Del said. He added, "Works for me, but you ain't gonna get a jury to buy it. Not on Lucas Davenport's say-so."

"Ah—but there'll be some hard evidence," Lucas said. "They bought something with the money. They paid something off. There was some residue on the body, or the sheet—some transmission fluid, and Ricky drove a wrecker. There might be some fingerprints . . . and I just thought of something else. Sonofabitch."

"What?"

"When I found the missing fifty thousand, I was at the Austin house," Lucas said. "I called up Alyssa and asked her about it, and she didn't know where it went. When we were talking, Helen was right there. Then I called Anson, and I mentioned that I might go back to the A1 that night. And that night, man, that cowboy cocksucker shot me. Ricky wears cowboy boots."

"Bonnie and Clyde," Del said.

"Ben and Jerry."

"Anthony and Cleopatra."

"Heather and Siggy." Lucas looked across the street: Heather was packing, all right. The boom box came on with Robert Palmer, "Addicted to Love." Lucas wondered, *Is that Heather's problem?*

"Anyway," he said to Del, "what else you got going?"

"Nothing you don't know about—except, did I tell you I'm trying to find George William Boyd?"

"George? Why?"

"He's been selling Level IV assault vests out his back door, along with Kevlar helmets and the occasional Mini—14 Ranch Rifle."

Lucas was annoyed: "What the hell is he doing?"

"Well, you know George," Del said.

"Yeah, but that was just paintball shit," Lucas said. "What's he doing now? Starting a war?"

"That's the question I plan to ask him," Del said. "Somebody said . . . hell, that some of the folks on West Seventh were getting antsy about the Republican convention."

"Ah, shit, Del." Lucas kicked his feet off the desk and came down on the floor with a *smack!* "We can't have people down there with undocumented rifles. The goddamn president is going to be there."

"So, we gotta find George," Del said.

"And tell the Secret Service," Lucas said.

"If we tell the Secret Service, we lose George as a source."

"Jesus Christ, if we didn't tell them, and somebody got shot, and they found out that we knew—we'd be living in Marion, Illinois, for a hundred years," Lucas said. Lucas ran his hands through his hair. Too much to think about. "Listen, I'm gonna pull Jenkins or Shrake to take over here. They both want a piece of Siggy. I want you to help me close down the Austin thing."

"What about Willett?"

"I got the bad feeling that Frank is telling the truth," Lucas said.

"Then how'd the knife get in his house?"

"That's a problem."

A moment later, Lucas said, "You want a scenario?"

"Sure."

"The other people who were killed were all friends of Frances," Lucas said. "Suppose that sometime during the confrontation between Helen and Frances, or maybe just from overhearing something that Frances has said, they come to believe that these three people knew something. They all knew something, even if they didn't know they knew it. Maybe all three of them knew that she was looking for the fifty thousand, that somebody had stolen it, and that fact had to stay hidden. In fact, somebody told me that the first guy killed, Dick Ford, the bartender, was hoping that Frances would help him start a club. What if that's why she looked at her Fidelity account? And found the money missing? Mentioned it to Ford, and maybe he mentioned it to Roy Carter, the kid . . ."

Del was shaking his head. "I buy the first scenario: they wanted money, they took it, they got caught, they killed her. Tried to shoot you when they thought you were figuring it out. But all these others . . . I mean, if your first scenario is right, Helen killed Frances because the knife was right there. If the knife hadn't been right there, there wouldn't have been a killing. Then, when they decided they had to do it again, they tried with a gun. These other three . . . the knife was a *choice*. A *big deal*. There's a ritual going on there."

Lucas sighed, looked out the window, and said, "I wish Siggy would come. Siggy's so goddamn simple."

SHRAKE SHOWED up with a machine gun, a putter, and a half-dozen golf balls. He stacked the M—16 case in a corner. "What you golfing retards never realized," he said, tapping the apartment carpet with the putter, "is that this floor here has four perfect breaks, toward the center, and the carpet stimps at nine. If I can putt for a week, I'll be in mid-season form. I'll get Jenkins out on the first day and rip him a new asshole. He'll owe me money for the rest of the summer."

"Golf is the stupidest game ever invented," Del said.

"That's true," Shrake said, pointing the putter at Del. "But you're not qualified to say it. You have to play it for twenty years before you can fully appreciate how exquisitely stupid it really is."

"If Siggy shows up and you become a hero, I'll fire your ass," Lucas told Shrake, jabbing a finger at his chest. "You call the duty guy, he'll get St. Paul SWAT rolling, you call me, and you wait. You pass that word on to Jenkins. I'm serious, Shrake, goddamnit, I don't need any of your macho shit. There's a child and a pregnant woman over there, and Siggy ain't Antsy. He's way past Antsy. This is no time to fuck around."

"Got it," Shrake said, his voice serious. "No bullshit. We'll get it right."

"You better," Lucas said. To Del: "Let's do it."

23

LUCAS AND DEL each took his own car, in case they needed to split up later on. On the way south, Lucas called Pratt, the Dakota County deputy who'd tracked the lab work on Frances Austin's body.

"We're going to look at a couple of trucks at Odd's Tow and Wrecking in South St. Paul. We may want your lab guys to come up and take some samples, if we find something good."

"Give us a call," Pratt said. "We got the lab reports back, and we're looking at wrecker kind of stuff—we've got that tranny fluid, some regular engine oil, some metal filings. Now that you're talking tow trucks, I'm thinking, the lift cables?"

"I'd buy that," Lucas said. "We'll call."

Next, he called Odd's Tow and asked for Ricky, and was told by the woman who answered the phone that Ricky wasn't working. Excellent.

ODD'S TOW and Wrecking was built on a hump of dirt off Highway 52, the dirt held together by a comprehensive coat of oil slicks. The office was a rectangular shed with one window and a hand-painted sign that said *Odd's,* and a red neon sign inside the window said *Open.* A dozen junked cars sat in the weeds next to a blue-metal garage. There were three tow trucks in sight, two inside the garage, one sitting in the yard next to the office.

Lucas parked on one side of the office door, and Del on the other, and Lucas led the way inside, where a fleshy woman with big dark hair sat behind a desk sorting by hand through yellow slips of paper. A plaque on her desk said *Linda.* She looked up when they came in, asked, "Can I help you?"

"Are you the manager?" Lucas asked.

"No . . . the manager . . ." She looked toward one of two internal doors and shouted, "Hey. Odd."

A chair scraped across a concrete floor in the office and a heavy-set man with pink cheeks and straw-colored hair stuck his head out of the office. "Help you?"

Lucas identified himself and said, "We need to ask you some questions about one of your employees."

"Welp"—it sounded like *welp*—"won't be the first time. Come on in. Is this about Jerry?"

"Why do you ask?" Del said.

"He's been sort of spooky the last couple days. I've kinda wondered if he's been up to something," Odd said. He was wearing an oil-stained flight suit, and took a pack of Marlboros out of a leg pocket and shook out a cigarette.

"Like what?" Del asked.

Odd settled behind a beat-up wooden desk, with a sign on it that said *Odd Angstrom,* pointed at a couple of plastic chairs, and said, "Well, you know, ever since he got out, we've wondered if he might go back to his old ways. Made some good money—heh, heh. EBay's the world's best fence, huh? No more ten-cents-on-the-dollar."

Linda had left her desk and came in and leaned on the door-jamb. "That goddamned Jerry. He's never going straight. Good worker, but he doesn't see himself getting along on forty thousand a year, if you know what I mean."

Del and Lucas looked from Odd to Linda, and then Lucas said, "We're not here about Jerry."

Now Odd and Linda looked at each other, and Odd hacked once, a smoker's laugh, and said, "I guess we coulda gone all day without mentioning Jerry," and Linda cackled and said, "Got that right."

Odd said, "So who's it about?"

"You gotta guy named Ricky Davis?"

Odd frowned. "Ricky, huh? What'd he do?"

"We don't know if he did anything. We're just looking around based on some lab work. Do you have any record of what he might have been doing—his calls—last December?"

Linda nodded. "Sure. What date?"

Lucas gave her the date, and she went back to her desk, and all three men stepped out to watch. She pounded on an old Dell computer, brought up a spreadsheet, rolled it for a couple of minutes, then put her finger on a greasy screen and said, "Yeah, he was working. Had three calls . . . let me see. Yeah, he came on at three o'clock, left at eleven. He was the only guy on that afternoon, sort of tangled up in the Christmas holidays. Must've been snowing—he had two ditch calls and one tow."

"Can you tell which truck he was using?"

"Yup." She touched the screen again and said, "He's usually in Two . . . yup, he was in Two."

"Could we take a look at Two?"

"Ain't gonna be anything left from December," Odd said.

"Like to take a look anyway," Lucas said.

★

ODD LED THEM back to the garage and pointed. Two was a black 2001 Ford 550 diesel with a dual winch on the back. They walked around it, and Lucas stuck his hand over the side and dragged his fingers across the bed, held them up in front of his face, rubbed his fingers. All the oil you could want. The winch lines were shiny, but gritty: there would be, Lucas thought, metal filings in the oil.

"What do you think?" Del asked.

"I think I gotta find a place to wash my hands; and we should call Dakota County, get their lab people up here," Lucas said.

"Not gonna take the truck, are they?" Odd asked.

"If they have to, you'd be compensated," Lucas said.

Odd brightened: "Welp, that'd be a benefit. What'd that boy do, anyway?"

Del asked, "So what's Jerry's last name?"

LUCAS WASHED his hands; and while they waited for the Dakota County crew, they got Linda and Odd around Linda's desk, and cross-examined them on Ricky Davis. "Used to work on towboats, down on the river, got tired of that, and decided to start a farm. He and his girlfriend are raising emus."

"Emus—like the bird."

"Yup. Ricky says that they got no cholesterol and no fat, and he's gonna sell them to high-rent restaurants in the Cities. They got a batch of chicks last fall, and they're gonna start harvesting them . . ."

"That means 'chop their heads off,'" Linda said.

". . . around next Christmas."

"Where's the farm?" Lucas asked.

"Down south of here, somewhere, what's the town?" Odd scratched his head.

Linda said, "Wanamingo—it's by Zumbrota."

LUCAS GOT ON his phone, called Carol, had her look at a map and figure out what county Wanamingo was in. She came back a minute later and said, "Goodhue. The county seat is at Red Wing."

"Get me the number for the county recorder, will you?"

"Let me get on the Net." Another minute, and she said, "Here it is . . ." and read out the number.

As he dialed it, he asked Linda, "Any idea what Ricky's full legal name is? Is it Richard or Ricky, his middle initial?"

She poked her computer a couple of times and said, "Richard William Davis, 01-07-75."

LUCAS GOT a clerk in the recorder's office, identified himself, and asked her to check the computer for any deeds, mortgages, or liens listed to Richard William Davis in the past year.

She was back almost instantly: "We have a deed recorded and a mortgage satisfaction on November twenty-one, forty-two thousand dollars for apparently . . . let me figure this out . . . forty acres out in Cherry Grove township."

"Is that near Wanamingo?"

"It is. Let me see . . . four, five miles?"

THE DAKOTA COUNTY crime-scene guys arrived a couple of minutes later, and Lucas and Del and Odd walked them out to Two. "You know what you're looking for?" Lucas asked.

"Yes." The older of the two guys looked into the truck bed. "We're gonna find it, too—whether or not it's *exactly* right, we'll have to see."

"I understand there were some oak leaf bits stuck in the plastic sheet," Lucas said.

"That's right," the older one said. "We'll look for them. What we'll do, we'll seal up the bed as best we can, then take it back to the garage and sample everything."

"How long before you know?"

"Lot to sample," he said. "Let's say . . . a preliminary read by tomorrow, something definitive in a week or so?"

"I'll give a preliminary read right now," the shorter guy said.

"Given what we found in the sheet, you couldn't even think of a better possibility than this truck. We had a mix of engine oil and transmission fluid and brake fluid and . . . shit, we should have thought of wreckers."

"Good enough for me," Lucas said. To Del: "Wanna go talk to Ricky?"

"What'd that boy *do,* anyway?" Odd asked.

THEY WERE only fifteen minutes from Lucas's place, so they went back into town, and Lucas dropped the Porsche and Del left his state Chevy in the street, and they took Lucas's truck. They got lost cutting across country, and didn't make the Davis farm until late afternoon.

The farm was not on what Lucas would have identified as farmland: it was a forty-acre hump of scraggly, sapling-infested meadow with a big wire cage in the middle of it, backed on one side by the foundation of an old barn. The barn foundation was tented with plastic; the pen itself was full of five- or six-foot-tall birds that Lucas would have called ostriches. A trailer, missing its wheels, sat on blocks to the right of the driveway, opposite the barn and bird pen, and a Dodge pickup was nosed in to the trailer.

They pulled into the driveway and parked fifty feet down the hump from the trailer; as they did, Ricky Davis stepped out of the trailer and peered at them. Lucas slipped his gun out of its waist holder and slipped it into his jacket pocket. "Watch yourself—that's the motherfucker who shot me."

"You sure?"

"Ninety-four-point-six percent."

DAVIS WAS watching them, a frown on his face. When Lucas stepped out, with Del on the other side, his face dropped, and then he looked both ways, up and down the hill, and Lucas yelled, "Ricky . . ." but Davis had thrown himself into his truck.

"Shit," Lucas said, and pulled the .45.

Davis fired up the truck and hit the gas, backing straight toward them, and Lucas yelled, "Ricky," and pointed the pistol, and Del, who was exposed, ran around behind Lucas's truck, and Davis accelerated, backward, past them, down the hill, all the way to the gravel road, across the gravel road, into the ditch on the other side.

Neither Lucas nor Del had fired a shot; they both climbed back into Lucas's truck and Lucas whipped it around in a circle. Davis was moving forward, but couldn't climb the steep bank of the ditch for a hundred yards or so, and bounced and ricocheted over the rough turf on the edge of the ditch, and finally coaxed the truck up the side and hit the gravel road. Lucas was a hundred feet behind him when they cleared the top of a hill, past a farmhouse where there was a woman standing on the lawn with a golden retriever. They were going way too fast.

Gravel dust made it impossible to see for more than forty or fifty yards. Every time Lucas moved to the side, to get out of the dust, Davis moved over in front of him.

"Gotta hard right coming up," Del yelled. "Coming up . . . Coming up close!"

Lucas hit the brakes and dropped back, the stability-control lights flashing on his dashboard, but Davis plowed into the intersection, too fast to hold. The back end of the pickup started to slide, the rear wheels frantically throwing rocks and dirt, and the truck almost went into the ditch again, but Davis at least got it straight, with two wheels down in the ditch and two on the shoulder. Then the ditch wall got steeper and he tried to stop; did stop. Sat for a moment, and then the truck slowly rolled sideways. Davis tried to steer into it, but failed, and the truck rolled, and stopped upside down.

"Hard right," Del said, climbing out behind the muzzle of his Beretta 9mm.

Lucas said, "Might be a gun in the truck. Watch it."

They boxed the truck, easing up behind it. There was no visible piece of sheet metal on the vehicle that hadn't been dented in the roll. All the windows were cracked, and when Lucas came up on the driver's side, he could hear Davis weeping.

He risked a peek: Davis was hanging upside down in his safety belt, his face contorted, tears running down his forehead into his hair. Lucas asked, "Are you hurt?"

Davis, out of control, asked "Wha-wha-what's gonna happen to the birds?"

"Are you hurt?" Del asked.

"No, I'm just upside down."

"Gotta gun?" Lucas asked.

"No."

"Let's get you out of there."

THEY'D GOTTEN him out, and Del had cuffed him, when a sheriff's car cut around a corner a half-mile away, out from behind the shelter of a stand of trees, and Del looked back at the farmhouse where the woman had been and said, "She must have called it in."

Lucas said, "Hang on," and climbed in the truck and hit the switch that activated the two red-LED flashers on his grill. The cop car slowed a bit, but came on, stopped thirty yards away and the cop got out with a shotgun, pointed to the sky, and Lucas shouted, "BCA—BCA," and he and Del held up their IDs.

"I'm so fucked," Davis said.

WITH THE Goodhue deputy standing there, they read Davis his rights, and Lucas asked if he understood them, and then Del said, "You scared the shit out of us, back there, man. What the hell was that all about?"

"I knew you were coming, someday," Davis said. "I knew you'd find out." He began to weep again, and the deputy seemed about to say something, but Lucas gave him a quick head shake.

"You almost shot me in the balls, Ricky," Lucas said. "Two inches over, and I'd be Nutless Davenport, wonder cop."

That made Davis smile, momentarily, shakily, and he said, "I didn't want to do it. That crazy bitch made me do it. We weren't trying to kill you."

Lucas was a little pissed: "Man, you shoot a gun at somebody."

"I was trying to wound you or something. Get you off the case. Didn't try to hit you in the nuts, though," he said, miserably. Then. "Look at my truck. Jesus, look at my truck. What's gonna happen to my birds? What's gonna happen to the farm?"

"Did you buy the farm with the fifty thousand?"

"Yeah . . . paid it off, anyway," he said. "We couldn't afford the mortgage when it rolled over. It was some kind of A-T-M or A-R-M or something. Couldn't make payments. We just got the birds, we were desperate."

"Who killed Frances?"

"She did," he said bitterly.

"Helen," Lucas said.

"Called me up at work and said there'd been a terrible accident and I had to get down there. Accident, my ass, she stabbed her about a hundred times. Big puddle of blood all over the place. I never knew she hated the Austins that much."

Del: "Hated them?"

"Hated them. They treated her like dirt. Paid her shit, and she was like, invisible. If I'd known all that shit . . . I don't know."

"So you didn't plan it out?"

"Hell no. I wouldn't have done anything to Frances Austin," Davis said. "I mean, we stole the money. She had so much, we didn't think she'd notice right away, or that she could figure out what happened. But she figured it out: came right out and told Helen that she was gonna be locked up for a hundred years, because that's what happened when somebody stole from the Austins. They started screaming at each other, and finally, Helen . . . stabbed her."

"And you came down and picked up the body with your wrecker, and put her in the ditch."

"I guess," he said.

"That's the goddamnedest thing," the Goodhue deputy said. "You should have gone right straight to the police."

"You weren't there," Davis moaned. "You weren't there."

"And you loved her?" Lucas asked.

"I did then, but that's gone away," Davis said. "That crazy bitch. I see her looking at me . . . she was scaring me. I think, I don't know. I didn't want to be around when she had a knife in her hand."

"When she killed the other ones, were you around for that?" Lucas asked.

"What?"

"When she killed—"

"She didn't kill anybody else," Davis said. "I mean, I know that. We were together when those other people were killed, and we weren't anywhere around there."

"What about Frank?" Del asked.

"Frank who?"

"Frank Willett?"

"I don't know any Frank Willett. Who's he?"

GOODHUE COUNTY was part of a sheriff's co-op and the deputy called in the crime-scene team, and they all trucked back to the trailer. Davis told them where the pistol was, the one he'd used to shoot at Lucas, and they marked it. And they dug out the folder from the Riverside bank, the one that would have Emily Wau's fingerprints on it.

"Whose idea was the Francis thing—calling you Frank, so the ID would be good?" Lucas asked.

"Helen figured that out," Davis said.

"Where'd you get the ID?"

He shrugged: "Trucker. Them things float around, you can get any name you want."

"Did you have one of Frances's credit cards or something? I understand you had to have two forms of ID."

Davis's head bobbed. "Yeah . . . Helen got one of those offers in the mail, for a credit card, already approved. She mailed it back, and the card came. That's what started the whole thing. That right there."

★

THEY WERE OUTSIDE, in the dark, about to put Davis in the deputy's car, when another car topped the hill by the neighbor's farmhouse, and Davis said, "That's Helen, coming home from work."

Sobotny's car slowed at the turnoff, as Lucas hustled back to the truck, and then straightened and continued down the road. Del piled into the passenger seat, and they went after her, caught her a mile away, flashers going, and she finally pulled over by a stop sign.

They came up behind her, slowly, carefully, and found her with her head resting on the center pad of the steering wheel.

Lucas said, "Come out of there."

She sat up for a moment, staring straight ahead, like she was considering other possibilities, then turned the key and shut down the car, and got out.

"Agent Davenport," she said.

"Helen."

"What's happened?"

"Ricky rolled the truck. You might have seen it back there in the ditch," he said.

"I thought . . ." she began. Then: "Never mind."

Del said, "Tell you what, ma'am. Ricky sort of spilled his guts."

"Yes, that's what he'd do," she said. She looked at Del and sighed. "We weren't smart enough to get away with this. We just weren't smart enough. Maybe I was, but Ricky . . . Ricky's a lunkhead."

"Why'd you kill the other three?" Lucas asked.

She frowned. "The other three? You mean . . . We didn't kill those people. We're not crazy. This has all been a mistake, that's what it was. We didn't want to hurt anybody—we certainly didn't kill anybody else."

Lucas looked at Del and said, "Ah, boy. I thought we had it wrapped."

And to Sobotny: "You have the right to remain silent . . ."

271

24

THEY PROCESSED Davis and Sobotny in St. Paul.

Sobotny asked for an attorney; Davis, miserable, declined an attorney, and made a statement, admitting that he'd moved the body and destroyed evidence: the knife used in the killing was in the woods, somewhere between the Austin house and the spot where the body was found, and he had no exact idea where.

He said that he moved the body in the wrecker, which made good the evidence taken off the plastic sheet, and out of the wrecker bed.

Sobotny actually hadn't driven to the Austin house that morning, because her car's water pump was out, and Davis had driven her to the Austins'. After the killing, they'd hastily cleaned up with paper towels and some "cleaning stuff" taken from the broom closet, which made good the crime-scene lab reports on the floor. Then they'd loaded the body into the wrecker, and Davis had taken it out a few miles and pitched it in a ditch. Sobotny had driven Frances's car back to Frances's neighborhood, and parked it, in an effort to conceal the fact that Frances had been at the house that afternoon.

"Honest to God, I was so freaked out that I didn't know what I was doing," he said. "She was telling me what to do, pushing me around, and by the time I got to thinking about it, it was all done and I was in the shit. I knew it wasn't gonna work. My dad said, 'If you ever do anything crooked, the 'thorities will get you.' He said that all the time, and we kids all believed it, and here it is, the proof."

"If you didn't plan to do anything bad, what about the money?" Lucas asked. "You had to plan the fifty thousand dollars."

Davis's tongue flicked out. "Yeah. I guess. I just kept thinking about them birds. No cholesterol, no fat. Them birds were gonna be my career."

He said he was sorry, that he would never do anything like that again, and asked who would feed his birds. They had to be fed that evening and again the next morning. Del called the Goodhue County Humane Society, and the woman who answered the phone said that one way or another, they'd take care of it.

The statement was recorded.

Lucas, Del, and the Goodhue cop made statements about the arrest procedure, the reading of the Miranda warning, which was critical, because Davis had simply blurted out the confession.

And when they were done, Del said, "I think we're good."

The Goodhue deputy, a cheerful farm boy with a blond flattop, slapped Del on the back, hitched up his gun belt, and said, "Man, I was in on a murder arrest. First time for that, eh? You're looking at the deputy of the month."

BY THE TIME they got out, it was nine o'clock, a small, cold-looking moon coming up in the east, with clouds ripping across it, almost like at Halloween.

They stood together in the parking lot while Lucas talked to Jenkins, who'd relieved Shrake at the drugstore apartment, watching Heather.

"She took a long hot bath tonight," Jenkins said. "Now I gotta find another woman."

"What happened to the last one?"

"Wore me out," Jenkins said. "And she always listening to that fuckin' piano music, that *Well-Tempered Clavier* shit. Enough to drive a saint to drink."

"But nothing going on."

"Well, I'd call that bath something, but in your cop frame of reference, no. No sign of anybody," Jenkins said. "But you know, I got the feeling that she's doing this on purpose: she's holding us here."

"She's a performer," Lucas said.

"She's a goddamn snake," Jenkins said. "Though I gotta say, that's the kind I like."

*

LUCAS HAD CALLED Weather to tell her about the arrests, and she was waiting to hear more when he got home. "I couldn't believe it—the case was like an egg that got broken. All of a sudden, *crack,*" she said. "What did Alyssa say?"

"I haven't told her," Lucas said. "I'm going to call her now, I'm going over there. I'd like you to come along."

"Me?"

"Won't take long," Lucas said. "You're cutting tomorrow morning?"

"Yes, but nothing big. I've got to graft some skin on a tumor site. I could do it in my sleep."

"So come on with me to Alyssa's," Lucas said.

LUCAS CALLED AHEAD, and told Austin they had some news, and that he wanted to come over. She'd be waiting.

They took the Porsche, and in the car, Lucas said, "When we get there, I'm going to leave you alone for a few minutes . . . maybe, I don't know, I'll think of something. Anyway, when it's just you two, I want you to suggest that I come back and get you, that you want to talk for a few minutes. Then, I want you to find out how she feels about these other three killings. About the three we don't know about."

"You don't think these two jerks did it?"

"I don't think so. And I don't think Frank Willett did it, either. I just don't have that feeling," Lucas said.

"So why . . ." Weather began. But she was no dummy. "Oh, no—you don't think Alyssa had anything to do with it?"

"I don't know," Lucas said. "For Christ sakes, don't ask her. If she's involved, she's nuts. You'll be okay, but I'd like you to get her to talk about it, and tell me what she says. She's gotten a little wary with me. I think with you, she'll open up."

"Because I'm a friend," Weather said.

"Yeah."

"So I can betray her."

"C'mon, Weather, you're not betraying her," Lucas said,

turning to her in the dark. "You're helping out in an investigation. I want you to bullshit with her a bit, and tell me what you think."

AUSTIN CAME to the door in sheepskin moccasins and an ankle-length white sleeping gown of a soft fine white cloth that might have been made from unicorn hair, and let them in with a blast of cold air. Lucas said, "I'm sorry, you look like you're ready for bed."

"I'd just gotten out of the bath when you called," she said. "What happened now?"

"We arrested Helen and Ricky for Frances's murder," Lucas said. "Helen won't talk to us, but Ricky has given a statement. There's not much question—Helen stabbed Frances when Frances accused her of taking the fifty thousand dollars, and Ricky helped cover up."

Tears began running down Austin's face, and as she backed down the hallway toward the living room, she said, "Why? Why would she do that? She was like a member of the family."

"Greed, basically—they were trying to start a business, and needed the money, and when Frances figured it out, she confronted Helen and there was a blowup. Helen stabbed her."

They sat down and Lucas took her through it, step by step, and she got up once to get some tissues and blow her nose, and at the end, she said, "So it's all done."

"Not quite done," Lucas said. He looked at his watch and said, "Shoot," and then back up at Austin and said, "I don't think that either Ricky or Helen, or Frank Willett, had anything to do with the other three killings—but I do think that the three killings are tied to Frances, somehow. And maybe Willett and Ricky and Helen are pulling my weenie, but I've been doing this for a long time and that's not the feeling I'm getting. We'll see." He looked at his watch again, and then said, "Uh, I've got something else going on. We've got a big dope guy coming through town, we've got a surveillance going, with all this excitement with Ricky and Helen, I forgot to check. I need to use your kitchen phone?"

Lucas stood up and Austin, blowing her nose again, said, "You know where it is," and Lucas left them, going down the hall toward the kitchen. Weather said, "It's over now. I really don't know what else to say—God, if I lost one of my kids . . . but you don't want to hear that. Now you've just got to hold on. If you need *anything* . . ."

They could hear Lucas down the hall on the phone, and Austin said, "Some big dope dealer?"

"You wouldn't believe what's going on with that—I can't tell you now, Lucas would kill me, but when it's over, we'll get a cup of coffee," Weather said. "Some of it's awful and some of it's hilarious."

"Unlike what happened with Helen," Austin said. "I can't get over it—why would she do that? I loved Helen."

Weather said, "My relationship with Lucas started—really started—when a little girl shot him in the throat and I was there to keep him breathing. Since then, we talk about his cases, and I'll tell you, the craziest stuff happens all the time. I always thought crazy stuff happens in medicine, but if you're not a cop, you can't even begin to conceive how weird people get. Lucas arrested a man who borrowed money from a neighbor, and then murdered the neighbor so he wouldn't have to pay him back—two hundred and twenty dollars that he used to get his snowblower fixed. He *killed* him."

"That's not even crazy," Austin said. "That's beyond crazy."

Weather didn't want to get into crazy cop stories—Lucas would kill *her*—and so she asked, "Is the funeral still on Saturday?"

"Yes. They'll release her, and it's Saturday morning. I just . . . I just . . ."

Weather said, "She's in heaven, now, Alyssa. She's fine."

Austin's chin trembled and she used another tissue on her nose and said, "I really don't believe in heaven, I'm afraid. She's been released from this incarnation into the next; I hope she found a good spirit guide. Maybe her father, if he hasn't yet been reborn. She was a good girl; she took care of people. I think her karma, her energy, will take her higher yet." She snuffled some more.

Weather said, "Well."

This time, Austin produced a small smile and said, "I know what all you good Christians think, and I just don't think that way. I think her spirit may still have been out there, waiting for satisfaction. I never conceived of the possibility of Helen . . . I just can't grasp it. Lucas is sure?"

"He got a detailed statement, and he tells me that it's all supported independently by laboratory evidence. They're sure."

"I was so sure those other three . . . there was negative energy about them, a black karma, I was *sure* they were involved." Austin had changed, and Weather sat back, disturbed by the look on her face.

"I have a friend, my friend Loren, who has, well, he's in a space that intersects with another plane, and he tells me that boats take our souls to the next life; and some boats are glorious, and some boats are dark and dank, like slave ships, going down the Mississippi. They load right there on the St. Paul waterfront, at night . . . Oh, shit."

She began weeping, rocking back and forth in her easy chair, and Weather stood up and sat on the arm of the chair and wrapped her arm around her and hugged her, and they both cried together for a bit, then they heard Lucas coming back, and Lucas stopped and looked at them and finally said, "Guys—this was a good thing that happened tonight."

"I know," Austin said. "But I'm sorry about Helen and Ricky, too. Oh, God."

"Should I call your parents?" Lucas asked.

"No, no, I'm fine. I'm better, really. It's over. It's all over. I'm going to go ustairs, take a couple of pills, and I think I'm actually going to get a good night's sleep for a change. God, I'm so tired. I'm so tired it feels like my heart is caving in."

*

BACK IN THE CAR, Lucas asked, "Well?"

Weather looked out the passenger-side window and didn't say anything for a bit, then, "I'm like you. I get a bad feeling. She thought the other three had black karma that indicated that they were tied to the murder of Frances. And she had a friend who thought the same way. If that's true, and if they were looking for revenge . . ."

"Revenge works as a motive. It's not as common as it is on TV shows, but it happens," Lucas said.

"She said this friend—she said his name was Loren—said there were riverboats of souls going down the Mississippi, and some of these were glorious riverboats, and some were like slave ships. The bad souls, obviously. She thought Frances might still be here, but on a different plane. Not on a boat yet."

Lucas interrupted: "Her friend was named Loren?"

"Yeah, that's what she said. A male Loren. She said, 'he.'"

"Her friend Loren is dead," Lucas said.

He explained in a few words, and Weather said, "She said he was in a different space. One that intersects with the plane of death. He's the one that sees these riverboats."

"I think Alyssa has a problem," Lucas said. A moment later: "She has a problem, and damned if I could prove it."

25

ALL OF ALYSSA'S nights were bad, even when there was only one of her. When there were two, and a ghost in the mirror, they were beyond nightmares. She struggled with the blankets, first too hot, then too cold. She fought the pillows: first they were too hard, then too soft, then too hot, and flipped over, blessedly cool, but only for a few moments. And she woke every few minutes to stare at the clock, where the hands moved at a snail's pace, grinding out the minutes, with hours that never ended.

The conversation went on endlessly, raging arguments— Loren, pushing to kill Davenport, to get rid of him. "He knows, he knows, he knows . . . Do you think Weather was gushing at you out of sympathy? Bullshit. She was doing it for him. And if she tells him that *I* believed that the other three were the killers, that Loren did this and that Loren did that, he'll remember that name. He will remember that I am dead and he will conclude that you are a psychotic. Once he convinces himself that you're guilty, he is the kind of man who will manufacture the evidence he needs to arrest you. He is crazier than any of us, he will do anything to win the game. He has to be eliminated. He's too dangerous to let go."

Alyssa resisted: "No. No, he's a friend of mine, he wouldn't do that to me. He's got no evidence."

"He will *manufacture* the evidence if he's convinced you killed the three."

"No, no, no . . ."

Fairy took Loren's side: "If we do it right, if we kill him, who's to know? A lot of people must want him dead. He must have enemies all over the Cities, all over the state. Killers. Drug dealers. Gang members. If we did it cleanly enough, who'd know? With a gun, not with a knife. In the dark. One shot in the heart, and run."

"I won't do it," Alyssa said.

"I will," Fairy answered.

"She will," Loren said.

"I know she will. She likes killing. She likes the taste of blood, for God's sake. She puts it in her mouth, sucks it off her fingers."

"It's self-defense," Fairy said. "As simple as that."

ALYSSA WOKE ONCE, in the middle of the night, shivering, and found that she'd thrown off the covers. Her mind was clear as glass—the clarity of insomnia, when she knew that immediate sleep was out of the question. She got up, turned on the light, got her tarot cards, shuffled them, laid out a Celtic cross, tried to focus: What would happen *if*?

The cards failed her—the answers all seemed obscure or trivial or irrelevant. She yawned, and thought about going back to bed, but knew better: the insomnia was trying to trick her. She had to be yet sleepier, to get any sleep. Had to seek exhaustion.

Downstairs, she had some milk. Thought about watching television, gave it up as a bad idea: she wasn't interested in television, she was interested in what she had to do.

Loren, reflected out of a window overlooking the lake, said, "You have no choice, Alyssa. I don't think you'd do well in the women's prison. You're not cut out for being locked in a cell, for that blue-collar misery, washing floors and working in a laundry. Year after year after year, until you turn into a hag. We have to kill him."

"Go away," she said. "You got me into this, you asshole, now go away and let me think."

Back upstairs, she stopped at the door to Hunter's bedroom, then pushed the door open and stepped inside. She could still smell him. He used an old-fashioned aftershave—Bay Rum, like that—and it clung to the room, as long as he'd been gone.

She noticed, in the dark, the small amber lights on the stereo: had they always been on? Maybe. She'd never been in the room for more than a few minutes at a time, after his death. On impulse, she picked up the remote control, clicked Play. After a few clicking sounds, Paul Simon came up: *"Still crazy, after all these years . . ."*

With the music playing softly in the background, she sat on Hunter's bed, not knowing exactly what she was up to. Closed her eyes, and let the karmic energy flow over her, through her, tell her what to do. The song ended, and she opened her eyes, and opened the bottom drawer on the bedstand.

The gun was there—a .38, with hollow-point bullets. When concealed carry became legal in Minnesota, Hunter had been one of the first to qualify for a permit. Then he carried for a while—the

.38, a Beretta 9mm, a .45, and then it all just got too heavy, and he started leaving the guns at home.

He took the .38 with him, though, when he and his biker buddies rode out to Sturgis—they actually cheated, and shipped the bikes to Bismarck in the back of a couple of Chevy vans, driven by wives sworn to secrecy, and rode into Sturgis from there, greasy jeans and leather chaps and dirty boots and four-day beards, aging Brandos right out of the executive suite. The .38, he told her, was a necessity should there be trouble: "Nobody knows that I've got it," he said with a grin, over breakfast. "Nobody knows where it came from. If I gotta use it, I can ditch it and be clear."

She'd said, "For Christ sakes, Hunter, you're a mechanical engineer, you don't shoot people. Leave the gun at home—it doesn't make you look like a gunman, it makes you look like an idiot."

That had annoyed him, and he hadn't spoken to her for a day or two; and he'd taken the gun.

SHE LIFTED THE gun out of the drawer, hefted it, put the muzzle to her temple, closed her eyes, started to squeeze, and Loren said, "Don't do that. Alyssa, please. The gun could go off, you might not even kill yourself, you could leave yourself with half a brain. You don't know what you're doing."

"Don't hurt me," Fairy pleaded.

Alyssa chuckled, and took the gun down, and now put the muzzle in her mouth—but it tasted bad, and she took it back out.

"I've got to think about this," she said.

"One shot, at night, and the Davenport problem is gone," Loren said. "We don't even have to hurry—just watch his place. If everything isn't perfect, we pass."

"Maybe he goes to bed at eight o'clock every night," Alyssa suggested.

"I don't think so—he's talked about working late. Weather says they're mismatched that way. She gets up early every morning, he stays up late."

★

ALYSSA TURNED OFF the stereo, carried the gun back to her bedroom and laid it on the nightstand next to the clock, where the green light of the clock, seen from her pillow, broke over the cylinder. Revolvers, she remembered from her lesson, were the simplest gun to use. No safeties—point and shoot.

And if they were cocked first, the trigger was a hair-pull. A breath would slam the hammer down, and the bullet would be on its way.

She lay back on the pillow, thinking.

Put the gun back in her mouth.

Or shoot Davenport.

AFTER A WHILE, they all went to sleep.

26

LUCAS GOT UP early, feeling lethargic, after a bad night's sleep.

In looking back over the pattern of killings—not counting the murder of Frances Austin—it still appeared to him that they had to be connected. Had to be connected to the Fairy, whether the Fairy had used the knife, or not.

He knew the Fairy was small, dark, and apparently in good physical condition. Some of the people who'd seen her had described her as young, but one woman said she wasn't as young as she looked—while a guy in the same conversation had said something to the effect that whatever her age, she had a young ass.

If, Lucas thought, you were looking for someone a bit crazy—perhaps even schizophrenic—with a powerful revenge motive, a somewhat older face but younger ass, you had Alyssa Austin.

But Fairy was dark, while Austin was blond. That would not, Lucas thought, be an insuperable barrier for a woman whose career was built on providing youthful images to other woman, through her spas.

A wig, some eyebrow pencil, youthful dress, a careful avoidance of prolonged contact with other people—it could be done.

And, in the murder of Patricia Shockley, there'd been the question of why she would let an unknown woman, who looked like the Fairy, whom she'd been warned against . . . why she would allow her in the apartment?

What if the unknown woman had shown up as the blond, unthreatening mother of Shockley's own murdered friend?

A long train of suppositions; not enough for an arrest. How about the burned car? Might that lead to her? Something that would pin her down? The only living person who'd seen the Fairy for more than a couple of minutes was the Xiong guy, if indeed he'd seen the Fairy at all.

HE WAS MOVING by eight, cleaned up, grumbled at the house-keeper and Sam, who'd already had breakfast, skimmed the papers. Neither one had anything on the arrest of Ricky and Helen, because, he knew, neither paper spent much time tracking the cops anymore. If the paper's main cop guy had gone home for the day, you could murder the queen of England, and the papers wouldn't know about it for eighteen hours.

He made it to the office a few minutes after nine o'clock, and immediately went down to see Jackson, the photographer—Jackson wasn't in, but had been in, was probably wandering around the building someplace, Lucas was told. Lucas grumbled more about that, as he sat and waited, and finally had the bright idea of calling Jackson on his cell phone—and it turned out the photographer was three offices down the hall.

"Be there in a second," he said, and he was.

"HOW LONG would it take you to Photoshop those pictures of Alyssa Austin, and turn her into a brunette?"

"Depends on how precisely accurate you want it to be,"

Jackson said. "I've got a half-dozen shots. If you want all half dozen, and you want good but not perfect . . . half an hour. From right now to prints on your desk."

"Get it done," Lucas said. "See you in half an hour."

WHILE HE WAS waiting for the photos, Lucas called Shrake, who was back at the Heather-watch apartment. "I was gonna call, but I didn't think you'd be up yet," Shrake said. "A weird thing happened—a guy showed up, looked like an asshole, talked to Heather, looked around the apartment. I'd seen him earlier on the street, walking around. Heather seemed to know him; didn't have a problem letting him in."

"They were friendly?"

"No, not especially. He just came in, hands in his pockets. Leather coat, black leather gloves. Looked around, mostly, and she just stood there. Then he left."

"Siggy's security," Lucas said.

"That thought occurred to me," Shrake said. "He gave off that feeling, like one of those Secret Service guys, checking the place out."

"Stay in touch," Lucas said.

"Look—what about overtime? I'd like to get Jenkins back in here, but he's not due until late afternoon. Then I'm supposed to be off, but I'd like to stay. I'd do it for free, but overtime would be nice."

"I'll fix the overtime," Lucas said. "Call him in."

JACKSON SHOWED UP at ten o'clock and slid a half-dozen high-resolution glossy prints across Lucas's desk. Lucas picked them up. He'd seen the photos of Austin as a blonde, and the brunette hair, in the new photos, had transformed her. "Tricky part was her eyebrows; they might look a little fakey," Jackson said.

"Look perfect to me," Lucas said.

"I heard about the arrests last night," Jackson said. "That picture of Davis help out?"

"That cracked it," Lucas said. "Everything came after that."

Jackson looked pleased. "I told them that the new gear was worth the money."

"If these turn out to be something," Lucas said, holding up the photos of Austin, "I'll talk to Rose Marie about making that van a permanent item on your equipment list."

"Ah, man—that'd be great," Jackson said.

XAI XIONG, the man who may, or may not, have sold the burned car to the Fairy, worked at a computer rehab place on University Avenue, fixing what could be fixed, putting in new hard drives. You could, he told Lucas, buy a good-as-new used Dell for $150.

"How long did you talk to the woman about your car?" Lucas asked.

Xiong was a small man with a brush cut and a pale burn mark on one cheek. He was maybe thirty. "Fifteen minutes? Twenty minutes? She didn't know nothing about cars."

"How'd you hook up with her?" Lucas asked.

"I had the phone number in the window of the car, and she called. I said I needed nine thousand dollars, and she said that was okay, if the car ran good. I told her the car ran perfect and even had good rubber on it. The seats were sorta screwed, we welded them down, but I told her a lady would probably fit pretty good. So she said she was interested, and we met out there, and we drove the car a couple miles up the frontage road to this Purina place, and then back, and she said she'd take it."

"Paid cash."

"Yup. Nine thousand dollars in hundred-dollar bills. Fresh in a bank envelope from Wells Fargo. Had me sign the papers, said she'd put them through, and that's the last I heard from her. The cops tell me she never did put the papers through."

"Was nine thousand dollars a fair price?"

Xiong's eyes drifted and he smiled. "That's what I was asking," he said.

"So maybe . . . she could have negotiated."

285

"Some," he admitted. "She never did. She just paid up."

She was rich, Lucas thought. As Frank Willett had said, the cost of a car was nothing. If Lucas could find a nine-thousand-dollar cash withdrawal from Austin's account, at the right date, that would be a big plus. Lucas took the pack of photos out of his jacket pocket, slipped them out of the envelope. He handed them to Xiong and asked, "Does this look like her?"

Xiong shuffled through them quickly, cocking his head back and forth, then handed them to Lucas and said, "That *is* her."

"You're sure?"

"Yeah, man—that's her," he said.

SO HE HAD Austin as the Fairy, but no connection between the car and the crimes—and if the car had burned to the ground, there wouldn't be one.

And what did she use the car for, anyway? To get back and forth from the killing ground, so that if anyone saw her, they couldn't say the killer had been driving a Benz or a Jag? Possibly. Probably.

Xiong's testimony would be challenged in court. Lucas would have to tie Austin/Fairy more tightly to the car, and to the Goth scene, before they could start pushing her directly.

He dipped in his notebook for names: a number of people had seen her. If he could get one or two more to make a positive ID . . . If he could figure out where she'd kept the car, and he could positively tie her to it, that would make good Xiong's identification . . .

A bell dinged in the back of his mind. Where was the car burned? He called South St. Paul, was told that Janice Loomis-Smith, the cop who'd called him about it, was off. He told the guy on the phone what he was looking for, and the guy said, "Just down south of 494, on Concord, on the east side of the road. Why?"

"Where's the South St. Paul airport? Isn't that down there, somewhere?"

"It's right up the hill. Six blocks, maybe. Why?"

"Making connections," Lucas said. "Thanks."

And that's where the Austins had an airplane hangar, but no airplane.

HE LOOKED AT his watch: noon, and he was hungry, and not too far from home. The refrigerator was full of healthy stuff—salads, tofu, yogurts, turkey breast. He stopped at Baker's Square Restaurant and had the French Dip without the dip, hold the fries, and a piece of raspberry pie as a replacement for the fries that were rightfully his.

He was finishing the pie when Shrake called from the Heatherwatch. "Maybe you better get over here."

"What's up?"

"Heather just took a call. She listened for five seconds, then she hung up, and right now she's sitting on the couch, with her arms crossed, looking at the door."

"Call SWAT. Tell them to stage up," Lucas said. "No goddamn lights or sirens. Let's get it on. I'm down on Ford parkway, I gotta get my vest, it's in my truck. I'll be there in ten."

He threw fifteen dollars at the cashier, said, "Use the rest for a tip," and ran to the car, pulled it around, headed up Mt. Curve and then over to Mississippi River Boulevard, running stop signs, punched up the garage door, ran up to the truck, grabbed the duffel bag with his vest, ran back to the Porsche and was out the driveway in four minutes. Eight minutes later, having parked around a full block, he was climbing the stairs to the apartment, hauling along the duffel bag.

Del was there, looking like a hippie except for his bulletproof vest, worn loose around his shoulders. Shrake and Jenkins hadn't yet armored up, Kevlar helmets sitting on the table like lost turtles, vests on the floor. Shrake said, "St. Paul says the SWAT will be at the church in four or five minutes. They were all briefed yesterday afternoon, they were ready, so if this isn't just a fuck-up, we oughta be good."

". . . in four or five minutes," Lucas said, standing on his tiptoes, back in the dark, trying to see the street. "Nobody out there. Looks like fuckin' *High Noon.*"

"I'm gonna feel like an asshole if nothing happens," Shrake said. "Calling everybody in."

"You *are* an asshole," Jenkins said.

"I want you to know, Jenkins made me do it," Shrake told Lucas. "I mean, if this doesn't work out."

"Anybody coming, anybody going?" Lucas asked.

"Two cars, two minutes before you got here. Nobody in the apartment. Heather just sits there."

"Well, something's happening," Lucas said.

TEN MINUTES. Lucas went to the bathroom to pee, came back out, said, "Somebody took all the paper towels."

"Here's something," Del said. "She's up."

Heather went to the door, opened it. A man was there in a dark blue peacoat and sunglasses, and she threw her arms around his neck, pulling herself up to his throat. He bent to kiss her, and two other guys crowded in behind him, and Shrake said, "Let's go, let's go . . ."

The guy walked past Heather, looked around, then moved up to the windows and pulled the shades. Lucas said to Del, "Put the glasses on him if he comes up to the window again. I don't think that's Siggy. He doesn't walk like Siggy."

"Then who in the hell was she kissing?" Shrake asked.

The guy pulled the shades on the second window, and Del said, "Shit, he looks like Siggy, but I think you're right. He's a dummy."

"Gimme the glasses," Jenkins said. "I know the fucker pretty good." The guy appeared in the last window on the left, the kitchen, and pulled the shade, and Jenkins, peering through the 12x36 image-stabilized binoculars, said, "Goddamnit. He does look like Siggy. And goddamnit, they're pulling our weenies. That's not him."

"You're sure?"

"Yeah—you know how? His earlobes are wrong," Jenkins said. "Siggy plays with his earring. He did it all the way through the bail hearing, kept playing with that diamond, big as a lemon drop, and he's got these great big fat fleshy earlobes. This guy's got no earlobes at all, and his mouth isn't quite right. Jesus, he looks like him. He's got the haircut, but that ain't him."

Lucas looked at Shrake: "Talk to the SWAT. This is just more security . . . he's coming in."

"How're we going to see him with the shades down?" Jenkins asked.

"The shades aren't down in the bedroom," Lucas said. "Siggy's a horny bastard, he's gonna nail her the minute he comes through the door. Unless they pull the shades down."

"Unless he's been getting some tail down in Miami," Jenkins said. "They got some primo stuff down there."

"He's a family man," Shrake said. "Even if he's been getting it three times a day, he'll try to prove to her he didn't. I know what the guy's like."

Del said, "But what if that tummy bump isn't his work? Then what?"

FIVE MINUTES.

Del said, "One of the guys was peeking at us, out of the kitchen window. He's got glasses."

"Can't see in, we're okay," Shrake said. When they took the apartment, they'd covered the windows with a thin gray 3M film. From the other side of the street, it looked like you could see in, but you couldn't.

FIVE MINUTES. Jenkins said, "They're in the street. One of them is coming right at the drugstore."

"You know what? He's going to ask about us," Del said.

"How many of them know about us?" Lucas asked.

"Phil and Ann. They're the only ones," Del said. He had his phone in his hand, and he was speed-dialing. A moment later, he said, "Phil? This is Del. There's a guy coming in the door. He'll ask you who lives up here. Let somebody else answer—get out the back or something. Get Ann out of the way, too. He's wearing a leather jacket, he's just coming up to the door, now. Just get out of sight . . . don't try to fake him out, he'll read your face."

TWO MINUTES. Phil called, Del listened. To Lucas: "The guy just left, he talked to Nancy, the pharmacist, she told him nobody lives here right now. Phil said it looked like he was headed around back, to the door."

"Snap-latch, should be locked," Lucas said.

They went quiet, listening. Nobody came up the stairs.

TWO MINUTES: they saw the guy come back around the end of the drugstore, and head across the street. He was talking on a cell phone.

"Get ready," Lucas said.

SIX MINUTES.

Siggy showed up, but they didn't know it. They found out later that he was in a raggedy ass Chevrolet that turned down into the parking garage entrance, and disappeared.

Jenkins wondered, "Why didn't she go to him?"

"Kid," Lucas suggested.

"Leave the kid with Mom. Meet in a hotel across town. She comes in at a preset time, his security is all set up, they see if anybody comes in behind her."

"Maybe you ought to suggest that for next time," Shrake said.

"He doesn't believe we'd still be here," Lucas said. "It's been too long."

"He knows we just busted Antsy."

"But that was Antsy's fault," Lucas said.

"He doesn't believe—"

"Wait-wait," Del said, urgently, and they all looked at the

remaining open window, and Heather was there laughing, in the arms of a big man who reached out and pulled the blind, and they were already tumbling toward the bed when the blind came down, and Jenkins said, "Hello, Siggy."

LUCAS TALKED TO the SWAT commander: "We know he's got at least three security guys—we've seen them. He might've had more people with him, when he came in. You gotta count on five or six guys. Just looking at them, I'd say they're cocked and ready to go."

The SWAT started in, and Lucas, Shrake, and Jenkins armored up, heavy stuff with drop-down groin protection and Level IV armor plates in the chest and back. Del slapped the Velcro bands around his vest and they all put on helmets. Shrake had an M16, Jenkins his 12gauge pump, Lucas and Del their pistols.

"It'd be stupid if they were all up there in that apartment, listening to Siggy and Heather getting it on," Lucas said. "I wouldn't be surprised if there was one of them on this side of the street, another one in the garage, another one on the other side of the building, couple in the apartment, plus Siggy. They'll all have phones. Let the SWAT do the hard stuff, keep your eyes on the windows . . ."

"Here comes SWAT," Del said.

A ST. PAUL undercover guy had photographed the interior of the apartment house, and had gotten keys for the lobby door. Since Heather's apartment was on the second floor, with street-side windows, the squad could be through the lobby, up the fire stairs, and in the hall outside the apartment in less than fifteen seconds.

As they came in, in three vans, the undercover guy, in plain clothes, would open the door and hold it: the squad would go straight through, up the stairs, and attack the apartment door, knocking down opposition with a couple of flash-bangs.

That was the theory.

If they killed the pregnant wife or the baby, they'd be, as the SWAT commander noted, permanent residents of shit city.

THE VANS ROLLED slowly down the street, and the undercover guy walked up the steps to the front door, working the key. Lucas said, "Let's go."

They went out the door and down the stairs in a rush, hit the outside door, and thirty feet down the alley and around the corner of the drugstore and down the width of the store and around the next corner and the SWAT guys were boiling out of the vans and into the apartment.

As they came around the corner, running into the street, Lucas saw a guy run out of a bagel shop across the street, seventy or eighty yards away from them, looking up at the apartment, a cell phone to his ear.

Shrake yelled, "Hey!" and the guy turned and looked at them and took off running, away, up Snelling, and Del said, "I'll get him," and took off after him.

Lucas, Shrake, and Jenkins ran across the street and up the sidewalk and heard the flash-bangs go off in the apartment, then the long, ripping stutter of a machine gun, and Jenkins yelled, "Holy shit," and the machine gun wouldn't stop and Lucas thought about drywall and plywood walls in apartment buildings, and hoped the shooting was being done by the cops, but it didn't sound like it, it sounded too uncontrolled and crazy.

Then Lucas picked up individual shots, and a man ran out the front door, looked at the vans, yanked up a small, short weapon, and fired a burst at the vans and then turned and ran away, up the street, where Del could still be seen chugging after the first runner, and Shrake said, "I got him," and lifted his M16 and Lucas shouted, "No, no . . ." and behind the runner, a car pulled out of the parking garage and stopped across the sidewalk and Shrake yelled, "Shit!"

A chair came through the end window on the apartment, and then a blanket dropped over the edge and Siggy looked out at them, saw them, turned the same weapon the second runner had, and fired a burst at them and they all went sideways behind parked cars and the bullets *patted* and *whanked* like bees.

Siggy dropped the gun out the window and threw himself over the edge, hung one second and dropped, ten or twelve feet into a flower bed, and Shrake stood up and the second runner, now eighty or a hundred yards off, opened up again and they all went flat again and then Siggy was running away with the gun, around the car still sitting in the driveway, behind it.

The driver came flying out the driver's-side door and sprawled on the ground and Siggy was in the car, fired another burst through the open driver's door, reached up and grabbed the steering wheel and pushed on the gas pedal with his other hand, and as the car started into the street, Shrake walked out into the street and said, "Fuck this," and dumped half a magazine into the front of the car.

The car straightened out and drifted across the street and ran into a parked car in front of the bagel shop, and sat there.

Lucas was running after the second runner, screaming, "Del, Del," and Del, at the top of a low hill, finally heard him, saw the second runner across the street coming toward him, ducked behind a car, and fired half a magazine at him, and the runner unloaded his weapon, whatever it was, the bullets pounding and zinging under the car that Del was hiding behind. Then he was out of ammo and he dropped the gun and started running again, and Del shot him, one long leading shot, and knocked him off his feet.

Lucas saw the second runner go down, then there were two more flash-bangs and the machine gun stuttered once, again, then a heavier, harsher sound erupted, and the higher-pitched shooting stopped.

All of a sudden, it was absolutely quiet in the street.

Lucas ran across and looked in the car Siggy had tried to take. Siggy was dead, his face a hash of blood and meat where Shrake's .223 slugs had torn into him. Jenkins was talking to the car's driver, a young guy in a blue suit, now wearing a pair of broken glasses and a stunned look.

Up the street, Del was approaching the man on the ground.

The SWAT commander ran out of the apartment and said, "We okay?"

"Got a loose runner, maybe two, got two down," Lucas said. "What happened?"

"Guy on the front room couch with a fuckin' M7 and we came through the door and man, he opened up and didn't quit; we shot him."

"Any of our guys . . . ?"

"We're all okay, got some cuts and splinters and shit."

"Heather and the baby . . . ?"

"They're okay."

DEL'S BULLET went through the second runner's triceps, his armpit, and into his chest, where it made a hash out of his heart and lungs. They called ambulances, but he was gone before Del even crossed the street.

They never saw the first runner again. The way they later worked it out, he'd run three blocks, spotted a passing cab, jumped in, and took the cab to Minneapolis. The driver said he dropped the passenger conveniently close to a light-rail station, which went to the airport, among other places.

They got Heather dressed and took her out in cuffs, and downtown to be processed, but she was already screaming, "I didn't know he was coming, I didn't know . . ."

She wanted a lawyer; and had his card in her purse.

Jenkins asked, "Where'd they get those fuckin' machine guns?"

Lucas shook his head: "They were coming in from Miami."

"But we got him," Shrake said.

THEN EVERYBODY in the world came down on top of them: TV and newspapers and even a public radio guy with a tape recorder and a boring voice, a dozen cop cars, the cops to check the neighborhood for any collateral injuries or damage, crime-scene people. The street and the various shooting scenes were cordoned off, and crime-scene guys landed in force, the ME's investigators, Jackson with his Nikon D3 and every lens in the world, the St. Paul police photographer with an inferior Canon camera, a variety of deputy chiefs, homicide investigators, and a partridge in a pear tree.

It all took forever, it seemed; and Lucas was there, the whole time, and they all talked about it over and over, what everybody had seen and done, and Lucas had this sense that he hadn't done much, but he was *there*, and it all felt pretty large.

By six o'clock, the activity was petering out, and most of the cop cars were gone, and the crime-scene people were turning off work lights, and the TV guys were peeling away.

LUCAS CALLED Weather and told her; and made sure that Del was okay, and that Shrake was okay, and they were, but now they were getting shaky with the realization that they'd actually killed people. Nobody knew exactly who'd killed the machine-gun guy in the apartment, because a number of cops had fired at him.

Lucas said, "Who'd have thought."

"Submachine guns," Del said. "Goddamn, if they'd been heavier, if they'd been assault rifles, we'd of had some dead guys."

"Saw the goddamn slugs powdering the street around you," Lucas said.

"Scared the shit out of me, it was like hail, but they weren't getting through the tires," Del said. "I don't know what they were shooting, but the tires went flat and the slugs weren't getting through."

"Thank God for steel-belted radials, eh?" Lucas said.

"I could hear them hitting those bricks around that bagel shop."

"That was a hell of a shot you made across that street."

"Luck, was what it was. Forty yards—I'd be lucky to hit a garbage can at that range."

"You all right?"

"A hell of a lot better than the alternative," Del said. "I didn't know he'd dropped that fuckin' gun until you told me."

"You see that guy come out of the store with that pie in the box?" Lucas asked. "He comes out and sees a dead guy laying there . . ."

"Hope it wasn't a cherry pie; he might be getting flashbacks about now."

In his mind's eye, Lucas saw Siggy's head, and the thick coagulating pool of blood underneath it. Imagined a fly buzzing around, though he hadn't seen any flies.

Fuckin' Siggy.

"SEE YOU back at the office?" Del asked.

"Yeah. We all oughta get something on paper tonight. This was a long way from perfect."

"See you there," Del said. "I'm gonna stop at home first. Cheryl's been barfing again."

"See you there."

27

FAIRY HAD THE gall and the will and even—maybe—the sense of humor that would make it possible to kill Davenport and get away with it. Alyssa herself was too fragile, and could feel the stress pecking at her even as Fairy, with her Valley-girl voice, called Davenport's home and spoke to Weather.

"Is Lucas Davenport there?"

"No, he's not—who is this, please?" Weather was using her surgeon's voice, with the crisp edge of command.

"Um, I'm an old friend of Frances Austin's. Do you know when Officer Davenport will be home?"

"Actually, I don't. There's been a big problem, a shooting, in St. Paul, and he's working it. You might be able to get him at his office."

At his office. The BCA. Where was that? Fairy was standing at a phone kiosk without phone books, or even a place to put them. Had to be some way—how did people get to the BCA, if they had an appointment?

FIVE MINUTES LATER, Alyssa, now in her office at the Highland Park spa, brought up the BCA website and got not only a map, but a photograph. The photograph gave her an idea, and she brought up Google Earth, homed in on east St. Paul, and two minutes later sent a satellite view of the BCA building and parking lots to her printer.

And it all came in handy: the BCA was located out of the city center, near a popular lake and park. She cruised the parking lot, spotted Davenport's Porsche. How many cops had Porsches? Very convenient.

She parked across the street, in an empty lot behind some kind of clinic, and let Fairy take over.

"Simple enough," Fairy said, meeting Loren's eyes in the rearview mirror. "If he's by himself when he comes out, I'll kill him here. If he's not, we follow him home, and we kill him at his garage. How far do you have to drive before you're lost in traffic? Not far, I think."

"But you're going as Alyssa," Loren said. "If Weather sees you . . . I'd be happier if we had time to get another wig. Have you go dark."

She shrugged. "If I bought a dark wig, and somebody ran it down . . . This is okay, because"—she tapped her forehead—"Alyssa's right here, and she's a big chicken. If there's any reason not to do it, she'll tell us."

"And you'll let her back."

"Of course," Fairy said. "Alyssa and I are very close now."

★

THEN SHE GOT a taste of cop work: she sat, and *sat*, and *sat*, and Lucas didn't come out. Three dozen people came and went, but the Porsche sat there, untouched. She got the gun out from the storage console at her elbow, turned the cylinder, looked once and then again to make sure each of the chambers was loaded, put it back in the console.

SAT SOME MORE, and after a while, became aware of her bladder and started looking at bushes by the back door of the clinic. If a cop saw her, and she was right across the street from about a million cops . . .

Alyssa didn't want to, but Fairy goaded her into it: "Two minutes, we'll feel a lot better."

"If anybody sees . . ."

"It's pitch-dark out there. We're wearing black. Who's going to see?"

The argument took a while. Fairy won, and she slipped out of the car with a handful of Kleenex, into the bushes, and back to the car a few minutes later, feeling much better.

"See. That's life, Alyssa," Fairy said. "Peeing is a natural function."

"Shut up."

THEN HE CAME. She recognized him immediately—a big guy, athletic, relaxed stride; with another guy, talking. Couldn't take him here—couldn't take him even if he'd been alone, she realized, because she'd misjudged the distance to the car. The two guys weren't especially hurrying, but they were covering ground, and Davenport would be at the Porsche before she could get close. Then he'd see her, and if he saw her . . .

"Shit! This was so stupid," Alyssa said. "What were we thinking? If he sees us coming, he'll know what's up. He'll kill us."

"So we take him home," Fairy said. "Hey: he's a cop. This is a first time we've done a cop. Let's calm down. Calm down and take him home."

LUCAS SAID to Del, "Okay, Cheryl's appointment's at ten? Let me know what happens."

"I will—I'm a little scared," Del said. "She's always been healthy as a horse. God only knows what you can get in a hospital now. They've got all these weird germs. And she used to assist with angiograms, who knows how much radiation she got? And she's really been feeling rocky. I thought she was better last week, but now it's back."

"Let me know," Lucas said. And, as Del turned away, "You're all right? About the shooting?"

"Pretty sure," Del said. He shrugged. "Maybe people like us can forget it. Let it go. Go get a cheeseburger."

"You'll think about it for a while," Lucas said. "I believe you'll be okay, but if you aren't, tell someone. They got pills."

"Yeah. Pills. Check you tomorrow, big guy."

LUCAS CALLED Weather from the car.

"Are we all over the TV?"

"Everywhere. Networks, cable. Lucas—we've gotta talk. This has been crazy, first you get shot, and then this."

"We'll talk," he said. "Maybe I'll become a humble carpenter. Or I could become the skate sharpener for the Gopher women's hockey team."

"Lucas . . . really, how're you feeling?"

"My ass is kicked, but I'm okay," Lucas said. "I'm still a little worried about Shrake and Del, but they say they're okay."

"See what happens tomorrow," she said.

"Yeah."

"So. Would you have time to stop at the SA? I just dropped a bottle of milk and it's all over the place. We'll need some for breakfast tomorrow."

"Sure. See you in twenty minutes."

HE TOOK it easy heading home. He had a Super America convenience store in mind, and headed down Maryland on remote control, thinking about the day. The Siggy investigation had been mostly a BCA deal, but when the final explosion occurred, St. Paul had carried a lot of the weight. They'd also been the guys in the sharp-looking BDUs and armor and helmets with the big guns, and they were the ones who'd gotten the TV time.

Which was fine with him.

Idled through a green light, heading down the hill toward the SA, flashed on the first animal he'd ever killed while hunting. It'd been a rabbit, and he was shooting a .410 single-shot shotgun, the first gun of his life. The bunny broke cover thirty feet ahead of him, at the edge of an empty, harvested bean field.

He remembered how cold it was then, in late October, and how he'd shucked one mitten and his father had said, "Take him." The rabbit ran away, as they do, but then, as they also do, began turning, a long curved run, as though the rabbit were inscribing a circle with Lucas as the center point. He led it by a foot or two, pulled the trigger, and the rabbit tumbled head over heels, dead before it hit the ground.

He thought about it because it was exactly the way that Del had shot the runner. Lucas had been watching it, the rest of them had too much background to risk a shot after him, and then he saw Del swinging with the man's pace and the single shot and the man went down like the shot bunny.

LUCAS FOUND HIMSELF standing in front of the SA store, hardly knowing how he got there.

He nodded at the counterman going in, got a bottle of one-per-cent and a couple of bottles of diet Coke. Checking out, the counterman said, "Looks like rain."

"Spring's coming," Lucas said.

"Wouldn't be surprised to see a little more snow."

"Won't last," Lucas said.

"Take it easy . . ."

He went out to the Porsche, carrying the grocery bag, popped the passenger-side door so he could put the bag on the floor . . .

FAIRY WHISPERED, to all of them, "Go, go . . ." And she was out the door, the car idling by the curb, across the verge of damp grass, coming up to the gas pumps where he'd parked, behind them, actually, out of sight, the gun heavy in her hand, around the pumps, and he was right there and he stood up and saw her and she was six feet away, the gun swinging up . . .

LUCAS CAUGHT A flash of urgent motion between the pumps and turned, still bent over the bag, saw her, recognized her, saw her hand moving, knew what was happening, had no chance for his gun or for anything, trapped by the door of the car and he reached onto the front seat and caught the vest and yanked it up and the gun went off and the blow hit him in the heart and he went down . . .

ONE BRIGHT FLASH and one horrifying bang and he was down beside the car and Alyssa was screaming, "Go, go," and she turned and ran before the counterman in the gas station could see her, and she was in the car and she swung in a U-turn . . .

LUCAS SAT UP, alive, breathing, holding his chest. The blow hadn't actually been heavy enough to knock him down, but he'd gone down anyway, because somehow, that's what you did when you were shot, and it took him a few seconds to realize that there was no blood and he staggered to his feet, the vest in his hand, realized he'd managed to smother the muzzle of the gun with the vest, and he looked toward the street and saw Alyssa's big green Benz swing in a U-turn and then he was in the Porsche and the counterman was running toward him, and he cranked the car and the anger clawed at his throat and they were out of there, a hundred feet behind her and he was gonna eat her fuckin' lunch . . .

SHE SAW HIM stand up, realized that she'd missed, and she screamed at herself, "Jesus, Jesus," and then she stopped thinking altogether and thought about getting home, getting somewhere safe, and she stood on the gas pedal and was through the light, swinging past skidding cars, left onto 35E, headed south, and a moment later she saw the blue lights of the Porsche behind her and Fairy rose out of her chest and took the car and pushed the gas pedal to the floor . . .

LUCAS WAS ON the phone, screaming at St. Paul: "Headed south on 35E, she's headed straight back into town, going past Pennsylvania, coming up on 94 . . ."

The dispatcher said, "We've got a car coming up. Aw, he says you're in front of him, he can see you," and Lucas flicked his eyes toward the rearview mirror and saw the lights, but they were falling back.

And the dispatcher said, "We've got another car coming east on I—94. Where do you want him, where do you want him?"

"I don't know yet, I don't know . . ."

They were traveling at a hundred and ten miles an hour through sixty-mile-an-hour traffic, through a big snarly intersection downtown, and Lucas saw flashing lights ahead to the right, then Alyssa's taillights flared and she cut left and Lucas shouted, "Headed east on 94 . . ." then he saw the curb coming up and went left and shouted, "Wait, wait, she's headed toward the Lafayette, she's coming up on the bridge, she's turning onto the bridge."

She crossed the Mississippi, speed climbing again, then, with more cop lights coming toward her, dropped off the exit onto the riverside Plato Avenue, and around the corner to the right, Lucas shouting into the phone all the time, bringing in more patrol cars.

Plato was an industrial street: not much traffic, and no homes. Lucas was on her bumper now, or nearly so, pushing her. If he pushed her hard enough, in the big car, she'd lose it, and instead of killing somebody else in another car, she'd take it into a phone pole or a fence or a concrete abutment.

She slashed a cross street without slowing, running the red light, and Lucas was forced to stand on his brakes, to avoid a pickup, and then he was across and behind her, dodging left, and up the river bluff, higher, higher, and there were more lights up ahead, flashers, and he saw her dodge right, slide through the intersection, bump over a sidewalk, cut a piece of lawn and then back on the street, Smith Avenue, onto the High Bridge, Lucas fifty yards behind her . . . and he saw her taillights come up.

At the bottom of the bridge, a few hundred yards away, a St. Paul cruiser pulled up, flashers going, and then, behind it, another. They backed into a blocking V and the cops got out, and then another cop turned onto the bridge . . .

FAIRY STOPPED the car on the bridge, looked back over her shoulder. She felt . . . exhilarated. All the boring stuff was over. The race through town had been the coolest thing she'd done forever . . .

Davenport was back there. Another cop turned onto the bridge behind the Porsche. Then Davenport got out of the car and was calling something to her, but she couldn't hear it.

She was still on the top part of the High Bridge, so cleverly named because it was high. From up there, she had a gorgeous view of downtown St. Paul, the buildings on the bluff over the river.

Loren was standing in the middle of the roadway, in one of his nineteenth-century ruffle-neck costumes. "Look there," Loren said, his voice coarse with stress. "Look there—the boat. The boat's there."

She looked, and down the river, an all-white riverboat with a big red stern wheel.

Loren said, "Frances is on it. I can feel her."

Fairy got out of the car, walked to the railing, looked over. A long way down; and the riverboat was there, coming toward her. Davenport was shouting at her—he was out of his car, walking down the bridge.

Carefully.

She smiled: Was he dead? He should be dead. But if he was dead, how'd the Porsche get there?

She slipped the gun—she had the gun in her hand—into the top of her pants, and did a two-handed push-up, and clambered onto the bridge railing, hanging on tight with her hands until she got her balance.

Then she stood up: a woman who'd spent some time on a balance beam. Now walking slightly uphill, toward Davenport, who was getting closer now, shouting, but she paid no attention.

If she jumped, she'd die. Then she'd be on the boat, with Frances.

Better than scrubbing floors in the women's prison, pushed around by a bunch of hard-eyed women guards.

Davenport was thirty feet away, and stopped, his voice clear now, and she listened for a moment. ". . . off there, Alyssa, for Christ's sakes, you're sick. You need medical help. They've got pills now, medication, get off the railing, for Christ's sakes . . ."

Loren had worked his way around behind Davenport, hovered there, smiling, and he shook his head and said, "Don't believe him. Better to go now."

Fairy could feel the hard edges of the rail under her feet, and as she stood there, she began to slip away; and Alyssa came up, the hard-edged executive, and she looked at Davenport and listened for a few more seconds and knew it was all lies.

Damnit, no way out. No way to explain Loren and Fairy. She'd killed Frances's three friends, all part of the silliness of Fairy and the ghost.

She looked down and shuddered.

Alyssa Austin wasn't going to jump. She wasn't even sure she was over water—as far as she knew, she might hit a concrete abutment and be torn to pieces, or she might hit the water and be paralyzed and drown, and the water would be freezing . . .

She said, to Davenport, very clearly, "Fuck it."

★

LUCAS STOOD THERE with his gun in his hand, heart thumping, thought he had talked her off the rail, was aware of every little thing, of the flashing red lights, of the cops running up the bridge, of the cop behind him, walking down, of more sirens, coming in, and then she said, "Fuck it," and hopped down off the rail. He thought he had her and then she stepped toward him and pulled the pistol out of her pants and whipped the muzzle at him and pulled the trigger and there was a flash and simultaneous crack as the slug went past his face.

Lucas shot her in the heart.

SHE KNEW she was hit; knew she was dying; could see the rail and the starless sky and then Davenport's face, looming above her, and she tried to smile and say to him, "Going with Frances."

BUT LUCAS couldn't make out any words.

All he heard as he crouched over her was a dying moan. Her eyes rolled away, and she breathed a final time, leaving on her full lips a thin foam of bloody bubbles.

28

THINKING ABOUT IT a week later, when he had time, Lucas realized that there had been two key moments in his life, in that one day, the day of the big Siggy shoot-out, the day that he killed Alyssa Austin.

The first had come when he'd driven home to get his bullet-proof vest, before the Siggy shoot-out. He'd jumped out of the Porsche, run into the garage, grabbed the duffel bag that contained the vest, and then had run back to the Porsche. He *could* have punched up the garage door, driven the Porsche inside, parked it, and taken the truck.

But he hadn't.

If he had taken the truck, he would have tossed the vest in the back after the Siggy gunfight. As it was, when he came out of the BCA building, the vest was sitting on the passenger seat of the Porsche. The duffel bag was still in the apartment across the street from Heather's. Anyway, the vest, with its armor plates, was right there.

The second key moment came when Weather dropped the bottle of milk. If she hadn't, he would have driven home, and he would have gotten out of the driver's side of the car, in the garage, and he would have been helpless, assuming that Alyssa was still following him.

He believed that she would have been. If she'd picked him up at the office, she had either been planning to kill him there, in the parking lot, or had been planning to follow him home.

So, he thought, he owed his life to an unconscious choice, and a slippery plastic bottle of yellow-capped one-percent.

WEATHER PREFERRED to lay things out in terms of cause and effect. Lucas thought all of the happenstances that day were exactly that: happenstances. He was alive because he was lucky, because he rolled a seven instead of snake eyes. Weather saw some kind of controlling hand; the victory of good over evil. Though she thought of herself as a scientist, she also had a healthy slice of faith.

Not that she wasn't horrified by what had happened.

LUCAS NORMALLY wouldn't have left the site of the bridge shooting in less than a couple of hours: the crime-scene people would have wanted to get everything nailed down, the St. Paul homicide guys would have wanted to dot some I's and cross some T's before he got out of their sight. But after talking for a while—and watching the TV trucks arrive—he pulled rank and told them that he was going home, at least long enough to talk to his wife.

Weather was not going to see this on TV.

AFTER HE SHOT Austin, and the bureaucratic stuff began, he'd neglected to call home. Weather had called him, wondering why he was so late.

He lied: told her he'd run into a problem, he'd be a while. When she pressed, he snapped at her, said he'd call.

He talked to St. Paul, then pulled rank.

WEATHER WAS IN the kitchen when he got home, wearing her ankle-length flannel nightshirt, one hand on her hip, irritated until she saw his eyes. Then her hands went to her face: "Ohmigod, what happened now?"

He gave it to her straight, as though he were reading a newspaper report, in declarative sentences and short paragraphs, from the time he pulled into the SA store until the shoot-out on the bridge.

She was reeling when he finished: "The whole family is gone. The whole family is dead," she said. "How could this happen? How could this happen?"

And the next stage: "What if I hadn't asked you to talk to Alyssa? I saw her that one day, after my workout, bumped into her, if I hadn't seen her, she'd be alive."

"More people might be dead," Lucas said. "She killed at least three. Who knows how many were on her list?"

"She tried to kill you," Weather said. "She *could* have killed you. She didn't kill you because . . ."

"I got lucky. I got so fuckin' lucky."

"Can't just be luck, Lucas . . ."

That would go on for a while; for two weeks.

HIS WARD, Letty, when Weather wasn't around, wanted the details. He gave them to her while she was eating a handful of carrot sticks, and when he finished, she gave him a couple of sticks and said, "That was good shooting. I think maybe . . ."

"What?"

Her eyes were cold as a teenager's could get: "I might have given her a double-tap. You're lucky she didn't get off another shot."

"You weren't there, you didn't see it," Lucas said.

"That's true," Letty said. She crunched on the last stick. "You done good."

SHRAKE AND JENKINS were freaked out, came and stood in his office door and peered at him the next morning. Jenkins asked, "You're not thinkin' too much, are you?"

"Nope. Don't believe so," Lucas said.

"Man, I looked at the paper," Jenkins said. "That was as good a shooting as I've ever heard of. You had—no—fuckin'—choice."

Lucas nodded. "I know. It was a good shooting."

Shrake said, "You're a brooder, though."

Lucas asked him, "Did you sleep last night?"

"Like a baby," Shrake said.

Jenkins snorted. "Your goddamn eyes looked like coal pits this morning. If you got ten minutes, I'll kiss your ass in Macy's front window."

"So we all gotta sit down and take it easy for a few days," Lucas said.

Shrake nodded. "Take it easy. Hard to stop thinking about it, though."

OVER THE NEXT week, the Ricky Davis–Helen Sobotny problem became more complicated. Davis had completely and comprehensively spilled his guts. Wouldn't stop talking. Wanted to get it off his chest. His story was that Sobotny had killed Frances Austin in an unplanned confrontation in the Austin kitchen.

She'd then called him, as he was driving the wrecker back from a ditch tow job, and told him what she'd done, and pleaded with him to come over. By the time he got there, she'd cleaned up the kitchen and had wrapped Austin up in her coat. Davis argued that they should call the cops. She told him that they'd go to prison forever, that she loved him, that they could get away with it.

He'd wound up getting a sheet of plastic out of the back of the wrecker, had wrapped the body in it, to keep any more blood from leaking out, and had taken off with the body. He dropped it in the ditch. Helen, in the meantime, had driven Austin's car back to Austin's apartment, and had then taken a cab back to Odd's towing service, where she'd picked up Davis's car to drive home.

Sobotny had heard Lucas talking on the telephone about the fifty thousand, and about going to the A1 that night. Davis had the gun, for home protection. She pressured him into attempting to shoot Lucas outside the bar. "I didn't want to shoot anybody, but she was all over me," Davis said. To Lucas: "I didn't mean to hit you. I was sort of shooting in the dirt."

His story wrapped up all the details and most of it was confirmed by the lab reports.

SOBOTNY WASN'T TALKING, but the representations from her lawyer suggested everything was as Davis said, except that Davis had killed Austin with the knife, and that he'd gone after Lucas on his own account, after Sobotny had told him about the phone conversation. She'd begged him, her attorney said, not to do that, but as a small woman alone in a trailer home with a killer, she'd been afraid to say or do anything that might get her own throat cut.

Her story also wrapped up all the details and was confirmed by the lab reports.

IF ONE OF them could cut a deal with the county attorney, he, or she, might spend as little as six or seven years inside. The other would spend thirty.

In either case, Del said, by the time somebody got out, the emus would be long gone—or way too fuckin' tough to eat.

THE PROBLEM WITH the Siggy shooting was that everybody whose name they knew was dead, except Heather, the baby, and her mom. Her mom was out of it. She knew nothin' about nothin'. Heather also claimed that she didn't know anything, until it was too late to call anybody. "I had a bunch of goons leaning on me and the baby, for Christ's sakes. What was I supposed to do, excuse myself while I called nine-one-one?"

They established that there had been two runners who had gotten away clean. One they'd seen—the man Del had chased until he got in the gunfight. The other, the man who looked like Siggy, they hadn't seen after the staged scene in the apartment. There'd been St. Paul guys covering the back of the building, and he hadn't gone that way. They'd checked every apartment in the building, and he wasn't hiding there.

One idea was that he'd run through the basement parking ramp to the far end, walked through a garbage pickup area, climbed a concrete-block wall, through some bushes and into a convenience store's parking lot, and simply walked away from there. There had been other people on the street, and not all had been accounted for.

WHEN PRESSED ABOUT the phone call at the Mall of America, Heather said she'd simply been shopping, heard the phone ringing, and had picked it up. Somebody with a wrong number, she said. Wouldn't anybody do that?

The county attorney eventually decided that they didn't have anything they could hold her with—she hadn't actually had time or space to commit any crimes. So she got the baby back from the social services people, and went back to her apartment.

WHEN THE BCA people were moving furniture and communications equipment out of the surveillance apartment, Lucas went over to pick up the duffel bag for his armored vest. He noticed that all of Heather's apartment's blinds were down.

Del had a theory.

"She knew we were there. She was doing a little stage play for us—holding us here. She got rid of Siggy. Siggy was a big liability—violent, on the run, in love with her. He thinks all the hidden money is *his*. So Heather let us see every damn thing that she did, that might make us think that Siggy was coming back. So we could nail him. Like we did."

Lucas and Del took that thought down to the Ramsey County lockup, and talked to Antsy, who had mostly recovered from resisting arrest.

"I AIN'T GIVING you shit," Antsy said, when they walked into the interview room.

"We don't need you to give us shit," Lucas said, pulling up a chair. "You're going to Stillwater. For a long time. That deal is done. We just want to chat about your sister-in-law. There's no criminal aspect to it. We just want to chat."

Antsy's lawyer looked at him and shrugged.

Antsy said, "What about?"

"That bump on her tummy, is that Siggy's work?"

"Why wouldn't it be?" Antsy asked.

"Because we happen to know that she was very friendly with another of Siggy's employees," Del said. "So: you think the baby was Siggy's?"

Antsy's brow beetled. "She was fuckin' somebody else?"

"That's an indelicate way of putting it, but, yes," Lucas said. "She was fuckin' somebody else. With a lot of enthusiasm. Christ, we thought they were gonna do it on the kitchen table, with the blinds up. We coulda made a porno movie."

"Ah, shit," Antsy said. "But—the bump was his. He snuck back here four months ago, they met at the Radisson over in Minneapolis. She said nobody was watching her." He gnawed at his thumbnail for a while, and then said, "You know what Sig was good at?"

"What?"

"He was good at getting the stuff out of Miami, talking to

those assholes," Antsy said. "He was good at keeping the dealers in line—making sure we got paid, at first. Later, we got the money up front. When one of the dealers had a problem with somebody, Siggy was good at smoothing that out."

"Yeah."

Antsy put his elbows on the table. "What Heather was good at, was moving the money. Figuring out how to get it into banks and into investments. That bitch knows where every nickel is. And when I called her up to get some cash for an attorney, she told me to blow it out my ass."

"She didn't give you any," Del said.

"Not that—it's not that she didn't give me any," Antsy said. He seemed deeply offended. "She laughed, and said what I told you. She said, 'Blow it out your ass, Antsy.'"

LATER THAT DAY, they went over and knocked on Heather's door. She came to the door with the baby. She said to Lucas, "I know who you are. I saw you on TV. You shot that woman in the heart. You were here when they shot my husband."

Lucas said, "This is completely unofficial. Everybody is happy that Siggy is dead. We just wondered, for our own selves . . . Did you set him up?"

Heather looked up and down the hall, as if checking for hidden cameras, then smiled and reached out with her forefinger, and scratched Del on the left tit, and said, "I hope you boys enjoyed the floor show."

She shut the door and Del laughed.

Lucas looked at his watch and said, "Want to go over to the St. Clair and get a milk shake?"

MARK MCGUIRE called Lucas and asked for the quarter-million dollars to start the website, offering a thirty percent interest in the business. Everybody called lawyers, accountants, and consultants.

★

DEL.

The day after Lucas killed Alyssa Austin, Del showed up in Lucas's doorway, knocked on the frame, stepped inside.

"How you doing?"

"Fine," Lucas said. "How's Cheryl?"

"Found out what's wrong with her," Del said. He was a little stunned. "She's pregnant."